SOUND OF BLOOD

LAWRENCE DE MARIA

Published by St. Austin's Press
(305-409-0900)

ISBN: 1470008688
ISBN-13: 9781470008680

Cover Art, Website Design and Editorial Services Provided by Nancy Kreisler

To Patti, without whose love, support and faith, this
book – and others – would not have been possible

‡

DANGEROUS MARINE ORGANISMS

"CAN'T WE SHOOT him?"

"What?"

"Just once, let's just shoot someone," Keitel shouted in frustration, as well as to be heard over the growling engine. "Or strangle him."

The outboard was the proximate source of his anger.

"How about a knife? I'm wonderful with a knife. Good with bombs, too. We could blow up his ridiculous car." He leaned precariously over the stern to untangle the cast net from the cowling, where it threatened to foul a propeller. "Somebody should." The net came loose suddenly and Keitel fell hard on his rump. His already abused coccyx throbbed with a pain reminiscent of bad landings in his paratroop days. He let out a string of curses in German, a sure sign of rage. "Why must everything be such a production?"

The 24-foot Dusky was pitching badly in the shallows off Sunny Isles beach. The man at the wheel glanced toward the shore 100 feet away. An old woman shooing children out of the water gave him the fish eye. Jesús Garza feared few things. A

Cuban abuela protecting her brood was one. They didn't need more problems. He and Christian were behind schedule; the light was going. So while he enjoyed Keitel's discomfort immensely, Garza gently throttled back the small sport fishing boat and gave the woman a friendly wave. Unmollified, she continued to direct a baleful glare at him. Christ, he thought, she could stop global warming with that look.

"This whole plan is the product of a deranged mind," Keitel groused. He was angrily refolding the dripping net. "Fucking *Pirates of the Caribbean!*"

"Watch your language. The wind is blowing toward shore. The children may hear you. Might I suggest you try hitting the water? There is an awful lot of it and we already have an engine."

"The hell with the children," Keitel said. But he lowered his voice.

Garza grinned broadly as his partner struggled with his footing. Shorter than his lean, angular friend, with a welterweight's balance and build, he had sturdy sea legs. Keitel, stubbornly ignoring the offer of a seat cushion, had taken the brunt of the bouncy ride up from the Key Biscayne marina. Cruising back and forth along Miami Beach for two hours in heavy chop before finding a patch of the slimy buggers had been no picnic either, Garza knew. They should have opted for the bigger Dusky with its twin 225 Evinrudes. He laughed. Christian could catch a bigger motor.

"I'm glad you find all this humorous," Keitel said.

"You're bunching it too tightly. Remember the video."

Both men had watched a homemade Internet tutorial on how to throw a cast net. The redneck fisherman in the video had a belly the size of a beluga whale but looked like Nureyev when throwing the net.

"It's not that easy, you idiot," Keitel snarled. "The expert fisherman! Salt water in your veins. You try it." He prided himself in his ability to hit whatever he aimed at. Missing the Atlantic Ocean was inconceivable.

"Then who would handle the boat? If you were up here, we'd be in Mindel's parking lot. No, today you are first mate, and barely passable at that."

"Eat a turd. Mindel's isn't even there anymore. He sold to a developer."

"Pity. I was quite fond of the pastrami and the pickle plate."

"And I'm fond of my spine." Water splashed over the gunwale and Keitel used a muscled forearm to brush blonde hair out of his eyes. "Did you have to hit every damn wave on the way here?"

If folded properly – and loosely – across one arm and thrown with a whirling bodily motion, a cast net, lined with dozens of small lead balls, opens into a circle before hitting the water. A good cast has a lot in common with a golf swing. Less effort typically produces better results. A hard toss usually leads to a clumped net. The thick gloves didn't help. They caught in the webbing. Most of Keitel's casts hadn't even cleared the boat. The most recent one did manage to clear the stern but didn't quite get past the engine.

But he finally got the hang of it and even managed to impart some savoir faire to the endeavor. Gradually his mood improved. After one ballet-like cast, he bowed to Garza's applause. The eighth toss was particularly fruitful and he did a count after adding the contents to the live well.

"Ten or eleven, I think. It's hard to be sure. Enough?"

"For a Cape Buffalo. Dump the net and wash your gloves. Keep them on."

Garza waited until Keitel sat – this time on two cushions, he noted – and opened the throttle, heading south past Bal

Harbour and Surfside. A few minutes later he slowed near the familiar high rise and reached for his binoculars.

"There he is," he said, cutting the engine just off a sandbar at 63rd Street.

As Keitel dropped anchor he glanced toward shore, where a surfcaster wading knee-deep in the water was expertly flicking his bait just short of a sandbar. The setting sun was blocked by the condo building and this section of beach was in deep shade. The few people still stretched out on blankets would soon depart. A bronzed old man with a metal detector scoured the sand nearby, his rhythmic sweeps regular as a metronome. Garza went to the stern, opened a Styrofoam cooler and pulled out a large white plastic bag. He leaned over the side and partially filled the bag with seawater. After testing the bag's strength and integrity by jouncing it several times, he reached in the cooler for a long-handled kitchen strainer and a pair of gloves. Then he peered into the well.

"What do you think? Intelligent design or evolution? I can argue either."

"I'm sure you could," Keitel said. "You always do. As if it matters."

"Christian, I'm always amazed at your lack of intellectual curiosity. Are you not interested in the wonders of creation and the universe we inhabit? You hail from a country that produced Einstein for God's sake."

"My universe is centered on my throbbing ass. And Einstein was a Jew."

"Do I detect anti-Semitism in that remark? I'm shocked."

"I'm no anti-Semite. You know I worked with the Mossad against the Syrians. That's how I met Lev. I know I told you about him."

Indeed he had, Garza thought, with the usual twinge of jealousy. He was sorry he brought up the damn subject at all. Keitel never missed a chance to mention his one-time Israeli commando boyfriend. The Israeli Defense Force was very open- minded. It didn't matter if you enjoyed screwing camels, as long as you also enjoyed killing Arabs.

"Gave me a commendation," Keitel continued. He saw the expression on Garza's face. "I know. Jews giving German soldiers medals. Crazy. Hitler was a fool. Should have made peace with the Jews instead of driving them into the hands of his enemies. The Nazis would have gotten the bomb. The world would be speaking German. Like all fanatics, he had limited vision."

"Thank God. German is too difficult a language. But I am impressed with your reasoning. I may have to reevaluate my opinion of you."

"Reevaluate my dick, and impress me with your silence. Let's do this."

"All right, if you insist. Hold the bag open. Wide open."

A rare December gale, far at sea, was roiling the shelf water. Breakers crashed over sand bars 30 yards out. By now the surfcaster could hear more than see them. But the phosphorescent foam told him they were substantial. So did the smell. The agitated water released the sea's essence, an intoxicating mixture of brine, minerals, seaweed, marine life – and death. A wave swelled up to the fisherman's waist. There was a splash of spray and the taste of salty spindrift on his lips. Something stuck to his cheek and his heart fluttered. A tendril came away in his hand. But it was all right; it was green. The wind-driven surf was pushing seaweed and flotsam toward land. By morning the beach would be rife with coral, sponges and sea fans, which local shore rats would sell to tourists for beer and butt money. From a distance the gunk piled at the tide line would look like a Normandy hedgerow.

The on-shore wind also brought the danger of the beautiful but toxic Portuguese Men-of-War. The distinctive dark blue "sail" that gave the little jellyfish their name caught the breeze and sent them toward land. At certain times of the year – this was one of them – hundreds of Men-of-War would be left high and dry by the receding tide. Their tentacles remained vital even when drying out. The little "bluebottles" attracted the curious, particularly children, and the fisherman always made a point of warning them.

He hadn't really thought the strand on his face was a tentacle but the stab of fear was instinctive. Weeks earlier, also while wading, his right calf had exploded in pain, as if slashed with a hot razor. The agony shot to his groin; he thought he was in real trouble. After scraping the four-inch tentacle off his leg with sand and seawater, he limped back to his apartment and washed the affected area with vinegar, one of several home remedies purported to neutralize jellyfish venom. (Another is urine, but pissing on demand was never one of his strong suits.) The throbbing remained intense and he finally went to Flagler General.

"The groin pain just radiated up a nerve," the emergency room doctor told him after giving him a shot. "Allergic reactions to jellyfish are rare. Your throat would swell and you'd have trouble breathing. The real danger is cardiac arrest caused by shock when a huge dose of toxin hits near the heart or head. But one bluebottle isn't going to do it. A box jellyfish, maybe, but this isn't Australia. Of course, now that you've been sensitized, you're next reaction might be different."

With that warning in mind, before fishing he looked to see if the aptly named blue "Dangerous Marine Organisms" flags were flying from the rescue shacks and kept a cell phone handy in his bucket. This wasn't South Beach; after dark he would be alone. Half the condos were vacant, owned by now-desperate speculators. Until the sun set, his main company had been the ubiquitous sandpipers pecking like typists on the keyboard of the shore and brown pelicans skimming the waves. There seemed to be more pelicans than usual. The fisherman wondered if some of them were refugees from the oil spill in the Gulf that had somehow traversed the Florida peninsula, or had been cleaned in the Panhandle and relocated. Then again, the mind saw what it wanted to see. Everyone in the country had pelicans on the brain. But he would check it out. Could be a great story.

As it darkened, all the birds flew off to wherever birds go at night. The only humans around were a couple of diehard bathers and an old man with a metal detector who, as he passed the fisherman, gave him a "me neither" shrug. There were also two men on a fishing boat just past the bars. Curious. Most small craft anchored further out, in calmer water. A man at the wheel swept the beachfront with binoculars, probably looking at a few skimpily clad women on the pool decks of nearby hotels.

The prospector and bathers were gone and the surfcaster could no longer see the boat. He didn't mind. New-found anonymity and Florida's milder climate provided a solitude he'd craved in New York. He religiously broke up his work week by fishing this stretch of beach every Wednesday. He'd even delayed his research trip to Antigua by a day so as not to break his routine.

A routine that had not gone unnoticed.

What we do with a drunken sailor?
What we do with a drunken sailor, early in the morning?

"Jesus, Jesús, not only can't you sing," an exasperated Keitel said as he lifted the plastic bag from the live well, "but the words are wrong."

Garza was undeterred by the criticism of his sea chantey.

"Cuban version. And look who's the music expert," he said. "The only song you know is *Deutschland über alles.*"

Keitel laughed and gave the bag a few hard shakes to test its integrity.

"It will hold. Are you sure it's dark enough?"

"Yes. You can see nothing from the buildings. Same moon as last night."

"I'll do it if you want," Keitel said quietly. "I'm the better swimmer."

Garza was touched. Christian was always full of surprises.

"Your heart isn't in it. And as you ungraciously reminded me, this is my lunatic idea. But I appreciate the gesture."

Slipping over the side, Garza found that he could almost stand. Keitel reached over the gunwale and handed him the tightly-tied plastic bag, holding it gingerly by its drawstring, which he wrapped around his partner's wrist.

"Buena suerte," Keitel said.

Garza smiled. The online language classes were obviously working.

"Danke."

He started side-stroking toward shore at a slight angle. As he disappeared from sight, Keitel could hear him singing happily.

Fifteen men on a dead man's chest, Yo ho ho and a bottle of rum...

†

The turbulent surf was a smorgasbord of organic matter and small crustaceans. That attracted baitfish, pilchards and silversides, whose sole purpose was to occupy low rungs in the food chain, where they provided a moveable feast for larger predators: small sharks, bluefish, barracuda, jacks and pompano.

There was too much seaweed to use lures so the fisherman baited his hook with a chunk of herring, to which he attached a strip of squid. Both had been purchased, rather guiltily, at a nearby Publix; he hadn't had time to go to the marina. Well, he mused, one man's sushi was another man's bait. He felt a sharp jab on his ankle. Reaching down he brought up a large, faded conch shell. He was tempted to put it to his ear, but recalled a recent run-in with a hermit crab that had taken up residence in another conch. The cheeky little devil nipped his lobe in annoyance. It wasn't even the crab's own shell! He'd tell Emma the story when she visited. She'd get a kick out of it. He smiled as the thought of her brought back a memory from their shared childhood, another beach, another shell – the first time he'd crossed swords with his uncle. But certainly not the last. Just wait until the old reprobate gets a load of what …

The rod tip jerked and the reel's drag started clicking wildly. The fisherman flipped the nondescript conch away (there were many more colorful specimens in his collection) and set the hook, using a wave to surf the seaweed-covered fish the final few feet. A bluefish flopped helplessly in the sand. It was small, maybe three pounds, with a streamlined body built for speed and a piranha-like head. The analogy was apt. Feeding blues easily topped the ferocity of the much smaller Amazon denizens and had even been known to bite bathers in their blood lust. The unfortunate bluefish suffocating on the beach was certainly not alone. Blues travel in schools of like-sized fish. If it was one of the smaller blues in its pod, he might get a five or six pounder! He dumped the flopping fish in the ice-filled bag inside his bucket, in his excitement receiving several nasty finger cuts from its razor sharp teeth. He rebaited quickly. The type of bait at this point was academic. Blues chomp anything. He could have saved money and bought a package of hot dogs.

The next cast into a trough only 20 feet from shore where a platoon of blues from a larger school swirled under the seaweed. Eventually they would head to deep water to rejoin the main pod, guided by senses that could detect a single drop of blood in a cubic acre of water. A savage hit! This blue ripped off line. He tightened the drag and worked the frantic fish back. Eventually it tired. A beauty, at least five pounds. He shoved the blue into his bag, where it thrashed violently against its deceased cousin. He would keep both. Blues this size tasted like real fish, not the sauced-up slabs of Chilean sea bass or tilapia passed off as haute cuisine in the tourist traps on Lincoln Road. And what the hell was monkfish? He bent down to cut more bait.

"Catch anything?"

Startled, he nearly baited his finger. He whirled around, dropping his knife in the sand. A man stood beside him holding a large plastic bag.

"Jesus, you almost gave me a cardiac!"

"To be quite accurate, it's Jesús," the man said, smiling. "I'm sorry." He didn't seem sorry. "I was swimming and saw you. I fish."

Slight accent, probably Cuban. Good-looking, with a small black mustache that matched his slick, jet-black hair. He looked like one of the rumba dancers on a cruise ship. Beaded with water, the stranger wore a tight black bathing suit that boldly outlined his genitals. At his hip was a small waterproof pouch. Rubber gloves were tucked into the other side of the suit. The plastic bag looked half full, with a watery luminescence. The man carefully placed it on the sand. Liquid spilled from the neck, and a strand of ... something ... slithered out. He opened his pouch and took out a cigarette. He did not offer one to the fisherman and took quite some time with a lighter, flicking it on and off several times before lighting the cigarette.

"These things will kill you," he said, laughing at some private joke as smoke hissed from his nostrils.

The fisherman heard a motor start up, and then a muted throbbing. He looked toward his apartment house, barely visible 200 feet away. There were lights in the high rise and on a calmer day he would have been able to hear the hum of traffic on Collins Avenue. But not tonight. The stranger's appearance unnerved him. This section of Miami Beach was in transition and just north Collins still had its fair share of cheap convenience stores, coffee shops, payday loan operations, burger and burrito joints with vinyl chairs, seedy beach bars and vagrants. This man was no vagrant, but that was small comfort. It's not easy to look sinister in a bathing suit, but the stranger managed it.

There was a thump as a fish tail flapped out of the bucket.

"Ah, bluefish," the stranger said, peering in. "They'll be delicious. How would you have prepared them?"

The fisherman relaxed, not noting the phrasing.

"I like to marinate them in key lime juice and dark rum. Then dust them with a little flour and bake then at 400 degrees. Maybe 10 minutes."

He was about to suggest an appropriate wine when the "Cuban" looked past his shoulder out to sea and said loudly, "He's alone. No one in either direction." He flicked away his cigarette and put on the gloves.

A clipped voice behind the fisherman said, "Make it quick."

He turned to see another man walking from the ocean. Sensing danger, he reached down to grab the knife, sticking hilt up in the sand. Too late. Garza lifted the plastic bag and in one practiced motion flipped it over the fisherman's head, pulling the drawstring taut. Seawater and slime filled the man's nostrils and ears. The seal wasn't perfect and most of the water gushed out the bottom of the bag, leaving only the congealed "things" that had been floating inside. Something in the fisherman's midbrain, just barely below the level of consciousness, a genetic remnant of primate fear, recognized the creatures. Although slimy, they seemed to be attaching themselves to his face.

Jellyfish! Something twirled up his nose. He dropped his knife as his hands flew up. He barely hooked his thumbs under the throat of the bag when dozens of tentacles almost simultaneously discharged their poison. It felt like scalding water. His eyeballs exploded. He inhaled reflexively to scream and the fire filled his esophagus, which closed in an agonizing spasm. The fisherman pitched backwards into the sand near the waterline, limbs twitching uncontrollably. Then he went limp, hooded head rolling freely in the waves.

Keitel reached into the dead man's bucket and pulled out a Ziploc bag. "Keys, wallet and cell phone," he said. "Convenient."

Then the killers each grabbed the corpse by an arm and started to drag it into the ocean.

"Wait," said Garza, dropping one arm, which started flopping grotesquely in the surf. He went to the bucket and retrieved the bag with the night's catch.

"Are you completely insane?"

"I like bluefish," Garza said. "He gave me a great recipe."

Once in the water, they flipped their victim over and then paddled him out to the boat, face down. No harm in being sure. After climbing into the Dusky, they carefully removed the fatal hood from the fisherman, whose bulging, spider-veined eyes stared at them in seeming reproach. The jellyfish slid into the water, but some blue, beaded strands remained attached to the dead man's face. Tendrils twirled out from his nose and covered his upper lip.

"He looks like Salvador Dali," Keitel observed.

"That's not a good look for him," Garza said. He gave the body a gentle, almost loving, push towards shore. "Now he belongs to the algae," he intoned solemnly. They had recently watched a History Channel special about the Lincoln assassination. "Get it?"

"It's not funny when you have to explain it," Keitel said.

Garza reached into his pouch and lit a cigarette, which he needed a lot more than the one he used on the beach as a signal. The corpse slowly sank from sight. The man had to be found. A mysterious disappearance might spur an open-ended inquiry. The body would wash ashore, but only after the sea and its creatures muddied the forensic waters. There would be no signs of man-made trauma. It was a murder using only natural ingredients.

"You know, Christian, Greenpeace would be proud of us."

"What are you talking about?"

"Never mind. Take the wheel. I'll put lures on the rods. We should look the part when we get back to the dock. Hell, we even have some fish."

He lifted the top of a seat and pulled out a tackle box. He knew what he was doing. As a boy in Cuba he fished the Guantanamo River with his father and uncles, near where the big waterway ran to the sea, splitting the now infamous American naval base in two. They often came so close to the base perimeter that Marine sentries fishing from the bulkhead waved. The perimeter searchlights, designed to spot intruders – mostly Cubans swimming to freedom – were an irresistible magnet to huge shrimp, which the Marines put on hooks.

"You wouldn't believe it, Chico," his father told him, "they get big jacks, tarpon, barracuda, because of those lights. I saw a 100-pound tarpon, a five-footer, leap like a sardine. Even the Marines jumped back. Then we saw the big shadow in the water. Tiburón, a hammerhead. Chasing the tarpon. At least 15 feet and 2,000 kilos! Eyes this far apart." His father held his arms as wide as he could. He was a fisherman, after all. "Only a fool would swim there."

Another time, he tried to step on a log jutting from shore. The "log" turned out to be a giant barracuda. Huge eyes rolled up to look at his foot, which he held in midair as his shaken father snatched him back and hugged him tight. And he recalled how his uncles passed him the rum bottle after a manta ray big as a Piper Cub jumped over their boat. What fun they had! Garza felt a twinge of remorse. His father would not have liked him killing a fisherman.

Christian was saying something.

"You should call them. Are you listening? You're a thousand miles away."

"Only 90," Garza said, picking up his cell phone from a bag at his feet.

In a luxurious penthouse in Coral Gables, a man teetered at his climax. The woman astride him was motionless but for the slight rise and fall of a small blue tattoo at the base of her spine as she clenched her internal sexual muscles. She had brought the moaning man close several times. Now she would end the sublime torture. She had a reservation at Joe's Stone Crabs. Not with him. A cell phone buzzed on the side table.

"Fuck! Leave it alone," the man gasped. "I'm almost there."

The woman climbed off. The man cursed and squirmed, all he could do with hands tied to the bedposts. She placed the phone to the man's ear.

"Yes," he gasped. "Wha... What is it?" He listened. "OK. OK. Fine."

The woman threw the phone on the table. Her face was expressionless.

"Well?"

"It's done," he replied, groaning as she remounted.

"One less thing for us to worry about. Any problems?"

"For the love of God, can we talk about it later?"

"We both agreed on this. Perhaps I should get these things in writing."

"I'll sign the goddamn Magna Carta if you want! Let's talk about it later!"

She laughed. The tattoo, of the Cross of Lorraine, resumed its rhythmic pulsation. She increased the frequency. A moment later her pinioned partner bucked upward violently, roaring in release. She gazed down at him dispassionately as his breathing slowly returned to normal and his eyes began to refocus. He could never be bored with her. That was the problem with all the men she slept with. True, he had been the most interesting. An affair that started with attempted rape had evolved into a lustful business relationship (in her mind, the best kind of sex). But she was ready to move on. They would still need each other, of course. There was a company to run. She wondered how he'd take it. Probably not well.

He was trying to say something.

"Shhhh, darling" she said, putting a finger to his lips. "Be right with you."

Her hips began to move slowly. The pace quickened. Her mouth opened and her head tilted back, throat taut. A flush spread across her breasts. Their nipples, always prominent, became rock hard. A series of guttural cries. A final shudder. Her face softened into a smile. The man was mesmerized, as always. It was like watching a swaying cobra.

"What did he say?"

"He couldn't talk." Garza laughed. "He was tied up."

He remembered the fisherman's wallet. The apartment and car would be sanitized but people kept important information on their person: locker and safety deposit numbers, even computer passwords. Using a penlight he went through the billfold and was mildly surprised to find several crisp $100 bills, which he happily pocketed. There were a half dozen credit cards. One in particular stood out.

"I thought this guy was a struggling journalist."

"That's what they told me," Keitel said. "Why?"

"He's got a Titanium American Express card."

"So?"

Garza didn't bother to explain. Christian left money matters to him. He wouldn't know a Titanium card meant its owner had a net worth of at least $10 million. He pulled the card out of its sleeve and read the name. Confused, he scanned the driver's license.

"Son of a bitch."

He reached for his cell phone.

†

Luke Goldfarb had a problem most 14-year-old boys only dreamed about. The three girls on the adjacent blanket were topless. That wasn't the problem. Unlike his grandparents, who looked like raisins after 30 years in Miami Beach, Luke, down from New York for a visit, was turning into the world's largest blister. He needed the umbrella that was back in the condo. His grandparents were out shopping for Hanukkah. Before the girls took off their bikini tops, Luke's thoughts had revolved around homemade sufganiyot – jelly donuts. Now all he wanted was to plant that umbrella like the Marines on Iwo Jima. *I love you, Nana and Gramps, but I hope the engine falls out of your Escalade.* He took a few deep breaths, thought about the Knicks to quell his erection and started to get up. Just then, the girls also stood and headed toward the ocean. Luke followed. Soon all four were standing side by side waist deep.

"Look at that," one girl said. For a horrible moment, Luke, embarrassingly aware of his excitement, thought he wasn't in deep enough. But then he followed her finger and saw something dark silhouetted by a wave. It was big.

"Probably a dolphin," he squeaked, unforgivably. He had never spoken to a half-naked girl, let alone three. "Maybe a sand shark," he was able to croak.

Luke thought that they would scurry to shore. He would stand his ground to impress them, although he did feel a thrill of fear. But these were Florida girls and edged out toward the object. It didn't look like a fish. A log? He was about to tell them to be careful when the wave rolled the object right into the girls. All erotic thoughts were blown out of his mind as they screamed and ran. He swore later that the tits on the middle girl, the one with the large, dark aureoles, "twirled" in opposite directions like a New Year's Eve party favor. It was sight Luke Goldfarb would remember the rest of his life, second only to the naked, bloated, almost faceless corpse now bumping gently against his hip.

A PLATINUM REFERRAL

THREE MONTHS LATER – *New York City*

THE PHONE WARBLED just as Scarne placed the last book into his London Library Cabinet. He ignored it and began arranging photo frames and plaques on the shelf, even though he knew Evelyn would eventually switch them around to her liking. Without his objection. In his relationships with women Scarne had long ago decided what few battles were worth waging. Decoration wasn't one of them. She had put her foot down about the antlers and now ruled the roost. The phone kept trilling. It was her choice of ring tone, too, and sounded like a Parisian ambulance. He *would* speak to her about that. Why didn't she answer it? Then he remembered she'd gone to buy last-minute office supplies. He reached his desk just before the answering machine picked up.

"This is Jake Scarne."

"Mr. Scarne, my name is Sheldon Shields. Don Tierney suggested I call."

Sheldon Shields? The name sounded familiar. Scarne pulled his laptop closer and sat down. He looked at the caller I.D. on his phone console: *Shields Inc.* One of those Shields? He began to Google.

"What can I do for you, Mr. Shields?"

"I may have something for you. Don said you can be trusted and have imagination."

"That was kind of him."

Scarne glanced at his computer. Sheldon Shields was the older brother of Randolph Shields, chairman of one of the nation's largest media companies. Good old Don. The gift that keeps on giving.

"The matter is rather delicate. Are you available to meet with me today?"

Scarne preferred meeting clients in his new office suite, which offered a stunning view of Rockefeller Center and the twirling skaters 20 stories below. Montpelier arm chairs flanked the Burford dresser that served as a magazine table in his waiting room, and the desks, tables and bookshelves in his office and conference room were in British Traditions style. Dark green carpets, maroon accent pieces and nautical paintings completed a décor meant to impress clients and hint at high fees. There were still boxes lying about, but they'd be gone by the afternoon.

"Let me check my calendar, Mr. Shields."

Scarne had barely begun riffing through a *Golf Digest* for sound effect when Shields said, "Any chance I could buy you lunch at the Federal League?"

Excellent chance, Scarne thought, the home field advantage of his office receding at the prospect of dining at one of the city's premier social clubs. Besides, a Shields was a Shields. Not easily impressed. Or worried about fees, for that matter. They agreed to meet at 1 P.M.

After hanging up, Scarne went deeper into the company website. Sheldon Shields held various titles, but from what Scarne could gather played a distant second fiddle to his somewhat notorious brother, and mainly hosted media events, investor conferences and other social or business functions. Sheldon also ran the grandly-named *Shields Foundation for Investors*, a unit that produced print and electronic investment newsletters. Scarne himself was often solicited for them and now recalled Sheldon's name on S.F.I. promotional flyers. Since annual subscriptions started at $1,000 – money better spent on a new set of golf clubs – the solicitations went into the circular file.

Randolph Shields held the real power in an organization that had grown exponentially since 1923 when their grandfather, Cornelius Shields, published *Shields*, the nation's first pure business magazine. The broad-based conglomerate now owned a dozen other magazines and newspapers, two cable television stations, a movie studio and some of the priciest real estate in Manhattan. Not to mention an ocean-going yacht and a Boeing 727.

Despite his ceremonial role, Sheldon surely had access to other investigative outlets. Scarne assumed the call involved a personal matter: perhaps something potentially embarrassing to his brother – although "Randy" Shields, as the tabloids dubbed him, was a hard man to discomfit. He called Tierney, who was at a meeting. His secretary said she'd relay the message.

Scarne went back to his shelving. The cabinet contained every book written by Churchill. The cabinet and its collection had belonged to Scarne's grandfather who, despite spending much of his career trying to torpedo ships of the Royal Navy, was an Anglophile.

"Very great race, the British," the old sailor once told him. "Seafarers have to be hard. Practical, too. They kept Winston on ice until their backs were against the wall. Trotted him out to fight. After they won they threw him aside. Better system than ours. Some men are made for war; some for peace."

Scarne smiled as he looked at Volume 4 of *Marlborough: His Life and Times*, the last section of the British Prime Minister's million-word biography of his famous ancestor, John Churchill, the first Duke of Marlborough. The volume was marred by a perfectly round hole in its spine that obliterated the last three letters of the Duke's last name.

"People will think it is about cigarettes," his grandfather had said as he surveyed the damage after calmly and carefully removing the target arrow. The shaft had flown through the open window of his study, narrowly missing the old gentleman's head as he sat reading court briefs. "But I suppose I should be grateful you weren't using hunting points. The tome would have been ruined." Then, turning to the speechless nine-year-old, he promised not to tell his grandmother if Scarne would confine his future jackrabbit hunts to the ranch's outer acres – as well as promise to read the skewered book. Which he did.

Not until years later, when reading an essay by Larry McMurtry, the *Lonesome Dove* author and book collector, did Scarne learn of the potential value of the *Marlborough* set. There were 155 copies of a limited first edition inscribed to the Prince of Wales, who was briefly King of England before abdicating in December 1936 to marry his divorced American mistress, Wallis Simpson. Scarne had immediately pulled his grandfather's *Marlborough* from the packing crate in which it languished in a (thank God!) climate-controlled storage facility. Sure enough, on a front page of each volume, the inscription: *"To the King, from Winston Churchill, October 30. 1936."*

Even after the economic meltdown of 2008-9, such an edition, albeit arrowless, brought nearly $100,000 at a Sotheby's auction. Scarne often wondered how such a rarity wound up in his grandfather's collection (although he suspected it was obtained prior to the outbreak of World War II when his grandfather had been a naval attaché in London). He also marveled at the old man's equanimity in the face of his grandson's desecration. Scarne now kept the undamaged first three volumes in his safe. But he enjoyed looking at Volume 4. He doubted anyone would steal a book with a hole in it. As to the value of the marred set? Scarne suspected that with more and more books being digitalized, even a slightly wounded Marlborough might command six figures in the near future.

On the top of the bookcase was a silver Cartier frame with a black-and-white photo of Capitano di vascello Giacomo Scarne resplendent in his Italian naval dress uniform. Next to that was a crystal frame containing a color photo of Scarne's parents flanking his grandmother, all on horseback. Scarne's gaze lingered on the faces of the young couple. What little recollection he had of them melded into a kaleidoscope of discordant impressions: fire, cold, utter silence, urgent shouts, men on snowshoes. Scarne could see his reflection in the glass covering the photo. Given the diverse gene pool from which he'd sprung, he was not surprised he looked so little like his parents. Save two features: the obsidian eyes and high cheekbones of his half-Cheyenne mother.

The phone rang, dissolving the ephemeral memories. It was Tierney. After thanking him, Scarne asked the lawyer if he knew what Shields needed.

"Haven't the foggiest, Jake. He wouldn't tell me. Hardly know the man. He apparently got wind of the Barnes thing at the club. He bought me a drink and I told him you were somewhat useful."

The "Barnes thing" hadn't started out promising. Tierney's firm was outside counsel for a large Wall Street brokerage house fighting an age discrimination suit. The broker was awash in securities violations and its regular lawyers had their hands full. The suit was small change. Tierney knew no one would second-guess a fast settlement. But he smelled a rat.

"Jake, this guy applies for a job as a 'wealth consultant,' whatever the hell that is, and gets turned down by a branch manager who sends him an email saying the company was looking for someone younger and with more zest."

"More zest?"

"Yeah. Talk about a million dollar word. Who the hell writes an email like that today? My five-year-old grandson knows better. Anyway, the guy sues post haste. You'll love this; he also claims that the manager is a homophobe."

"He's gay?"

"And over 60. Thank God he's not a transvestite. That would be a hat trick. As it is, it's a slam dunk before any jury in this city. Hell, I'd find for the guy."

"What's the problem? Your client has deep pockets and certainly doesn't need any more bad press."

"That's what bothers me. They're just too easy a target. Something stinks. Do me a favor; take a run at the guy. I know it's a long shot. Can't keep you on it long. Two weeks, max. My client wants to settle before the rags get it."

Scarne thought about a lucrative month-long personal security assignment for a visiting rock star he would have to forego.

Tierney, who missed nothing, said, "If you can't, don't sweat it."

"Don't be an ass, Donald."

"Sorry, it won't be much of a payday, Jake."

Tierney wasn't wrong about many things, but he was wrong about that.

Jackson Barnes had recently moved to New York from San Francisco. Unemployed, he and a roommate shared a one-bedroom in Greenwich Village. Scarne tailed him to Rugby's, a Village hangout. He confirmed that the man was voraciously gay. No great detective work was involved. Barnes propositioned him. Scarne demurred, hoping he wouldn't be sued for bar-pickup discrimination. But Barnes was actually a pleasant fellow, and kept talking to Scarne. After they got past the normal prattle about the Knicks, he brought up his case. Scarne clucked sympathetically and kept buying drinks to loosen the man's tongue. All he managed to do was get more people involved in the conversation. By the time he left, he was out a hundred bucks and half the bar was telling Barnes to "sock it to those corporate cocksuckers."

He next concentrated on the roomie, Byron Taliger, who had moved from San Francisco with Barnes and was also unemployed. Tierney had run Barnes through the appropriate databases in New York and California to see if he was litigious. Nothing. Scarne decided to run Taliger's name. He hit pay dirt.

"A Byron Taliger brought a sex-discrimination suit against a local brokerage house," a lawyer at a San Francisco firm affiliated with Tierney's shop told him. "It was settled out of court. Taliger claimed he was fired because he was gay."

"In San Francisco?"

"Yeah, I know. The case was never going to a jury. The guy who fired him put something in an email about Taliger's 'lifestyle.' I kid you not. The settlement was sealed, but a friend told me it was for a good piece of change. Out here that's lawyer-speak for more than $250,000 and less than a million."

A few more questions revealed that the brokerage in question had been accused by the Government of insider trading. Another easy mark anxious to shove unrelated dirty laundry under the rug. Scarne was convinced Barnes and Taliger were running a scam. But how did they get managers to be so devastatingly stupid with emails? The obvious answer was that the managers were part of the con. Since it was a stretch to believe Barnes and Taliger planted them over the years, Scarne suspected blackmail. He asked Tierney to set up a deposition for the manager who refused to hire Barnes in New York.

The man's name was Alfred Webster and he appeared with both a lawyer from his brokerage firm and his own attorney. After 15 minutes of typical deposition background blather Tierney went for the jugular.

"Was it Byron Taliger or Jackson Barnes who first suggested the scheme to defraud my client with this lawsuit?"

The mention of Taliger did the trick.

"I want to see a lawyer."

"You have a lawyer," Tierney said. "In fact, two of them." He waved his arm to encompass the other attorneys present, both guppy-mouthed.

"I want a criminal lawyer."

From there it was easy. Alfred Webster, married with three kids in Colts Neck, NJ, where he coached little league, frequently stopped for a drink after work and just happened to run into Jackson Barnes. Webster occasionally, and secretly, swung from the other side of the plate and was in bed with the suave Barnes when Taliger burst in, digital camera in hand. SLR, 12 mega pixels, no shutter lag. Faced with suburban humiliation, he was only too happy to entertain their scheme. They had, of course, targeted him specifically because he was in the position to hire people at his firm. As an added inducement, he was promised 25% of the "profits." After all, he might lose his job for the email idiocy.

Barnes and Taliger had run the operation for a decade. New York was their sixth city. They started out with sex-discrimination, but as they got older added age discrimination to the mix. They had little trouble finding victims, who soon became paid accomplices. They concentrated on troubled companies with deep pockets, and averaged a $600,000 settlement every 18 months or so.

Once Webster turned on them, they cut a deal to avoid criminal prosecution. Tierney saved his New York client at least a million dollars. And he succeeded in recovering $4 million the pair had bilked from other companies and insurers. (The two con men were also savvy real estate investors; even in a weak market they had no trouble coming up with the money for restitution.) He negotiated a huge bonus for Scarne from the New York brokerage. And since Tierney's firm received a third of the recovered funds from the other cases, he made sure Scarne saw a piece of that as well. The money helped pay for Scarne's new office but wouldn't last forever. Of more permanent value were platinum referrals like Sheldon Shields.

Scarne had just finished with the *Wall Street Journal* when he heard the outer door to his office open. He read both the *Journal* and *The New York Times* every morning and was quite convinced that their respective editorial writers did not live on the same planet. But somewhere down the middle of their polemics, he reasoned, was common sense, and their reportage was miles ahead of the drivel available on the Internet.

"Thought you might enjoy a crumpet," Evelyn Warr said, standing in his doorway in coat and scarf. She was holding two shopping bags. One said *Office Max*. The more promising bag said *Starbucks*. "I'll be there in a jiff."

A moment later she walked to his desk carrying the *Starbucks* bag. She was wearing a brown pleated skirt and a tan cashmere sweater. She ran a hand through her thick brown hair and shook her head until her tresses fell back into shape. "Bit of a wind out there," she said, reaching into the bag, producing napkins, coffee and two blueberry scones. To Evelyn, all pastries were crumpets. She slid one across to Scarne, then broke hers in half.

Scarne suffered gum-chewing products of the city school system before finding her. She was recommended by a friend in City Hall who admired her volunteer work after the Twin Towers attacks. It was by pure chance she was on holiday in Devonshire on 9/11, instead of the 90th floor of Tower 1. Her fiancé wasn't as fortunate. In addition to superb administrative skills, Evelyn's cultured English inflection, which would have stopped Rommel, charmed clients. And it didn't hurt that she bore more than a passing resemblance to Kate Winslet. Early on, Scarne had debated making a pass at her, balancing his natural inclinations (and the belief she would be insulted if he didn't) against the possibility he'd lose her. Eventually, after one too many bourbons at a Christmas party in a neighboring office, he'd explained his quandary to Evelyn, who'd laughed and soothed his male ego by revealing she had a lover. That was several lovers ago. Their relationship had evolved into a professional partnership tinged with healthy sexual tension. Now he told her about Sheldon Shields, all the while glancing hopefully at the uneaten portion of her scone.

"Any idea what it's all about?"

"No. See what you can dig up. I only did a cursory search on the web."

"Well if he's half the rake his brother is it's likely to be scandalous and lucrative. At least you will get a good lunch among the swells. Oh, damn!" She brushed some crumbs off the slope of her lovely left breast. She saw Scarne's appreciative gaze and smiled. "I know what you want." She passed the remainder of her scone over to him.

†

Scarne stopped by Evelyn's desk on his way out.

"Considering the splash his brother makes," she said looking at her computer, "Sheldon barely creates a ripple. The only relatively recent news concerns the loss of his only son in December in a drowning accident and his wife's death last month. Cancer. He's certainly going through a rough patch."

"I'll say. Thanks. I should be back around three."

"Be a good lad and try to be sensible about the martinis. And take your raincoat. It's chilly out there."

"I thought you Brits were tough."

"But not dumb."

"I'll be fine. It's not supposed to rain."

‡

A BOY AT GETTYSBURG

NEVER DOUBT A Brit about nasty weather, Scarne vowed as he trotted head-down through the icy needles of rain on Park Avenue. He rounded the corner at 37th and bumped into a man walking rapidly in the other direction. It was Scarne's fault. He'd been thinking of the club's signature bay scallops in sherry. He started to apologize, but the man, whose face was partially obscured by a purple ski hat and upturned jacket collar, didn't stop. Scarne shrugged and crossed the street toward the Federal League's entrance, where Henry Mosely stood scowling.

"Why the sour puss, Henry? Was I jaywalking?"

"Mr. Scarne, how are you?" The scowl dissolved into a smile. "Wasn't you I was looking at. Been watching that fellow almost knocked you over."

Scarne shook the uniformed man's hand warmly as they went inside. As is common with retainers at great private clubs Mosely remembered regular guests. After 30 years of service he was an institution. From a cubicle just inside the door he served as a concierge and keeper of club protocol. It was said that if you didn't pass muster with him, you needn't apply to the club.

"What did he do?" Scarne asked, looking back and catching a glimpse of the man's back as he rounded the corner. "Nip the club silver?"

"Not on my watch, sir. But I spied him loitering across the way. Gave him my evil eye. That did it. Probably nothing. But one must be wary these days."

Scarne wished he had gotten a better look at the man. Oh, well.

"By the way, Mr. Shields is running late. Track fire in the Village. Do you believe that a gentleman like him still takes the subway? Don't make them like that anymore. You can wait in the bar. Just mention his name."

"I'll just head to the library. Can you tell him?"

Christian Keitel was in a bind. It wouldn't do to be rousted by some flatfoot. New York City cops were a serious bunch after 9/11. He was no terrorist, but his prints would light up their database like a Christmas tree. He circled the block, reversing his jacket in case the damn doorman happened to be looking out when he passed. All that accomplished was to get the both sides of the jacket soaked. He figured he had at least an hour before Shields emerged from the club, so he ordered a coffee and a dirty-water hot dog from a vendor. (Recalling Garza's frequent teasing about his normally fastidious diet, he actually had two wieners, which were excellent.) But now he had to find a spot where he could watch the entrance.

Scarne walked up the famed double staircase to the elevators. Although he'd been to the club many times, he felt the familiar tug of history. For while it was not as grand as some of the city's other moneyed bastions, the Federal League had an honored reputation none of them could touch. Founded during the darkest hours of the Civil War "to cultivate and strengthen a devotion to the Union," its importance was not lost on Abraham Lincoln, who gratefully accepted a membership. The club's founders opened their hearts and their purses; one fundraiser sent half a million Thanksgiving turkeys to soldiers at the front. They also opened their gun cabinets, sheltering the Negroes who were the main targets of the city's infamous draft riots. And when the city government refused to allow blacks to participate in the funeral procession for Lincoln in 1865, the Federal held a separate ceremony. The club chose its original staff from the ranks of free black men or freed slaves and kept hiring their descendants, instituting one of the earliest retirement plans in the city, becoming, in effect, the black man's Fire Department. Political sensitivity and the upward mobility of blacks eventually dictated a break with tradition. But the staff was still overwhelmingly black. Over the years, the club's influence grew; it counted 16 United States presidents among its members.

After an interminable, creaking ride on an ancient elevator Scarne exited on the third floor and headed down a long hallway, passing a steam room, sauna, squash courts, gym and health club. The Federal's devotion to fitness, however, had its limits. The pungent odor of fine tobacco seeped beneath one closed door. The club's battles with municipal authority didn't end with the Civil War. Its infamous smoking parlors, stocked with illegal Havanas, continued to rankle the city's billionaire mayor, a reformed smoker.

Scarne entered what was perhaps the best private library in the city. It was empty save for one old fellow who was quietly snoring in a deep leather chair. With his head on his chest and an open book in his lap, he sounded like a purring cat. Scarne moved to the other side of the room where he selected a bound volume titled *Maps of the War Between the States* and sat in a leather chair next to a glass case containing colorful miniatures of the 5th New York, a heroic Zouave regiment. He was tracing Sherman's march to the sea when a voice behind him said, "I'm glad he spared Savannah. There's not much charm left in the South. Most of what's left is in Savannah."

"I'm fond of the mint juleps myself," Scarne said, rising from his chair.

"I'm sorry I kept you waiting." Sheldon Shields offered his hand. "I love this room, too. But you must be starved. Let's head downstairs."

On the way out Shields stopped and gently patted the shoulder of the sleeping man, who came awake with a snort.

"I think they may start the game without you, Clyde," he said as the man looked at his watch and mumbled his thanks as he rushed out.

"Gin rummy," Shields whispered to Scarne. "Every Friday."

Next to the elevator was a portrait of a severe-looking Civil War general leaning on the hilt of his saber.

"Joshua Chamberlain," Shields said. "College professor at Bowdoin. They wouldn't give him a leave of absence to enlist so he quit. Joined the 20th Maine Volunteer Regiment along with his brother, Tom. Joshua rose to command the unit. At Gettysburg the 20th was holding Little Round Top when an Alabama regiment tried to overrun them. Chamberlain's men were out of ammunition. So he ordered them to charge down into the rebels with bayonets! Those big rawboned Maine men thoroughly demoralized those tough Alabamans. The amazing thing was that those Union soldiers knew what was at stake. If their flank is turned, the whole Army of the Potomac is rolled up and the battle, maybe the war, is lost. Less than 400 men decided the fate of a nation."

"I read McPherson's book and saw the movie *Gettysburg*," Scarne said. "I loved that line in the movie when Chamberlain tells his brother not to stand too close to him 'or it could be a bad day for mother.' He looked up at the portrait. "He doesn't look at all like I pictured him. I guess I imagined him more like the actor who played him in the movie, Jeff Daniels."

"Don't let Chamberlain's dour expression fool you. He was in considerable pain when he stood for this painting. He was wounded at Petersburg in 1864, 'low down' as they used to say delicately, which means he was shot near where no man wants to get shot. Miracle he lived. And yet he was with Grant at Appomattox. By that time he'd been wounded four times and had six horses shot from underneath him. Then he went home, raised his family, was elected governor of Maine several times and then named president of Bowdoin. How that pleased him!" They reached the elevators. "Of course, the war never left him. His wounds constantly re-infected and he died of complications in 1914."

"You seem to know an awful lot about Chamberlain," Scarne asked.

Something creaked behind the elevator door but nothing happened.

"When I was a boy, I read a book, *The Twentieth Maine,* by John Pullen, and was hooked. Actually met him recently. Unbelievable luck. He wrote an article for one of our magazines and I asked him to lunch." Shields smiled. "He died a couple of weeks later. Hope you have better luck."

Scarne laughed. "Have you visited the battlefields?"

"When my son was young," Shields said, "we took him to Gettysburg. We walked the town. Would you believe there's still some bullet holes in the older buildings? Then we went out to Little Round Top."

As Shields spoke, Scarne took the opportunity to study the man. He was at least three inches taller than his guest.

He might have lost weight recently. But he had a full head of white hair, and was immaculately groomed and dressed, with a brown tweed jacket and darker brown slacks. His tie was Ferragamo and his loafers Gucci. His thin face was set off with bushy eyebrows.

"Josh ran ahead, like kids do, and spotted a monument. On it was the regimental crest of the 20th Maine, with a roster of the men who fought at that exact spot on July 3, 1863. He was so excited. I had regaled him about the battle many times. That was our best time together, other than our fishing." Shields was quiet a moment. His features softened and his voice grew husky. "I recognized Chamberlain's name right off, but then some of the other names from the book started coming back to me. Sergeants and privates even. I started to weep. My wife and son were embarrassed. Came out of nowhere."

"You weren't crying for the soldiers," Scarne said. "You were crying for the young boy who read the book."

Shields, whose eyes had glistened, gave Scarne an appraising glance.

"Let's have drink at the bar in the lounge before lunch. We'll take the stairs. A man could give up drinking waiting for this damn elevator."

Once on the ground floor they walked through the billiards room. Two of the six green-felted tables were in use. Scarne was surprised; he'd never seen anyone playing at the club. Then he recalled a recent article in *New York Magazine* about a couple of Hollywood stars opening a new pool hall/wine bar in the Village. Billiards was now all the rage.

The lounge itself, up a few stairs from the pool room, contained a dozen small tables arranged around a buffet featuring an assortment of meats and cheese, cold salads, chafing dishes with egg rolls and Swedish meatballs and bowls of various types of nuts. A large plasma TV hanging from a bracket in the far corner was tuned to a cable business news channel. An attractive blonde anchor was pontificating silently – the TV had been mercifully muted – above a continuous stock scrawl. No one sitting eating at the tables near the TV would have paid any attention to her anyway. Scarne knew for a fact that the woman, whom he'd met, barely knew the difference between a stock and a bond, let alone the esoteric derivatives that had recently brought the economy to heel. Scarne wasn't a financial misogynist; the anchor's well-coifed male counterparts were also universally clueless about the workings of the markets they allegedly covered. How else to explain their missing the greatest business stories in history while touting the brilliance of the financial "geniuses" whose activities threatened to destroy the world economy.

Several people were standing at the bar, talking quietly amid the tinkling of ice and stirrers against glass. In the background was the faint clack of pool balls being struck or racked. Despite the faint aroma of the premium Brazilian Rosewood wax the club used exclusively on all its wood surfaces (adopted by Scarne for his own office), the bar area mainly smelled of old oak and cherry – and even older money. All in all, Scarne thought, not a bad place to be on a frigid day. Shields asked him what he wanted to drink.

"Grey Goose martini, straight up. Twist."

"Make that two, Eddie," Shields said.

The drinks came, and they made small talk with the others at the bar, including a few well-dressed women who openly sized Scarne up. A shade over six feet tall, with a dark complexion and a face that would have been more handsome had he not taken his college rugby so seriously, Scarne knew he didn't quite fit in. Most of the younger men at the bar were in decent health-club shape but they looked soft. He didn't look soft, and the women noticed. Shields introduced him as a "friend," and no one had the temerity to ask him what he did for a living. One by one, the crowd drifted off. Most walked up a small staircase to an intimate dining room behind the bar. Shields ordered two more martinis and told the bartender to send them to the main dining room on the fourth floor.

"Eddie makes the best drinks in the house," Shields said as they walked out. "You know what they say about martinis? They are like women's breasts. One is not enough, and three are too many."

Scarne made a mental note to repeat that dictum to Evelyn.

"Actually, at my age, Jake, two, in either category, may be too much."

The walls of the cavernous dining room were adorned with landscapes and portraits, creating a museum-like atmosphere. They were led to a corner table. Nearby, the Cardinal sat with the Police Commissioner, who glanced at Scarne and rolled his eyes. Scarne grinned at his old friend and sometime nemesis.

"I reserved stone crabs for our appetizers," Shields said as they were handed menus. "They don't often have them and they go fast. Wonderful with ice-cold vodka. Of course, you can have anything you want."

"What did Pullen order?"

Shields looked confused for a second and then laughed.

"I love stone crabs," Scarne said, turning to the waiter. "And I'll have the bay scallops."

Shields ordered Dover sole.

"I know you are curious about why I asked you to lunch, Jake. But before I get to that, I wonder if you would tell me something about yourself?"

Scarne hesitated a moment, as if concentrating his thoughts.

"Not much to tell. I've been doing private investigative work for almost eight years. I don't always get my man, but it's not for a lack of trying. I win more than I lose and I have references from people who don't even like me."

Scarne realized he had been using the same spiel for quite some time. It sounded a little stale and a bit too pat. He'd have to work on another.

"Some people think you are a bit of a cowboy."

"I come by that honestly," Scarne said evenly. "I was born in Montana."

The crab claws arrived, along with martinis in frosted glasses. The claws were cold and plump, set off perfectly with lemons and the traditional mustard-laced dipping sauce. Both men tucked into the delicious meat.

"I never feel guilty eating these," Shields said, waving a huge claw. "Totally renewable. They pull off one arm and throw the crab back. The appendage regenerates completely in two years. Season is closed from May to October to give the buggers an additional break. Look at the size of these. Even with one claw the crabs can defend themselves against most predators."

"Anyone ever ask the crabs how they feel about being so renewable?"

"I suppose you're right," Shields said as he vigorously split a shell with a nutcracker. "It all depends on one's perspective. Hell is probably full of one-armed crustaceans with a long memory."

When their entrees came, Shields ordered a bottle of Cakebread chardonnay. The room began to fill up. Only an occasional laugh or rattling cocktail shaker rose above the murmurs of the well-to-do and politically connected diners. After they finished they both ordered coffee and brandy.

"Tierney told me a little about your background," Shields said as two waiters cleared their table. "And about your grandfather. He must have been quite a man. How in the world did an Italian submarine captain wind up in Montana?"

"He liked to joke that they gave him the wrong charts. The truth is almost as good. His sub was rammed by a British destroyer in the Mediterranean. The crew was eventually rescued by an American merchantman. He wound up in a P.O.W. camp in Montana near my grandmother's farm. They fell in love and after the war he went back to Montana, became a citizen and married her."

"He never returned to Italy?"

"Grandpa loved the West. As a boy in Sicily he was devoted to dime novels about cowboys and Indians. He became a lawyer, eventually a judge. He always said he always wanted to find the British captain, to thank him."

"Don said your grandfather basically raised you."

"Yes. My parents died when I was very young and my grandmother soon afterward. So it was just the two of us."

"A plane crash. I mean your parents. Which you survived. It must have been quite traumatic."

"I barely remember it."

Which wasn't quite true, Scarne knew. But those nightmares were less frequent now, replaced by those spawned by more recent horrors.

"Why didn't you stay out West?"

"My grandfather thought I needed some polishing. He also wanted to keep me out of the hoosegow. My friends growing up were real cowboys and I had cousins who were real Cheyenne Indians. We were always getting into scrapes. A hundred years ago we'd have been hung from the nearest tree, Judge Scarne or no. So he sent me off to Providence College in Rhode Island."

"Why Providence?"

"Good Catholic school. But mainly because he had cousins in the city, men he respected for having the good sense to leave Italy before the war while, as he put it, "I stayed to fight for that fat, bald shit Mussolini.'"

Shields laughed.

"Don said you also have an admirable war record. Marines, right?"

Scarne felt the familiar feeling of withdrawal, the barrier going up, whenever his war was mentioned. He never considered blood, fear, filth and death admirable. Or some of the things he had done to other human beings. His medals were in a drawer. He wished he could put his memories in with them.

"You guys had quite a chat, didn't you?"

Shields noticed the subtle change in Scarne's demeanor.

"Don't be offended, Jake. I asked Don a lot of questions. He thinks highly of you and broke no confidences. For the record, he's not the one who told me you were suspended from the District Attorney's office for throwing a City Councilman off the balcony in City Hall. By the way, is that true?"

Scarne smiled, his humor restored.

"An exaggeration. I had him by his ankle."

Shields picked up his brandy glass.

"I'd like to hear the reason."

"He bought off one of my witnesses with a patronage job. My case went down the tubes and a rapist, a cousin of a big contributor, went free."

"It cost you your career."

"But now people buy me stone crabs and brandy at fancy clubs."

"No regrets?"

"Only that I didn't drop the bastard. Is this a problem for you?"

"Quite the opposite. I need someone who can shake things up, who is not afraid of ... consequences. There is an element of danger in what I want you to do. Professional, for sure, and maybe more than that."

"Is this where I say, 'danger is my middle name' Mr. Shields?" Scarne smiled reassuringly at the old man. Everyone thought their problem unique and intractable. Must be woman trouble. Some gold digger has gotten her claws into the recent widower. Blackmail? He noticed that Shields wasn't smiling. "I'm sorry. I shouldn't be flip. Why don't you just tell me what this is all about? I'm sure I can help."

Shields took a large swallow of his brandy.

"I think Victor Ballantrae killed my son."

'JOSHUA HIDLESS'

SCARNE WASN'T SURE he'd heard Shields correctly.

"Victor Ballantrae?"

"I take it you know who he is."

"Of course. Doesn't everyone? Wall Street's latest darling." Up until now, the old man had seemed so rational. "Your own magazines have run glowing profiles on him. '*At the Top from Down Under*,' was one story I recall."

Shields waved his hand dismissively.

"At one time or another we've run glowing profiles on Ivan Boesky, Bernie Madoff and Allen Stanford. Business journalism is an oxymoron. We shill for these crooks until they're caught. Then we blame the regulators."

Scarne thought the same but was surprised by the man's candor.

"Not what you expected from someone in my position, is it Jake? Let's just say that I don't agree with my brother's editorial policy as it applies to Wall Street. And neither did my son."

"I heard about your recent losses, Mr. Shields. I'm sorry. I would have said something earlier but I didn't think it was my place. We didn't know one another. But I was given to understand your son died accidentally."

"That's bullshit!"

Scarne saw Condon and the Cardinal glance in their direction.

"When they told me Josh apparently drowned while fishing, I couldn't believe it. I can see by the look on your face that you are wondering about his name. Yes, I named him after Chamberlain. Anyway, it's always a shock when your child dies. But it seemed inexplicable. Josh was at home around the ocean. They said he got knocked over by a wave and panicked in the dark. A rip current surprised him. Or he got stung by a jellyfish. Maybe it was the tooth fairy. All sorts of theories. All nonsense. Nobody drowns in two feet of water in Miami! My boy was an excellent swimmer. For God's sake, all he had to be was an excellent wader."

"Mr. Shields," Scarne said gently. "Anyone can be unlucky." Or stoned.

"I know what you are thinking. But Josh rarely drank and there was no alcohol or drugs in his system. They said he might have had a heart attack or seizure, since there wasn't much water in his lungs. And there were jellyfish stings on his body, even on his face. I understand how they would assume it was an accident." Shields hesitated. "They even suggested suicide."

"Can you dismiss that possibility?"

Shields took in a lot of air.

"You have children, Jake?"

Scarne shook his head.

"Well, you'd be surprised how often parents think about their kids killing themselves. Rich or poor doesn't matter. When Josh was growing up, and torn about his sexuality, my wife and I worried constantly that he might do something to himself. But it doesn't make sense, not now."

"Josh was gay?"

"Yes. And happy in his own skin."

Scarne reserved judgment on that. Parents see what they want to see.

"Was he in the family business?"

"For a while, on the magazine. But he grated on my brother." Shields took a sip of his brandy. "Please don't misunderstand me. Randolph didn't give a hoot about Josh's lifestyle. People in glass houses and all that. But Josh never met a CEO he didn't think should be indicted. He loved skewering them."

"Including some of your advertisers?"

Shields smiled ruefully.

"The biggest. To be fair to Randolph, Josh could be a rant. He knew he was becoming an embarrassment to me. So he moved to Miami and joined the *South Florida Times*, what they call an alternative weekly."

"Were you estranged?"

"No, nothing like that. I was quite proud of his independence. Children have to find their own way. It's the way of things. He was doing good work down there. After oranges, corruption is Florida's biggest crop. With his business savvy, he got stories other reporters found too complicated. We used to discuss his scoops all the time. We were planning a fishing trip this spring."

Shields leaned forward.

"If Josh wanted to kill himself, why take his fishing gear to the beach?"

"To make it look like an accident, to spare you and your wife."

"His wallet, his keys and cell phone weren't among his things on the beach. And they weren't in his apartment or car."

"Perhaps they fell out of his pockets...when he...in the ocean."

"Rubbish!" Shields waved his hand dismissively. "That's what the police said. I told them that no surfcaster forgets to empty pockets. Everything goes in a watertight plastic bag. Taught him that myself."

"Someone could have stolen them after the fact."

"Cops said that too. Seemed logical at the time. But a thief probably would have used Josh's credit cards right away, before they were canceled. There were no charges, ever. And I've left them active."

"What did the police say about that?"

Shields gave Scarne a disgusted look.

"Catch 22. Josh's cards were either in the ocean or were stolen after he died. The fact that they weren't used means they were probably in the ocean."

They were interrupted by the Cardinal and the Police Commissioner, who stopped by their table as they were leaving.

"How are doing, Sheldon," the Cardinal said. "I was saddened to hear of Adele's passing. She is in my prayers. As are you."

"Thank you, your Eminence. That's very kind."

The Cardinal looked at Scarne, who stood. Shields made the introduction. The last time Scarne had met a Cardinal was at his confirmation and he'd kissed his ring. He was relieved when this Cardinal stuck out his hand for a manly shake. Condon winked at Scarne as they left.

"Where does Victor Ballantrae figure into all of this?"

The old man's shoulders slumped. He waved to the waiter.

"I will have another brandy."

The waiter looked at Scarne, who shook his head. Shields took a healthy pull of his drink and then reached across and gripped Scarne's arm.

"Josh was investigating the Ballantrae Group." He sagged back in his chair. "And it's my fault."

"I don't understand."

"I know Ballantrae. Hosted him several times on our yacht. That's one of my responsibilities. One of my few responsibilities. Randolph – I should say we – may need some deep-pocket partners. Our company is not immune to the inroads of the Internet. Ballantrae has offered us a substantial infusion of capital for a minority stake."

"That would also explain the glowing profiles."

"Yes."

"So, what was the problem?"

"Randolph thinks Ballantrae is a hale fellow well met. Blinded by his money. No, that's not quite fair. They have a lot in common. Bigger than life, buccaneers. Talk women and golf incessantly. You know the sort. But something about him just didn't sit right with me. I can't put my finger on it. Call it intuition."

"Surely your brother did his due diligence."

"If a check clears, that's all the due diligence Randolph needs. Especially now, with other sources of money drying up."

"Did you tell him about your doubts?"

Shields sighed.

"My brother doesn't have a high opinion of my financial acumen. Or my intuition. I needed some ammunition. I asked someone in our cable news division to discreetly look into the Ballantrae organization. He wasn't discreet enough and Alana Loeb got wind of it."

"Alana Loeb?"

"Ballantrae's chief of staff. She called Randolph and demanded an explanation. He naturally didn't know a thing about it and denied any involvement. When he tracked down the reporter and found out it was true, he was justifiably outraged. I'd put him in a bad spot."

Scarne thought about that. His sympathies were with Randolph. Just what the man needed: a meddlesome, passed-over brother second-guessing efforts to save the family company. Moreover, everything he'd read about Victor Ballantrae was positive, even discounting the public relations hype. He was becoming a national icon for funding rehab facilities for wounded veterans. The Ballantrae Invitational was one of the premier events on the pro golf tour, raising millions for childhood cancer research. Scarne had been lobbying with friends to get an invitation to the tournament's Pro-Am for months.

"What happened?"

"It was all I could do to save the reporter's job. And I had to fly down to Miami – that's where Ballantrae happens to be headquartered – and apologize in person. I was humiliated. And angry. So while I was there I told Josh what happened. I should have known he'd follow up." Shields took a sip of his brandy. "Maybe I did. Maybe I wanted him to."

"But you both must have realized Ballantrae would find out."

"Josh wouldn't trade on his name. He wrote under the byline 'Joshua Hidless.'" Shields spelled out the last name. "It's an anagram of Shields. I'm afraid it's also a dig at my brother, a rather poor pun indicating that now he could write what he wanted."

"Did he come up with anything?"

"I think so. He called and asked me if any deal with Ballantrae was imminent. I told him that it was some months away. He was relieved. He said he had gathered information about Ballantrae that was too explosive to talk about over the phone, but if it were true there was no way our family should get in bed with him. I pressed him on the details, asked him to send me what he had, but he was reluctant. Given their past battles, Josh knew my brother would question his objectivity. He was probably also trying to protect me. He would have wanted ironclad proof." Shields finished his brandy. "Josh was a good journalist. He wanted to give the company a chance to respond. He said he was heading down to Antigua to tie up some loose ends."

"Why Antigua?"

"Ballantrae International Bank is domiciled there." Shields took out a handkerchief, blew his nose and wiped his eyes. "Sorry. He never made it."

Scarne gave Shields a moment to compose himself.

"He must have left copies of his story or notes. Did you call his paper?"

"Not right away. When I didn't hear from Josh, I assumed he was traveling. It was two days...before his body...washed ashore. We were in shock. Flew down to bring him home. Went to his apartment to gather his personal things. It was particularly tough on Adele, seeing the shell collection he'd started as a boy. Magnificent specimens, some quite rare. She insisted on taking most of them home."

Shields took a long sip from his water glass and stared at Scarne, his eyes clear. When he spoke, his voice had a new determination.

"Losing Josh killed my wife. She didn't even bother to fight the cancer. These last few months, I just concentrated on helping her. No time for anything else. But after she passed, I decided to see what Josh had found out about Ballantrae. Not only might it help the company, but it could also be a fitting memorial for my son to get his story in print."

"What had he discovered?"

Shields shook his head and looked exasperated.

"I don't have a clue! When I called Josh's editors they said they knew he was working on something about Ballantrae but didn't know what it was."

"Isn't that a bit unusual?"

"They apparently give their reporters a lot of leeway. Besides, Josh probably kept things close to his vest. He wouldn't want anything leaking out. And their reporters typically wrote their articles on laptops and emailed them. They didn't have his laptop. Wanted to know if I did."

"Didn't you?"

"No. In hindsight, we should have wondered about that. But we were half out of our minds when we went through his apartment. Even if I noticed it missing, I probably would have assumed it was at his office. I called the building manager and asked him to go into Josh's apartment, which hasn't been touched except for a monthly cleaning. I haven't had the heart to sell it, or his car. Anyway, I told him to look for the computer. It wasn't there."

"Sometimes cleaning people help themselves," Scarne interjected. "And maybe it wasn't the first time the super had been in the apartment. It happens."

"I thought of that. So I flew down. Looked everywhere. No computer. No flash drives, notebooks or anything like that. A computer is valuable, but scraps of paper? It was as if Josh never existed as a journalist."

"Did you check his car?"

Shields smiled.

"Almost didn't. It was Mario who suggested it."

"Mario?"

"He's the building concierge. He was fond of Josh and took care of his car. Still does. Solid fellow. Helped me search the apartment and the car. Nothing."

Scarne had to admit the whole thing smelled a bit off. But still...

"Mr. Shields, respected, hell, even crooked, billionaires hire lawyers, not hit men. What could Ballantrae possibly be involved in that justifies murder?"

"I don't like the son of a bitch but I can't imagine what it could be. I obviously don't have anything I can bring to the authorities. They think I'm a crackpot. Randolph is the only reason they humored me as long as they did. But they convinced him it was an accident. When I told the police about the computer and missing notes, they were barely polite. Apparently Miami doesn't have a shortage of murders that are easier to solve."

He reached in his pocket and took out a thick envelope, placing it on the table and pushing it to Scarne.

"Bottom line, I've got nowhere else to go. Here's $20,000 to start. I'll pay your expenses, too. Go to Miami, turn over some rocks. Maybe something will slither out. You will find much of what you need to start in that envelope. Josh's address, employer and so on. You can stay in Josh's apartment and use his car. I'll call Mario. He'll have everything ready. If you turn up something, we can make further arrangements. But this money is yours to keep for trying."

"You can't be serious."

"Why, isn't it enough?"

"That's not the point. Mr. Shields, I think you may be grasping at straws. What you have told me is interesting. But this is all pretty thin. I don't want to take your money on false pretenses."

"Are there any other kind of pretenses, Jake? If you conclude that Josh's death was indeed an accident, or perhaps a random act of violence, I'll have to live with it. But if Victor Ballantrae thought Josh was just a no-name, two-bit reporter for a Florida weekly...well, I don't know. I can't live with the thought that I may have caused my son's murder. I have to find out."

"And what about your brother? I can't be discreet about this."

Shields smiled.

"I finally told Randolph what Josh said about Ballantrae. And the missing computer, everything. He said I had no right to do what I did. He said Josh thought everyone was a crook. Was exaggerating, trying to please me. He raised many of the points you and the police have. We had a huge row. Claimed

I was jealous of him and wanted to run the company. Victor Ballantrae was a dear friend and I was going to destroy everything. If Emma wasn't there, I think we might actually have come to blows."

"Emma?"

"Randolph's daughter, Emerald. She and Josh grew up together and were always thick as thieves. More like brother and sister than cousins. Hell, Adele and I practically raised her, what with Randolph always scooting around the world, and usually between wives and mistresses. Emma took Josh's death particularly hard. I'm not sure she agrees with her father."

"How did you leave it with your brother?"

The old man looked at his brandy glass, twirling it as he spoke.

"I was angry. I didn't like what he said about Josh, although now I'm sure he didn't mean it the way it sounded." He finished his drink. "I told him that I wasn't going to drop it. I was going to find out what Josh meant."

"Sounds like you've burned your bridges."

"Randolph and I aren't speaking. It is what it is. I've lost my wife and my son. If Josh was right about Ballantrae, and I can prove it, Randolph will come around. It's still family, after all."

"And if you can't?"

"Then I assume Randolph will put me out to pasture." Shields smiled. "Or follow through on his most recent threat – and have me committed." He looked at Scarne. "Will you help me?"

Now Scarne signaled for another brandy. A $20,000 payday doesn't come along every day, he reflected while the waiter poured. But the potential risks for going up against one of the most powerful media personalities in the world as well as a rising Wall Street star were incalculable. And for what? A wild goose chase to ease a grieving man's conscience?

"Sure," Scarne said, without knowing why.

‡

FIRST CONTACT

KEITEL CONSIDERED HIS *new vantage point on the median on Park Avenue a miserable compromise. The constant stream of traffic made surveillance difficult but he was probably far enough away not to be spotted by the nosy doorman. As an added precaution he put his cheap and garish cloth ski hat, hastily purchased earlier from an inexplicably cheerful Pakistani street vendor, in his pocket. As a result his hair was now plastered against his head and he looked like he was wearing a yellow helmet. Icy rain rivulets trickled down his neck. He was so bedraggled two people dropped coins in his empty coffee cup! Where had this sleet come from? It was April, for Christ sake. Someday he was going to kill a weather idiot on general principles.*

What the hell was Shields doing in there? Eating a side of beef? A passing car splashed more slush on his legs. We must have felt this way at Stalingrad. You'd think we'd learn. He decided that his blood had indeed thinned in Florida. No wonder the Dolphins lost most of their games north of the Mason Dixon line. Of course, he reflected, they lost a lot south of the line, too.

Henry Mosely held the door as Scarne and Shields walked out of the club together. They quickly retreated back inside.

"Can you rustle us a couple of umbrellas, Henry? We're good for them."

"Oh, I know you are, Mr. Sheldon. But this fellow looks pretty shady."

Mosely disappeared into his cubicle and came out with two Totes from an endless supply of lost or forgotten umbrellas.

"I don't know as these will be much help. It's blowing pretty good out there. Why aren't you gentlemen in Florida?"

"Thanks, Henry," Shields said. "Believe it or not, we're working on that."

The two men walked to the corner together.

"To get to Ballantrae, Jake, you'll probably have to go through Alana Loeb. Remarkable women. Brilliant mind and truly stunning. Randolph's tongue hits the deck whenever she's on the yacht." Shields shook his head. "I don't know what she's doing working for Ballantrae."

"Maybe it's not all work."

"God, I hate to think so. It would be another reason to dislike the bastard." He put out his hand. "I know you will find out what happened to my boy, Jake. I believe you are a man I can trust."

Shields turned and started walking downtown. Scarne watched him bend his umbrella into the wind. He was soon lost in the crowd.

Keitel spotted them coming out of the club, deep in conversation. He didn't recognize the younger man but he looked like a hard case. Cop?

Keitel knew where Shields was headed. He decided to follow the other man. At least now he could cover his head.

Scarne started back to his office, changed his mind, and crossed Park Avenue to St. Christopher's, one of the oldest Catholic churches in the city. The loss of their only son and his wife in an air crash had not dimmed his grandparent's faith and as a child Scarne was herded to mass every Sunday. But he was not now particularly religious, despite, or maybe because of, four years at a Catholic college. And in more introspective moments Scarne suspected he was not as forgiving as his grandparents.

An old woman in the church vestibule was robotically feeding quarters into electric votive "candles" that blinked on as the coins registered. Either she had a huge family, Scarne surmised, or thought she was playing a celestial slot machine. He recalled standing in front of a bank of real candles with his grandmother as she showed him how to use the long taper to light the wicks in the small jars. The wax and soot smell of those candles were rooted in his memory. They always said a prayer for his parents although he was quite sure they hadn't spent even a moment in purgatory on their way to heaven and thus didn't need any indulgences. But it was a comforting ritual for a little boy and he always picked candles that looked like they would burn the longest. He assumed the modern versions were on timers set to maximize donations. The old woman turned her head toward him, her face a mask of sorrow. Her hand kept moving and the votives kept clicking.

Scarne took a seat in a pew half way down the aisle. At this hour many of the churchgoers were pungent street people seeking temporary shelter and warmth. Although he now rarely saw the inside of any church save for weddings and funerals, St. Christopher's held a personal significance. It was Kate Ellenson's favorite church – and where they had planned to marry. He looked toward the altar. If it hadn't been for the war...

He rose abruptly, disgusted at his mawkishness. He spotted a man staring at him, caught unawares. The man quickly bent down to look at some missals in the slots on the back of the pew in front of him. He hadn't been in the church when Scarne walked in. As Scarne passed him he noted that the man's ski hat. It was the same color as the one worn by the man he bumped into outside the club. The one Mosely had stared away. He wasn't sure about the jacket. Blonde hair stuck out under the back of the cap.

Scarne loitered in the vestibule. The old woman was gone. He put a $20 bill in the poor box, hoping it would get to the poor. The Church had enough real estate, not to mention all those pedophile lawsuits to settle. He immediately regretted that facile condemnation, recalling the sturdy Hispanic priests of his youth, who taught him much about life, including how to throw a wicked slider. Out of the corner of his eye he spotted the man in the ski hat glance his way before turning around.

Scarne darted through a side door. Once outside, he peeked around the corner of the building, his face hidden by his open Tote. A moment later "ski hat" ran out of the front of the church, looking both ways.

"They are giving a class in Surveillance 101 at the New School," Scarne said as he walked towards the man. "You might think about it."

Ski cap was not into witty repartee. He bolted down Park at a respectable clip, considering the traction. Scarne was taken by surprise. He gave chase but the man's sneakers easily trumped tasseled loafers. Running with an umbrella made Scarne feel ridiculous and he closed it. After half a block he assumed a shooter's stance, put the umbrella across the crook of his left arm and sighted on the back of the fleeing figure.

"Bang," he said as the runner turned the corner, where a man who appeared to be studying a map fell over. Momentarily disoriented, Scarne actually thought he had plugged someone with his Tote. Then he realized his quarry had knocked the man off his feet. The downed man started yelling in French.

"Man, you know better than to shoot a loaded umbrella into a crowd."

A hatless vagrant with a toothless grin stood next to him. They both started toward the corner where the sputtering man was already being helped to his feet. The vagrant picked up a small brightly-wrapped parcel and handed it to the tourist. He turned to walk away, water beading on his scruffy beard.

Scarne handed him the Tote.

"Be careful with it," he said. "It's got a hair trigger."

It was 4 PM when Scarne got back to his office. Evelyn was paying bills.

"Any calls?"

"Just Dudley. He wanted to know about Sunday dinner."

Scarne motioned Evelyn into his office and filled her in on the lunch and the incident at the church. She took notes to be transcribed later onto a computer and copied to a flash drive, a routine followed for both legal and billing reasons. But Scarne also wanted to leave a trail, especially for Dudley, should something happen to him. Evelyn wasn't happy about the church thing.

"Do you think it had something to do with you and Shields?"

"I don't know. It's a stretch, unless someone knew I was meeting him, and that would have had to come from him. I'll check it out. It could also be a hangover from an old case, or something else I'm working on now."

Evelyn's mouth turned down slightly.

"I don't suppose it was an angry husband. He didn't shoot you, after all."

"Book me a flight into Miami Tuesday or Wednesday. Then go home. It's turned nasty out there."

"It has?" She smiled sweetly. "I didn't notice."

After Evelyn left, Scarne dialed Dudley Mack's cell. Got a message. He called another number. A husky and familiar voice answered.

"Mack-Sambuca Funeral Home. How may I be of assistance?" Very proper.

"I kill 'em, you chill 'em," Scarne replied.

"Jake, how are they hanging! Where you been? I was just talking to Alice about you." Not very proper. Scarne laughed, as he always did when the "real" Laura Mack came out to play.

"Is your miscreant brother around?"

"Oh, Deadley's somewhere, being a miscreant, whatever the fuck that means. When are you gonna learn to speak English? Did you try his cell?"

"No answer. Left a message"

"Probably getting a nooner. Want me to track him down. Be my pleasure."

"Good God, no," Scarne laughed. "Just tell him I'm on for dinner Sunday."

"Great. We can catch up on our sex lives."

"I'm afraid you and Alice will be doing most of the talking."

"You better believe it. Hey, did you hear me and Bobo are an item?"

"Bobo?"

"Don't be a snot. I could do worse. And have. See you Sunday, sweetie."

MARIA BRUTTI

GARZA DIDN'T LIKE to kill women, let alone this woman. If he'd had more time to plan the operation, perhaps he could have avoided it. But Victor was insistent. Their West Coast clients had to be distracted, and quickly. The big Australian was getting more reckless.

From long experience Garza knew hasty actions often backfired. They were dealing with some very dangerous people. He'd thought about taking his concerns to Alana. Christian had never warmed to her, but Garza had come to respect her judgment. Ballantrae had specifically told him to keep her out of the loop on this one. Something had changed in their relationship. It was obvious that they were no longer having sex. But it went deeper than that. Ballantrae had fallen in love with her. Now spurned, he was listening to her less and less. As ruthless and calculating as Alana had proven to be, she had somehow managed to rein in Victor's more impulsive propensities. And the simple truth was that it was usually Alana's coups that were the most profitable and least risky.

Garza sighed and rubbed his shoulder as he followed the woman out to the parking lot. I hope it's not a rotator cuff. I'll never make fun of Christian and his Pilates again. One class and I can feel it. That instructor must have trained with the Green Berets. I must be getting old. He put on his gloves.

Maria Brutti was tired. Perhaps Pilates three times a week was a bit much, especially after teaching recalcitrant fifth graders all day. But her husband was proud of her. She lifted the rear hatch of her S.U.V. and threw in her gym bag. Carlo thought she was crazy. Which was funny. Because her brother *was* crazy, though she loved him. He liked the way she looked as is, probably because she reminded him of their mother, who died young and still beautiful. Maria knew she was attractive, but would not consider herself beautiful until she lost the 15 pounds her last (definitely the last) baby had added to her frame. Seven more pounds to go.

"Maria, you dropped your wallet in the locker room!"

She turned toward the voice and saw a man in a black sweat suit running up to her holding something in his hand. She strained to make out his face. It was the good-looking Spanish guy who had worked out next to her. It was his first time and she had given him some help with his form. They had chatted amiably and he said he was going to sign up again. She waved hello and then instinctively looked down and started going through her pocketbook. What was his name? She was always doing that. Exchanging names and then forgetting the other person's. So lame, especially when they remembered yours.

Her wallet was right where it was supposed to be.

"I have my wallet," she said. "It must belong to someone else."

Only then did she wonder why he hadn't checked the name in the wallet. But it was too late.

"I know," Garza said. "I'm sorry, but it won't hurt much."

He quickly and expertly drove the ice pick through the fabric of her sweat suit under her left breast and into her heart, up to its hilt. He caught her as she sagged and lifted her into the back of the vehicle, grunting at the pain in his shoulder. As she fell back she said, "My babies."

Garza grimaced as he took her car keys, still clenched in her hand. He gently folded the body into the back around a small child's car seat.

"You had to say that. As if I didn't feel bad enough about this already."

He left the ice pick in her. It was a common tool in the area where she would be found. As the hatch closed Maria Brutti's last conscious thought was not of her children or husband, but of Carlo, who had protected her from their schoolyard days.

Garza drove the dead woman's S.U.V. from the parking lot. Like most suburban mom vehicles it was filled with the detritus of childrearing: hand wipes, empty juice boxes, animal crackers, Star Wars figures, plush toys, games and enough electronic gadgets to manage a nuclear war.

"I don't know how you do it," he said to the dead body in the rear.

Since it was Seattle, of course it had started to rain. The roads were slick and he drove cautiously. An accident wouldn't do. He'd be hard pressed to convince a cop that Maria Brutti had died in a fender bender. The rain got heavier, which actually worked to his advantage. He doubted there would be anyone out and about in the dock area.

When he pulled up to the warehouse next to the pier 20 minutes later the area was deserted. The only sounds, other than the steady patter of rain, were from straining hawsers and lapping waves. The building itself was dark. He would have been surprised by the apparent lack of security but for the fact he knew who owned the warehouse. Nobody in their right mind would trespass.

There were several large containers lined up along the dock. He hoisted Maria Brutti up over the side of one of them. It smelled of fish. She landed inside with a sickening thud. Then he drove back to the gym parking lot and parked next to his rental.

Garza checked the back of the S.U.V. Not a drop of blood. He wasn't worried about any other fibers or D.N.A. There wasn't a forensic scientist on the planet who could find anything incriminating among the stains and crumbs in that S.U.V. The police – and her brother – would assume Maria had been snatched after her class.

Garza was starving. He got into his own car and let the on-board G.P.S. system guide him to Eliot's Oyster House. He had programmed the unit before heading to the gym. He was sore and wet. Nothing a dry martini couldn't fix.

Garza assumed Maria Brutti's body would be discovered almost immediately and given its location her brother would draw the obvious conclusion. The assumption was wrong. Busy dockworkers didn't notice the corpse and the container in which she lay was filled with a load of iced fish. It was almost a full day later when a worker culling the catch inside the warehouse stuck his hook into one of her legs. The delay, which normally would be of no import, would prove catastrophic to the Ballantrae organization, validating Garza's misgivings about hastily planned operations.

THE WILD EAST

"BEHIND EVERY GREAT fortune, there is a great crime," Dudley Mack said after Scarne told him about the Ballantrae case. "Balzac."

It was cool on the deck but it felt like spring was finally gaining a toehold.

"Stop showing off," Scarne said, warily watching his friend fiddle with the pilot lights on a gas grill the size of the USS *Nimitz*. "I know who said it. Behind a lot of small fortunes too."

"Well," the big Irishman said with a wolfish grin. "I try." He kicked the gas canister beneath the grill. "Come on, you son of a bitch. I just replaced you."

Scarne leaned down and turned the tank's handle and was rewarded with a confirming hiss.

"Thanks, Cochise. I was just about to do that. What do you make of the old man's story?"

"I don't know what to think. I like the guy, and he's obviously hurting. But it all seems so improbable. There's probably a rational explanation to all his suspicions. What do you think? Other than quoting dead French novelists?"

"My gut tells me Shields is on to something. So does yours. That's why you took it on."

"He's paying me $20,000 and promised me as much as I need."

"Irrelevant, to you, I'm sorry to say. Most guys wouldn't take five times that to get on the Randolph Shields shit list. You didn't get a good look at the guy in the church?"

"Blonde hair, light skin and quicker than a lap dance in one of your Jersey Shore dives."

Scarne was getting distracted by the continuing gas hiss.

"Turnover, my boy. It's all about turnover." Mack started scraping the grill. "Kind of funny coming right after meeting Shields. I'm not crazy about coincidences. What the hell were you doing in St. Christopher's anyway? Oh, yeah. That's where you and Kate... A trip down memory lane, huh. Nostalgia is dangerous, Jake. Guys who look back never see who kills them. Course, you getting aced in a church is as likely as my ex-wives dying in a kitchen."

"He didn't seem to want to do me any harm."

"Just the same, I'd be careful. Want to borrow Bobo a couple of days?"

Scarne shook his head and poured himself some bourbon from the Maker's Mark bottle kept expressly for his visits. Mack's usual pitcher of martinis sat on the rail near the grill. Scarne had made an early ferry, hoping to catch Patricia Mack in the kitchen so he could snare some fried meatballs before they went into the sauce. For some unknown reason Dudley's Irish mother excelled at Italian cooking. Dinner would start at 2 P.M. and last into the evening.

"Well, watch your ass. If it's connected to the Miami thing, that means you're already in somebody's sights."

"You just watch that damn grill," Scarne said. "It's filling with gas. We're going to wind up in low orbit."

Mack pushed the starter. The grill whooshed to life explosively, sending him staggering backwards across the deck.

"Son of a bitch!"

The kitchen window off the deck opened.

"What in the name of God was that?"

"Nothing, Ma," Mack said, laughing. "Grill's ready. Send out the steaks."

I'll get them," Scarne said as the window slammed shut. "Try not to immolate yourself."

"You try to leave the rest of us some fuckin' meatballs."

After returning with a huge platter of steaks, Scarne watched Mack lovingly prepare the rib-eyes with a variety of his "special" sauces and rubs before consigning them to the fire. Dudley Mack was a carnivore of the first order. When home, he usually could be found searing some kind of meat. Year round. One Super Bowl Sunday, wearing a snow parka, he grilled in near-zero temperatures in a blizzard. Even the family dogs, fierce-looking creatures straight out of a Jack London novel, refused to venture out of the house, scraps or no scraps. Scarne now reminded him of the incident.

"No sense owning stupid dogs," Dudley said.

The hounds of the Super Bowl had long since departed into legend but two fierce creatures that resembled wolves were now watching their master's every move. He flipped the steaks. When they were done, he cut off some big chunks and put them in a bowl that he set on the railing. The dogs, which had started to stand, eased back down. The rest of the steaks went on a fresh platter.

"Feed the boys their meat after it cools. I have to give these to Mom. She finishes them in the oven. It's her secret thing."

Scarne leaned back on the railing and filched a cigarette from Mack's pack. The dogs followed the big platter, but once the sliding door closed returned to their new best friend.

"You guys are easy," he said, looking at the Mack residence.

The house was a reflection of its owner. There was more to it than met the eye. It sat on a one-acre parcel on Howard

Avenue in Grymes Hill, just down the street from both Wagner College and the Staten Island campus of St. John's University. From the street, the dwelling was unremarkable, with the appearance of a large brick ranch. In fact, it was three levels deep in the back, as the property sloped down a heavily forested hill to Van Duzer Street 100 feet below. The third, or top, floor contained a living room, dining room, kitchen, library, master bedroom and two baths. A 40-by-80-foot deck supported by 30-foot steel beams jutted out of the hillside. One could jump from the deck to the top of 70-foot trees, if suicidally inclined. One of the highest points on the east coast from Maine to Florida, it was cool in the summer, and on a clear day the view was remarkable, stretching from Coney Island and the Verranzano up the Narrows to the Statue of Liberty and Manhattan. The middle level of the house contained three bedrooms, two more baths and a 3,000-bottle hermetically controlled wine cellar. The bottom level had a game room and small cabana and bath that opened out to an in-ground pool on a rock promontory set away from the house to catch the sun.

Jake Scarne and Dudley Mack met as juniors at Providence College, a small liberal arts school run by the Dominican Order. Both their families separately hoped the good friars would have a salutary effect on the wild boys.

They initially despised each other. "Deadly" Mack – as he was known to friends and foes alike – was the chief enforcer on the varsity hockey team that frequented the saloon Scarne managed for one of his relatives after school. It was his job to maintain a semblance of order in the bar. After a few drinks, Mack liked to hit people. One night he punched Scarne, who was trying to evict him. Scarne's temper, legendary in Montana, finally made its eastern debut. Although outweighed by his beefy opponent, Scarne fought him to a memorable "no decision" that left both battered before Mack's friends, who didn't want to be barred from their favorite watering hole, broke it up.

Mack, never one to let sleeping dogs lie, came back a week later for a rematch. It was early Monday night, typically slow, and he figured he'd have Scarne all to himself. When he walked in, he found his nemesis already being pummeled by four sailors. One of them, face bloodied, had Scarne's arms pinned so the others could use him as a punching bag. None of the winos in the bar was inclined to interfere. Mack did, on general principles. The boys won but wound up on adjoining chairs in the local emergency room.

"Nice fucking bar you run," Mack said, "Every time I walk in, I get the shit kicked out of me." He extended his hand. "Dudley Mack."

"Jake Scarne." They shook hands, and both winced in pain and laughed.

"I owe you" Scarne said. "I was about to be turned into hamburger. What were you doing there?"

"I came in specifically to kick your ass. I didn't know I had to take a ticket. What's the deal with the Atlantic Fleet?"

"Great minds think alike," Scarne said, smiling. "I threw them out last week too. Listen, we should soak these hands in ice. I know just the place."

Dudley Mack now had those hands in most of the illegal activities on Staten Island, which because of its longtime isolation from the other boroughs, had developed a small town culture alien to the rest of "the city." As college buddies do, Mack and Scarne visited each other's home turf. Mack spent a summer working construction on the reservation in Montana, where he became a favorite with the local lunatics, one of whom even taught him how to scalp. (That would come in handy on one still unsolved occasion back home.) And Staten

Island became Scarne's home away from home during and after college, especially after his grandparents died. He dubbed it "the Wild East."

For most of its history, Staten Island had been a bucolic refuge from the grime and crime of the greater metropolis, ignored by the Manhattan elite. It became a haven for city workers, especially police and fire officers, lured by affordable single-family homes that had plenty of room and land for kids to grow. It also attracted mobsters for the same reasons. The Island's cops and resident robbers were equally intolerant of local crime and violence was a rarity. That began to change in 1964 with the opening of the Verrazano-Narrows Bridge connecting the borough to Brooklyn and the rest of the world. Political corruption became rampant, fueled by the easy money in a real estate boom that rapidly made much of Staten Island unlivable.

In the decades following the opening of the "guinea gang-plank," as Mack delighted in calling the bridge in Scarne's presence, the Island's population quadrupled to almost half a million people. (In fact, many of the hundreds of thousands of post-bridge "immigrants" flooding the borough were Italian-Americans fleeing the crowded and racially charged confines of Brooklyn and Queens.) Unscrupulous developers crammed townhouses on top of townhouses. Huge swaths of the Island fell to the bulldozers of builders whose every project was approved, thanks to bags of cash exchanged in Hero Park on a bench next to a marble tablet listing the names of honored war dead from Staten Island. The money eventually wound up in Caribbean banks or Florida condos. In return for unbridled development, scarring of pristine hillsides, traffic snarls, crumbling roads and the obliteration of centuries-old neighborhoods, Staten Islanders were granted free ferry service. The politicians who orchestrated the carnage named the ferries after themselves.

Dudley Mack avoided real estate entanglements. A seventh-generation Staten Islander, he loved the place. "There's enough honest crooked money to be made," he once told Scarne. "I want to be able to sleep at night."

The Mack clan had started out in the funeral business in the 1890's. But when Dudley took over he sold the two parlors they owned in declining drug-infested neighborhoods. As he put it, "You don't go to a funeral home to get killed; besides there was never enough parking." He opened up newer funeral homes in safer neighborhoods and eventually merged with the Sambuca Home for Funerals. The Macks and Sambucas had long been close. After bloody confrontations in the early part of the 20th Century between the first Italian immigrants and the more established Irish, truce evolved into trust. In the handful of local public and parochial high schools, loyalty to teams soon outweighed loyalty to nationality. Many a refrigerator-sized Sambuca opened a hole in the line to running backs named Mack at Curtis or St. Peter's. Lifelong bonds formed. It was the same for other families. Then came the war. The guy who saved you on Iwo Jima was no longer a Mick or a Dago. He was your Mick and your Dago. And while boys loved their sisters they lusted after their friends' sisters. Wedding bells united families that had once shot each at other.

Dudley Mack branched out into nursing homes and hospitals ("not much of a stretch") and made a fortune, which he plowed into a city-wide string of massage parlors and hot sheet motels. ("I get them coming and going.") His reputation for a ruthless integrity made him a power broker. The Italian mob, weakened by RICO prosecutions facilitated by the propensity to talk into every listening device the Feds could plant, was fighting a losing battle with Russian gangsters who saw the Island as the Promised Land. ("The Ruskies have been landlocked so long they can't believe they can drown people in every direction.") Mack knew there was money to be made in a competitive environment. He financed the Italians to keep them in the game and formed joint ventures with the Russians. The local District Attorney, by Island tradition Irish, concentrated on drunk drivers and his golf game and left everyone else alone.

The sliding door opened and a deep voice rumbled, "Jake, come on in. I think they're gonna let us eat at the table for a change."

He looked up and smiled at Bobo Sambuca, who filled the entire doorway.

Bobo, one of many Sambuca nephews, wasn't cut out for the funeral business. He tried his best but after a widow fainted when he hefted a casket to his shoulder and the other pall-bearers came off the ground, Dudley found him a spot in the inhospitality end of his organization. He excelled as a bouncer in Mack's toughest bars. Mack claimed he'd leave his own bar if Bobo insisted. But one night he bounced too hard and killed a biker who mistakenly equated tattoos with toughness. Bobo jumped his bond and Mack asked Scarne, then with the Manhattan DA's office, to find him before the cops did.

"Bring the dumb shit back in one piece. He's not a bad guy. All he did was throw the loudmouth out the door, which unfortunately was locked. Cracked his skull like a quail's egg. I'm gonna put a sign up. 'Helmet law applies inside the premises, too!'"

"Why don't you let the local cops handle it? The D.A. won't be thrilled about me stepping on their turf. O'Connor hates my guts."

"Hell, I hated your guts and got over it. I squared it with O'Connor. He owed me one. Besides, Bobo's a hothead and he hates Island cops. Thinks they've forgotten where they came from. They used to hang around with Bobo in the same gin mills. They're pissed because he beat them in arm wrestling."

"It wasn't arm wrestling, Deadly. It was extortion. Bobo never lost. Just the weight of his damn arm was enough half the time. Hell, he took ten bucks from me every time I walked into the bar. It was like a cover charge."

"Listen, Bobo might shoot any cops trying to bring him back. He probably won't shoot you, you're family. I'm sure we can get him off on second-degree manslaughter. He didn't mean to kill the guy, who was an asshole by the way. He punched a waitress."

So that's how Scarne and a resigned Bobo Sambuca wound up on an early flight out of Las Vegas on September 11, 2001. Scarne had just nodded off when Bobo nudged him awake.

"Wake up Jake, something is wrong."

A flight attendant raced up the aisle. The seat belt light flicked on and the captain asked all passengers to return to their seats as the plane banked sharply. What the hell!

A man on an Airfone in the next aisle said, "You've got to be shitting me." He looked at Scarne. "They're attacking New York and D.C."

Before he could reply, Scarne noticed the flight attendant who had been on the intercom stride purposely toward him. She leaned down and whispered.

"You are a police officer, right? Can you come with me please?"

"What's going on?"

She leaned down and whispered, "There have been several hijackings. They destroyed the World Trade Center. The captain is worried about some of the people on board. He wants everybody out of first class and his door guarded." Her lips were trembling. "Can you do it? I'll see if I can get help."

"Don't you worry," Bobo said. "You ain't gonna need anyone else. They'd just get in the way." He let the blanket covering his hands slide to the floor. "Jake, take these fucking things off. Sorry, miss."

Jake unhooked Bobo. The girl's eyes widened at the sight of the handcuffs.

"I ain't no choir boy, honey, but I'm just what you need."

"Follow me."

She walked to the first class cabin and asked everyone to move to coach.

"These two police officers need this section."

Sharp girl, Scarne thought. He looked at Bobo, who was grinning at his recent promotion. Some of the passengers had already heard of the attacks and were ready to follow any orders. Those that grumbled took one look at "officer" Bobo and became instantly docile. A few minutes later the attendant brought two off-duty Marines to sit in the first seats of coach. They looked in at Bobo, who nodded at them. They turned and started scanning the rest of their cabin. U.S. Marines know when their flank is secure. The flight was diverted to Indianapolis. The people the pilot was worried about proved harmless, or were rendered harmless by Bobo's presence. By the time they landed, Scarne had gotten most of the details of the catastrophe and was anxious to call his secretary. At the time his office was at One Liberty Plaza, directly across from the Trade Center complex. Bobo was also frantic.

"My cousins work a boiler room in the North Tower. I hope they made it."

Bobo wasn't talking about a maintenance shop. It was an open secret that Mack and the Sambucas controlled a small brokerage house that specialized in pumping shares of companies that had no products, revenues, earnings or future. The boiler room also ran the biggest football pool in lower Manhattan. After landing, they jumped in a cab and headed into town. Scarne figured they'd have a better chance of renting a car outside the airport. They almost struck out. The clerk at the rental counter in the Indianapolis train station claimed all his cars were reserved. Fortunately for them (and unfortunately for him), he was of Middle Eastern extraction, and Bobo was having none of it. They left in a brand new Volvo, unlimited mileage.

On the ride out of town, Scarne got through to Maria Marquez, his secretary at the time.

"You're gonna need a new office," she began without preamble. Puerto Rican girls were tough once they brushed the dust off.

After 12 grueling hours, they arrived on Staten Island, where Scarne was supposed to deposit his "prisoner" at the 120th Precinct in St. George.

Bobo wasn't happy. "I gotta see my family, Jake. Then I'm gonna go into the city and look for my cousins. You can't turn me over."

A sworn officer of the law, Scarne knew he couldn't let Bobo go.

"Here's my cell number. Check in with me every day. I'll square it with the D.A. He's got other things on his mind right now. But if I tell you to surrender, get back here. I'll be in the city, too. I'm trusting you, Bobo."

"Don't worry, Jake. My word is good. And I'll never forget this."

It was, and he didn't. Bobo spent a month at Ground Zero even after he learned that his cousins survived. He was worth four men. The D.A., who acted honorably for once, finally pulled the string and Bobo surrendered. His rescue efforts, attested to by dozens of firemen and cops, were acknowledged in his sentencing report. He did a year on an involuntary manslaughter plea.

At that, he got off easier than Scarne or Mack. They both enlisted, something neither of them let him forget.

†

As Scarne and Bobo walked into the dining room, Mack and his father were already seated at the huge table and, as usual, debating politics.

"Scumbags, all of them."

"Well put, Dudley" George Mack said. "Very profound." He smiled at Scarne. "Jake, there are more horses' asses in this country than horses."

"I recall you telling me that once or twice Mr. Mack. I could be wrong."

That brought a gentle slap to the back of Scarne's head from Patricia Mack, who was walking by carrying a large tray of lasagna, which she put down next to a round platter of antipasto. Jake found it curious that she served the antipasto and pasta together. He had mentioned it to her once. And only once.

Now she said, "You know George has a dozen more piquant sayings to go through before dessert. Might as well let him get them all out."

Then, addressing her husband, she added, "And you shouldn't call your own son a horse's ass in front of company."

"Jake's not company. He's family."

"And truth is a defense," Scarne added helpfully.

"What about Bobo?"

"Oh, for God's sake, Pat, I got the expression from old man Sambuca. And I wasn't referring to Dudley. Besides, Bobo's almost family from what I hear."

"Oh, shit," Bobo said. "Sorry, Mrs. Mack."

"What a fine bunch of idiots," she said. "Dig in. I got the antipasto from Stanzione's. Think of it as your salad." She shot a look at Jake. "The lasagna's mine. The steaks will be ready in a minute. Girls, get the side dishes and the kids, not necessarily in that order. Bobo, open the wine."

Most of the meal conversation revolved around the athletic prowess of the various Mack grandchildren produced by Laura and Alice and their ex-husbands. The marital record of the girls had for years provided cover for both Mack and Scarne when the subject of their own love lives was broached. Most of their kids were at the table. The extended clan, consisting of parents, stepparents, grandparents, in-laws (and a few outlaws), aunts, uncles, cousins and others usually made up the largest cheering section at any parish game. It also made for some very unhappy refs. After dinner, the youngsters headed to the game room. Scarne and Bobo helped the girls clean up

When he got back to the table, father and son were back talking politics.

"You weren't always so cynical about things," George Mack said. "Both you and Jake served your country."

"I think he drugged me when we enlisted. Anyway, that was then. The people who run things now are a ferry ride away. Not that I give a rat's ass. This is a great climate to make money. But it bothers my pal, Jake, here. He's a romantic. Want to hear him recite the Gettysburg Address?"

"Put a sock in it," Scarne said equably, pulling up a chair. Dudley's war had also been short and brutish. He dealt with it by joking.

"No more politics," Patricia Mack said sternly as she sat down, casting a worried glance at her son. She knew he and Jake didn't talk about the war. "Or no coffee and dessert. So, Jake, how's your love life. When are you going to get married?"

"Ma, give it a rest," Laura said.

"You give it a rest. Jake's getting long in the tooth to be catting around. I thought Italians were all about family and Sunday dinner."

"How about them Knicks," Bobo murmured.

"Mom, don't be insulting," Dudley said. "You're stereotyping Jake. He's part Indian. All he wants to do is get drunk, roam the prairie and rape white women, or maybe just women. Or is it buffalo, I never could get that straight."

Pat Mack ignored him

"Oh, Jake knows how we feel about him. Bobo, too. There's nothing wrong with keeping with your heritage. And I realize that this family hasn't exactly produced poster children for the sacrament."

Scarne didn't like the way this conversation was headed either.

"If you ever stop feeding me, Mrs. Mack, I'd probably have to get hitched. When the right girl comes along, who knows? If I could have caught one of the Bobbsey twins here between husbands, it might have happened already."

"You wish," the sisters said simultaneously.

"The right girl came along," Patricia Mack continued. "You let her get away."

"I need a smoke," Dudley interjected quickly.

The four men retreated to the deck.

"Thanks for the rescue," Scarne said, taking one of the cigars his friend passed around. "Even if you did suggest I screwed buffalos."

Soon a cloud of smoke hovered around the four men as they puffed quietly. The breeze was against them and it drifted toward the kitchen window.

"For God's sake," Patricia Mack said as she slammed the window closed.

The men laughed.

"Hell," Dudley said. "I'd rather get porked by a buffalo than get cross examined by Ma."

"She means well," George Mack said. "But women have to get men married. It's in their DNA. But, Jake, if you don't mind my asking, how's Kate?"

"She's in LA. Won't talk to me."

"I'm sorry I introduced you two," Dudley said. "She poisoned your head."

"Nonsense," his father said. "It's the ones that make you crazy that matter. Never be cautious in matters of the heart, Jake. Remember one thing."

"I sense a piquant remark coming," his son said and they all laughed.

George Mack patted Scarne on the shoulder.

"A faint heart never won the chorus girl."

†

SEATTLE SLIME

THE THREE MEN and one woman stood silently in a small dimly-lit room facing a large window. Folding chairs bracketed a dull-gray metal table on the opposite wall. The water cooler and wastebasket by the door were also gray. A bright red ashtray on the table and the white blinds covering the window seemed out of place.

Two of the men were from Seattle's elite Homicide Unit, which consisted of three squads of six detectives each who worked full time on the 30 or so murders that the city of 570,000 people generated every year. Seattle homicide cops were proud of their 80% one-year clearance rate. Given the circumstances and the people involved in this particular crime both cops hoped for a quick resolution. Their superiors obviously expected one. The squads usually caught murders in random rotation. Not this time. These two detectives had the highest closure rate in the division and were specifically assigned to this case.

The woman was a new assistant district attorney. She tried to look professional but was falling a bit short. Although it was purposely cold in the room, there was a slight sheen of sweat on her face and she was taking exaggerated breaths. One of the cops, a large dark-skinned man with a sad face named Noah Sealth, exchanged a knowing glance with his younger, white partner. She wasn't bad looking for a D.A., Sealth noted. He hoped she wasn't a fainter. Supposed to be an up and comer. The first one of these is always the toughest. She'll adjust. He was wrong. This would be the woman's last time at the window. Within a month she'd be doing wills and trusts, and in therapy.

The third man in the small room was almost as impassive as the detectives. Only his rigid posture suggested a coiled tension. He even offered the young woman his handkerchief, which she almost took before realizing the absurdity of the situation. For the man was well known to all three law enforcement officers. Ordinarily, none of them, particularly the cops, would have given him the time of day. Today they were very solicitous, which he appreciated.

A fan kicked in with a rattle that settled into a hum. It was part of the facility's primitive positive-pressure air-circulation system designed to keep the interior environment protected from outside contaminants. Sealth knew its limitations. They weren't making computer wafers in there. At best, the system helped to suppress particularly noxious odors. But what was that smell? He sniffed the air, hoping not to be too obvious. Then he remembered where the woman was found. He said a silent prayer that Brutti wouldn't ask him.

A buzzer went off as a small red bulb over the center of the window lit. The woman gave a visible start. There was no reaction from the men. The white detective said gently, "Carlo, are you ready?" The man didn't turn his head, but nodded. The cop reached for the drawstring that controlled the blinds and started pulling. On the other side of the window was a gurney on which was draped the form of a woman, made clear by the gentle mound of her chest under the sheet. A white-haired and bespectacled man in a light green medical smock stood at the head of the gurney. Around his forehead was a visor that had a small light attached. He looked like a coal miner, Sealth thought. I guess he is going to do the post himself. Kind of unusual for the chief medical examiner, notorious for not working weekends, but this was an important case. Glad he held off on the mask and the gloves until this part was done. The M.E. was not known for his social skills. Would have been just like him to show up with a blood-stained apron and a surgical saw in his hand. The presence of the M.E. also explained why there were two other people near the foot of the gurney, a man and a woman in their 20's. Trainees. The woman held a spiral notebook; the man a clipboard. Their pens were poised. They had serious looks on their faces but were obviously nervous. The cops looked at each other. Of all days for show and tell! They knew that the M.E. was a stickler about on-the-job training, but at the same time they felt some sort of adversarial professional courtesy for the victim's brother and didn't want a circus. Sealth, who was still worried about the A.D.A., was thankful that this viewing promised to be a piece of cake. It wouldn't do to have city employees on both sides of the window dropping like flies in front of this particular relative.

If Brutti noticed the extra audience, he didn't react. The only noticeable effect to the sight of the body was an increase in the depth of his breathing. The cop at the window pressed a button on an intercom and said, "OK." The M.E. reached across the body and pulled the sheet back from the head, draping it modestly well above the woman's breasts. The dead woman's skin was very white. Sealth reflected briefly that even for a corpse she looked exceptionally drained of color. Probably the immersion, he thought. His eyes met his partner's.

"Is that your sister, sir?" the younger cop said.

Brutti said nothing. He stared at the face. Then the tough-guy veneer broke.

"Maria!" he said. "What did they do to you?"

"Is this your sister?"

Brutti got control of himself and nodded. Then, realizing that the officers probably needed a verbal response, he said. "Yes, that is my sister."

"Sorry for your loss," Sealth said, as his partner reached for the intercom and the drawstring. "Let's go outside and see about her personal effects."

It was an obvious attempt to distract the bereaved man. Again, he was thankful for their consideration. This was not pleasant for them, he realized, no matter what their feelings about him. A young woman was dead and they would do everything they could to find out what had happened. The fact that she was the sister of a notorious local gangster might complicate their investigation but not alter their dedication to find her killer. In that they would make common ground. He knew they wouldn't even bother telling him to leave it to them. This would not be the first time Carlo Brutti tried to save the state the time and money of a trial.

"Where was she found," Brutti said.

Shit. Sealth hesitated.

"I will find out anyway, detective, so you might as well tell me now."

"In a warehouse near the docks."

"What warehouse?" Brutti's eyes bore into his. Double shit.

"Seattle Seafood Distributors."

"Boyko!" Brutti spat the name out.

"Don't jump to any conclusions, Carlo. We don't know anything yet." Sealth decided not to tell Brutti his sister was found under a half-ton of halibut.

The detective who was lowering the blinds heard something clatter on the other side of the window. He looked into the other room. The male student had dropped his clipboard. His mouth was agape. This had barely registered with the cop when he noticed the young A.D.A., who had stopped in her tracks and was now staring at the gurney with one hand at her throat and the other bracing herself against the window, knees buckling. Sealth also saw the prosecutor sagging and took a step toward her. But a shout drew his gaze into the scene on the other side of the window. The medical examiner and his two students now had all their attention focused at a point about two-thirds down the table. The male student had started backing away.

"What the fuck!" the younger cop said. "Noah!"

The A.D.A. screamed. Both cops forgot her and rushed to the window. The draped body was motionless, but the sheet was billowing upward and undulating. The people on both sides of the window were frozen. Only their heads moved as they followed the swaying "bulge." They looked like spectators at a tennis match. Finally, the medical examiner, forgetting the proprieties and the brother, ripped the sheet completely off the body.

"Mother of God!" Sealth exclaimed, instinctively reaching for his weapon. He stopped in mid draw. A slithering pinkish grey eel-like creature was crawling down the corpse's right thigh. A bubbling excretion started to spread from the animal. It rolled off the table onto the floor, although the whitish slime made it seem like it was still tethered to the woman. When it hit the tile floor it made a disgusting smacking sound, clearly audible through the glass. It was at least two feet long, thick as a garden hose.

There was a loud crash from inside the viewing room as the A.D.A pitched backward into the folding chairs, almost upending the metal table. None of the men even turned. In the morgue itself, both students had now fled to a far corner. The boy was vomiting. Even the M.E. had retreated a few feet.

But once over his initial shock his scientific training took over and he began to advance on the "thing." Its movements were slowing. It's horrible mouth, rimmed by serrated teeth and short thick rubbery tentacles, opened and closed spasmodically. Then it was still.

The total silence which accompanied the final moments of the terrible tableau was shattered by the sounds of fists pounding on the window. Only then did the detectives remember Brutti, who seemed to be trying to claw through the partition. The white officer pinned his arms back while Sealth shouted, "Get him out of here!" Then he turned to the A.D.A., who was moaning feebly and bleeding from a nasty gash on the back of her head. He put his handkerchief against the wound. She was coming around. He took off his jacket, rolled it up and made a pillow for her head. Uncharitably, he hoped she wouldn't bleed through. It was his favorite. Scalp wounds were the worst. He heard his partner and Brutti shouting in the hallway. Other voices, shouts. An alarm began clanging. He looked up and saw the M.E. gingerly prodding the slimy creature with his booted foot. The two assistants were slowly walking towards the table on which a now totally naked woman lay indelicately exposed. For some reason he noticed her bright red toenails, so incongruous against her pale skin and the horror of her condition. It made him think of the ashtray on the table. He'd been off cigarettes almost two years but now he felt like he might kill somebody if he couldn't get a smoke.

One of the kids, showing amazing spunk under the circumstances, reached for the sheet. Sealth punched the intercom and shouted, "Don't touch anything. I want a crime scene unit in there!" He reached for his cell phone. Christ! What a colossal fuckup!

PEST CONTROL

THE GULFSTREAM II leveled off at 42,000 feet just as its sole passenger finished his first glass of wine.

"Would you like more Cabernet?"

"I'd be a fool if I didn't," Jesús Garza said, holding out his glass to the smiling Miss Universe lookalike that Victor favored for his fleet of three corporate jets. As usual the wine served aboard the company's planes was superb. "And what is that scrumptious aroma?"

"Lamb cutlets. They'll be ready in a minute. Can I get you a salad first?"

Having a "getaway jet" at his disposal certainly made things pleasant, Garza thought, stifling a yawn. What the wine started the food would finish. He'd sleep most of the way to Florida. After a mostly wet week in Seattle, he was looking forward to some time off in Naples, where he and Christian maintained their permanent residence. The Florida Gulf Coast town was 90 minutes by car and a world away from the Miami madhouse. Naples was surprisingly open to other lifestyles and had a small but vibrant gay subculture. Garza and Keitel chalked that up to the basic practicality of Midwesterners, who dominated the town. They had many friends of all persuasions and were fixtures at the town's annual Wine Festival, which raised millions for local schools and drew the elite of Hollywood and Wall Street. Garza was hoping to surprise Christian with an invitation to one of the private dinners prepared by Emeril or Martha in one of the hedge fund mansions in Port Royal. Yes, Garza thought, Naples was a sweet place to unwind, with its 100 golf courses and world-class restaurants. He hoped Christian had called the cleaning service.

In fact, Keitel had just made the call after discovering a *Periplaneta americana* swimming in one of the condo's four toilets. The palmetto bug (the Chamber of Commerce name for the huge cockroach) was not primarily a house dweller, but lived in the lush vegetation that the tropics provided and made an occasionally memorable domestic foray. Too big to squash, the bug was now ensconced in a small Tupperware container. Keitel carried it out to the pond on the golf course bordering their house. He could see the breakfast swirls of the pond's fish. Opening the top of the container, he flipped the creature into the water. Its six legs started kicking up ripples in every direction. The vibrations were like a dinner bell. A huge bass blasted into the bug, coming halfway out of the water. Apparently, it didn't find palmetto bugs disgusting. Damn, that was a big fish! With all the chemicals draining into the water, Keitel thought, the pond's bass could hit 70 home runs in the majors.

Christian Keitel and Jesús Garza had been together for five years. They met in one of Miami's hotter clubs, which, while not catering exclusively to gays, was a reliable place to find lovers of any sex. The German had recently arrived in the country, and was looking for work. He had done some modeling but it was soon apparent that his talents lay elsewhere. Garza gave him surveillance jobs and an occasional debt collection. The ex-commando proved adept at both. Any doubts about his potential were put to rest one night after he was accosted by two men who tried to relieve him of his night's receipts.

"They used to work for the pig that owed the money," Keitel told Garza the next morning, sporting a bruise above his right eye.

"Used to work?"

"Here's the money."

"This is more than he owed," Garza said.

"I cleaned out their wallets after I killed them. The idiots pulled knives. I'll take care of the pig tonight. It will be on me."

Garza, the more reflective of the two, occasional wondered at the odds of two homicidal gay men of such differing backgrounds winding up together. Actually, he had to admit, it probably wasn't all that remarkable given the incredibly varied and bizarre nightlife available in Miami. Some of their hangouts reminded him of the cantina in Star Wars.

Both were well liked within the Ballantrae organization by the majority of their fellow employees – who knew them only as "Financial Consultants" – for their good humor and consideration. They remembered birthdays, were the life of office parties and avoided the politics and backstabbing prevalent in most financial services firms. (Frontstabbing was another matter.) They shared a large corner office on the 40th floor overlooking Biscayne Bay. They also shared a beautiful secretary whose main function was to book their trips. They were often out of town. She wondered how brokers could spend so much time out of the office. But that was not unusual in this company. The entire floor was seemingly staffed by receptionists and secretaries. The plush executive offices were usually vacant. Garza and Keitel did no mailings, gave no seminars and rarely made a phone call. But business seemed to be thriving. It was the same for many of the other brokers. At least her "boys" kept her busy with their travel and active social life. She was always ordering tickets to some play or gallery opening for them, or catering one of their parties. The other secretaries and assistants rarely had anything to do. Over lunch or in the coffee room some of the girls complained about being bored. Once in a while somebody wondered where all the money was coming from. But since some of that money was coming their way – the pay was excellent and everyone got a nice bonus at year's end – the talk never went past the donut stage.

It was well for them that it didn't. The whole operation was a sham and hemorrhaging money. The brokers – the men and women who occasionally showed up – were all legally registered with Series 7 and 63 certificates and were licensed to buy and sell securities. But they rarely did that. True, there were a couple of old-timers hired as window dressing. Any clients they brought in, any assets they gathered, any trades they generated, were gravy.

For the main business of the financial services section was laundering money. So much that the brokerage operations could afford to "lose" $30 million a year. Jesús Garza and Christian Keitel had their Series 7, but also a few Glock 9's. They would argue that of all the executives on their floor, they were the only ones with real jobs. The company employed many tough characters in its Security Division, but Garza and Keitel were the problem solvers. They took pride in their work and made it as entertaining as possible, believing traditional assassinations too dangerous. A double tap to the back of the head with a silenced .22 aroused suspicions even in the dimmest cops. But bizarre, hard-to-explain deaths were usually written off as bad luck. Garza, with his experience in Castro's service, was by far the more innovative. That rankled Keitel, whose only real coup involved the impregnation of one target's toilet paper with tetrodotoxin, an instantly fatal nerve poison. And even that he'd borrowed from the Mossad, something he neglected to tell his partner.

Keitel was lying naked on his stomach on a lounger, his head hanging over the end, where he had placed a Kindle on a wooden stand. He was half way through *The Old Man and the Sea*. Garza had started him on Hemingway; like many Cubans he revered the American author.

Keitel's body was muscled and golden, broad shoulders tapering to an absurdly thin waist. His buttocks were taut; he was an accomplished runner, both at sprints and distance. At the base of his spine, where there was a small knob, a tuft of golden down waved gently in the breeze provided by an overhead fan in the covered part of the lanai a few feet away. Keitel knew that the prominence of his tailbone was caused by too many rough parachute landings (and idiotic boat rides). It was, literally, a pain in the ass, but the hard little knot couldn't be surgically repaired without risk. Besides, he knew that many of his lovers found the little "tail" attractive.

Keitel barely remembered his parents, who died when he was very young. He and his older sister were taken in by an aunt and uncle who were as kindly as they were dull. The couple had no children of their own, and apparently few friends, the result, Christian suspected, of the Keitel family's rather checkered past, which included a distant relative who had been Hitler's chief of staff. That was a Keitel who didn't run fast enough; his wartime service earned him a trip to the gallows. The aunt and uncle were farmers, so both Christian and his sister, Hannah, grew up strong. There was plenty of good solid food, but farm work melted off the calories. He rarely saw Hannah anymore, but recent photos indicated that she should not have given up milking cows. Still, she was a pleasant enough woman. Keitel regularly sent her large amounts of money with the understanding that half would go into German and French real estate, and the rest to educating her ever-growing brood of children.

A track star in school, Keitel immediately distinguished himself as a non-commissioned officer and eventually wound up in Germany's elite KSK, or "Special Power Commando" battalion, the equivalent of the British SAS. He participated in several secret combat operations, often with allied units.

Keitel stopped reading. He watched a small lizard feasting on ants. It was fascinating. The lizard, a dark green anole, was perched on the bottom rung of the umbrella table next to Keitel's chaise. The ants were trying to navigate a no-man's-land between the pool and the small flower garden bordering the lanai. The ants often stopped in patches of dappled shade caused by the leaves of nearby plants. Some even paused near drops of water that had sprayed from Keitel's body after his frequent cooling-down swims. Were they drinking? Or just made momentarily cautious by the change in their almost microscopic environment? The tiny reptile stayed motionless, but for its bobbing head, until an ant wandered into the killing ground. Keitel estimated that the distance between the lizard's ambush site and the ant trail was three feet. Once the anole targeted an ant it was over in seconds. A few lucky ants veered away under Keitel's chaise before the lizard pounced. Their good fortune annoyed Keitel and he finished them with a finger. The only other part of his body that moved was his head, moving up and down in rhythm with that of the lizard.

Garza dropped his bag on the kitchen counter and grabbed a Dos Equis from the refrigerator. Kicking off his shoes he padded silently out to the pool.

"Christian, I believe you have finally gone around the bend."

"Be quiet. Don't frighten him. It's almost in his kill zone."

Garza ignored him and sat down in a chair next to the table. That was too much for the anole, which shot into the garden.

"Thank you very much."

"Just what are you doing?" Garza was exasperated.

Keitel told him.

"I know this is Naples, Christian, but aren't you a bit young for a retirement home?"

"Show some respect. We are amateurs compared to that little assassin. Look at how far he had to traverse. It would be like one of us running a city block for a bite and back again in ten seconds."

"Remarkable. But I prefer our diet, no? Which reminds me, I am hungry. Get dressed. Let's go out for dinner. I will tell you how it went in Seattle."

"Let's try that seafood place on Third Street," Keitel said, springing up.

"Good God, no! It will be some time before I can look a fish in the eye again. I want French food. You can satiate your blood lust by stalking a snail. By the way, what are you doing home? I thought you had jury duty again."

"I did. Criminal trial. A redneck pederast from Everglades City who raped a little Hispanic boy in Immokalee."

Garza lit a cigarette as they walked into the house.

"I remember the story. As if those poor people out there don't have enough trouble. What happened?"

"The guy pleaded out before it went to the jury. Lucky for him. We were ready to kill the bastard ourselves."

"Don't worry; it's a death sentence for him. They don't mess around with that kind of scum down here. The cons at Raiford will deal with it. But tell me, Christian, what do you say in court when they ask about your occupation? I've always wondered."

"Pest Control Specialist."

They both laughed.

AN ADORING PRESS

"WATCH YOUR ASS in Miami," Dudley Mack said as he drove Scarne to catch the 7 A.M. ferry to Manhattan Monday morning. "It's a rough town, despite all the Chamber of Commerce bullshit. Third world. If you get jammed up, I know people who owe me down there. Big time"

"I'm sure you do. Some of them may even be out on bail. If I spot anybody following me wearing a ski cap, I'll call 911."

"Anybody ever tell you you're an asshole?"

"You, all the time," Scarne said as he got out of the car and with a wave waded into the throng of half-somnolent commuters.

He was in his apartment by 8 A.M. He had purchased the one-bedroom at 2 Fifth Avenue, just above Washington Square Park in the East Village, with most of his inheritance. Now, he probably couldn't afford to sell it. The flats in the 40-year-old, 18-story building apartment were almost twice as large as those in newer buildings. Scarne had almost 1,600 square feet of living space, and that didn't include all the closets, two of which were walk-ins. To get comparable value, he'd have to move back to Montana.

The apartment was sparsely furnished. He told people it was "manly" or "Spartan." In truth, he couldn't make up his mind on the décor. Living in the Village didn't make a decision easier. There were so many antique and specialty shops around he found himself changing his mind every week. The women who occasionally slept over were not Spartan in their opinions or suggestions. A couple had even "dropped off" paintings or accent pieces, most of which quickly took up residence in the back of a closet (unless the gifter was scheduled for a return visit). That didn't happen often. Scarne valued his privacy. Besides, the majority of his flings preferred their own beds.

The apartment was not totally bereft of refinement, thanks to the burnished St. George Rosewood chess set on a Staunton pedestal game table in his living room. He had debated putting the set in his office, but thought that would be a bit much. Both table and set had belonged to his grandfather and were non-negotiable in any redecorating scheme. At the moment Scarne, a good college player whose game had improved under fire in pick-up games in Washington Square Park, was engaged in a tough battle with an Internet player who was using a confounded Ruy Lopez defense. It was Scarne's move, and he had been mulling it for days.

He was just getting out of the shower when Evelyn called.

"I just got off the phone with a fellow named Nigel Blue."

"As in red, white and..."

"Yes. He works for Randolph Shields."

That didn't take long, Scarne thought.

"What did he want?"

"Mr. Shields would like you to be his guest tonight on the corporate yacht. La dee dah."

"That's the name of the yacht?"

"No, you goose. That's my comment on your recently exalted status. The name of the yacht is *Emerald of the Seas* and she is supposed to be a beauty. Anyway, Randolph is hosting some sort of party. Starts at six. They can send a car for you. What do you want me to tell Mr. Blue?"

"That I will be delighted. It will give me a chance to wear my tie with the little sailboats on it."

"The 52-story *New York Times Building, designed by noted Italian architect Renzo Piano and constructed almost exclusively with recycled steel, is the seventh-tallest building in the United States and one of the most energy efficient in the world. Located on the east side of Eighth Avenue between 40th and 41st Streets across from the Port Authority Bus Terminal, it features a natural gas cogeneration plant, an exterior tinted-glass curtain wall that gives the illusion of transparency and 18,000 individually-dimmable fluorescent lights. It also has under-floor air distribution, a free-air cooling system that brings outside air inside and mechanized shades to reduce glare."*

Robert Huber looked up from the glossy brochure.

"I really like the next part."

"There is no on-site parking, although building managers recently established indoor space for 20 bicycles."

"This is all very fascinating," Scarne said, passing a coffee and bagel across the desk. "Cinnamon with a smear, right?"

"They never should have built the fucking thing," Huber said, biting a huge chunk out of the bagel. "They sold the old building for $175 million in 2004, and in 2007 the new owners, a bunch of sharks, resold it for $525 million. This joint cost a billion. Do the math. I warned them."

Indeed he had, Scarne recalled. With 34 years at "the paper of record" Huber was a true journalistic dinosaur. Even though he favored grey three-piece suits, maroon ties and cordovan wingtips, he had the waspish mien of a tough police reporter. He kept his white hair in a buzz cut and his stocky build hinted more of muscle than fat. All you had to know about Huber was the legendary – and documented – incident when he demanded cab fare from a pistol-wielding mugger who had just relieved him of his wallet. And got it.

He was also a fearless and prescient reporter. In a series of articles in the *Times* business section he had explained why the nation's real estate boom could not be sustained. The extensively researched stories noted that even if Manhattan prices held up better in a crash, media companies facing new competition should preserve capital or invest only in new technologies, not bricks and mortar. While he never mentioned *The New York Times* by name, it was clear who he meant, especially within the walls of the old building at 229 West 43rd Street, where he lobbied against the new edifice. Huber was something of an embarrassment to management, which was now shedding staff and drastically cutting costs to service a huge debt load. Not surprisingly, they offered him a buyout. Also not surprisingly, he refused and with a George Polk business award in his quiver, they had to put up with him. He was moved off the real estate beat, however, and now covered Wall Street. ("Same catastrophe, different pew," he said.)

Scarne and Huber were sitting in a starship-like newsroom overlooking the ground-floor gardens. All around them were the accoutrements of modern media. Reporters sat in front of the latest computers, working their iPhones, Blackberries or more advanced wireless devices (Scarne found it hard to keep up), occasionally glancing at wall-mounted plasma televisions and their streaming news: An electronic sea of instant information designed to make the organization they worked for obsolete. Some of the brightest minds on the planet were in this building, Scarne knew, and while he often disagreed with the "paper of record," especially its frequently facile dismissal of the traditions and collective memory of the society that protected it, he believed that its demise would be one more indication that the barbarians at the gate had the code that would unlock civilization's protective keypad. To his mind, too many people relied on the Internet, which for all its power and promise was becoming a lowest-common-denominator sewer of libel, scandal and vulgarity.

"What's the pastry bribe for," Huber mumbled with a mouthful of bagel.

"What can you tell me about Victor Ballantrae?"

"Why?"

Scarne sighed. Over the years the two had traded favors, but Scarne was at least one down to Huber and the reporter wanted to let him know.

"When you ask about someone," Huber said, "it's usually because a bowel movement is about to hit the fan. So, I get curious. It's what they underpay me for. Why do you want to know about Ballantrae?"

"I think he landed in a spaceship at Area 51 and is really a lizard."

"Well, that's OK, then. As long as there's not a story in it for me."

"So, what about him?"

"You're not going to tell me, are you?"

"Nope."

"That's it? I bend over for a fucking bagel?"

"And I'll buy you dinner at The Waverly Inn."

"This century? No way. You ain't got the clout."

"Yeah, I do" Or rather, Dudley Mack did. "And I'll renew my *Times* subscription."

"Now you're talking. Every little bit helps around here. But why don't you just Google the guy? That's what these numbnuts do for background." Huber made a dismissive wave at reporters nearby, making sure he could be overheard. An attractive young woman at the next desk gave him the finger.

"I did. Mostly PR stuff. He's apparently the second coming. I thought you might provide something more down to earth."

"To tell you the truth, I've been thinking about pitching a piece on Ballantrae to the bullpen." Huber smiled and lowered his voice. "After I Goggled him, I made some calls. I hear he's looking to make a big move into the media. Couple of interesting names being thrown around. Tri-City Communications, Shields, even this place, though management insists the Old Grey Lady isn't for sale."

Scarne kept his face impassive at the mention of Shields, but Huber must have noticed something.

"Is that it, Jake? You doing some due diligence for a takeover target? I could use some confirmation. My editors get nervous when I look into anything to do with the media."

"I don't work for any potential takeover target." It wasn't really a lie, Scarne rationalized. "Satisfied? Now can we get to it?"

Huber reached into his desk, pulled out a reporter's notebook and began flipping pages.

"Victor Ballantrae is 45 years old, born in Australia and a billionaire. He's also a citizen of Antigua, which may knight him, so he'd be Sir Victor."

"Antigua has knights?"

"Days, too. Sorry. Yeah. It's an honorary thing. If you have enough money, you can get the title. You know what I say, at my age once a knight is enough."

Huber's cell phone buzzed. He picked it up and listened for a minute.

"Oh, for Christ sake! Just find out who it is and tell 'em we'll evict them if they don't stop. I know it's a stupid fuckin' law. But we have to be purer than Caesar's wife. Caesar. Julius. He was – shit, never mind. Just do it."

He flipped the phone onto his desk and looked at Scarne.

"My super. Can you believe it? Indian guy in my building is bitching about another tenant smoking. Threatening to go to City Hall. Says it's coming through the vents." Huber and a couple of older editors owned a small SRO building in the Bowery. It didn't surprise Scarne that Huber handled complaints. "Might not even be on his floor. I don't know how he can even smell it. You can smell the curry crap he makes in Hoboken." Sighing loudly, he went back to flipping pages.

"Anyway, Ballantrae recently applied for American citizenship. He's his own fucking UN. Apparently never been married, but his early years are a black hole. According to the corporate bio bullshit he led a hardscrabble life in the outback then made a fortune in mining and insurance before getting into banking. Arrived in the U.S. with a shitpot of money and then branched out into the Caribbean, setting up a big international bank in Antigua. Also very successful in the Texas oil patch, real estate and in insurance again. Over the last five years or so, he has moved aggressively into financial services. He owns homes in Houston, Miami, Colorado, Antigua, and London, and a 120-foot yacht. You ever see it? It's over at Chelsea pier."

"No, I haven't," Scarne replied. He didn't mention that he would be on the Shields yacht in a few hours.

"Then there's the three jets and, if you count all the dough he's spread around, Antigua and several American Congressmen who oversee offshore banking."

"Sounds like a self-made man," Scarne said. "Nothing wrong with that. Anything make you suspicious? Why were you thinking about doing a story?"

Huber threw his notebook on his desk and sat back.

"Ballantrae may have cut some corners moving so fast into financial services. There's been a few minor run-ins with the S.E.C. But he's never been accused of any criminality. My sources tell me that he's getting a reputation on Wall Street for sharp elbows. Could be sour grapes. He's beginning to grab deals from established players and snapping up their talent. But even his rivals give him credit for his philanthropic work. A lot of people think he's a breath of fresh air on Wall Street. The new paradigm after what we've been through."

Huber picked up his coffee and tilted his chair back.

"That sets my bullshit antenna tingling. Tell you a story. When I was covering Wall Street the first time in the mid-80's, I sat in on a meeting with the top editors, people who couldn't find their asshole with a GPS system now. They wanted their reporters to prepare glowing profiles on the brilliant financiers who were then changing the paradigm – there's that word again – of Wall Street. They asked my opinion. I said it was a marvelous idea because when the people we profiled got indicted we'd scoop everyone else." Huber sat forward and laughed, almost spilling his coffee. "You'd have thought I farted in church! I told them that I didn't know what their superstars were doing but it had to be illegal. Couple of months later, Boesky, Milken and the rest were busted. Twenty-five years later, it was Madoff, Drier, Stanford. All of whom got their balls licked by an adoring press before the cuffs came out. Things never change. Ballantrae may be legit, but he fits my profile for shysterism. He has a piece of a couple of casinos in Vegas and the Caribbean. They say he's his own best customer and drops two, three hundred grand a night. He's also a fanatic golfer and plays at all the best clubs, usually for very high stakes."

"So what? So do I."

"Ten, twenty grand a match?"

"Well, no."

"Didn't think so, hotshot. Then there's the broads. Always a model on his arm. Not a bad looking guy. Big bastard. Don't know what more I can tell you. If you come across anything you'll let me have it, won't you? You owe me."

"I gave you Barnes and Taliger before anyone else," Scarne said.

"Yeah. Great story. I got to like those fruitcakes. Completely unrepentant. Told me it wasn't like they put fingers in the chili at a restaurant. Only sued 'blood-sucking brokers,' as they put it. Personally, I'm glad they didn't do any time. By the way, they think you had something to do with that. Did you?"

"I put in a good word for them, but I think their restitution had more to do with it." Scarne laughed. "They sent me a Christmas card."

"Me, too. Well, they know real estate. Helped me on a couple of stories. More than you've done lately."

They walked out of the newsroom together.

"I can't believe it's so quiet in here," Scarne said.

"Newspapering went to hell when they switched from hot to cold type," Huber said. "When I started, it took time for the composing room to punch out the linotype and arrange the words. We had a couple of hours between editions and could run out for a real dinner and some drinks. Hell, I could go to the Village, Chinatown, Little Italy. Mix with people; find out what the fuck was really going on. Now, with computers, there's maybe a half hour between editions. These kids rarely get out into the real world. They're glued to their computers. Of course, it may all be academic. We're facing extinction."

"Why don't you take a buyout?"

"And give up my bicycle slot?"

†

EMERALD OF THE SEAS

THE SLEEK BLACK limousine pulled up to the 23rd Street dock next to Chelsea Piers. Scarne got out and gazed in admiration at the *Emerald of the Seas,* the magnificent seagoing yacht that was the most visible symbol of the Shields media empire. At a time when corporate bigwigs were shedding private jets and other the trappings of their wealth, the family stubbornly held on to the yacht, which for years had entertained advertisers, lobbyists, politicians and movie stars. It had been featured in both Bond and Bourne movies and its lounges and staterooms were the staple of architecture and fashion spreads in two-pound coffee-table books that invariably highlighted the huge oval bed on which Randolph Shields reportedly entertained many starlets half his age.

Other limos and taxis pulled up, disgorging a cross-section of New York's cultural, media, political and financial elite. Scarne recognized at least two of Wall Street's recently disgraced CEO's heading up the gangplank with their slim and spectacular trophy wives. Not the gangplank they deserve, he thought.

"Mr. Scarne?"

He tuned to see a thin black man wearing a Hugo Boss suit.

"I'm Nigel Blue, Mr. Shields's assistant. Thanks for coming on such short notice. Please follow me. Have you ever been on the *Emerald*, Mr. Scarne?"

"No. She's a beauty. Must be 200 foot."

"Just under. Mr. Shields named her after his daughter, Emerald...Emma."

"Beats the hell out of *Randolph of the Seas*."

Blue started to say something but was drowned out as a helicopter circled the ship, hovered and finally landed on a small pad behind the bridge.

"Mr. Shields is hosting a short cruise up the Hudson tonight," Blue explained as the copter's whine decreased. "It's the first of the season and rather special. Some guests have flown in. We pick them up at the airports."

Two white-coated stewards were checking in guests at the top of the gangplank. Both wore little blue berets. Blue nodded at them and he and Scarne jumped the line. As they walked down the length of the yacht Scarne peered into several lounges where bars were already doing a good business and more stewards were passing canapés.

"We have bars and buffet stations set up on every deck but there is a V.I.P. cocktail party on the fantail," Blue said. "Mr. Shields will join you there."

"I'm honored," Scarne said. "Is Sheldon Shields on board?"

Blue looked at him and smiled.

"No. He is otherwise occupied."

"I thought he hosted these types of events."

"Not tonight, apparently," Blue said easily. "He recently lost his wife."

"A pity."

There were only a few people on the fantail, situated just below a deck on which two rakish cigarette boats hung from davits. Most were sensibly congregated near a bar. It was warm for the first week of April but Scarne noticed a couple of space heaters, which would undoubtedly come in handy when the cruise got underway. The guests all seemed to be drinking wine or champagne and Scarne was momentarily discouraged until he saw a tall, auburn-haired woman standing alone at the rail sipping a martini.

"I have some duties to attend to, Mr. Scarne," Blue said. "Can I get you a drink before I leave? Mr. Shields will be along shortly."

"I'm fine."

Scarne was particular about his martinis and after Blue left went to the bar and ordered one to his liking. Then he walked over to the rail and stood next to the woman. He tilted his glass at her.

"Until I saw you," he said. "I feared this might be a wine-tasting cruise."

She laughed.

"When you've been on enough of these," she said, "you learn that a stiff drink is the only thing that makes them bearable."

"Well, I'm not sure that sentiment would go over well in Rwanda," Scarne said dryly as a steward offered them some smoked salmon. "But I can see where all this could be a burden. Let them eat canapés!"

"Oh, God. You're right. Listen to me. Marie Antoinette on the Hudson."

"I'm just teasing you. I wouldn't worry about the Rwandans." Scarne adroitly snared a small beef Wellington from another passing tray. "But you might not want to tell Randolph Shields how you feel."

"Oh, I already have. Many times." Before Scarne could react to that, she said. "Speak of the devil."

"Is that anyway to speak of your father, Emma?"

Scarne turned. Randolph Shields could have used a few of his brother's inches to spread his weight more attractively on his frame. He wasn't fat, but even his expertly tailored Armani suit couldn't hide the fact that he's earned his reputation for good living. But his fleshy face, with its prominent eyebrows, strong nose and piercing blue eyes radiated power and privilege. With him were the city's billionaire Mayor, Police Commissioner Richard Condon and the President of the City Council, a weasel-faced man named Michael Grubber. A trio of plainclothes bodyguards hovered nearby, as inconspicuous as white rhinos.

"I see you've met my daughter, Mr. Scarne."

"Yes, we were discussing the situation in Rwanda."

Shields looked confused, but said, "Tragic, tragic. Those poor people."

He turned to his guests and introduced Scarne, who shook hands with the Mayor and Condon, who said, "Like a bad penny, Jake."

Grubber, whose face had turned splotchy red, didn't offer his hand. Rather, he said, "You son of a bitch," turned on his heel and stormed away, startling everyone except Scarne and Condon.

"What the hell was that about," Shields said.

"Perhaps you shouldn't have tried to throw him off the balcony at City Hall, Jake" Condon said, trying, unsuccessfully, to suppress a smile.

"Man is overreacting. I had a good grip on him. Of course, had I known he would become President of the City Council, I might have dropped him."

"Too bad," the Mayor said. "Would have saved me a lot of trouble with the budget. Well, come on Dick. Let's go smooth his ruffled feathers."

"I'd better go along too," Shields said, staring hard at Scarne. "Emma, will you entertain Mr. Scarne for a moment?"

He walked off without waiting for a response.

"I suspect I may not be invited to too many of these shindigs."

Emma Shields smiled. "It was shaping up to be your only one, anyway. I guess what my father says about you is true."

"And what's that?"

"You are trouble."

"Some women think that's my most endearing quality."

"They probably don't own stock in Shields Inc."

Scarne didn't have a witty comeback for that, and was relieved when several couples walked over to them. Amid air kisses Scarne drifted a few feet away and studied Emma Shields. She was a very pretty woman with an angular, athletic frame. She wore her rich hair long, a style that often does not work in a woman in her mid-30's, as Scarne guessed her to be. It worked for her. Her face radiated intelligence and a bit of mischief. She wore little makeup and was dressed sensibly for the weather. The night air and slight breeze brought out color in her cheeks. When she was alone again he approached her.

"Why do I feel as if I'm going to walk the plank tonight?"

"Perhaps because you should. My father thinks you are taking advantage of Uncle Sheldon."

"Do you?"

"I'm very fond of my Uncle. And I loved Josh."

"More than your portfolio?"

Emma's face hardened.

"Grubber is right. You are a son of a bitch."

"You brought up your stock position in the company, Ms. Shields. I'm a simple gumshoe hired to find out what happened to your dear cousin. If that means trampling on people's sensibilities and jeopardizing Wall Street's next big scheme, so be it.

You can help or hinder me, but that won't change the outcome. I'm going to find out."

"I suppose that means you are going to Miami."

"Yes. And Sheldon tells me you and Josh were close. I was hoping you might be able to answer a few questions."

Before she could reply, they were interrupted by Randolph Shields.

"Will you excuse us, Emma? I'd like a word with Mr. Scarne in private."

"Of course, Dad." She extended her hand to Scarne. "Will you be joining us for the cruise up the Hudson? We sail at eight."

"I think Mr. Scarne..."

"Has other plans," Scarne finished.

Randolph's stateroom was the size of a large hotel suite but still managed to be dominated by the famous circular bed, which was covered by a thick, dark red comforter. Photos of Randolph Shields and various dignitaries and beautiful women were arrayed on walls and ledges. The two men sat opposite each other in leather lounge chairs.

"How much is my brother paying you?"

"Don't beat around the bush, Mr. Shields"

"I asked you a question."

"None of your business."

"Whatever it is, I'll double it."

"I seem to be having a good week."

"Then it's a deal?"

"No. I sense a conflict of interest."

"How much do you want?"

"To do what?"

"Drop this nonsense about my nephew."

"Let me ask you something Mr. Shields. How do you know your brother hired me?"

"It's wasn't all that hard. He withdrew a considerable amount of cash from his office account. I have contacts at the Federal League Club."

Probably monitors his calls, too, Scarne thought.

"My brother is sick...delusional. Understandable, with what he's been through. I have to protect him from making a fool of himself....or being taken by some shyster looking for a big payday."

Scarne stood.

"Thanks for the drink Mr. Shields. You've got a nice little boat. I think I'll go below and visit the galley slaves."

Shields stood and blocked Scarne's way.

"Victor Ballantrae is a respectable businessman and a valued friend. I won't have him harassed by a cheap gumshoe."

"Just for the record Shields, I'm an expensive gumshoe. Do you need Ballantrae's dough so badly, you'd risk covering up your nephew's murder?"

"You arrogant son of a bitch!"

"We seem to be reaching a consensus on that."

Shields jabbed Scarne in his chest.

"I loved Josh. He and my Emma grew up together, like brother and sister. But his death was an accident! And if you don't drop this lunacy I'll make your life miserable. I'll get your fucking license. I promise you."

Scarne didn't like to be touched. Or threatened. The combination was too much. Blood roared in his ears and everything seemed to take on a reddish haze. His mind barely registered a knocking sound, growing more insistent. Shields saw something in Scarne's face that made him stagger back. The knocking grew louder and finally the stateroom door flew open. It was Emma Shields, with a worried-looking steward standing behind her.

"Daddy, is everything all right?"

Randolph, his face red, turned to her.

"Scarne was just leaving."

†

On his way off the yacht, Scarne spotted Dick Condon at a buffet table.

"Where's the Grubster?"

"Last I saw, he was getting smashed on the poop deck, or whatever they call the goddamn thing." Condon laughed. "I thought he was going to poop his pants when he saw you. What the hell are you doing here, anyway?"

"I was invited by Randolph."

"This have anything to do with your lunch with his brother?"

Scarne tried to avoid lying to Police Commissioners whenever possible.

"I'm doing some work for Sheldon."

"Not for Randolph?"

"Actually, he just threw me off the boat."

Condon stared at him.

"It's complicated. But don't be surprised if you get a call from him. In the meantime, can you do me a favor?"

"What is it?"

"Isn't your pal Timoney still the police chief in Miami?"

"Yeah."

"Give him a call and see if he can put in a good word for me with the local homicide cops and the medical examiner's office down there."

Scarne could almost see the light bulb go on above Condon's head.

"Sheldon's kid?"

"I told you it's complicated."

"I didn't think you could piss off any more people in this city, but I never fail to underestimate you."

†

Once ashore, Scarne headed to a line of cabs still dropping off guests.

"Mr. Scarne!"

He turned to see Emma Shields walking toward him.

"I'm sorry about what happened," she said when she reached him. "I'll have Nigel call you a car."

"That's not necessary. I'll catch a cab. I'm just glad I wasn't keelhauled."

"We stopped doing that years ago." She smiled. "At least inside the 12-mile limit. Can I ask you a question, Mr. Scarne?"

"Of course."

"Do you think Uncle Sheldon may be right...about Josh?"

"I wouldn't take his money if I didn't think there was a possibility. What do you think?"

"I don't know what to think."

"Emma!" Randolph Shields was standing at the top of the gangplank. "Our guests are waiting." Some of those guests looked surprised and embarrassed at the tone of his voice.

"When are you leaving for Miami?" Emma Shields said.

"Wednesday morning."

"I'm teaching some courses tomorrow at the New School but I'll have a break at lunch. Can you meet me?"

"Just say where and when."

"Noon, at the Rose Café in the Village? It's at Fifth and..."

"I know it. I'll see you there."

She headed up the gangplank and Scarne made sure to look at her legs the entire way. He probably would have done it anyway, but the thought of "Randy" Shields watching him gave him a perverse, if childish, pleasure.

†

BABY'S BREATH

THE BEAUTY OF Georgia is wasted at 80 miles per hour. So, after a lunch at a Cracker Barrel – a chain restaurant, to be sure, but ridiculously satisfying – Garza left Interstate 16 at Dublin and headed southeast on local roads. That prompted a steadily stream of robotic remonstrations from his already programmed GPS system, which didn't suffer fools gladly. But it eventually threw in the towel after one desultory "calculating new route."

Garza decided to put the top down on the convertible and really enjoy his new route, which would add at least 45 minutes to the trip to Claxton. Then he'd have another 30 or so to Statesboro. But Bradley Cooper wasn't going anywhere. Nor was he expecting any visitors. Garza figured he'd arrive by 3 P.M., when most residents would presumably be sleeping off their chicken, soft rolls, gravy and Jell-O.

The speed limit on the local roads was 55, but could suddenly drop to 35, even 25, in and around small towns. Wary of speed traps, he paid attention. There was no hurry. The rich red Georgia earth was speckled with green, and variegated buds sprouted on trees and bushes awakening from winter. The air smelled sweet and the horses in the pastures seemed to be having a lot of aimless fun. At one point he pulled over and walked over to a fence near where a mare and her foal were grazing. They were beautiful animals and from the look of their glistening black coats well cared for. The mare's tail was swishing back and forth slowly. The little guy's tail was going a mile a minute.

Garza had hoped for such a moment and had come prepared. He emptied a few Cracker Barrel sugar packets into his palm and stuck it through the fence. He was surprised at how quickly the foal bounded over to him. His was undoubtedly not the first hand through that particular fence. The foal, which had a white star on its forehead, lapped the sugar as the mare watched cautiously. The baby's tongue was warm and surprisingly soft. It almost tickled. Garza kept very still and made no sudden moves when he opened more packets. Sensing no danger, the mare eventually sidled over and began nuzzling his hand as well. She towered over him. She didn't interfere with her foal's treat until Garza moved his hand under her muzzle. A mother, after all, is a mother. Her tongue was rougher and he could feel her teeth. Her breath was hot against his palm. He produced more packets, wishing he had some apples or carrots. Or even some fruitcake. They probably would love that. But it might not be good for them.

"It has nuts," he said to the mare. "Might not agree with your little fella. Besides, I'm not coming back this way."

At the sound of his voice the mare twirled a huge brown eye toward him, dipped her head and nickered, as if in appreciation at his thoughtfulness. Garza knew he was anthropomorphizing; horses weren't as intelligent as they looked. But it was a charming moment nonetheless. Not for the first time he wondered what, if anything, animals thought. He had, by necessity, spent many hours with people whose cognitive faculties had deteriorated to the level that basic awareness could not be assumed or proven. Was this horse now more "intelligent" than those poor sods in the nursing homes he visited? Garza realized he was teetering on a rationalization. He reached up and rubbed the mare's neck.

"Stupid," he said.

The mare's nostrils flared.

"Not you, beautiful. Me."

Garza left the pasture reluctantly. He checked his watch. He hadn't meant to stop that long. But the interlude had been worth it. He loved horses. When he wasn't fishing much of his youth had been spent riding the mountains meadows and hills of Cuba. Again, memories flooded back, but no regrets. He had come to believe that there was no place on earth as beautiful as the American Southland in spring.

Garza abandoned his sightseeing to make up some time, but slowed when he reached Vidalia, home of the famously sweet onions, as the de rigueur billboard announced. He smiled. Sometimes it seemed as if every town in the South was famous for something. If it wasn't a Civil War battle (pardone! *The War for Southern Independence*), it was some form of produce.

He was startled from his reverie by a pair of motorcyclists who overtook him just as he left the town. They roared by him, cutting in front so closely he had to brake. Neither wore helmets.

"Organ donors," he muttered.

His normal good humor was restored when he reached the outskirts of Claxton (*Population:* 2,391 the welcome sign stated) and spotted the familiar 50-foot water tower with its "Fruitcake Capital of the World" slogan. Claxton, he knew, was famous for only two things: fruitcake and a meteorite that crushed a resident's mailbox in 1984. He'd read someplace that the mailbox, the only one in history believed to have been hit by a celestial object, brought $83,000 at auction.

Garza wasn't interested in meteorites. He turned off Route 301 onto Main Street and three blocks later pulled into the parking lot of the Claxton Bakery. He visited the bakery whenever he was in the area and knew the Claxton story by heart. How the bakery was started in 1910 by an Italian immigrant named Salvatore Tos, who made a special fruitcake for Christmas. How Tos sold the business to his longtime apprentice, Albert Parker, when he retired in 1945. How Parker decided to concentrate on "old family recipe" fruitcakes rather than compete with supermarket bakeries sprouting up after World War II.

A brilliant move, as it turned out. The Claxton Bakery and its rival Georgia Fruitcake Company (started by another Tos apprentice) have since shipped millions of fruitcakes all over the world. The United States military is one of their largest customers. That, Garza was sure, generated plenty of jokes about fruitcakes being used as weapons. Certainly a Claxton fruitcake dropped from a drone on some Taliban fighter would do the trick!

Most civilian customers, including a thousand charities that sold Claxton fruitcakes at fundraising events, probably ordered them through the company website. Garza occasionally did as well. But he also liked to visit the store, where he could soak in the ambiance and sample new products. Like most Cubans, Garza had a sweet tooth. He was always bugging Christian to remind his sister to send extra Stollen at Christmas. He'd received his first American fruitcake as a gift, and now considered himself an aficionado. He had come across no finer fruitcake than the ones made in Claxton. He ate them, gave them as gifts, shipped them to relatives back home, left them in every nursing home he visited and expounded the glory of the recipe to anyone who would listen. Christian naturally bore the brunt of his enthusiasm, and often reminded him of the time a bar of the dense mixture of nuts, candied fruit and pound cake in Garza's carry-on was mistaken for plastic explosive by airport security.

"It has the same consistency," Christian said.

Garza opened his trunk. He stood back for a long moment and then took out a large bouquet. After checking it for leakage, especially around the stems, he placed it on the back seat of his car. A little fresh air wouldn't hurt the flowers. He also didn't want to risk the bouquet being crushed by his purchases. With rising anticipation he entered the modest store that fronted the huge bakery complex. The smell of fruitcake was overwhelming. He'd once asked a sales clerk if he could view the production facilities, only to be told that the company's insurer now forbade the once-popular tours. Damn insurance companies ruin everything, the clerk had griped. Garza, while not mentioning that he occasionally worked, in a manner of speaking, for an insurance company, wholeheartedly agreed with the man.

The walls and shelves of the store were lined with fruitcakes. Platters of samples, each on a small doily, were everywhere. Most people, Garza included, preferred the regular Claxton fruitcake over the dark variety, made with more molasses. But the dark variety was useful for one of Garza's favorite treats, which involved soaking several loaves in Myer's Rum for a month in his refrigerator. Even snotty Christian usually asked for a loaf.

One of the platters featured "Nut-Free Fruitcake." Garza didn't remember ever seeing the product. Must be new. A small placard next to the platter read: *Southern Original Fruitcake, For Those With an Allergy to Nuts*. He tried a piece. Not bad! He thought of the mare and her foal. What a pity.

He took his time, tasting a sample, sometimes two, from every platter. A clerk finally came over.

"Can I help you, sir?"

Probably thinks I'm just here to eat the samples, Garza mused.

"Let me have 40 regular, 20 of the dark and 10 of the nut-free, all in individual one-pound loaves." The man stared at him as he picked up another sample. "And perhaps you can help me carry them out to my car."

He gave the clerk a generous tip for loading the fruitcakes into his trunk and a half hour later pulled into the parking lot of the Bartlett Home and Hospice on Pine Needle Road in Statesboro. With a bouquet in one hand and a Claxton fruitcake in his jacket pocket he walked up the stairs to the nursing home's large veranda and said hello to a small group sunning themselves in rockers and wheelchairs. Bradley Cooper wasn't among them. Most were asleep but a few smiled, probably hoping he was visiting them. One elderly lady put out an onion-skin hand to him. He took it, careful not to squeeze too hard. It felt like a trembling little bird in his hand.

"Lawrence?"

"No, ma'am. I'm sorry."

She quickly lost interest and he went through the door.

As he walked past the central nursing station, the duty nurse said, "Those sure are lovely flowers, honey."

Every woman below the Mason-Dixon Line said "honey," either at the beginning or end of a sentence. Garza really loved the South.

The bouquet certainly was spectacular. Figuring it was the least he could do, Garza had spared no expense. Bradley Cooper was one of the insurance unit's most important clients. If anything, the florist had gone a bit overboard with the Vanda orchids, spray roses, gloriosa lilies and chrysanthemums.

"Thank you," he replied, handing the fruitcake to the nurse. "You are very sweet."

She smiled indulgently. The nursing home was only a few towns over from Claxton. It was not her first fruitcake.

Cooper was in Room 126, down a long hallway. Garza came to a recreation room. Inside a young man in a wheelchair sat at a table, moving some blocks around with his right hand. His left arm was folded awkwardly in his lap. He seemed to be having trouble holding his head up. Stroke victim, Garza assumed. He'd always been surprised at how many younger residents were confined to assisted-care facilities.

There was nobody in the hall and none of the other patients appeared to have visitors. As he walked past rooms his senses were assaulted by a variety of human and mechanical smells and sounds unique to nursing homes. One never got used to them. Nothing out of the ordinary, to be sure. Bartlett was immaculate, unlike some of the assisted-living facilities he'd been, where residents sat in dirty pajamas amid overflowing trash receptacles. After those visits he'd sent off scathing anonymous letters to the authorities. But no matter how nice some nursing homes were, Garza had long ago decided he would shoot himself before it ever came to that.

When he finally reached Room 126, he walked in, closed the door and smiled at Bradley Cooper, who was watching a television on a small ledge at the foot of his bed. The old man looked up and nodded, trying to place Garza. When he couldn't, he went back to his show.

"What are you watching?"

"CSI," Cooper answered, sounding annoyed.

Of course, Garza thought, suppressing a laugh. While no spring chicken – he was 81 – Cooper looked surprisingly healthy. His skin tone was good and his voice strong. Garza knew that recent surgery on a blocked intestine had laid Cooper low. That and some leg troubles had forced him into the nursing home. There was nothing terribly wrong with Bradley Cooper.

Cooper had a roommate and Garza walked over to his bed. Compared to this shriveled old fellow, Cooper looked like Derek Jeter. The man looked up with rheumy eyes and Garza gently patted his arm with his free hand.

"How are you, old timer?" Garza said.

"The clams are flying."

"That's wonderful," Garza replied, and turned back to Cooper.

"He never makes any sense," Cooper said. "Alzheimer's. I keep asking for a roommate with some marbles left, but all I get is the wackos."

Garza knew the old goat was feisty. He frowned and Cooper apparently had second thoughts.

"You here to see him? Sorry I said that. He's not as bad as the last one. Least he's quiet most of the time. But I'll be glad to get out of here. Soon as they reverse this damn colostomy." Senior citizens, Garza knew, showed no hesitation in discussing the most intimate details of their medical condition, even with total strangers. "That's a hell of a bunch of flowers. But they're gonna be wasted on him."

"Actually, Bradley, these are for you."

Cooper looked at the massive arrangement. He was obviously confused, but also pleased.

"Who are you?"

"A friend of your cousin. Asked me to drop them off. Here, why don't you smell them before I get a nurse to put them in water?"

"My cousin?" Cooper scrunched up his face in thought as he leaned in to take a whiff. "Which one? Gladys?"

"Yes. She's quite fond of you."

"You'd think she'd visit once in a while. Decatur ain't all that far."

"I'm sure she'll be seeing you soon," Garza said. "Here, let me prop those pillows for you."

"What's those little white thingamajigs?"

"Baby's breath," Garza said as he put a handkerchief to his own face and pressed the turkey baster's bulb at the bouquet's stem. The little spray of liquid hit Cooper squarely in the nose.

"Jesus," he managed to gurgle.

"Actually, Mr. Cooper, it's Jesús."

Despite the flowers, an almond odor began to permeate the room. The old man's eyes rolled back. His chest heaved and his face turned purple. Garza wasn't worried about the color. It would soon fade to the light blue hue typical among the recently deceased in nursing homes. Cooper fell back on his pillow with a plop, quite dead. A bolus of some recently eaten glop dribbled out the side of his mouth. That, too, was consistent with a sudden stroke or cardiac event. Nothing like a little verisimilitude, Garza thought as he went to open a window. A few drops of cyanide on the rose petals nearest the center of the bouquet glistened in the afternoon sunlight as they quickly evaporated. The odor soon dissipated. He looked out the window, which faced a broad expanse of lawn at the back of the nursing home. Perhaps a dozen or so residents were sitting on benches or in wheelchairs facing the sun. A large black man dressed in whites moved among them, checking their blankets, occasionally stopping to pat an arm or a shoulder. The orderly laughed at something one of the residents said. This was a very nice facility, Garza decided.

When he turned from the window he noticed the roommate, who was now sitting up and staring at the arrangement.

"Want to smell them?"

"I don't think so," the man said.

Jesús Garza laughed softly and walked out, dumping the flowers and turkey baster in separate trash bins. They would leave no traces, and, even if they did, the chemicals involved would be indistinguishable from many of those found in any medical establishment's refuse. More than likely they would be in a landfill or incinerator before anyone questioned the death of an old geezer like Cooper. The fruitcake would be opened and eaten in short order. Besides, Garza's fingerprints, which weren't on file anywhere, were now interspersed with those of hospice staff. So, he could have his little fun and leave tasty calling cards.

Garza had long ago decided that the lack of security at nursing homes was second only to that at funeral homes. The closer to the grave the less one's personal safety mattered. If anything, assisted living facilities in the South were more laid back than their counterparts elsewhere. Southern hospitality. Flowers and fruitcake got him the run of every nursing home he visited. (Christian was partial to Russell Stover chocolates when on similar assignments.) Yes, nursing homes were easy. Of course, not all the clients were in nursing homes. That called for a little more creativity. They occasionally had to deal with clients so active and vital they were threatening to become centenarians and blow a hole in the bottom line. Christian still bragged about the skydiving accident he'd arranged for an 88-year-old!

But Bradley Cooper's sudden death, not exactly a stop-the-presses event at a nursing home, would be written off as a massive infarction or embolism. There would be no autopsy. Within a month, his insurance company would pay off on a $4 million policy owned by a subsidiary of the Ballantrae Group that had purchased the policy from Cooper in return for $450,000 in upfront cash that allowed him to afford assisted living care. Such arrangements were perfectly legal and not unique to Ballantrae. According to actuarial tables, even after paying premiums in some cases for up to 12 years, a company could make a nice return, of say, 15%, on its investment when the insured finally passed away. Of course, if the insured died much sooner, the new beneficiary could make a real killing. In the instance of Bradley Cooper, who succumbed after only six months at Bartlett, Ballantrae realized almost $3.5 million in profit on its $450,000 investment, or about 777%.

Of course, killing codgers *was* illegal. But Ballantrae had suffered some severe reversals in the economic downturn.

Garza didn't know all the details, but knew that the company's mortgage department, in particular, had taken a shellacking. Victor had been pressing Garza and Keitel to increase the body count among insurance clients who were surviving long past their expiration dates. They argued that it was risky and took them away from more important assignments. Victor was adamant, arguing that the death of 20 or 30 seniors, spread out among the 16,000 nursing homes across the nation, would go unnoticed. It would be a rounding error. "A drop in the bucket list," he joked.

But not on the profit statesment. Garza estimated that their insurance activities were easily generating $100 million in much-needed cash a year.

Given all of Ballantrae's schemes, their workload was getting onerous. He and Christian might have to join a union. The teamsters would probably be a good fit. Or maybe ask for a piece of the action from the River Styx unit, as Garza dubbed the operation.

He headed out of Statesboro. A company jet had dropped him in Macon but he planned to drive the six hours to Miami, stopping off for a restful night in St. Augustine, one of his favorite cities. He knew a restaurant that served the best frogs legs and shrimp in Florida. His cell phone buzzed. He saw the name.

"What are you doing for the next few days?"

Alana Loeb rarely wasted words.

"Nothing important," he sighed. So much for the frog's legs.

"I want you to go to New York. I need some background on a private investigator there."

Because of his intelligence background in the Castro government Garza was given all Ballantrae's sensitive research assignments. Victor and Alana considered him the brains and Christian the muscle. That rankled the German and even bothered Garza, who, despite his frequent teasing, knew how innately smart his partner was and didn't like him denigrated that way.

"What is his name?"

"Jake Scarne."

"Why the rush?"

"He's heading to Miami any day now. And he may be a problem."

Garza listened for a moment, asked a few questions and then hung up. Alana, as cool a fish as he'd ever encountered, sounded worried. She was putting too many fingers in Ballantrae's dikes. And she was plugging only the leaks she knew about. Victor hadn't told her about his insurance scheme. Alana didn't draw many lines, but euthanizing old people for profit was probably one of them.

So Sheldon Shields was suspicious of the "accident." Garza wondered why. But if the old man was willing to buck his brother – Alana said Randolph called Ballantrae to warn him about the private investigator – it meant serious trouble. It wasn't that he and Christian didn't have experience dealing with private investigators. Some of Ballantrae's business practices attracted them like flies. But they'd always been able to buy or scare off the ones that somehow got through Victor's lawyers. They certainly never even came close to killing one. Let's hope the lawyers can deal with this Scarne character, because with Sheldon's money behind him it was unlikely he could be bought.

Garza called his secretary on his iPhone. He told her to book him a commercial flight out of Jacksonville, two hours away, with a return to Miami. He also told her to do an Internet search on Scarne, as a "potential client." She had access to the sophisticated legal and law enforcement databases Ballantrae's in-house lawyers used.

"Email the results to me," he instructed her.

He'd start making calls to his contacts in New York while driving to Jacksonville. And once in New York he'd do some legwork on the ground, and also break in to Scarne's apartment. By the time he got back to Miami he'd know everything about Scarne, including his shoe size.

His secretary called him back. He was booked on an 8:20 P.M. nonstop to Newark. He had time to kill. Just as well. He'd have to find a UPS store to ship the damn fruitcake to his home. He'd expense it. It was their fault after all. He had another thought and called his secretary again.

"I don't want to stay at one of our regular places. Get me a room at the Waldorf." He then gave her the name of his three favorite Manhattan restaurants. "Reservations at 8 P.M. for the next three nights, in any order. You're a doll. I have some fruitcake for you."

Garza's stomach rumbled. Could his system stand two Cracker Barrel meals in one day? Every cloud had a silver lining. It was still light out. Garza smiled. He decided he could make a quick stop at the pasture and treat the mare and foal to some nut-free fruitcake.

It was now on the way.

A ROSE BY ANY OTHER NAME

"THERE IS A wonderful story about Charles De Gaulle. After World War II he visited Stalingrad at the invitation of the Soviets. Viewing the devastation, he was heard to mutter, 'What a magnificent people. What a magnificent people!' His hosts, making the natural assumption, proudly began to recount the valor of the Russians who had prevailed. 'Non. Non. Not the Russians,' De Gaulle said. 'The Germans, that they could come so far.'

There was an appreciative twitter and Emma Shields looked up from her notes on the podium and smiled at the 40 or so students sitting in the front rows of the New School auditorium. At least a few of them knew their history.

"Sometime it takes an enemy to see an opponent clearly. In De Gaulle's case, he saw past the atrocities of war to praise the underlying character of a misguided and misled nation. Would that the peoples of today's world – friend and foe alike – pay Americans the same compliment for our accomplishments, not in war or conquest, but in furthering the advancement of mankind in so many realms. It has long been apparent that the character of the American people is a distillation

of all the races, creeds, languages, hopes, angers and histories of the world.

"America is – and has always been– different. Americans have confounded statesmen for hundreds of years. Bismarck, with unconcealed envy, said that Providence watched over 'fools, drunks and the United States of America.' How else could the Iron Chancellor, or anyone else, regard a country that grew in might and prosperity despite cataclysms that included a Civil War that would have torn any other country asunder? To understand America – and the character of its people – one must not look at the country through the pragmatic political prisms used by the Bismarcks of the world. America was, and is, more than merely lucky. It has forged a political and cultural society that has molded citizens who – despite inevitable disagreements – have one thing in common: Love of country. Not the jingoistic patriotism so many people assume they have, but a deep love and respect that comes from an understanding that they are stewards of something special.

"Americans are not necessarily braver or smarter than other people. But you can make an argument that, given their country's power and influence, they are often more responsible. Yes, responsible. They make mistakes, sometimes terrible mistakes. But in a time when a world left to its own devices produced some of the most savage regimes and madmen in history, Americans usually came down on the side of the oppressed and the vanquished. And they have righted many wrongs. Not always, but surely enough times to register on the global conscience. Historically, Americans have been generous with aid and comfort during natural disasters. Over the last century, American science has saved, conservatively, a billion lives that would have been lost to disease or starvation. It is certainly one of the great ironies of history that many people alive today in the Third World want to destroy the very country that saved them. Is every American innovation – particularly in matters of culture – a step forward? Of course not. But Americans walked on the moon, and can usually be trusted to broaden the human experience more often than not.

"It is undeniably true that Americans, whether native or immigrant, have been blessed with a fertile continent protected by oceans that allowed the development of stable political system rooted in democracy. But they have used their legacy wisely. They have not wasted the world's time."

Emma Shields closed her notebook.

"And I hope I haven't wasted yours. Are there any questions?"

A hand shot up.

"How can you be so naïve? The rest of the world hates our guts. We attack anybody we want. Our bankers bleed us while their CEO's make millions. We're the richest country in history and we don't have universal health care or free college education. I don't buy this crap."

The kid who delivered this diatribe was thin, scrawny and long-haired. He didn't stand up. In fact, he was slouched in his seat with one foot perched on the back of the seat in front of him. He was wearing the uniform of the day for college: jeans, ratty shirt and some sort of cowboy vest. Scarne wanted to punch him, even if he had made a couple of good points.

Emma Shields gripped the podium with both hands and looked directly at the boy, scowling in mock seriousness.

"Jeremy, it's considered bad form to embarrass your teacher with facts."

Even Jeremy, who sat up straighter, joined in the laughter.

"Oh, you know what I mean," he said.

"Sure I do. And I'd be lying if I said I didn't agree with some of the things you said. But you're smart enough to know that your view of the United States is colored by your age, your friends, your current position in life. I'm not happy about a lot of what is going on either, and I get pretty discouraged. But I wasn't talking about the United States or its policies and politicians today. I was talking about the country we want, the country at its best. The ideal. The United States as it may be remembered. You might do well to recall what Napoleon said: 'History is a fable agreed upon.' It may be too early to judge."

A few of the students started to stand, slinging their backpacks. Emma Shields gathered some papers and walked down the stairs at the side of the stage and started up the aisle, chatting with kids as she went. Jeremy said something to her and she swatted him playfully on the back of the head. Scarne stood as she passed him.

"Ms. Shields. I hope you don't mind, but I had some time to kill and crashed your class. Caught the tail end."

"I saw you come in. Did you get anything out of it? And how about Emma and Jake from now on?"

"Sure. I liked the De Gaulle story. I'd heard it before. I hope it's true. Sounds like something he'd say. He wasn't noted for his diplomacy."

"I see you know your history. Churchill said that of all the crosses he had to bear in the war, the heaviest was the Cross of Lorraine."

"But they sure can cook. Which reminds me, I'm hungry."

They had just been seated when Emma Shields said, "Do you know why this is called the Rose Café?"

"Is this a riddle?"

"Of sorts. I figured it out my second time here. You're a detective. Let's see if you can do better."

Scarne looked around. At the wallpaper, which was a pale yellow. At the flowers on the tables and in the windows. They weren't roses. At the lights and fixtures. The tableware and tablecloths. The linen. The wait staff uniforms.

"I presume it's not owned by someone named Rose."

"No, you're not getting off that easily. All I will say is that the clues are in this room."

"Can I have until the end of the meal?"

"Sure."

They turned to a hovering waiter. Emma Shields ordered the café's signature "Five-Napkin" burger, rare, with fries. She saw Scarne's look.

"I'm starving," she said.

"You'd better be. I'm not sure I could finish one of those." Looking up to the waiter he said, "I'll have the lamb chops. Rare. Mint jelly. Enough grilled asparagus to share. And a bottle of the Chateau Mouton Bordeaux."

Without preamble Emma said, "Josh and I were very close. We grew up together. I adored him. He was kind of shy and I was pretty outgoing so we complemented each other. Sometimes cousins of a certain age get along better than siblings. We didn't have to see each other every day and fight over toys or for attention. What a sister would have found annoying about him was cute to me. And I'm sure it worked that way for him as well. We told each other our deepest, darkest secrets and presented a united front to the world."

Her eyes glistened.

"Josh was my best chum. I spoke to him a couple of days before he died. We were planning my visit. I was bereft...especially coming so soon after my husband passed away."

"I didn't know about your husband. I'm sorry."

"Mike died a year and a half ago. Cancer. Josh had helped me through that and, well, that made our bond even stronger."

Scarne decided that money wasn't buying the Shields clan much luck.

"How often did the two of you speak?"

"Once or twice a week. Josh was my rock. He did everything he could to keep my spirits up." Emma Shields started to laugh, then caught herself. "Sorry. I was just remembering. Josh had a ribald sense of humor. I told him some of his emails were going to get us arrested. Over the phone he did his best to keep my spirits up. He said he spent so much time cultivating straight guys for me to sleep with it was crimping his love life."

"What about his love life? Any problems?

"Well, over the years, he had his heartbreaks, like everyone."

"Emma, could Josh have taken his own life? Rejection can be cumulative."

She bit her lip in thought, then shook her head.

"Josh wasn't depressed. I can never recall him being seriously down. I was on medication after Mike died and he was concerned that I would become dependent. He hated medicines. I don't think he'd ever been in therapy. He was fine on the phone. It was obvious he was still worried about me and couldn't wait for us to get together. Josh didn't kill himself."

The waiter arrived with their wine and Scarne went through the tasting ritual. They clinked glasses and drank appreciatively.

"Your uncle thinks Josh's death was connected to a story he was writing about Victor Ballantrae."

"I know."

"Have you met Ballantrae?"

"Once. On the yacht. We threw a party for him. He's a phony. And a boor. Now, the Dragon Lady, she's the real deal."

"Dragon Lady?"

"Alana Loeb. His chief of staff. One of the most beautiful, accomplished women I've ever met. Ballantrae is a forceful figure, but she could shut him up with a look. She was the center of attention for every man there. And every woman on the yacht wanted to pitch her overboard."

Emma's eyes took on a look that any man immediately recognized. The Green Monster.

"Every woman?"

"It was my first big social function since Mike died. I was dressed to kill. You'd think I'd have a home field advantage on my own fucking yacht. But Alana stole my thunder." She paused and smiled. "The bitch."

Scarne took a sip of wine and tilted the glass in her direction.

"You were probably just a little out of practice. When you're on your game you could launch a thousand ships."

"Thank you," she said, coloring slightly.

"Is there anything else you can think of that might help me? Your father believes Josh was tilting at windmills. As usual."

"No. But I can't believe Josh would make something up, or even exaggerate. If Ballantrae is a legitimate investor an infusion of cash would have been in Josh's best interests, too. And he prided himself on getting things right. When he wrote for us he knew that as a Shields his work would be scrutinized for errors or prejudice. His stories annoyed the hell out of Dad, but no one ever said they were inaccurate, including Dad." Emma Shields hesitated. "My father was wrong about Josh. I was angry when he left and I blamed him. That was unfair. Josh was his own man. He even made me apologize to Dad. That was so like him, worrying about us."

She looked away. When she turned back to Scarne, her eyes were wet.

"I'm sorry," she said.

"You needn't be, Emma. You've lost a husband and a best friend in short order. And now you're caught between your father and your uncle. This is just a job for me. For you, it's more than that. I'll try to remember that."

Emma Shields smiled and nodded. Their food arrived. She took a long pull of wine. Scarne suspected the conversation had been more draining than she anticipated. But she tucked into her burger with gusto. She looked at him.

"What are you thinking about?"

"*Jurassic Park.*"

She laughed so loudly that other diners looked over.

"I told you I was hungry."

Scarne started to pour more wine but she waved him off.

"I have a class at 2. The students already think I'm full of it."

"I doubt that. Those kids seemed to really like you. But why do you do it?"

"Teach? Well, for one thing I love it. My husband was a professor of history at Columbia. I wasn't sure that I was going to stay in the family business so I got my Masters and am working on my doctorate. I have two stepbrothers who were assumed to have an inside track at the company."

"Were assumed?"

Emma Shields smile did not extend to her eyes.

"The issue is now in doubt."

Over coffee, Scarne got her to talk more about herself. She was a graduate of both Chestnut Hill in Philadelphia and the Sorbonne. Fluent in French and conversant in German and Spanish, she worked as a correspondent in various European bureaus of *Shields* before returning to the States, where she met, and married, her late husband. They had a daughter, now seven.

That took Scarne by surprise. She read his face.

"Disappointed? Why does that matter to a man?"

He suddenly felt defensive. And he was damned if he knew why.

"That's silly. I'm not disappointed. I'm a bit surprised you took so long to mention it, that's all. It certainly doesn't matter to me."

"Don't be disingenuous. Sure it does. A man looks at a woman who has a child differently than a woman who is, shall we say, un-tethered."

Scarne hated being called disingenuous, especially when it had the ring of truth. He started to say that since his only interest in her was professional, it didn't matter what ties she had.

But he suddenly decided not to go there. That might really be disingenuous. What he did say turned out to be the right thing.

"Emma, if you were having lunch with a woman, how long would it have taken you to bring up your daughter?"

She gave him a long, appraising look, and smiled.

"Touché. Want to see her picture? Her name is Rebecca."

Please let the child be pretty, Scarne thought, as she handed him the photo. This woman reads me like a book. I don't need a Seinfeld moment now.

The child was stunning. Thank God.

"She will break a lot of hearts."

Emma Shields smiled at the gallantry.

"Becky is the reason I decided to talk to you. My father wants me back in the company. For all his perceived male chauvinism and arm candy, he will leave the company to the best qualified heir, man or woman. If I go back, it will be to protect my daughter's future. My father may be right about Ballantrae, but if he's not…."

Her stepbrothers better watch out, Scarne thought.

"And there's something else. Rebecca loved Josh. In many ways he replaced her father. Last summer she found a large shell on the beach. Josh put it to her ear so she could 'hear the ocean.' I guess every kid is told that."

Scarne smiled. He still did it himself. The familiar hollow roar was a straight line back to childhood innocence few adults could resist.

"She ran to my father, so excited. But Dad was never much of a romantic. Despite, or maybe because of, his many escapades. He told her it wasn't the sea she heard. The shell reverberates the sound of our own blood rushing past the tympanic membrane. The inner ear. Rebecca was crushed. Later that afternoon Josh took her to the library in town. At dinner she marched up to my father holding a science book and the shell, which she passed around the table. She looked at my father and said: 'Human blood has the same chemical makeup as sea water, from which all life springs. So we do hear the ocean!'"

"That's a wonderful story."

"Josh put the magic back in her childhood. I know my father tried to buy you off. Not many men would turn him down. If anyone killed Josh, I want them punished. But I love my father. I hope you won't do anything to hurt him...or Uncle Sheldon."

Out on the sidewalk, Scarne turned to her.

"I'm sorry I made that crack about your portfolio."

"You had every right."

They shook hands. Scarne held hers for a moment.

"The pictures on the wall. Rose Kennedy. The woman working in a war plant, 'Rosie the Riveter.' The stripper, Gypsy Rose Lee. The woman with the microphone in the dowdy dress. That was tough. Tokyo Rose. Every photo in the place concerns a woman named Rose. Very obscure and very clever."

Emma Shields smiled.

"I'm impressed. Now let's see how you do up against the Dragon Lady."

With that, she turned and walked briskly up the street.

‡

MIAMI LICE

SCARNE WALKED DIRECTLY to the taxi line at Miami International.

"Take me to 63rd and Collins in Miami Beach, please," he said to the driver of a yellow minivan that pulled up. "Place called La Gorce by the Sea." He threw his carry-on into the back seat.

"Sure thing. You from New York?"

Russian accent. There were a lot of Russians in Miami who immediately took to a city surrounded by ocean, bays, rivers and canals and full of women not swaddled in layers of sweaters and coats. They exchanged tales about the crummy weather "up North" as Scarne looked out the window on the drive through downtown.

"Building boom still going on? Thought the easy money dried up."

"Don't get me started. The speculators and developers were like lice. Started all these condo projects and now have to finish them. Can't give them away. Serves them right. All this construction clogged the streets. Takes forever to get around. Costs me money. Same in New York, no?"

"It's the same all over. Where do you live?"

"Miami Lakes. Near Shula's. You know, the golf resort with the steakhouse? I rent. It's cheap, so many apartments on the market. But I'm gonna buy a two-bedroom on Brickell. Flip it when the market recovers."

Scarne's amusement showed on his face in the rear view mirror.

"I know," the cabbie said. "I'll be one of the lice. Can't scratch 'em, join 'em, I say."

They entered the Julia Tuttle causeway, one of several that connected Miami to Miami Beach. As they rode above Biscayne Bay Scarne enjoyed the spectacular view of downtown Miami's glistening skyline. The cabbie left the Tuttle and cut over to 41st Street, also known as Arthur Godfrey Road, which would take them to Collins Avenue. He began pointing out restaurants.

"That's the Forge, most expensive restaurant in Miami. Wednesday nights, it's nuts. Would embarrass Caligula. Local rich bitches and the studs. Anything goes. I've dropped off some unbelievable women. Went in once just to see the bar. Cost me $15 for a drink! Took a look at the menu. Want a $100 steak, that's your place. Not me. The steer would have to blow me."

From the outside the Forge looked like a bank in Zurich. Scarne made a mental note to stop by for dinner before he left Miami. He'd read about its famous wine cellar, one of the largest in the world. And he knew something of the restaurant's colorful history from friends in law enforcement.

As if on cue, the cabbie said, "Meyer Lansky, you've heard of him, right, opened it in the 1920's. The mob controlled this town. Some say they still do."

"I can't believe you know who Lansky was," Scarne said.

"Oh, sure. A lot of these rich old Jews around here brag about the good old days. Rich ones. Not poor Russian Jews like me driving cabs."

"What's it like inside?"

"The Forge? Beautiful. I could have sat at that bar all night, if I hit the lottery. Very baroque. Hah! That's the word. You go baroque eating there."

The cabbie roared at his joke. They crossed over the Indian River onto Collins Avenue. Scarne's cab headed slowly northward, dodging cement trucks. Huge cranes loomed dangerously overhead, dozens of stories high, swinging girders into place. There was hardly any room to walk on the sidewalks, and dust was everywhere. Huge waste chutes spewed detritus into dumpsters. The racket was unceasing.

"You couldn't pay me enough to work on one of those buildings," the cabbie said. "Last week three guys in Bal Harbour were working on a floor that collapsed and they fell down to the next floor into wet cement. They drowned in it. Their buddies started digging them out but the cement hardened and they finally had to use picks and jackhammers. Can you imagine dying like that? No, I'll stick to my cab."

"Accidents happen."

"This ain't New York, my friend. It's Miami. Buildings fall down without planes crashing into them. The building code dates from the Flintstones."

They pulled into the driveway of La Gorce.

"Looks solid enough," Scarne said casually.

"This place? No, this is a good building. I know the guys who run it. I mean the concierge and like that. They love it. You'll see. It was built a few years ago before all the lice came." He turned in his seat and leaned toward Scarne. "Hurricane hits, you can hole up here unless the city forces you to leave. It's a rock. Just be careful if you walk down the street past one of the new monstrosities. Might fall on your head."

An attendant walked over, took Scarne's Dakota and exchanged pleasant insults with the cabbie in Spanish.

"What did he say?" Scarne asked.

"Who the hell knows?"

Scarne paid his fare and walked into the lobby. A uniformed man and a woman stood behind the counter of the concierge station facing a bank of security cameras. When Scarne told them his name, the man offered his hand.

"I am Mario. We've been expecting you. Did you know young Mr. Shields? A wonderful man. We were all very sad about what happened."

"I'm a friend of the family, here to clear up some personal and legal matters. I understand you have apartment and car keys for me."

Mario reached under the counter and brought out a thick manila envelope. He shook out some metal keys and plastic disks.

"The keys are for the apartment and car. These disks open and close all the security doors in and out of the building, garage and grounds. Mr. Shields had me stock the pantry and refrigerator with the basics. I'll take you up."

The Shields apartment was on the 29th floor, just below the penthouse level. Outside the door were *The New York Times* and *Wall Street Journal.*

"These never stopped coming," Mario said, picking them up. "I told Mr. Shields about it, but he said to let the subscription run out and pass the papers on to other tenants. I told the boy to deliver them up here while you were staying. A little bit of home, no?"

"That's thoughtful. But they may never stop. I'd bet they are automatically renewed by a credit card, charged yearly. And I think the cards are still active.

Mario looked pained.

"I never thought of that. I'll call Mr. Shields and tell him."

"Don't worry about it. I'll take care of it before I leave. If I don't speak to him, I'll just call the papers. There is a code on the label I can use."

Mario gave Scarne a quick tour. The two-bedroom apartment featured a living room with wrap-around, floor-to-ceiling glass windows. Scarne walked right up to the glass. He felt as if he was jutting out over the Atlantic Ocean. Looking down he could several women sunning themselves on a pool deck. The master bedroom had a bathroom suite as large as some Manhattan studios. There was a pass-through bar between the kitchen and living room. An outside terrace connected the master bedroom and kitchen and was accessible from both through large sliding doors. The entertainment center in the living room had a large plasma TV, DVD player and a sound system surrounded by a large bookcase whose shelves alternated between books and sea shells of all varieties and sizes. Josh may have worked for an alternative newspaper, but he lived like a Shields.

"The cleaning lady was here Wednesday. She comes once a week."

Scarne walked to the bookcase and picked up a shell.

"Mr. Shields liked his shells," Mario said. "These are what's left. The family took a lot back home with them. He never went to the beach he didn't bring back some shells. He gave me some nice ones. The gym, sauna and steam rooms are on the seventh floor. Do you want to see them now?"

"No, this is fine. I want to unpack. You've been very helpful."

Scarne reached into his pocket and took out a $100 bill. Mario held up his hand and said, "That isn't necessary. Mr. Shields takes good care of the staff."

Scarne pressed the money into the man's hand.

"I'm sure. I'd feel better showing my own gratitude. Don't fight me."

Mario smiled and took the bill.

"When you need the car, call me at the desk and I will take you to it. The garage can be confusing."

After he left, Scarne wheeled his bag into the master bedroom and unpacked. Then he went to the kitchen and opened the folding doors to the liquor closet. The "basics" included Kendall Jackson wines, and bottles of Grey Goose vodka, Meyer's Dark Rum, Glenlivet 20-year-old single malt scotch, Bombay gin and Remy Martin cognac. Mixers for all. Thoughtful. Six real Cuban cigars lay in their metal tubes. Very thoughtful. He was hungry. There were enough provisions to last a month. He made himself a ham sandwich, opened a bottle of Sam Adams and went out on the terrace, picking up the two newspapers off the coffee table where Mario had dropped them. He'd have to remember to cancel them. Even the wealthy shouldn't have to pay for eternal subscriptions. Then he had a thought. He pulled out his cell phone and called Evelyn Warr, getting the answering machine. He left a message, which included the account numbers he read off the subscription labels from both the *Times* and *Journal*.

After finishing his lunch, Scarne put on a bathing suit and T-shirt. He found a pair of flip-flops still in their wrapping next to the Jacuzzi bathtub. He hesitated. He detested flip-flops. These were light blue with a flowery tropical motif. What the hell, he thought. At least they're not pink. He grabbed a gaudily colored beach towel from a rack, thought better of it, and took a solid white bath towel instead. On the way out he stopped at a small bookcase. All the books were devoted to nature. He picked out the brightly illustrated *Sport Fish of Florida: 231 Species: Food Values, Methods and Ranges* by Vic Dunaway. He took the elevator to the seventh floor and followed the signs to the pool deck.

The pool was crowded. There was a nice breeze off the ocean. A small group of men and women had pulled some lounges and chairs together and were smoking and speaking

French. Scarne had intended to take a quick swim, until he noticed several fathers dipping their squealing diaper-clad infants in the water like teabags. He resigned himself to a deck chair far from the maddening crowd. He opened his book to the chapter on marine predators. There were plenty of sharks in Florida waters, and many of them, especially the Hammerhead, Tiger, Mako and Bull, were man killers. The section on *Carcharodon carcharias*, the Great White, noted that it was only an occasional visitor to southern Florida. Under "Food Value" the author wrote: "From whose viewpoint, the angler's or the shark's?"

A thin but pot-bellied man wearing a red-checkered boxer bathing suit walked over and stretched out on a lounge chair next to Scarne.

"You a renter or an owner?"

Scarne looked over at the man.

"I'm sorry."

"Just wondered if you rent or own here."

The man looked to be in his mid-30's. He had a concave chest and what little hair he had left on his head was blonde and wispy.

"Just visiting," Scarne said, turning back to his book.

"I own three condos in this building," the man said, undeterred. "Total of about 20 up and down the coast. Gonna buy more now, with prices dropping like they are."

Scarne couldn't see any way out of the conversation.

"A lot of speculators are getting burned."

"Last time I looked, God ain't making any more beachfront. But I'm no speculator. I mean, I think I'll make out in the long run, but I've got to put my dough someplace. Ran a hedge fund in Connecticut. Made a fucking fortune. Retired at 36, can you believe it? Just having fun. Women down here are hot."

If it wasn't for his wallet, Scarne thought, they'd have to be blind.

"Why Miami Beach," Scarne said. "You have that kind of money, I'd think Palm Beach would be more your style."

"Don't like the people," the man said seriously. "Nouveau riche."

Scarne didn't have a reply for that. Fortunately the man soon walked away. But the respite was short-lived. Almost immediately two women took adjacent lounges. One was incredibly pregnant and wore a thong. She wouldn't have been the thong type nine months earlier. Her stretch marks looked like an Amtrak route map and her blue-veined, bulbous breasts threatened to burst the trace of fabric that held them. She started slapping suntan lotion on all her exposed skin. What she couldn't reach the other woman, apparently her mother, did. It sounded like a butcher flattening cutlets. It was all too much for Scarne. He decided to chance the sharks.

He took the beach elevator to the ground floor. He waved is electronic key in front of a pad to use the elevator and again to get through the rear door to the tropical garden that led to the beach. The garden had a small bath house, as well as a children's playground and barbecue pits surrounded by wooden or stone picnic tables and benches. A half dozen or so feral-looking cats eyed him suspiciously as walked to the beach gate. They undoubtedly were tolerated for their ability to keep the rat and palmetto bug population under control. A narrow trail led through the dunes to the beach.

Scarne spread his towel, dropping his keys at one end under his book. He had to walk out 30 yards before it was deep enough to swim. He glided through the water, occasionally jackknifing to touch bottom and gauge the depth. Glittering schools of bait fish scattered. At one point, a large shadow passed just below Scarne. He felt a trill of fear in his groin. After a half mile he stroked towards shore and beached. He walked back and found his towel, book and keys untouched.

THE BEST MOJITOS IN TOWN

AFTER SHOWERING, SCARNE called the Miami Beach Police Department and after the usual bureaucratic wrangle was connected to its Homicide Unit. After another 10 minutes of explanation and name dropping, one of the detectives who investigated the death of Josh Shields came on the line. They made arrangements to meet. Scarne then called Mario, who told him to take the elevator to the parking garage on the sixth floor. Scarne hoped that the lush Shields lifestyle would be reflected in Josh's choice of car. He didn't want to be saddled with a broccoli-fueled hybrid.

The concierge was waiting when the elevator door opened and led him to a low-slung vehicle covered by a tarp – a good sign. The La Gorce garage extended from the sixth through the ninth floor. The walls were latticed with openings, which meant a strong breeze would bring in both salt and sand. Josh Shields thought enough of his car to protect it from the elements. Scarne helped Mario pull the tarp off the car.

" What the hell?"

"This was his baby," Mario said. "Limited-edition Rouche Mustang Convertible. I just had it detailed and tuned. Full tank of gas."

"It's a beauty," Scarne said, somewhat dubiously, as he looked at the bright red 400-horsepower muscle car. "But not exactly inconspicuous."

"Don't you watch C.S.I.? This is Miami. Everybody has a crazy car."

Scarne, a car buff, liked nothing better than seeing what a high-performance auto could do. Even so, the Rouche took some getting used to as he headed down Collins Avenue toward South Beach. The manual transmission was a dream, but he doubted he'd have to get out of second gear before leaving Miami Beach. He assumed he could pass the Space Shuttle in sixth gear.

As a rule, homicide detectives don't like to talk to private investigators, who they believe will pollute their cases. If they must, they prefer to do it outside their offices. Not only won't they be seen by their colleagues but there is also the chance they can get a free meal, drink or at least a cup coffee. Still, Scarne hadn't expected Detectives Frank Paulo and William Curley to pick the Fontainebleau. Newly renovated at a cost of $1 billion to recapture its past Rat Pack and *Goldfinger* movie glory, the hotel, although reportedly again facing bankruptcy, was once again the centerpiece of Miami Beach high life.

From his perch at the glass-enclosed "Bleau Bar" in the lobby Scarne watched a seemingly endless parade of bikinied beauties gamboling in the pools below.

"You Scarne?"

He turned to see two men in sports coats and floral shirts. They both gave him the cop stare. Despite Condon's intervention with the Miami police, second-guessing a police investigation would not endear him with any cops.

"You guys must be Crockett and Tubbs. How did you know it was me?"

The cop who addressed him, a short, redheaded man with thick arms, looked at his partner and sighed.

"I'm Curley. This is Paulo. You weren't hard to spot. Hotshot Big Apple dick looking for clues out there at the pool."

"You picked this place. I guess you didn't want to be seen with me."

"Crap. We come here all the time. Best mojitos in town."

Scarne decided that being a homicide cop in Miami Beach had its perks.

"Can't argue with you on that," he said, lifting the mojito he'd ordered and signaling the bartender for three more drinks.

"Captain says that you are looking into the Shields case," Paulo said. He was a tall thin man with a dark complexion and a beak nose.

"That's right," Scarne said, "just trying to tie up some loose ends."

"You working for the old man?" Paulo said.

Scarne nodded.

"Guy just won't leave it alone," Curley said. "No disrespect, but he can be a pain in the ass."

"Which is why he sent me. He knew you probably wouldn't take him seriously anymore."

"And we're supposed to take you serious?" Curley said.

"You're here aren't you?"

"Only because somebody made a phone call," Paulo said, "and that only got you a courtesy visit. Timoney ain't our chief. Miami Beach is a separate jurisdiction."

The drinks came. Nobody clinked glasses.

"Look, let's cut to the chase," Scarne said. "I used to be a cop so I know that you're not overjoyed being here, mojitos aside.

But Timoney asked a favor from your boss, who has banked it for the future. So you have to talk to me. I don't want to step all over your investigation but I have a job to do. The boy's father thinks he may have been murdered. You're convinced it was an accident. From what I know so far that seems the more likely conclusion. I'll make just as much money proving you right, so there is no downside in talking with me."

The partners looked at each other and shrugged.

"Fair enough," Paulo said. Both detectives pulled up bar stools and faced Scarne. "Why'd you leave the cops? You look too young to be retired. Disability?"

No matter where he went, cops quizzed Scarne about New York's disability and pension policies, which were the envy of other jurisdictions.

"I wish. Got suspended for holding a city councilman off a balcony."

The two detectives looked at each other.

"You must have had a reason," Paulo said.

Scarne told them an abbreviated version of the story, which he knew wouldn't hurt his standing with them.

"Prick," Curley said.

"Listen, we won't have much for you," Paulo said. "Homicide wouldn't have even caught the squeal except for the lack of I.D. on the vic and then him turning out to be semi-famous. Family pressure kept us on it longer than it deserved, but you know how that goes. We closed it. Opened it. Closed it again. Came out the same. No signs of foul play. No apparent motive. No witnesses. No suspects, unless you count jellyfish. M.E. wrote it up as accidental and we agree. I feel sorry for the old guy, but he should let it go."

"Nothing about it bothered you?"

The bartender put a couple of bowls of nuts on the bar.

"Thanks, Hal," Curley said as they all took a handful. "Look, you've been there. You know how it goes. Young guy dies, you always look a little closer, even if his family isn't prominent. Guy is gay, even closer. I mean we probably shouldn't cause it's kind of discriminatory to do that, but it is what it is. In this case, the circumstances weren't all that mysterious. I mean, he wasn't found in an alley behind a stud bar or anything. He was fishing in the ocean at night and washed up crab-eaten a couple of days later. You know, sometimes even healthy young gay guys die naturally or accidentally. Believe me, our captain would have loved to make the Shields family happy by catching a murderer. But there was no murder."

"What about the missing wallet and keys? His father doesn't believe they fell out into the ocean. Said his son would have left them in his bucket."

"Probably stolen," Curley said.

"Credit cards haven't been used."

"Then they're in the drink. Guy forgot to put them in his bucket. We're lucky the bucket was still there. Tide ran high and the water was rough that night. I think there were even small craft warnings out that day. I know the lifeguards were worried about rip currents."

Scarne suddenly thought of something.

"What about his fishing rod?"

"What do you mean?" Paulo said.

"Did you find it?"

"Yeah. It was in one of the rod holder things you stick in the sand, next to the bucket. Where you going with this?"

"Well, if he was fishing, and got stung by jellyfish or pulled in by a rip current or had a heart attack, why was his rod on the beach?"

The detectives looked exasperated.

"Hell, we don't know," Curley said. "Maybe he had two poles working. A lot of guys do that. Maybe he was looking for seashells. There was a pile by the bucket. Or he just went into the surf to wash his hands off."

"Or kill himself," Paulo said. "I know the father doesn't want to hear that, but it was my first thought."

"And all of it was still there?'

"Look," Curley said, "I know this is Miami, but nobody is gonna steal a fishing rod, a bucket and some shells. That stuff might still be there if we hadn't found it."

"What about his computer?"

"What about it?

"His laptop is missing, along with all his notes."

The cops looked at each other.

"We didn't know that," Paulo said. "The family went through the apartment. Never said anything to us."

"They were distraught. Didn't think about it at the time. Maybe you guys should have. Shields was a reporter, for Christ sake. Didn't you think it odd that there was nothing related to reporting in his apartment?"

Paulo's face reddened. He started to say something but the other cop put a hand on his arm.

"He's right, Frank. Maybe we should have spotted that." He turned to Scarne. "You saying there was something on that computer that might have gotten him killed?"

Scarne hesitated.

"I don't know. Just makes me curious."

Curley spotted the lie.

"You wouldn't hold back something in a homicide, would you?"

"I thought it was an accident."

It took another round of mojitos to mend fences after that remark. But by the time they left, they were all, if not pals, at least on the same side of the case, whatever it was. They exchanged business cards and the cops said they would go back and review their file, which Scarne assumed they would. For his part, he promised to keep them informed, which they half believed. He also asked if he could get a copy of their final report. They glanced at each other. The councilman story had probably done the trick because Paulo said, "Why the fuck not?" He said he would email a copy later that day.

Scarne was hungry. He left the bar and went to the beach. After a short walk along a boardwalk he came to the Eden Roc, another recently renovated Miami Beach landmark. He sat at the bar at the hotel's Cabana Club and ordered conch chowder and a grilled grouper sandwich, washed down with a Sam Adams. After which he picked up his car at the Fontainebleau valet and drove back to La Gorce.

In Manhattan, Garza was just about to leave Scarne's apartment. The man was either extraordinarily neat or the maid had just been there. Probably the former, given his Marine Corps background. Garza had known about his service. Finding the medals buried deep in a sock drawer told him something else about the man. There wasn't much else to learn in the place. Garza had gotten more off the Internet and from his contacts.

It would be obvious to a trained detective that the place had been tossed, but Garza tried not to leave too much of a mess. He thought about pocketing a few small valuables to make it appear more like a random burglary but quickly shelved the idea. Scarne would see through the ruse.

Garza paused before the beautiful chess set. Like many Cuban boys, he had been brought up on the tales of José Capablanca, the charismatic Cuban grandmaster who dominated the chess world in the 1920's. Garza played a mean game himself and he studied the position before him. There was a notepad next to the set. It was Scarne's turn. The move was obvious. What the hell was he waiting for? Garza's gloved hand hovered above Scarne's white bishop, then picked it up and moved it across the board to capture his opponent's remaining knight. Scarne would lose the bishop on the next move, to a pawn, but according to Capablanca, Scarne's remaining queen and knight would prove more powerful than black's remaining queen and bishop, both of which traveled in a straight line. A knight, however, could jump over pieces and wreak all sorts of havoc.

Just for good measure, Garza made a note on the pad and circled it. Then he left the apartment and went to dinner.

†

THE SOUTH FLORIDA TIMES

THE NEXT MORNING Scarne called the *South Florida Times* and made an appointment to meet its editor, John Pourier, at 10 A.M. at the paper's Hollywood headquarters. He had picked up a copy of the weekly the night before in the lobby of the apartment building and read it cover to cover before going to bed. He thought it compared favorably with New York's famed *Village Voice*. Within its 128 pages were movie, book, restaurant and club reviews; sports and business columns; community notices and news, and, considering the moribund media environment, an incredible amount of classified and display advertising. Most of its stories dealt with local political shenanigans and the blights of overbuilding and traffic congestion. Miami's hedonistic lifestyle and its extensive gay community were prominently covered. The editorials pulled no punches. From what he knew about Josh Shields, it was not surprising he'd found a home there.

Following directions given him by the editor, Scarne took Collins Avenue up through Hallandale Beach and cut over on the Lehman Causeway to Ives Dairy Road. Pourier said the route would help him avoid the rush hour madness on Interstate 95 near Miami. Great plan, didn't work. He stopped at a small Jewish deli on the way and the short delay allowed a freight train pulling at least 100 cars to get to Ives Dairy just before he did. He killed 15 minutes munching a bagel, sipping coffee and calling his office.

"I checked with both papers," Evelyn said. "Josh apparently stopped delivery when he was going away for more than a couple of days. He had the *Times* and *Journal* donate the issues to schools." She didn't mention that she was the one who arranged that for Scarne, who invariably forgot.

"What about the time he was scheduled to go to Antigua?"

"He arranged for a halt of service, just for a week."

It wasn't conclusive he knew, but one more argument against suicide.

He thanked Evelyn and rang off just as the railroad gate started to open. Once on I-95 he made good time and exited at Hollywood Blvd., heading west. He soon spotted the building he was looking for at the Presidential Center, in the center of a huge traffic circle. The building was at least 20 stories with four towers surrounding a large enclosed courtyard filled with benches, trees and sculptures. The effect was more artful than utilitarian, and Scarne liked it. He entered an elevator serving the South Tower, holding the door for two short-skirted, long-legged women chatting happily in Spanish. Their clothes were high quality and cut short. In New York they might have been criticized for dressing in hooker chic but in the Miami area they were in uniform. Cuban girls set the style and were among the sexiest women in the world.

The *South Florida Times* occupied the entire 10th floor. Scarne walked in through double glass doors. A receptionist was on the phone, transferring a call. When she finished, she looked up at him and said, "Can I help you?"

She was cute but wasn't going to win Miss Elevator in this building.

"I'm here to see John Pourier. My name is Jake Scarne."

"If you will take a seat, I'll let me him know you are here. Coffee?"

Scarne declined and sat down next to a rack of magazines. Two men sat on a couch across from him. They both had coffees and as the aroma drifted his way he regretted his decision. He began leafing through *Florida Sportsman,* which had numerous photos of attractive women in bikinis holding large fish.

"Mr. Scarne? I'm John Pourier."

Scarne stood. Pourier belonged in a bank boardroom, right down to the suspenders and club tie. He was a good deal shorter than Scarne and well fed. He pointed at the photo Scarne was looking at.

"Hell of a snapper."

Scarne laughed as they shook.

"Let's go back to my office. Want some coffee?"

This time Scarne accepted. On the way through the cubicled newsroom, Scarne remarked that it seemed strangely quiet. Half the desks were empty.

"It's always like this the first couple of days after we put out an edition. We use a lot of stringers and part-timers. It will pick up, believe me."

After stopping at a small room to get coffee (and half a donut for Pourier – "I can't resist these things, as you can probably tell") they walked to an expansive corner office. A window ran the length of the room and Scarne could see the traffic swirling around the circle below. In the distance glistening high rises dotted the Atlantic beachfront. Pourier sat down, chewing his donut and spilling crumbs on his blotter. Scarne sat across from him.

"Now, what can I do for you? I understand that you have some questions about Josh Shields. His father called by the way. Said you would probably stop by. Very nice man. I've spoken to him before, of course, after Josh died."

Scarne looked around the office. Everything was expensive, down to the silver Movado clock on the bookcase. A full set of the newest Cobra golf clubs leaned up against the wall. Picture frames lined the ledge in front of the window. There were shots of Pourier with a tall blonde woman and children in various venues: beaches, ski slopes, lakes and athletic fields. Interspersed with the frames were plaques and trophies. Scarne spotted one statuette of a man on a polo pony, in the act of swinging a mallet. He couldn't read the inscription.

"Am I in the right office?"

Pourier laughed.

"Yeah, I know. I bet you didn't think alternative journalism could be lucrative. This is a great market. We have to fight off advertisers."

"With a polo mallet?"

Pourier laughed.

"Oh hell, I have to fess up. I don't make that kind of money doing this. I made it the old-fashioned way. I inherited it. Bought a piece of the paper and made myself editor. Took a while to win over some of the longhairs out there" – he hooked a thumb toward the newsroom – "but they came around after I skewered some fat cats. Most people at my clubs don't know what I do, for which my wife is eternally grateful."

"Did you know Josh Shields was looking at Victor Ballantrae?"

"Not until his father called."

"Did he tell you why?"

"No. Just that he'd appreciate any help I could give you. I was surprised. Ballantrae Financial is a big deal in these parts. Even advertise with us, which is a bonus. We don't get much advertising from banks, drug companies and the like, as you might imagine. But Ballantrae is trying to make a splash in South Florida and is covering all the bases, especially in the Latin community. Young Cubans are the hippest people on Earth and our club coverage is the best in Miami. And we have a growing South American population. They have a god-awful amount of money. Own half the condos on Miami Beach."

"What kind of ads?"

"The usual stuff. Financial planning, trusts, insurance, banking. Ballantrae also sponsors golf and tennis tournaments and ran promos about those."

"Would you have printed an unflattering article about Ballantrae?"

Pourier looked offended. He hooked a thumb at his polo trophy.

"I said his advertising was a bonus. We don't need it. We exist to piss off the powerful and it hasn't hurt our advertising. It's something the mainstream press hasn't grasped. Getting in bed with the people fucking the country doesn't sell papers. They never learn." Pourier sat back in his swivel chair and put his feet up on his desk. "We run an exposé a week. South Florida has no dearth of scoundrels. You might have heard about the city councilman who shot himself in the lobby of the *Herald* after being caught with his hand in the till? Everybody was shocked. Who kills themselves for stealing in Florida? Anyway, I just told my staff to start looking into Ballantrae."

"Come up with anything?"

"Mr. Shields asked me to cooperate with you. But professional courtesy only goes so far. What's in it for me?"

"Maybe we can help each other out?'

"How?"

"I might find out things you can't."

"And of course, you'll rush right over and tell me."

"If it doesn't hurt my client."

"I don't seem to be getting much out of this. Lots of quid, little pro."

Scarne knew that telling Pourier of Sheldon Shield's suspicions was risky. Borderline irresponsible, particularly if Ballantrae was innocent. But getting information from the editor could save a lot of time. He assumed that Pourier wouldn't risk a lawsuit from a billionaire without hard evidence.

"Off the record?"

"Sure," Pourier said.

"Josh's father thinks Victor Ballantrae might be involved in his death."

Pourier's feet came off his desk and he sat up. He stared at Scarne.

"You must be joking. I thought it was an accident."

"Probably was. But there are a few things bothering the old man, and I have to admit they bother me too."

"Such as."

Scarne told him. Pourier started taking notes halfway through.

"Two feet of water? Jesus Christ. I didn't know that. Maybe I should have. And the business about his computer and notes is inconsistent with the reporter I knew. Josh was a good journalist. With his financial background and contacts, he stood out down there, not that he flaunted it. I'm not sure how many people the 'Hidless' thing fooled inside the building but he got some great stories on people who didn't know who they were dealing with."

"Like Victor Ballantrae?"

Pourier nodded. "It's possible." He picked up his phone and punched a button on his console. "Lois, can you come in here? And bring whatever you've got on Ballantrae." He listened for a moment. "Yeah. The man and the company. I know. Anything at all. Just bring it in here. Thanks."

He hung up and looked at Scarne.

"Why isn't Shields, the company, doing something?"

"Randolph Shields thinks his brother is crazy. Ballantrae is also planning to buy into the family business."

"Good God, man. I don't know what Sheldon is paying you, but it can't be enough. Randolph Fucking Shields is nobody to screw around with."

There was a knock on the half-open door and a young woman walked in holding a manila folder. Without asking she sat on a chair next to Scarne.

"Meg. This is Jake Scarne. He's a private eye. Jake, this is Meghan Pace." He saw the look on Scarne's face and laughed. "Oh. Meg is our Lois Lane. Just a nickname. My best reporter and soon-to-be deputy editor."

Scarne shook hands with Pace, a compact brunette wearing jeans and a sweater.

"Now, what do we have on Ballantrae?"

She hesitated.

"It's OK. We're working on something together, so you can talk freely."

She did. Alternately glancing at her notes and documents in the folder, she painted a picture of Ballantrae and his organization. Scarne knew much of it, from his talk with Huber, but he didn't interrupt.

"Ballantrae seemed to arrive in Southern Florida full-blown about five years ago," she said, "simultaneously opening a flagship office on Brickell Avenue in downtown Miami for its Financial Services subsidiary; satellite offices in Coral Gables, Kendall and Lauderdale, and a research division with 40 stock and bond analysts in Boca Raton. The investment banking unit has made some small deals locally, mostly with high-tech startups in Port St. Lucie. It's the offshore bank that interests me. According to the company it has almost $10 billion in deposits and is growing by 20 percent a year. It seems to be generating the most revenue, selling certificates of deposit to rich South American expatriates in South Florida. They're apparently a hot item since they offer an interest rate a couple of points higher than anyone else is."

"I can vouch for that," Pourier said. "Some of my banking and broker friends at the club are bitching. Ballantrae is cutting into their business."

"Isn't that suspicious?" Scarne asked.

"According to the sales brochures," Pace said, "the bank is treated differently tax wise and since they market directly to the public there is little overhead. They also claim that as an international company they can invest in foreign markets for higher returns. The CD's aren't FDIC insured, by the way, so there is risk. Which they disclose. But investors are apparently willing to take that risk because Ballantrae has never missed an interest payment on a CD. Whatever they're doing, it's been approved by the SEC and a whole slew of state regulators."

"An S.E.C. imprimatur doesn't impress me," Scarne said. "Madoff, Stanford and some of the other crooks bragged about how the S.E.C. gave them a clean bill of health. That's how they suckered so many people."

"Look, I'm just starting to look into Ballantrae. It's hard to get any info out of the company other than their approved brochures. You have to go through their lawyers in Houston and an in-house PR firm. If you ask them anything about finances they say its proprietary and they don't want their competitors to know how and what they are doing. Same with Victor Ballantrae himself. There is very little on him, except what's in the corporate bio, which basically describes him as a wonderful human being."

She saw Scarne and Pourier exchange looks.

"What is this, a fraternity house? What do you guys know that I don't? Why the sudden interest in Ballantrae? Why is a private eye involved?"

The men were silent, but then Scarne said, "She probably has a right to know, if something did happen to Shields."

Pourior told her. Her expression went from interested to incredulous.

"This has Pulitzer written all over it," she finally said when he'd finished.

"Or lawsuit that will bankrupt me," Pourier said. "It may be total bullshit."

"And it may be dangerous," Scarne said.

"Josh Shields was a friend of mine," Meghan Pace said quietly. "I don't know if his father is right but I'd like to find out. I'll tell you one thing. If Josh said Ballantrae was bent, you could take it to the bank. Well, maybe not a bank. And I don't like his computer and notes disappearing."

"You know," Pourier said, "you might want to talk to the guy who puts out *Offshore Confidential*. Real piece of work named Reginald Sink."

"Offshore Confidential?"

"Yeah. It's a newsletter that tracks fraud, money laundering and such around the world. Lots of stuff on Africa, the Caribbean and South America."

"Is he nuts?"

"In addition to putting out his newsletters," Pourier said, "he runs conferences that a lot of law enforcement types attend. Probably figures that gives him some protection. For my money he's still crazy. Something happens to him they'd have to put all the suspects in the Orange Bowl."

"I've never heard of him."

"Not many people have, but Reggie's a legend among cops and crooks. He was actually one of the latter. Got nailed for insider trading and did time."

"Fox in the henhouse," Scarne said.

"We've checked his website," Meghan Pace said, "and there are several citations for Victor Ballantrae and his companies. But it's a pay-as-you-go service. To get more than headlines we'd have to lay out serious cash."

"That's not going to happen," Pourier said. "The money wouldn't bother me but I like to generate my own copy. We do use the website as a tip sheet. Reg doesn't mind." Pourier riffed through his Rolodex and wrote on a pad. "Here's Reggie's number and address. He's in Weston. I'll give him a heads up. It might help if I let him know you may be dropping by. Good luck. Say hello to Reggie for me. Just don't stand too close when he starts his car."

EXPENSIVE TASTES

IT TOOK SCARNE a half hour to drive to Weston, an inland suburb of both Miami and Fort Lauderdale that bumps up against the Everglades. The town allegedly marked the limit of the megalopolis's expansion west, although according to Pourier few people believed that Florida's rapacious developers would stop short of the Gulf of Mexico 90 miles away.

Offshore Confidential occupied a storefront between an Edwin Watts golf superstore and a Ruth's Chris steakhouse in an upscale shopping plaza. The woman at the reception desk smiled pleasantly at Scarne. He hadn't known what to expect at a newsletter devoted to ferreting out financial sleazebags but it wasn't a stunning blonde who looked like just stepped out of Vogue.

"Oh, yes. Reginald has been expecting you." Boston accent. "Coffee?"

Scarne said black would be fine. The woman disappeared and returned with a steaming mug that said "Money Laundering Expo – Caracas - 2008" on its side. As they started down a hallway he pointed to a wall rack filled with various newsletters: *Offshore Confidential, Bermuda Confidential, Caribbean Alert, Swiss Watch* (presumably not about timepieces) and *Frauds & Fakers*.

"Do you publish all of those," Scarne said.

"Those are just our print products," the woman said. "We also have several web-only newsletters. We provide real-time information on the Internet, which, as you might imagine, comes in handy when you are dealing with people who, how should I put it, tend to move around a lot."

They passed a small office in which a boy and a girl sat facing each other across a desk. They were dressed in jeans, tee shirts and sandals. Both had hair down to their shoulders. The boy, who needed a shave, ignored them, but the girl glanced up from her computer and waved. Scarne returned the gesture.

"They look like college kids."

"They are. Interns. University of Miami. Honor students."

They entered an office where a man was working on a computer with his back to the door. He was dressed much like the kids and had a brown ponytail. Only when he turned around did Scarne realized that there was plenty of gray in his hair and a lot of miles on his face. He looked like the quintessential aging hippie. But he flashed a friendly smile and stuck out his hand.

"Mr. Scarne, I presume? Reggie Sink. Well, you fit Pourier's description, so I guess it's you. John's a good sort. We steal from each other."

He waved Scarne into a seat.

"Now, before you go into your spiel, I have to tell you that we sell everything we print or put on the web." Sink spoke rapidly, as if his mouth couldn't keep up with his brain. "I don't feel comfortable giving away for free what other people pay for. Which brings me to your subscription."

"My subscription? I don't have one."

"You will, if you want much information out of me. Listen, it will be worth every penny. It will open up a whole new world of potential business for you. Come on, for a thousand bucks a year you get all my publications, print and electronic. Less than a set of good golf clubs."

"Do you take American Express?"

"Certainement! Doesn't everyone. Allison here can take your order."

Scarne gave her his credit card information and mailing address. Well, he thought, so much for saving a thousand bucks by not subscribing to a Shields newsletter. At least it's Sheldon's money.

"Now you can buy that new dress, sweetie," Sink said.

"What a wonderful idea," the woman said, and walked out.

The eyes of both men followed her.

"Allison is another reason I charge so much. Wellesley gals have expensive tastes. But she's worth every cent. And not just for the obvious reasons. Harvard Law. Writes a lot of our stuff and vets the freelancers."

"Looks like you are doing OK."

"It's like stealing money."

"Again."

Sink laughed.

"So you know about that. Well, I don't hide it. Actually, it helps me. People assume I can spot the frauds, having been one. And they're right."

"How did you get into this business?"

"After I got out of the slammer, I had to start over. Lost my securities license, of course. But also my family. First wife took most of my remaining assets and the kids. I don't blame her. What money I had left was going up my nose. I was headed downhill until I found Jesus." He laughed. "Only kidding! Just wanted to see if you're paying attention. What I found was Allison, that babe you keep leering at. Worked for the firm that defended me. Saw a lot of each other. Wouldn't marry me until I went straight. She came up with the idea of starting a newsletter tracking investment fraud. Only I didn't have to."

"What do you mean?"

"One already existed here in Florida. Guy had a small rag tracking the offshore banking world in the Caribbean. He practically gave it away so no one took him seriously. I bought him out and started charging big bucks. I still had a lot of contacts on the Street. They were happy to feed me dirt on their illegal competitors, who, after all, are siphoning billions away from their legitimate scams. Subscribers flocked in. People don't value information they get for free. Then came 9/11 and *Offshore* became a must read for the intelligence community." Sink spread his arms wide. "And the rest, as they say, is history. Now, what can I do for you?"

Scarne liked Reggie Sink.

"First, let's get one thing straight. I just paid for you. Not the other way around. I don't want anything I tell you to appear in one of your newsletters unless I say so. Is that clear?"

"No problemo."

"What can you tell me about Victor Ballantrae and his company? I know you have run some stories on him."

"Ballantrae, huh? It's about time somebody other than us got interested in the bastard. Mainstream press treats him like Nelson Mandela. But something is rotten in Denmark."

"How so?"

Sink leaned forward and put his elbows on his desk.

"Let me tell you about Wall Street. All the crap of the last couple of years – the huge profits, the collapse and then the bailouts – were the result of so-called new products, derivatives and collateralized mortgage whatsists. And, of course, a total lack of regulation, which is insane. You can deregulate the airlines and safety isn't compromised because the guys running those airlines know that nobody will fly if the planes keep falling out of the sky. But deregulate Wall Street and they don't care if your investments aren't safe. The big guys make money on the way up, and on the way down. Sometimes more on the way down, cause that's where the bargains are. And the American taxpayer will bail them out no matter what happens."

Sink stood up and started pacing. He was getting into his subject.

"But I digress. In the normal course of events, using traditional securities, it's tough to beat the market, which actually does level the playing field. Insider traders can do it in stocks, as I well know. But if you stick to the rules, or anywhere close to them, you're not going to be able to separate yourself from the pack, unless you think long-term, like Buffet. Short-term, there are too many smart brains doing what you are doing, using the same computers. Of course anyone can get lucky in one or two short-term trades, but when someone consistently outperforms his peers, or claims to, I get suspicious."

"And you're suspicious of Ballantrae?"

"He offers CD's with interest two or three percentage points higher than other banks and brokers, including the biggest in the country."

"Doesn't seem like all that much."

"What are you talking about? If I'm offering a CD at six percent and you're offering one at eight percent, that's 33 percent higher than me. At low rates, say three percent versus two, that's a 50 percent premium. Normally, if one banker is offering a CD at six, his rival across the street might offer it at 6.1 percent and throw in a toaster. You might even cross the street for that tenth of a point. For three points you'll cross the fucking galaxy."

Sink sat back down.

"How can he do it?'

"He can't. That's my point. He's doing something that's not kosher."

"Wouldn't the SEC or other regulators spot that?"

Disdainful didn't cover the look Sink gave Scarne.

"Jesus. Did you step out of the room when I was talking about regulation? There was none. Now, of course, they're playing catch-up. But Ballantrae isn't selling mortgages. He's selling CD's. Too dull for most prosecutors."

"He says his bank in Antigua gives him tax advantages that mainland U.S. banks don't have," Scarne said, "and that he can invest overseas for higher returns. Also his direct sales operations have a low overhead."

"You've been reading his marketing malarkey. All big American banks are international and they are all pretty good at evading U.S. taxes. Giving Ballantrae credit for the direct sales crap, I'd say he could offer, at most, a quarter of a percentage point over his rivals. On the outside. If the wind is blowing the right way."

"A Ponzi?"

Sink slapped his hand on his desk.

"Give that man a cigar! It's nice to talk to an educated man. Yeah, I think Ballantrae is running a sophisticated Ponzi, paying high rates to old investors using cash from new investors who, of course, are lured by those very rates."

"You've actually run stories about this?"

Sink shook his head sadly.

"We've run some stuff on Ballantrae that we could document. He's making a major push in investment banking and has taken some shortcuts. A few of his brokers and advisors have been involved in minor securities violations. But he always disavows any knowledge of their actions and promptly fires them. Nothing sticks to him. He pays fines and the matter goes away."

"That's it?"

"Here's how it works around here. We report lawsuits, court cases, depositions, administrative investigations and arrests. My interns monitor news agencies, regulatory and legal websites and blogs for anything smacking of offshore illegality and we print what we can confirm. We're not staffed to do much investigation ourselves. What could we do, when the C.I.A., F.B.I., Interpol, the S.E.C. and all the rest are overwhelmed by the avalanche of deceit out there? There's a trillion fucking dollars floating around offshore! It's all we can handle to report the hard stuff. And that's enough to make me rich. We're one-stop shopping for people who want to know who's been caught doing what. We don't print innuendo and rumors. Or my gut instincts. That's why we don't lose lawsuits. If formal charges are filed against Ballantrae, or if he's even sued by his investors, we'll use it. I think Ballantrae is as crooked as my dick, but he's got a gazillion lawyers. He's super litigious. He even threatened to sue me when I ran some stuff that was already public record."

They were interrupted by Sink's wife, who handed Scarne a receipt and a small shopping bag filled with newsletters.

"I gave you the last three issues of all our newsletters," she said. "You can access the online editions with a temporary password you can change later. Instructions are in the bag. More coffee?'

Scarne declined and thanked her. After she left, he turned to Sink and said, "I want anything you have on Ballantrae, even what you can't print."

Sink considered that.

"I'm not real comfortable with that. Your thousand bucks doesn't buy you that kind of information. Forget the legal angle. I like to know what I'm dealing with. Who are you working for?"

"Didn't Pourier tell you?"

"Nah. Just asked me to see you."

Scarne told him. Sink's expression went from benign interest to incredulity.

"And Sheldon Shields thinks his son's death is connected to a story he was preparing about Ballantrae?"

"He's convinced his son was murdered by someone. I'm keeping an open mind. If Josh Shields had proof of a Ponzi, it might be enough to derail Ballantrae's investment in Shields Inc. He'd be a real threat."

Sink looked dubious.

"Look, I think the worst about everyone, from Mother Teresa to Santa Claus, but I can't see it. Ponzi guys don't kill people. Madoff, who was facing life, didn't go that route. These guys always think they can turn things around, or lawyer things away. Plus, unless they do it themselves, or have access to reliable hit men, too many people would know. If the old man is right, it's gotta be something else. Something Ballantrae knew would be catastrophic."

"Any guesses?"

"Hold it a second." Sink picked up his phone and dialed an extension. "Barry, come in here, will ya?" He looked at Scarne. "Barry's one of my interns. The in-house bomb thrower. Likes to collect dirt on people, very little of which I can ever run. He's my Ballantrae expert."

A moment later the scruffy kid with the ponytail slouched in.

"Tell this gentleman everything you know, or think you know, about Victor Ballantrae and his operations."

He gave Scarne a suspicious glance.

"Who the fuck is he? A cop?"

"Someone whose cash may allow me to keep you the fuck on as an intern."

Barry shrugged. "This can get complicated, you may want to take notes." He picked up a legal pad from Sink's desk and flipped it toward Scarne. Then he started talking, as if from memory.

"Ballantrae International is an international holding company trying to get its fingers in everyone's pie. Victor Ballantrae is Australian. His antecedents are murky, as is his personal and business life Down Under. Had some minor scrapes with the law that were ascribed to youthful indiscretion. Apparently straightened himself out and moved to England to get a degree in finance. Returned home. Bounced around and then went into banking, if you can call it that. Opened up shell banks in Niue and Nauru, two rock-sized islands in the Pacific with a combined population of 12,000. But they domiciled 500 banks, some of which reportedly washed millions for Russian mobsters and officials stealing the former U.S.S.R. blind."

Scarne's initial opinion of the kid slowly gave way to awe. Behind the scruff and ponytail was a real brain.

"The banks, of course, were just pieces of paper. If you could fog a mirror and pay the fees, you could open a bank. Ballantrae supposedly transferred a lot of cash from the islands to a bank he started in Australia. All quasi-legal, by the way. Before 9/11, Australia was pretty Wild West in banking circles. Lots of money went into the kangaroo's pouch dirty and came out squeaky clean. Aussies are big in offshore Internet casinos, too, and I hear Ballantrae had a piece of that as well.

He paused to let Scarne finish what he was writing.

"Anyway, Australia finally started cracking down on the money launderers and Ballantrae set out for friendlier climes. And no place was friendlier that the Caribbean after Ballantrae bought off Congress – both sides of the aisle, by the way – and torpedoed legislation restricting offshore banking. Ballantrae International Bank in Antigua is now one of the largest offshore banks in the region. My bet is that a lot of those Russian rubles found their way there. As with any offshore bank there are rumors of money laundering for South American drug dealers. Then, of course, there is Pavlo Boyko. Heard of him?"

"No," Scarne said, still writing. "I hope there isn't going to be a quiz."

"Boyko is the former Prime Minister of the Ukraine who fled to the U.S. in the late 1990's after wiring $200 million from his treasury out of the country. He sought asylum but was instead arrested and is now serving a long stretch in Marion. But the money was never recovered and the suspicion is that it eventually wound up for safekeeping with his brother in Seattle. Andriy Boyko is a fish wholesaler but he also runs the Ukrainian mob on the West Coast."

Barry paused for effect and even did a credible drum roll on Sink's desk with a couple of pencils.

"But here's the interesting part. Andriy supposedly needed someone to launder all that money. He's smart enough to know that the Feds were one step behind. He had to get it out of the country again. After all, you can hide only so much cash under dead mackerel. And that's where Ballantrae comes in, or so my sources tell me. He's the new banker for the Ukrainians."

"Why did they pick him?

"Word is that he came highly recommended from the Seattle Mafia, which got to know him through his Internet casino operations. He handled a lot of their money and the Ukrainians went to them for advice."

"Where did you get this?"

The kid looked at Sink, who nodded.

"The stuff about Pavlo is public record. And his brother is all over the papers out there. But a lot of it comes from disgruntled competitors and pissed-off ex-employees who say something is fishy, pardon the pun, but don't want their names used."

"And none of this has appeared in the newsletter?'

"Nah. Reggie is a pussy."

Sink snorted derisively.

"Mafia, Ukrainians, why not throw in al-Qaeda while you're at it. I only act crazy. It's good for circulation. When you get something you can prove, snot ass, let me see it."

The intern laughed. "Sure, boss." He started to walk out.

"Let's suppose," Scarne said, "that some of what Barry suspects is true. Would it change your mind about what Ballantrae might do to suppress it?"

"Yeah, sure," Sink said. "If the Shields kid had something solid tying Ballantrae to the Ukrainian mob it would do more than queer an investment deal. It could be all over for him. Even the Feds couldn't ignore that."

Barry stopped at the door and turned around.

"Who's the Shields kid?"

"Reporter who worked for the *South Florida Times*," Sink said. "Used the name Hidless, was looking into Ballantrae."

"You mean Josh? His real name was Shields?"

Both Scarne and Sink stared at the kid.

"What? What'd I say?"

Finally, Scarne said, "You knew him?"

"Sure. Had some drinks at Michael Collins, a pub on Lincoln Road. Hangout for underpaid media types." He looked at Sink. "Like me."

"Did he ever mention Ballantrae?"

"All the time. We'd compare notes. Talk on the phone a couple of times a week. He even came by here once or twice. Haven't heard from him in a while. Want me to give him a call?"

"Don't bother," Scarne said.

Sink walked Scarne out.

"You realize that none of this proves anything," he said. "Two kids exchanging conspiracy theories."

"Josh wasn't a kid. He had serious investigative creds. He might have run down those rumors and sources Barry fed him. Maybe they're not rumors."

"You think he had proof? So they killed him?"

"I don't know. Maybe all it took was him being right."

Well, if it's true I hope you nail the bastard. I'd love that story."

Huber and Pourior had said virtually the same thing.

"I'm thinking of starting a news service," Scarne said. "In the meantime, tell those kids not to be too curious about Ballantrae. Just to be safe."

"Shit. I didn't think about that. You're right. But what about you?"

"I'm not even sure Ballantrae did anything. I may be thinking zebras when I'm hearing horses. But if he did, making a run at me would be a red flag for too many people. Including Randolph Shields. I'm pretty sure he's probably spoken to Ballantrae about me by now."

"I'd still be careful. Are you going to see Victor Ballantrae?"

"That's the plan."

"He's a hard man to get a hold of. Do you have an appointment?"

"No."

"Well, you're in luck. He's in town, giving a luncheon speech tomorrow at the Biltmore. Some organization called the Caribbean Basin Free Trade Alliance. Probably launders money for some of its members."

DEATH BY MISNOMER

IN SCARNE'S EXPERIENCE, medical examiners looked nothing like the quirky, handsome or beautiful actors who portrayed them on television or in the movies. Most looked just like everyone else in any other profession.

Eric Fonthill was the exception. He was an M.E. from B-movie central casting in the era before Hollywood made the profession so sexy. He'd given Scarne a general description and told him where he'd be sitting at the outside bar at Monty's, a seafood restaurant at a marina just short of Coconut Grove proper. And that's where he was, hunched over a menu, sipping a beer and looking like Ichabod Crane's twin. He was even dressed all in black. Although there was a decent lunchtime crowd, the stools on either side of him were empty, as if people instinctively sensed something foreboding in a man leafing through entrees with hands that had probably just been in somebody's entrails.

Despite his grim reaper demeanor Fonthill had a pleasant smile and a warm, firm handshake that Scarne, not wanting to give away his thoughts, returned vigorously. And he didn't smell of formaldehyde. Still, Scarne was happy to be eating outside. They grabbed a table by the water, sitting on benches opposite each other.

"Sorry, I'm late," Scarne said. "Took me almost an hour from Weston."

"Yeah, traffic is getting out of hand down here."

Small boats in their berths made bumping sounds against the dock and water lapped over the walkway. They ordered a pitcher of beer, a basket of boiled shrimp to munch and two grilled grouper sandwiches. Fonthill had also been primed by a call from the N.Y.P.D. and even knew some M.E.'s in Manhattan so they talked shop for a few minutes. The shrimp came and Scarne was relieved to have his own dipping sauce. They were halfway through their grouper when Scarne got around to Josh Shields.

"What killed him?"

Fonthill reached into his jacket pocket and brought out a thick envelope, which he handed to Scarne.

"Copy of the report. You didn't get it from me. My boss would throw a clot. The death looked pretty straightforward. Body hadn't been in the ocean all that long, and apparently the water was a bit chillier than normal. But it's still Southern Florida and there are all sorts of creatures out there on the chow line. Poor guy was nibbled over some. Tox screen was pretty normal. No blunt trauma injuries, bullet holes, knife wounds, striations, reticular hemorrhages or anything else to indicate the proverbial foul play."

"You didn't list it as a drowning," Scarne said, sifting through the sheets.

"There wasn't much water in his lungs. He died quick, if miserably. Cause of death was cardiac arrest, an arrhythmia, either natural or caused by a shock. My own guess, and it's only a guess, he got stung by jellyfish in the dark, got disoriented, fell into the water, got stung some more and it overwhelmed him."

"Newspapers said it was a drowning."

"You know how that goes. It was an 'apparent drowning' in the first stories and that's how it stayed. Nobody followed up but the family, and I guess they're still unhappy, which is why you're here. But it's not like the Miami Beach cops or the local rags would broadcast the possibility that a swarm of jellyfish blobbed him to death. The Chamber of Commerce would go nuts."

"Was it possible?"

"Well, he had a lot of Men-of-War stings on his face and neck. Even had some damage to his eyes and the inside of his mouth. Found a jellyfish in his throat." He looked at Scarne, who had stopped eating his sandwich. "Could have been post-mortem. Bottom line, I think Josh Shields died of the world's worst case of bad luck. Couldn't put that down. So arrhythmia it was."

Scarne, thinking of the jellyfish, had trouble swallowing his beer.

"This is going to sound crazy to you, but is there any way a jellyfish could have been forced into his mouth?"

Surprisingly, Fonthill took the question seriously.

"Let me think. I suppose if someone held your mouth open and someone else dropped one in, it's possible. But that's an awful lot of trouble. More likely it just kind of drifted in when he was floating around with his mouth open. You wouldn't believe some of the things that I find in people after they've been in the ocean. One guy, I thought it was his tongue hanging out, all purple and everything, except it had eyes. That was weird."

Scarne put the remains of his fish sandwich permanently aside.

"Of course, he could have just kind of inhaled it reflexively, in kind of a spasm, when the other Men-of-War fired off."

"Fired off?"

"Yeah. The term 'jellyfish' is a misnomer. A Portuguese Man-of-War is a hydrozoa, made up of four different animals. Each has its own job. The blue sail is one animal, the tentacles another, and so on. Like a commune, except without sex, at least not the kind we'd appreciate. The poison is in the nematocysts in the tentacles, which can stretch out several feet from the main body, which might only be six-inches long." Fonthill picked up a large pickle from his plate and placed it on the table. Then he arranged some coleslaw so it looked it was a bunch of tentacles. Their waitress swooped by, took one look, and swooped away. "This is not to scale, of course, and the colors are all wrong. Anyway, when the nematocysts hit something or become irritated they explode and release the toxin."

For this part of the demonstration, which had now attracted the attention of nearby diners, Fonthill used a leftover boiled shrimp, which he dropped into the coleslaw tentacles.

"Bam! Brutal stuff, about 75% as powerful as cobra venom and made up of all sorts of enzymes that are hard to spell. Smaller doses than a snake bite, of course, and not injected as deeply. Paralyzes small fish and shrimp that are then drawn into the part of the colony that digests." He picked up the shrimp and popped it in his mouth. "So Shields probably got hit with a bunch of tentacles from a dozen Men-of-War and spazzed out. One sting has been compared to getting hit by lightning, so a lot of simultaneous stings would be unbearable. He might have been particularly sensitive because he apparently had a run-in with a Man-of-War a couple of weeks earlier. The cops found a discharge slip from an emergency room. You gonna finish the other half of your sandwich?"

Scarne pushed it across to him.

"I don't think the toxin killed him," Fonthill said, biting into the grouper. "No sign of anaphylactic shock. But from the look of the welts, there would have been incredible pain in his face, eyes, neck and chest. And that probably caused the arrhythmia. Like I said, I think the poor guy was just unlucky."

"I take it the family wasn't told about the extent of the jellyfish stings."

Fonthill looked thoughtful.

"I doubt it. I mentioned the stings in my report, but it might have gotten lost in all the other medical and marine verbiage. Don't forget, we couldn't be sure it was the jellyfish. Maybe he was drowning, and just died before he could do a good job of it."

"Chamber of Commerce has that much clout down here?"

"I'm just glad he wasn't eaten by a shark. I hate it when I have to put down that the victim cut himself shaving."

"I didn't mean..."

"Hey, no sweat. I'm kidding. We write them up as we see them. But this was too ambiguous to go off half cocked. There hadn't been any other serious jellyfish incidents. I would have been irresponsible saying jellyfish were the cause of death when I wasn't sure. You asked me what I thought. I told you. What I know is that his heart stopped in a way that suggested an arrhythmia. Maybe they wanted to spare the family."

Scarne thought of something else.

"Even if he was seriously stung, would death be so instantaneous he couldn't make it to shore? Instinctively try to get help."

Fonthill took some time thinking about that.

"Maybe he waded far out. It's real shallow there. Course, it was supposed to be pretty dark and the surf was up that night. Wasn't there some talk of suicide? You know, like Norman Maine in *A Star Is Born?*"

Fonthill looked like the kind of person who watched old movies.

"I'm not ruling anything out. The kid's father thinks he was murdered."

"Whoa! That's a stretch." Fonthill looked thoughtful again. "But it's one of those things you can't disprove. Lots of things could have stopped his heart and left no trace. We're pretty good, but finding a needle puncture or something like that in a shriveled corpse that's been chewed on by crustaceans is almost impossible, unless you're on TV. And like I said, the only thing on the tox screen was jellyfish venom. Lots of it. I will admit that the gap between when he died and when the body was found is troubling. He must have been in pretty deep."

"Could someone have dragged him out and drowned him?"

"No water in the lungs, remember?" Fonthill paused. "And no obvious trauma to the body, which we'd pick up even given the condition of the body. He was a young guy. Probably would have fought back. Of course, if he was already dead...." Fonthill finished his beer and wiped foam off his upper lip. "Let's see. Someone kills our boy with something we can't trace. Then swims his body out to deeper water." He was talking to himself. "A lot of trouble just to kill someone. The nearest public beach access is blocks away. He'd be chancing getting spotted going back through one of the apartment gates. Make more sense if he had a boat. Even more if he someone to help him."

Fonthill popped a final shrimp in his mouth.

"But my money is still on the jellyfish. Listen, thanks for the lunch. I don't get out all that much."

Scarne could believe that.

"I appreciate your help. Want some more beer?"

"Nah. I have to get back. Got to keep my hands steady. Don't carry malpractice insurance." He cackled. It was apparently an old morgue joke.

A FREUDIAN SHIP?

SCARNE DROVE BACK to Josh's apartment and changed into shorts and a T-shirt. He spent a punishing but much-needed hour in the building's exercise room, starting on its Nautilus circuit and finishing with free weights. After a steam and a shower he was about to start reading the Sink newsletters when his cell phone beeped. It was Evelyn.

"I just got a call from the state licensing board. A very nice man said that they were looking into some 'irregularities,' and wondered if you could come in for a chat."

"What kind of 'irregularities?"

"He wouldn't say, but he said it was merely pro forma."

"That's Latin for 'you're screwed'."

"I told him you were traveling. That's when he used the subpoena word."

"Call Don Tierney and ask him to stall them. Tell him it's probably Randolph Shields applying the pressure."

"Are you making a nuisance of yourself again?"

"I've just begun."

After ringing off, Scarne sat on a couch and started reading some of the articles in the Sink newsletters:

"Czech Republic Seeks Extradition of Nigerian in $60 M Internet Scam"

"British Virgin Islands Hedge Fund Collapses; Investors lose $140 M"

"PwC (Bermuda) Partner Met Madoff; Gave Him Clean Bill of Health"

"Offshore Bank Refuses to Turn Over Records, U.S. Says"

"Accounting Firms Agree to Pay $30 M to Settle Nevis Fraud Action"

"Turkey Seeks Evidence from Massachusetts in $100 M Ponzi"

"Belgium Seeks Identity of Website Casino Fraudster"

"Montserrat Banker Allegedly Embezzled $14 M"

"$10 M Judgment Entered Against Barbados Insurer; Minister Resigns"

He was astounded at the sheer variety and sophistication of the Ponzi schemes, money laundering, investment frauds, securities violations and other scams the world over, not to mention the colorful rogues who perpetrated them. Some of the bilk-artists had been caught and prosecuted but skipped town. They now operated under new names, using dummy or shell corporations in friendlier jurisdictions, trying to keep one step ahead of overmatched regulators and cops. A section in *Offshore Confidential* entitled *"Reggie's Regulators Hall of Shame"* contained profiles and photos of various government ministers who looked the other way – and got rich – while the banking and securities laws of their nations were flouted. Another column detailed the status of all the libel actions brought against Sink. According to a note at the bottom of the column, *Offshore Confidential* never lost a libel suit.

After two hours Scarne just stopped reading. Since Sink only reported on confirmed cases in a trillion-dollar sewer of offshore corruption, that meant there were hundreds, maybe thousands of crooks still undiscovered. The fact that Victor Ballantrae owned an offshore bank didn't mean he was one of them, but it begged the question: Why own an offshore bank?

Scarne needed a drink. He went to the kitchen and took a quick inventory of the refrigerator and pantry. Meyer's Dark Rum, limes, orange juice, grenadine and maraschino cherries. Bless you, Mario. Five minutes later he was sitting in front of his laptop sipping a Planter's Punch. After a workout it was important to replace electrolytes he told himself.

As he expected, the Ballantrae Group website was a font of useless information. The company had $56 billion under "active management," whatever that meant, up from $40 billion a year earlier. The interests of its clients "always came first" and its management team included "the best and the brightest" of financial advisors, research analysts and trading specialists who offered "a unique spectrum of expertise and investment products."

The company's 128-page, four-color corporate magazine, the Ballantrae Eagle, could be downloaded as a PDF file, and Scarne did. The corporate logo, a golden eagle's profile surrounded by Olympic-looking torches, dominated the cover and graced every page of the magazine. The logo was also prominent on the many shots of buildings, plush offices, corporate jets and the Ballantrae yacht, the *Botany Bay.* A Freudian ship, Scarne wondered?

Victor Ballantrae, a large man with a red beard, was pictured with American Presidents, past and present; dictators; prime ministers; governors, mayors; members of Congress; Hollywood stars; famous athletes, and, of course, children of all colors, both healthy and sick. Ballantrae's philanthropic deeds were well documented, but Scarne soon tired of Ballantrae's expansive smile, which he thought looked piratical. I'm being unfair, he admitted. I'm looking for a reason to dislike the guy. But there's just something...

The next section did nothing to allay Scarne's discomfort. The Ballantrae Group's corporate structure was diagrammed in a "tree" chart that looked like something Darwin would have designed for *The Origin of the Species*. The Ballantrae Group was represented by the trunk and scores of subsidiaries branched out from there: Ballantrae International Bank, Ballantrae Trust, Ballantrae Financial Services, Ballantrae Investment Banking, Ballantrae Bank of Panama, Ballantrae Aruba, Ballantrae Groupo Mexico, Ballantrae Venezuela Ltd., Ballantrae Group Suisse, Ballantrae Français, Ballantrae Development Corporation, Ballantrae Bullion and so on. There were so many branches and sprouts that Scarne had trouble reading the small type. He counted 23 that were in boldface. A note at the bottom of the page proudly stated that the subsidiaries in bold had been added within the previous year. Rapid expansion like that took a lot of cash. How did a company continue to pay those high C.D. rates? Could it really be a giant Ponzi?

The rest of the magazine and the bulk of the website itself were devoted to brief profiles of the subsidiaries and some of their directors. All were apparently doing wonderfully although any references to revenues and profits were vague. The offshore bank in Antigua rated only a few lines and no photo, which Scarne found curious. He also found it strange that he came across no photos of Alana Loeb, or at least none that were identified as her. She was listed by title in a corporate directory (in addition to being Chief of Staff, she was the Ballantrae Group's Corporate Counsel and a director of several subsidiaries). There were dozens of attractive women on the website in group photos who were not named in captions. Scarne wondered if Loeb was among them. Sheldon had described her as stunning. None of the women in the pictures quite qualified. He remembered Sheldon's age and reserved judgment on his taste in women. Of course, Emma Shields had also been impressed.

Scarne was thoroughly sick of reading about Ballantrae. And he was hungry. Fonthill had eaten most of his lunch. He closed the site and made himself a couple of sandwiches. He grabbed a beer, went back to his laptop and opened his emails. He was mildly surprised to see that Paulo and Curley had already forwarded a copy of their investigation.

The report appeared to be a thorough job (a certainty once they found out who the victim's family was) but there wasn't much in it that he didn't already know. Beach crowds change, so the two detectives had a tough time finding someone who remembered seeing Shields that specific day.

A local character who patrolled the beach every day with a metal detector saw Josh before he left for the night. The prospector, who was not a suspect (he was 73), remembered him because he was always in virtually the same spot, at about the same time, every Wednesday. There was no one else around except two men in a small boat anchored just offshore. It was getting dark and the boat was bouncing up and down so he couldn't give a good description of the men, other than to say one was taller than the other and had blond hair. The boat was either a Dusky or a Grady White. He couldn't be sure.

Scarne was about to put the report aside when he thought of something. He reread the section about the men in the small boat bouncing around and recalled one of the detectives telling him there were small craft warnings out that day. The prospector didn't mention any other boat, so it was probably the only one there. Why would a small boat be so close to the beach in such rough water? He recalled Fonthill postulating how a boat and a partner would have made it easier for a killer.

It wasn't much to go on, and Scarne also didn't like the part about Josh's rigid routine. But he still had trouble envisioning a murder.

‡

'HE WAS LUNCH'

IN SEATTLE, NOAH Sealth was having no such problem. He didn't think that Taras Rudnyk, now splayed naked across a desk in the warehouse office, had accidentally cut himself open from forehead to ankles. He counted at least 14 major knife wounds and at least twice that number of minor slices. Sealth would have to wait for the M.E. report but he was pretty sure that most of the stabs had been torture related. The facial and genital mutilation would have been particularly effective. He assumed the dead man eventually talked.

"I would have," he said aloud.

The smell of blood and what had been in the man's bowels and bladder even overwhelmed the odor of fish in the building. The forensic team was snapping pictures, placing yellow markers and swabbing away, so Sealth left to get a breath of air. When he got outside he walked over to a group of men being warily guarded by uniformed cops. One of the men was Andriy Boyko.

"Who found him?"

Nobody said anything until Boyko nodded. Then one of the others said, "I did." He looked at his chief who nodded again. "I came here to look for him."

"Why?"

"I sent him," Boyko said. "He wasn't answering his cell phone. That wasn't like him." Boyko smiled. "Although he apparently had a good reason."

About the only reason Boyko would accept from Rudnyk, Sealth thought. The dead man was one of the Ukrainian mob chief's closest lieutenants and would never be out of touch long.

"Why did you think he was here?"

"I didn't think anything. It was one of many places we looked."

"How long were you looking?"

"Since noon. He did not show up for lunch."

Sealth knew Boyko and his chief henchmen made a habit of lunching together, usually at a busy restaurant where it would be difficult to be overheard. Unlike the Mafia, which was partial to their "social clubs," the Uke mob liked to move their strategy meetings around. The random selection of restaurants, chosen at the last minute, made it almost impossible for local police or Feds to eavesdrop electronically. It also thwarted potential assassins.

"From the looks of it," Sealth said, "he *was* lunch. Why was he here?"

"I don't know, Detective. But since you can't possibly believe I would slaughter one of my men in my own warehouse and then call the police, perhaps we can go now."

More police vehicles were pulling up, as well as the morgue wagon.

"Your men can leave after they give their names and addresses to these officers. I'd like to talk to you for a minute. Let's take a stroll."

The two men walked over to a bulkhead. They stood facing the busy harbor. A seagull standing on a piling swiveled its head toward them briefly and then went back to looking out over the water.

"No rain for two days," Boyko said.

In Seattle, that passed for news.

"I'm worried about my lawn," Sealth said. "Any idea who did this?"

"Please, Detective. I saw the body. We both know. I heard about the autopsy. It's already a legend. Were you there?"

"Yeah. Brutti went berserk, and I can't blame him."

"So, he thinks I killed his sister and came looking for me."

"She was found in one of your warehouses under your fish. Your buildings have become very unhealthy all of a sudden."

"We don't target families." Sealth turned to stare at him. Boyko smiled. "As a general rule. And even if I had killed her, there are better places to dispose of a body." He gestured toward the Pacific Ocean. "So, I've heard."

"Look, Andriy, we both know it was a setup. The question is, 'What are you going to do now?' My chief is worried about a mob war. I already have two murders to solve. I don't need any more."

"You believe I should do nothing? Let the police handle it? That will really endear me to my men."

"My partner is out looking for Carlo. So is his family. All I'm saying is that the man is unhinged. He acted on his own. If you saw what he did at the morgue you'd have lost it too. Perhaps your men will understand that if you explain it to them."

Boyko took out a pack of cigarettes. He offered one to Sealth, who took it. He'd been dying for one ever since Maria Brutti's autopsy. They stood smoking for a while. The seagull apparently disapproved and flew away.

"Perhaps. Whoever killed the woman and planted her body in my warehouse did not count on the hagfish."

"Hagfish?"

"That's what came out of her, Detective. I was given a clear description. They are parasites. Occasionally get dredged up with bottom fish, like halibut. We try to separate them out but some slip through. It must have been in the same container as her body."

"Brutti believes it was torture."

"They do not feed on living creatures. She was dead when it entered her."

"I'm sure Carlo will be happy to hear that. If he doesn't already know. He spent a lot of quality time with your friend in there before he finally finished him off. I'd guess he got more than name, rank and serial number. He probably knows a lot of things now."

"Then he knows I had nothing to do with his sister's murder. So I do not think I have anything to fear from him anymore."

Good point, Sealth admitted.

"Any idea who might?"

The seagull returned to its perch. At least Sealth thought it was the same seagull. They all looked alike to him.

"Can I go now, Detective? I have a business to run."

"One more thing, Andriy. You don't seem to be particularly broken up by the mutilation and murder of one of your closest associates."

Boyko shrugged.

"He would be alive if he had been where he was supposed to be."

Sealth didn't buy it. There was something else going on. He suspected that Boyko didn't know why Rudnyk was in the warehouse office. The Ukrainian turned to leave.

"Boyko!"

"Yes, what is it?"

"Let me have another cigarette."

Boyko laughed and threw him the pack.

NO EXAGGERATION

SCARNE WOKE EARLY the next morning, stiff from the previous day's workout and from falling asleep on the couch reading more newsletters. He changed into shorts and a sweatshirt and headed to the beach, where he began jogging north near the waterline to take advantage of the harder sand. After a half hour the stiffness abated and he cut through a public park and began walking back along Collins Avenue. He resisted the smells emanating from the many restaurants along the way as long as he could and then popped into a small Cuban coffee shop for a delicious breakfast of tostada, ham croquetas and a café con leche. When he got back to the apartment, his cell phone was beeping. There was a message from Don Tierney: "Call me."

"How bad is it?" he asked the lawyer when he got him on the phone.

"Did you really kidnap the Lindberg baby?"

It seemed that the state licensing board was pulling every case Scarne ever worked and was reexamining every piece of regulatory paperwork he ever filed. Randolph had probably called Councilman Gruber after the incident on the yacht.

"Can you stall them?"

"Sure. And I can probably take the death penalty off the table. But not forever. You have pissed off a very powerful man. You know what they say about picking a fight with someone who buys printing ink by the barrel. Can you tell me what this is all about?"

Scarne did.

"I take it back about the death penalty."

Ballantrae's Miami headquarters was in a high-rise on the northern end of Brickell Avenue just short of downtown. It was set among a score of modern buildings that were redefining Miami as a center of international commerce and finance. Even among all the glass, aluminum and angular architecture the office tower stood out, with what appeared to be a large rectangular hole in its middle about a third of the way up its 40 stories. The gap was three floors high and wide enough for a helicopter to fly through. Circular red stairways inside the gap led to floors above, and Scarne could see large palm trees swaying inside the structure, perhaps an interior courtyard. He assumed that people at the same level in buildings across the street could see right through to the bay. The visual effect would be unique. But not a place to be caught in a hurricane, which would turn the void into a wind tunnel.

After parking his car in a nearby lot, Scarne walked back to the building, where workmen were placing a large bronze plaque over a name chiseled in the side of the building. The old name was "Biscayne Bank & Trust." The name on the plaque was "Ballantrae International." He walked into the lobby.

"Can I help you?"

The girl behind the reception desk was another Cuban stunner. He was beginning to think Miami was just a huge set for a *Stepford Secretary* movie.

"I would like to see Mr. Ballantrae."

"Do you have an appointment?"

"No, I'm afraid not."

Scarne sized up the look he got. Charm was out. He decided on bluster.

"I'm investigating a possible homicide," he said, opening his wallet and flashing his investigator's license, which he hoped the kid would be too flustered to scan closely. It worked. She hardly glanced at his "credentials" before the wallet snapped shut. Eyes widened, she stammered something unintelligible, dialed an extension and began speaking rapidly in Spanish. There was a moment's silence. Then the girl straightened her back. She looked confused, then chagrined. Scarne guessed that someone else had come on the line and was reading her the riot act. She turned to him, hand over the receiver.

"I'm sorry sir. What did you say your name was?"

"I didn't. It's Scarne." He pointedly looked at his watch.

"Detective Scarne," she said into the phone.

She listened for a moment, then put the phone down gingerly. She tried a brave smile, which came up a few watts short.

"If you will take the elevator up to the 18th floor, Miss Loeb will meet you."

When the elevator opened, Scarne just stood there. Sheldon and Emma Shields had not exaggerated Alana Loeb's beauty. Then the door started to close and she put out her hand to break the electronic eye.

"This is the right floor, Mr. Scarne," she said, "unless you are looking for ladies lingerie or home furnishings." Not "Detective" Scarne.

Scarne stepped out and took her hand. It was warm to his touch, and dry.

"I'm Alana Loeb, and you are not a police officer. Why the subterfuge? Isn't it illegal to impersonate a real law officer?"

She smiled sadly. It was a look he recalled from grammar school when his excuse for not doing his homework fell on a nun's practiced ears.

"I didn't have an appointment. Just happened to be in the neighborhood and took a shot. I never said I was a cop. What the hell? Got me this far, so I guess it was worth it. Why it got me this far is the question."

"The word 'homicide' tends to open doors. Even then, when I realized who you were, I almost told that silly girl to send you away."

"Why didn't you?"

"What the hell?" Her smile was radiant. "Took a shot."

"I'm glad you did. I would have had to try my 'building inspector' routine on her. And that's usually beneath me."

"How does that one work?"

She gestured for him to walk with her down the hall.

"I would have said that there is a big hole in the building and it's unsafe. You do have several floors missing. I hope you didn't overpay."

Alana Loeb laughed. It was a good laugh, deep and throaty.

"It would have worked with that one. She's won't be there long."

"Listen, I didn't want to get the kid in trouble."

"Don't worry. We won't fire her. She was hired as an office assistant. We had to plug her in down there until we recruit more people. Soon as we do, she'll come back upstairs. Besides, I was young and dumb once, too."

"I doubt that."

They came to the end of the hallway and Scarne heard hammering.

"My office is that way." She pointed down a corridor where workmen were laying carpet. "We'll be better off in one of the smaller conference rooms. Watch your step. We're still doing a lot of work."

He followed her. Electricians and painters seemed to be everywhere. If the conference room was meant to impress, it succeeded admirably, with plush carpeting, heavy, dark wood furniture, deep-backed chair and a wonderful vista of Biscayne Bay.

"Nice view."

"Yes, isn't it?" She waved him over to a large leather L-shaped couch in the middle of the room. She sat down on the shorter part of the "L" and crossed her wonderful legs and turned to face him when he sat at the other end. Scarne, concentrating on the beautiful woman sitting near him, didn't notice the small red light blink on in the "security camera" recessed in a bookcase on the opposite wall.

Alana Loeb was not a classic beauty, not that any man – or woman – noticed. Like many women with a commanding presence, she gave the impression of being taller than she was. She was thin without being scrawny and even her conservatively-cut business suit could not hide her figure. Blonde hair was cut short and framed her face. It looked natural and Scarne had a thought that would have been common to any heterosexual male on the planet: he wanted an opportunity to find out. Her skin tone spoke to a life comfortable with the outdoors. She wore little makeup and obviously didn't feel the need to camouflage the few small freckles that framed her nose and made her look younger than the woman in her mid-to-late 30's that Scarne assumed her to be. She had a full mouth. But it was her grey eyes that made her face. Widely set and almond shape, they had a slightly oriental cast. She had a habit of ducking her head and looking up at an angle when she spoke.

"Can I get you anything," she said, motioning to a phone on the small table in front of them. She did everything slowly, without wasted movement. "The lunch room is still a work in progress, but we have a coffee machine. Miami runs on coffee. It was the first thing we brought into the building."

Her voice had a pleasing, dulcet timber, with almost perfect English diction. There was the vaguest trace of an accent but Scarne had no clue what it was. She spoke softly but he had no trouble hearing her. Nor did the microphones that she knew were hidden strategically throughout the room. Every word of their conversation would be recorded.

"Coffee would be nice," Scarne said.

The volume was too low. In his office Victor Ballantrae adjusted the sound on the display. Alana had positioned Scarne perfectly on the couch and Ballantrae felt a twinge of jealousy as he caught him looking at her legs. Too bad this wasn't the movies. I could just push a button and the nosy private eye would be electrocuted where he sat and his corpse would slide down a chute, leaving behind a puff of smoke and charred upholstery.

Ballantrae smiled grimly. Given Alana Loeb's capabilities the poor bastard might be better off in the long run.

✝

VICTOR BALLANTRAE

VICTOR BALLANTRAE WAS a big man, broad across the shoulders. Well-tailored suits hid a midsection growing paunchier as he got richer. An Aboriginal grandmother accounted for some darkness of complexion; a passion for golf, the rest. His thick reddish brown hair tended to curliness. A trim beard framed a roguish face dominated by a prominent nose laced with early signs of rosacea. A not unpleasant visage given a piratical cast by the misshapen corner of his right eye, the result of a bar fight in which a sheepherder used a bottle of Fosters before Ballantrae beat him to within an inch of his life. He refused plastic surgery and his eyelid drooped when he was stressed.

Ballantrae's family tree could be traced directly back to one of the 19th Century prison ships that disgorged in Australia the refuse of London when Mother England decided to solve the problem of its overcrowded gaols and poorhouses. But no further back than that, as a young Victor discovered in a rare moment of retrospection when attempting some genealogical research. His antecedents in England were either so poor or so criminal there was no record of them prior to the entry of a "George Ballantrae" in the ship's manifest. The fact that George was arrested shortly after stepping ashore for picking the pockets of people who had nothing in them at least had the effect of getting the Ballantrae name on paper and Victor was able to trace the family's subsequent misdeeds. For unlike most of the poor wretches who became solid citizens after being dumped Down Under the Ballantrae apples never fell from the diseased tree. George was the primogenitor of a long line of horse thieves, con artists and embezzlers before he was hanged an overdue 10 years after setting foot on Australian soil.

Victor was not even sure "Ballantrae" was the man's real name. The entry for a George Ballantrae on the manifest was followed by a note that said, "Died at sea." Either the record keeping on prison ships left something to be desired or George appropriated the name of a dead man. And since there were many ways for someone to have "died at sea" it was possible that he'd had something to do with the demise of the old "George."

The Ballantrae corporate history and personal biography was a mix of half truths and outright fabrications that the American financial press swallowed whole. After emigrating to America well-financed by his offshore activities in the Pacific, Ballantrae made more millions buying and selling Canadian oil and gas leases, many of dubious provenances. He soon realized that with deregulation of the American securities markets some of his more worthless holdings could be cut up into tiny pieces and sold as limited partnerships. The partnerships were always structured so that a few producing wells could generate enough returns to lure in subsequent investors and even provide the semblance of an aftermarket.

This aftermarket came in handy when, against all odds, drillers actually hit an oil or gas pocket, or because a spike in energy prices made marginal holes profitable. Then Ballantrae, through third parties, bought back those properties, which ended up in his portfolio. Many of his limited partnership shares were marketed by "respectable" Wall Street firms through sales departments whose due diligence never went further than their hefty commissions.

Ballantrae's Wall Street contacts proved useful for his next scheme, "La Vuelta," a Spanish word meaning "The Return." It had its origin in a quasi-legitimate arbitrage business started after Venezuelan President Hugo Chavez refused to pay off certain creditors of Petroleos de Venezuela (PDVSA) who had backed a crippling strike against the state-owned oil company in an effort to destabilize his regime. Some local businessmen arranged to buy up the unpaid debt at 10 cents on the dollar. Using corrupted PDVSA officials, the business group managed to get full payment on the debts behind Chavez's back. The businessmen soon ran out of their own capital, but loath to lose an investment stream returning 90% they cast about for new funds. They had little trouble attracting investors locally, who were promised *monthly* returns of up to 20%. Word of mouth about this incredible investment opportunity spread throughout families to the United States, creating a frenzy among South American expatriates in Florida and Louisiana.

Enter Victor Ballantrae, who knew a burgeoning Ponzi when he saw one. He created a financial subsidiary that sold interests in La Vuelta to thousands of South Americans living in the United States. For a time, this new influx of cash kept the scheme going and old investors indeed reaped good returns generated both by the initial 90% arbitrage and dollars provided by new investors. Given the underlying cash flow from PDVSA it might have worked for years. Then Hugo Chavez caught on to the duplicity within PDVSA, had the corrupt conspirators arrested and cut off all dollar payments to the creditors. ("Fucking Communist bastard," Victor raged.) Ballantrae continued to sell interests as long as he could find suckers – he knew that the S.E.C. could care less about South Americans getting ripped off in Venezuela – but without government petroleum funds the fraud soon fell of its own weight.

Most of Ballantrae's clients lost everything, but since the majority had invested less than $100,000 (each interest sold for "only" $25,000) there were few lawsuits. It was just too expensive to take on Ballantrae's legal legions. But a few large investors with millions at stake did bring suit. Alana Loeb was able to clean up the mess with hefty payouts tied to confidentiality agreements. Only one investor, a former general with ties to right-wing death squads in Ecuador and a penchant for vengeance, wouldn't be bought off. He sent Jesús Garza, who was then making a name for himself as a hired "negotiator" in Miami, to collect all his money from Ballantrae, with interest.

"The general doesn't believe in lawyers," Garza told Alana Loeb at their first meeting. "He's prepared to be very unreasonable."

She looked at the swarthy man who relayed this message so calmly and saw the killer. She knew such men from "before." He wasn't going away.

"Let me see what I can do."

She found out all she could about Garza and went to Ballantrae.

"For Christ sake, Alana, that's a lot of money."

"It will pay dividends down the road, Victor. Trust me on this."

She called Garza and met him for mojitos at the bar in the Fontainebleau.

"You can have $250,000."

"He wants his million, plus interest," Garza said, smiling. "Abróchense los cinturones, senorita." *Fasten your seatbelt.* He started to rise from his chair.

Alana put her hand on his arm.

"I said *you* can have $250,000." She paused "A year. Plus bonuses."

The police said the explosion on the general's yacht was likely caused by a leaky fuel pump. No bodies were recovered. Many in Miami's expat community assumed that a vengeful Ecuadorian family caught up with him.

A year later, Garza brought Keitel into the firm. There was more than enough for them to do, as scam begat scam. Victor Ballantrae was at heart a con man. Nothing intrigued him more than a good Ponzi scheme. Alana Loeb, on the other hand, was a financial genius. She came up with the idea that there was a lot more money to be made in Venezuela – this time with Hugo Chavez's unwitting help.

In the early 1980's, a Venezuelan agricultural development bank, Banco de Desarollo Agropecuario, better known as Bandagro, went bankrupt, leaving creditors holding zero-coupon bonds with a face value of $800 million. Few investors went near the bonds until 2003, when Chavez said that the country would honor the bonds when they reached maturity. Neither he, nor the investors who now snapped up the Bandagro bonds, knew that they were sophisticated forgeries, part of a brilliant scheme engineered by a group of Panamanian con men. Bandagro had intended to issue the bonds as part of a last-ditch effort at solvency, but the bank's scrupulous treasurer, knowing the bank was going under in any event, refused to sign them. But *someone* signed his name, and many people bought them in good faith.

Ballantrae, through his connections from his first Venezuelan scam, knew the bonds were forged. (Indeed, the forger now worked in one of his companies; good men being hard to find.) Ballantrae and Alana Loeb created a hedge fund and sold tens of millions of dollars worth of the Bandagro bonds short. When the time was right, they provided, through intermediaries, proof of the forgeries to the government and leaked the news to the press. As expected, Chavez reversed himself and renounced the obligation, making the bonds worthless. Ballantrae's hedge fund closed out its positions for pennies per bond, reaping obscene profits. ("Always liked that Chavez bastard," Victor said. "Salt of the earth.")

The scheme made so much money that Ballantrae was forced to hide it by expanding rapidly in investment services and other businesses in the United States, where decades of deregulation and regulatory shrugs made any sort of financial enterprise appear to be legitimate. He had discovered that the only thing safer than breaking the financial laws in third-world countries was doing it in a country whose citizens naively assumed that their Government was watching out for them.

But Ballantrae was always looking for new sources of revenue. The offshore bank in Antigua proved useful in laundering money for powerful criminal elements on the West Coast of the United States.

Unfortunately, against Alana's advice he had taken some risks and the relationship with those elements had recently soured, which was why the *South Florida Times* story had to be stopped in its tracks. It might have brought their West Coast problem to a head. Of course, had they known the reporter's real identity, they might have taken a different approach. Of all the rotten luck!

But that was spilled milk. Now it was even more important that Sheldon Shields and his annoying private investigator be derailed. Garza's trip to Seattle had presumably bought some more time. In a month or two the bank funds would be replaced and he'd have a powerful minority interest in one of the world's largest media empires.

He'd be untouchable then. Especially since he didn't plan on being just a minority owner forever.

DO YOU GOLF?

"WHAT DID YOU mean when you said you knew who I was, Ms. Loeb?"

Alana Loeb wasn't smiling. But she didn't look angry.

"Randolph Shields called us. We were expecting you. There was no need to play cops and robbers, or even a building inspector."

"Then you know I'm looking into his son's death."

She shook her head sadly.

"Poor Sheldon. I'm not sure how Victor will react to this insanity."

"I'm not so sure it's insanity, Ms. Loeb."

"You think we had something to do with it," she said coldly. "I would be careful, Mr. Scarne. There are laws against slander."

"Look," he said. "I'm not saying he's right about Ballantrae being involved. Makes no sense to me either. But I've spoken to a lot of people, including the medical examiner, and I can no longer dismiss the possibility that Joshua Shields was murdered. His computer and notes are missing. He was preparing an unflattering article about your organization. Perhaps there are other explanations but the fact remains that the article never got printed."

They were interrupted by a woman carrying in a tray with a coffee service.

She placed it on the table and started to pour.

"Thank you, Maria," Alana Loeb said. "You can leave it. I'll take care of our guest."

Which she did, quickly and efficiently.

"Reporters keep a lot of stories on their computers, Mr. Scarne. Maybe he was writing about dope rings or ghetto gangs. Miami has a vibrant criminal subculture. Companies don't kill people to prevent unflattering articles. There would be daily massacres. Why pick on us?"

"If I find out that he was working on other stories, I will pursue them. But you're all I've got for now. If there is nothing here, I go away. But I have to start somewhere."

Alana Loeb looked exasperated. She put down her cup and leaned forward.

"You seem like an intelligent man, Mr. Scarne. I don't doubt that you have Sheldon's best interests at heart. You proved that by turning down Randolph's offer to drop the case. Oh yes, he told us. I, for one, find your actions admirable. I'm sure Randolph rarely has anyone turn down his money. He must have been shocked." She smiled and sat back, crossing her legs elegantly. "So I don't think we will make you an offer. More coffee?"

"I'm fine."

"Sheldon has obviously become undone by the deaths of his son and wife in such short order. I know he had been indiscreet and you are aware of our interest in investing in Shields Inc. There is a tremendous amount of money involved. I hope we can rely on your discretion in that regard. But there is much more at stake. Your investigation has the potential to rip a family apart and humiliate a fragile old man. I hope I'm not talking out of school here, but Randolph told us he's thinking about forcing his brother to seek psychiatric help, perhaps even have him committed. Are you really willing to risk that?"

"It's not my call, Ms. Loeb. Surely you can see that."

"Well, surely you can understand that it's not in our interests to encourage you in this matter. I speak now as chief counsel and I think that from here on out you will have to deal with our legal department."

"Gee, I was hoping to meet Mr. Ballantrae."

"I'm afraid that isn't possible."

From the doorway a voice said, "Oh yes it is."

Scarne stood as the man walked in the room. Alana Loeb remained seated.

"I'm Victor Ballantrae." His dark eyes bored into Scarne's. "What's this all about, Alana?"

She stared at Ballantrae for a moment and then told him, in a few clipped, concise sentences. Her tone was businesslike and lacked deference. As she spoke, Scarne took the measure of the man. Ballantrae was at least four inches taller than he was and a good deal heavier, broad shouldered with a hint of a belly. Good suit, strange, overblown face. Thug at the core, he decided. Ballantrae listened with apparent indifference and then turned to Scarne.

"I usually refer matters like this to my lawyers. I have a passel of them. No one wants to further complicate a family tragedy but I have a reputation to uphold. My company is expanding rapidly. We are in the financial services industry. Trust is what we sell."

The snake oil sincerity grated on Scarne.

"Mr. Ballantrae, Sheldon Shields asked me to look into his son's death, not specifically your company. I agreed to do so with the proviso that I was to be given a free hand. I'm just going over old ground but that's the way I operate. Don't read too much into it and please spare me the Wall Street sales pitch. I've been around the block and done some research. You may sell trust, but you get a commission. But for what it's worth, I'm not here to embarrass anybody because you screw your competitors or inflate your profits. If you had nothing to do with the Josh Shields's death – and I'd guess you didn't – then you should want to help me. If you don't, it will only make me more curious. You'd be better off stonewalling the cops. They have many priorities. This case is my only one. I won't stop until I'm satisfied I've covered every base."

"I don't appreciate threats."

"Neither do I. Randolph Shields is trying to put me out of business. I don't like that. I intend to give his brother his money's worth."

Ballantrae looked like he was making up his mind. Then he let out a guttural laugh.

"What the hell! Do you golf, Mr. Scarne?"

"Excuse me."

"I would like you to be my guest at my club tomorrow for a round of golf."

This is bizarre, Scarne thought.

"I golf."

"Great. I don't have time to talk now. I'm giving a speech at the Biltmore. What do you say? I can arrange clubs for you, shoes and the like."

"I won't need anything. Just tell me where and when."

"Pelican Trace, in Boca Raton. You may have heard of it. Let's say noon. We can have a bite of lunch first." Ballantrae put out his hand. His grip was hard and meant to intimidate. "Alana can show you out." As he left, he said over his shoulder, "Don't forget your checkbook."

At the elevator, Alana Loeb said, "Victor is very competitive, Mr. Scarne."

"So am I. I'm looking forward to our match."

The doors opened.

"And I hope to see you again, Miss Loeb."

"Alana."

She extended her hand and smiled faintly as he stepped into the elevator.

†

Alana Loeb walked to Ballantrae's office. He had his feet on his desk and was watching a replay of the interview.

"You make a lovely couple," he said.

"Victor, what are you doing? Golf?"

"What about it?"

"He's dangerous. And smart. He's highly regarded in New York, with powerful friends. You're not going to charm him or buy him off. Just refer him to our attorneys while we figure out what to do."

"Our lawyers would only antagonize him. I want to see what he's made of. Golf is a great way to size up a man."

"Don't insult my intelligence. This is about dick size and you know it."

"I don't need advice from you on that subject. Not any more. Besides, I'm not going to charm him, you are. He couldn't keep his eyes off of you."

"Stop talking like a pimp, Victor."

"I'm not asking you to fuck him. I know you've become very choosy about who you sleep with. I want to know what he knows, if anything. You should want that, too. I don't have to remind you what's at stake."

He looked at her bitterly. She realized Victor had yet to accept the change in their relationship. He still wanted her; that much was obvious. How much of that desire was caused by hurt pride? Did he love her? As always, she began to calculate how to use his vulnerability. Love, what a terrible affliction; what a weakness. She had never made that mistake and never would. But not for the first time Alana Loeb wondered if there was something wrong with her.

"What's the matter, Alana?"

Ballantrae was looking at her strangely, and she realized she had been someplace else for a moment. He slowly came back into focus.

"Nothing, Victor. Maybe you're right. It can't hurt to get to know Mr. Scarne better. He's not hard to look at and certainly is in good shape. I'll see what I can do."

She enjoyed the sulky look he gave her.

When Alana Loeb got to her office, Garza was standing at a window looking at the ocean. There was a folder and a small box on her desk.

"It's all in there," he said.

"What's in the box?"

"A fruitcake."

"Thank you, I think. Just give me the highlights."

Garza picked up the folder and flipped through the pages.

"Quite a character. Exotic background. Only child. Orphaned in grade school when the small plane his father was piloting went down in the mountains. The boy miraculously survived. Hardly a scratch." He looked up. "His mother was half-Cheyenne Indian, by the way." Garza started reading again. "He was then raised by his grandparents, Giacomo and Elizabeth Scarne. Giacomo, a decorated Italian sub commander imprisoned in Montana in1943, met Elizabeth, maiden name Bairn, while with a P.O.W. work crew that grew its own produce on the Bairn farm in return for day labor."

Garza looked up.

"Giacomo was repatriated to his native Sicily. He apparently came from a prominent Palermo family, old nobility, much like the one in Giuseppe di Lampedesa's book."

"The Leopard."

Garza smiled in appreciation. He liked Alana Loeb, more for her intelligence than her obvious beauty.

"Yes," he said. "Giacomo could have lived a comfortable life in Sicily, but he returned to Montana, married Elizabeth and become a citizen. They had the one son, Adam. Elizabeth died a few years after the plane crash so it was basically just Giacomo and the boy."

Garza closed the folder and looked at her. She had a strange expression on her face.

"What?"

"Nothing, really. I find it interesting about the grandfather raising him."

Garza shrugged.

"Incidentally, 'Jake' is not a diminutive of his grandfather's name," he said. "It is his given name. His full name is Jake Bairn Scarne."

"How did you get all this?" The former Cuban intelligence officer never ceased to amaze her. Castro's loss was Ballantrae's gain.

"The grandfather earned a law degree and eventually became a county prosecutor, then a judge. Apparently highly respected. Even for Montana it's a unique story. The family was profiled in the local press and some state magazines. It's now all on the Internet, and I made a few calls."

"What else?"

"The old judge died while Scarne was recuperating from wounds. Marines. Detached to Army Special Operations. He's a damn war hero. Silver Star. Must run in the family. Apparently he was captured in Afghanistan but managed to escape.

That's the Indian blood in him," Garza said admiringly. "But he wasn't treated gently by the towel heads. From a description of his subsequent medical care it was pretty obvious he was tortured. Bottom line, he's been a hard man to kill, from the plane crash onward. Anyway, after getting out he joined the N.Y.P.D. Attended Fordham Law at night and eventually wound up as an investigator with the Manhattan District Attorney. Left suddenly and went private."

"Why? Anything we can use?"

Garza sat back and stretched.

"Something political. Still waiting to hear back about that. You thinking about hiring him?"

As she filled him in, Garza reached into his jacket pocket and took out a gold case with the initials "F.C." It was, she knew, one of Garza's prized possessions, given to him personally by the Cuban dictator in better days. He took out a small cigar and lit it. She didn't object. The scent of fine tobacco was an indelible memory of her childhood, along with the smell of oak casks and lovingly waxed saddle leather. After she finished speaking, the Cuban blew a perfect smoke ring toward the ceiling and leaned forward.

"You want my advice, Alana, don't screw around with him," Garza said. "He's no fool. He spotted Christian tailing him in Manhattan."

"You're sure?"

"The description fits some photos I found in his apartment."

"Can he identify Keitel?"

"I doubt it." Garza laughed. "Christian said that after standing in the rain for two hours wearing a ski hat he looked like every other derelict in Manhattan. But seriously, this Scarne has a reputation as a straight shooter. Worse, he's persistent. And anyone who is part Cheyenne and part Sicilian is probably all trouble. Let us handle this."

“Too dangerous. For now.” She smiled. “Victor wants to play golf with him, find out what he knows.” Her mouth went down at one corner. “To see what he’s made of.”

Garza rarely looked surprised. He did now.

“Perhaps I should give Victor the fruitcake.”

Things were moving more quickly than Scarne had imagined. For some reason Ballantrae was taking him seriously. He had, in fact, overruled his own legal counsel. Despite her icy calm Alana Loeb had not managed to suppress her surprise – and anger – at the golf invitation. Something in her eyes had flashed a warning to Ballantrae, which he chose to ignore. It was almost as if he was taunting her, or reestablishing his authority in the presence of another man. A sign of insecurity? Jealousy? Stress? Scarne had also noticed the slight twitch in Ballantrae’s damaged brow. Whatever the reason, it was a mistake. Alana Loeb had been right. Despite his challenging words, or perhaps because of them, Scarne should have been shown the door. That was what an innocent man would have done.

On the drive back to La Gorce he called Evelyn and told her to go to his apartment and ship his golf set overnight to Pelican Trace. He had indeed heard of the club; it was one of the premier courses in Florida. Many touring pros were members. If she hurried, he’d have them by 10 AM the next day.

“Won’t that be expensive? Can’t you get some at the club, or rent?”

“Not as expensive as losing a big money match with unfamiliar clubs.”

“How do you know there will be a large wager involved?”

“I know Ballantrae’s type. He won’t be happy just beating me. He’ll want to grind me into the dust.”

"My, that sounds like fun."

"Actually, I'm looking forward to it. I'll be here longer than I thought. Stuff my golf bag with some extra underwear and golf socks."

"It will be an honor to pick through your unmentionables, Jake."

DEAD MAN'S LOCKER

IT WAS JUST before noon when Scarne drove under the porte cochere at the clubhouse entrance of Pelican Trace. A valet in white shorts and shirt gave him a ticket for his car. He was wearing a pith helmet.

"Many tigers on the course, my good man?"

"Occasionally one, sir," the man said. "Between tournaments."

Scarne pulled a small bag and some fresh clothes on hangers from the back seat. The men's locker room was everything he expected, given the club's reputation. It contained a small card room, a television lounge and a bar. There were two barber chairs set up in a small alcove. An attendant sat behind a counter in another alcove stocked with towels, plastic shoe bags and golf shoe cleaning and repair equipment. He came out and walked over to Scarne.

"Can I help you, sir?"

"Yes, I'm a guest of Mr. Ballantrae. Do you have a locker I can use?

"We've been expecting you. Come this way. Let me take your things."

The man led Scarne to a bank of lockers. All but one had large brass nameplates. The attendant opened the locker that had no nameplate, but still showed its outline and four small screw holes. It was between the lockers of an aging rock star and the head of a Wall Street investment bank now under investigation by the S.E.C.

"Don't tell me this one was convicted," Scarne said, pointing to the locker.

"Actually, this was Mr. McGillicuddy's locker. Dropped dead after a hole in one. His first after 50 years of golfing. Hope you're not superstitious."

Scarne started to laugh, but caught himself.

"Too bad. I'm sorry to hear it."

"Well, at least he didn't have to buy a round of drinks," the attendant said. "By the way, if you have a cell phone please leave it here. Not allowed on the course. Put your street shoes outside the locker and I'll shine them for you. The showers, steam room and sauna are right through there. If you need a massage after your match, I can set it up for you. Compliments of Mr. Ballantrae."

"Thank you, but no. Just tell me when the Dallas Cowboys are due back."

The attendant drew a blank for a second, and then laughed.

"The Cowboys wish they had a locker room like this. Best I've worked."

Scarne put on his golf shoes. He stopped by to thank and tip the attendant.

"Thank you, sir. Enjoy your round. By the way, your clubs are at the starter's shack. Mr. Ballantrae is waiting for you in the Grill Room."

After Scarne left, the attendant dialed the house phone.

"It's Danny. He just left. His phone is in the locker."

"I'll be right down," Jesús Garza said.

"How about grabbing me a sandwich? I missed breakfast waiting for him."

"What am I, Meals on Fucking Wheels?" Garza looked over at Christian Keitel and rolled his eyes. "All right, what do you want?"

†

Ballantrae was sitting at a table with Alana Loeb.

"How are you today, Mr. Scarne," she said, extending her hand. "Has Victor told you that you will be playing for your first born?"

"I don't have children, Alana, but if I lose, I'll adopt. And it's Jake."

Both she and Ballantrae laughed as he sat.

Ballantrae had on bright yellow golf slacks and a blue short-sleeve shirt. His massive arms were covered with rust-colored hair. The effect was slightly ridiculous. But Scarne realized it could have been worse. If Ballantrae's legs were equally hirsute, the result would be borderline grotesque.

Alana Loeb, on the other hand, radiated elegance – and sex. She was wearing white shorts and a short-sleeve coral blouse. Barely visible fine downy blond hairs speckled her well-tanned and toned arms and legs.

A waiter approached the table with menus.

"I'll have my usual, Jorge," Ballantrae said. He glanced at Scarne. "The house club. It's great. Made with Russian dressing and coleslaw."

"Sounds a bit heavy before a match," Scarne said.

"Why don't you get it," Alana said. "I'll help you out. I'm just going to have some lobster bisque. It's wonderful here. I'll let you have a taste."

"Done," Scarne said.

They all ordered "Arnold Palmers" – half ice tea, half lemonade.

Ballantrae said, "Alana is going to play with us, Jake. I hope you don't mind. She won't be in our match. She'd probably beat our pants off."

"Not at all," Scarne said. "I'd be delighted." He wasn't being polite.

Ballantrae switched gears. "All right, Jake. You have questions?"

Scarne again saw a slight tremor of the right eyelid. Tension? Or just a result of whatever had caused the scar above it? He decided to press the issue.

"Josh Shields was investigating you. He told his father to stall your investment in Shields Inc. Your company rubs a lot of people the wrong way."

"There's a big difference between rubbing people the wrong way and rubbing them out," Ballantrae said angrily. "What would be my motivation? Fear of publicity? Fear of the S.E.C.? They're a joke. Read the papers."

"You own an offshore bank. Some people might assume you launder money. You have South American clients. People could think drugs."

"Are you out of your fucking mind? That bank is totally legitimate. Why don't they go after the Swiss, for Christ sake? They've been hiding money forever. Or the Vatican? And hinting at drugs is defamatory. You're profiling. Hasn't anyone told you that you can't do that anymore?"

His voice had risen an octave. A few heads at nearby tables turned.

"Victor, keep your voice down," Alana Loeb said quietly.

"Let's consider another possibility," Scarne said. "Perhaps someone who works for you took matters in his own hands. Are you sure of all your employees?"

"Nobody is sure of everyone who works for him," Ballantrae said. Then he looked at the woman. "Present company excepted, of course." He appeared thoughtful. "You think someone in my employ might have harmed the boy?"

"It's possible."

"He may have a point, Victor," Alana Loeb said.

"Or it could be entirely something else," Scarne continued, "not related to journalism. Something personal. I have an open mind. It would help me to know just exactly what kind of business you operate. Maybe meet some of the people Josh interviewed."

Ballantrae assumed an air of bored resignation.

"I invest my clients' money using offshore banks and various trust instruments, all designed to keep asshole regulators off their backs and limit confiscatory taxation. They can pass their assets down to their heirs without some banana republic government eviscerating their estate. That pisses off a lot of people on Wall Street who stole money the old-fashioned way and don't want anybody else getting rich. It's pure jealousy. And hypocrisy."

He paused while their lunch was served. Scarne put two of his sandwich quarters on his bread plate and pushed it toward Alana. She only took one and pushed the plate back with a smile. Her bisque smelled wonderful. She slid the bowl toward Scarne.

"You have to try it."

He did and it was excellent. Ballantrae looked annoyed. He resumed his spiel with a mouthful of food.

"Do you really believe Wall Street is legit? They give you this bullshit about revenues, earnings and share value and it's all just paper and promises. Stocks are traded like commodities in bushel baskets. A lot of it is done by computer. A stock hits a certain price, it's sold or bought. What does the company produce? Who gives a rat's ass? It's a financial shell game. The hell with the companies, their workers, their prospects or the poor slobs who buy the stock. The Dow drops by a thousand points in six minutes. Investors lose a half trillion dollars and the regulators say 'oops.' The bond market is no better. Wall Street repackages bad loans as new debt securities with higher interest rates to attract buyers. At some point the buyers get wise and dry up, with the last jerks holding the paper stuck with it. It's the world's largest Ponzi scheme, with the possible exception of the American Social Security system."

"Some would say that's how a free market system works," Scarne said. "Let the buyer beware."

"You think it's a free market system? Bullshit. It is American socialism reserved for hedge fund managers, investment bankers and private-equity hotshots. And if something comes along to upset the apple cart, the Fed steps in to save the hides of the very people who screwed the pooch."

Ballantrae jabbed a finger at Scarne.

"And I love this crap about derivatives and how only sophisticated investors can get hurt, not little old Aunt Sadie in Idaho. You think some billionaire is going to risk his own dough on some synthetic security with no real assets behind it? Many of those so-called sophisticated investors are institutional traders representing banks and pension funds and they are gambling with the money thousands of small investors gave them for safe keeping. Why? Because they get a cut of any profits they make and don't get penalized when a deal goes down the toilet. And people question my business ethics? If your bankers and regulators pulled this crap in China and North Korea, they'd be shot. Bullet to the brain and their families would have to pay for the bullet. Here, they keep their jobs or resign with a $100 million payout. Give me a fucking break."

It was a marvelous rant. And, Scarne thought, the big oaf was probably right about most of it.

“There are no rules, Jake, except for suckers. And I’m not a sucker.”

“That’s a matter of opinion, amigo.”

Scarne looked up and immediately recognized the man who had just walked up to their table. It was Lee Rodriguez, the famous professional golfer. “I don’t want to intrude, Victor, but I must say hello to the beautiful Alana.”

“Nice to see you again, Lee,” she said as Rodriguez bent to kiss her hand. “You’ve just rescued us from one of Victor’s moral lectures.”

The pro golfer laughed and then joined an adjacent table with three men who had ‘CEO’ all but stamped on their foreheads. Ballantrae pulled back his chair a bit so that what he said would include the men, as well as Scarne and Alana Loeb.

“You hear about the guy who meets this gal at a bar. He asks her to dinner. She’s bright, funny and a real looker. Can talk to her, you know. He mentions that he’s a golfer and she says she loves the game too. He’s in heaven. So he asks her to his club and they play a round. And she’s good! Even beats him. He can’t believe his luck in finding such a companion. She becomes his regular playing partner. She usually wins, but what the hell, he’s falling for her. After dinner one night she invites him back to her place. After a couple of drinks, they tumble into bed. He can’t believe his good luck. He slides his hand down her panties, and feels a pair of balls! And they ain’t Top-Flites! He jumps out of bed and starts yelling, “How could you do this to me. How could you deceive me like this? I let you play from the ladies’ tees!”

All the men laughed. Alana Loeb smiled indulgently. Ballantrae slid back to his own table and turned to Scarne.

“By the way, Alana hits from the men’s tees. And she’s all woman. Played golf for the University of Miami.”

The room was filling up. There were greetings and loud forced laughter.

"A lot of new money here," Ballantrae observed. "Not as refined as some of the older clubs. Funny how money stolen a hundred years ago is quieter than money stolen recently. Speaking of money, now that I've fattened you up for the kill, Jake, let's talk game. What's your handicap?"

"I'm a 10," Scarne replied. "U.S.G.A."

"And I'm an 11. You'll have to give me a stroke."

"Nice try, Ballantrae. But I'm not a sucker either. This is your home course and I'm at a disadvantage. We'll play even, how about it?"

The United States Golf Association handicap system was supposed to level the playing field among amateur golfers but there was always a little room for horse trading. It was a ritual repeated thousands of time a day among honest golfers and thieves, and everyone in between.

"Sure, why not?'

Scarne nodded at the false generosity. Ballantrae had undoubtedly checked Scarne's handicap on the computerized stroke system most courses used. And why not? Scarne had checked him out, too. Ballantrae was telling the truth. So even given the home field advantage, it should be a pretty square match, made even more interesting by the presence of a beautiful woman, who was now staring at Scarne with a curious look on her face.

"So, Jake," Ballantrae said smoothly, "what's your poison?"

Scarne, thoughts elsewhere, said distractedly, "Your regular game is fine."

Ballantrae smiled like a barracuda.

"This is the big leagues, my friend. I don't usually play anything less than a $5,000 Nassau, front, back and overall. Hard to get my juices flowing for anything less. Lost a bundle to Lee over there last week. Anxious to get it back. You game?"

A Nassau is the most traditional of golf wagers. Ballantrae was proposing three separate matches over the 18 holes. The front and back nine holes would each represent a $5,000 match, based on who won the most number of holes on the respective nine. And the entire 18 holes, the overall, would be a third $5,000 bet. Scarne was no longer distracted.

"Victor, Jake is your guest," Alana said, an edge to her voice. "And he's here on business."

"I know. I know. Truth is, he's down here to give me the business. Just returning the favor. Hey, if that's too rich for his blood, I'll understand. We can play for drinks for all I care. I don't need the man's money."

This last was said so dismissively that the men at the adjoining table, who had been talking animatedly, quieted. Scarne was being put down cruelly, in public. The fact that Ballantrae threw such a huge bet in his face in front of a beautiful woman was churlish. Ballantrae didn't expect him to take the bet.

Scarne heard himself saying, "I don't like Nassaus. You obviously want to clean my clock. Let's make it an even $20,000 for a straight 18-hole match. If you're as good as you think, you'll close me out six and five and we can go home early." It was his fee from Sheldon Shields. Easy come, easy go.

The conversation at the next table had stopped completely. The four men were now openly staring at Scarne and Ballantrae. There was obviously something else going on between them. Probably the woman. A nice afternoon had turned sinister.

Ballantrae's laugh was short and harsh.

"How do I know you are good for the 20 grand?"

As soon as he said it, he knew it was a mistake. His hustler roots were showing. A gentleman would rather lose money rather than question another man's honor in public.

"Victor!" Alana's voice was like a whip.

One of the men at Rodriguez's table said, "Jesus."

Ballantrae tried to recover. He looked at Alana.

"Hey. I'm kidding. I'm not worried about it. What's the matter, can't anyone take a joke. I know he's good for it." But he couldn't leave it at that. "He can always expense it to Sheldon Shields. Right, Jake."

Scarne took a deep breath and smiled. His voice was icy.

"I'll call my secretary and have her wire the money into one of your accounts. You'll know it's there before we even tee off."

"Jake, that's not necessary. Let's drop it. We'll just play for fun, OK?"

Scarne continued as if he hadn't heard.

"The bet stands, Victor. And just so you know, I'm playing with my own money on this. I don't risk other people's money to satisfy my own pride."

The inference was obvious. Ballantrae stood abruptly.

"I have to use the little boy's room. Then I'm going to take a few swings on the range. I'll have your bag put on Alana's cart. You can ride together and talk about what a pain in the ass I am."

"We're only playing 18 holes, Victor," Alana Loeb said sweetly. "That's hardly enough time to do the topic justice."

Ballantrae laughed again and slapped Scarne on the shoulder and walked away, stopping at other tables to trade a jibe with the men and peck a few women on the cheek. Once again the consummate charmer.

Scarne looked over at Alana Loeb, who had a bemused look on her face.

"Men," he shrugged.

"Boys," she said.

THE WHEELS COME OFF

ON THE WAY to the course Scarne stopped in the golf shop to buy some new balls and a fresh glove. Like most golfers he was particular about the balls he played. In his case, Pinnacles. Even though deep in his heart he knew it didn't make a damn bit of difference at his skill level. As the cashier rang up the sale, Lee Rodriguez walked over to him.

"Watch your ass out there," the great golfer whispered. "He cheats."

As he walked to the starter shack, Scarne reflected on his consummate idiocy. He was about to play a $20,000 match with a man who probably had tried to cheat Lee Rodriguez. Scarne was by nature a gambler who reveled in pressure. Dudley Mack frequently accused him of making bad situations worse, just to see how he could get out of them. Oh, well. Ballantrae was right. If a golf game for $20,000 with a beautiful woman watching can't get a man's juices flowing, what could? I can take this jerk, he thought.

"What are you smiling about?"

He looked up to see Alana Loeb standing by their cart.

"Oh, nothing," he replied.

She called one of the attendants over.

"Switch the bags, please. I'm driving."

"Yes, ma'am. I just assumed..."

"I know you did," she said curtly.

She turned to Scarne.

"I hope you don't mind. But I know the course and you don't."

After the boy had switched the bags, she walked after him. Scarne thought she was going to further berate him. Instead she reached into her pocket. He tried to resist the tip, but she said something and rubbed the back of his neck. He laughed and took the money. When she rejoined Scarne, she said, "He's just a kid. He'll learn."

She busied herself with her bag, pulling a glove out of a side pocket and taking the head covers off her woods. Her movements were clean and efficient. She knows how to handle men, Scarne thought. Icy one moment, warm and caring the next. The dichotomy would be irresistible to any male with a pulse.

At the practice range, Alana began stretching, totally oblivious to the stares of the men nearby. She bent from the waist and put her hands flat on the ground, then did a series of leg and arm stretches. She stood on one leg and pulled her foot to her delectable backside, then alternated with the other leg. She put a short iron behind her neck and did several body twists. She tilted backwards and not for the first time Scarne noted her high, tight breasts. Selecting a wedge, she gave the club a slight waggle and hit a high arching shot toward a red flag on the range that was about 100 yards out. She had an athletic golf swing that nevertheless looked effortless. He noted that her hips were moving toward the target just ahead of her downswing. Classic Hogan. Then like a well-oiled machine, she worked her way down to her low irons. He looked in her golf bag. No hybrid or "rescue" clubs. The woman was a player.

Scarne was already pretty loose and didn't want to overdo it, having spent much of the previous afternoon at a range at a Miami municipal course using rented clubs. Unlike the muni, where he'd pummeled 200 beat-up practice balls, each stand at Pelican Trace was supplied with a large pyramid of brand-new Titlists. Concentrating on the wedge, 7-iron and driver, and reveling in the feel of his own clubs, Scarne grew more confident by the moment.

Alana had switched to her driver. It was soon clear why she played with men. Despite a tendency to push her ball to the right, she was very long and would kill any male weekend player if she hit from the woman's tees. Scarne objectively noted that her power came from her excellent tempo. Less objectively, he noted Alana's taut buttocks, legs and flat stomach. She caught the look and smiled.

"See any flaws ... in my swing?"

"You're perfect."

Ballantrae strode over. His gaze shifted between them.

"You ready? Let's play some golf."

The first hole was a dogleg left par 5, playing 517 yards. Lakes lined both sides of the fairway. The golf carts were equipped with a GPS screen that showed the position of a cart on an electronic replica of each hole. Hazards, traps, trees, water and slopes were all depicted. A digital readout gave the exact distance to the center of the green. Ballantrae pushed the button to start his GPS and turned to Scarne.

"And it took them 10 years to find Bin Laden."

The men flipped a coin to see who had first honors in their match and Scarne won. But they agreed to let Alana lead off on every hole. She chose a driver and split the fairway about 220 yards out.

"I told you she could play," Ballantrae said.

Scarne glanced at his own GPS, pulled his 3-wood and hit a high fade just short of a fairway bunker also about 220 yards out, but in the first cut of rough.

"Nice shot," Ballantrae said politely. "But I'm not afraid to use a driver."

He lashed a towering shot that ran through the fairway and bounded into the lake bordering the right side. "Fuck!" He looked at Scarne and smiled. "Jake, do you know how to make 30 old ladies say "fuck" at the same time?"

Scarne shook his head.

"Have one old lady yell out "bingo!"

On the way to their balls, Alana said, "Victor can be disarming. He'd rather hit it far than straight. Great short game. He'll probably make par from there. But don't expect his good humor to last."

Ballantrae did make par after dropping outside the hazard with a one-stroke penalty. He hit a beautiful fairway wood onto the green and two putted. Scarne, who laid up to 90 yards with his second, also managed a rather sloppy par. Alana badly misjudged her birdie putt and hit it three feet past the cup. She refused the conceded putt and missed the come-backer for a bogie 6. She snatched the ball up, eyes flashing. She looked at the men, who knew better than to say anything.

"Bingo," she said.

The men laughed. But Scarne was annoyed with himself. Halving the first hole when your opponent hits into the drink was an inauspicious start.

†

They had reached the tee at the seventh hole next to a small pond.

"All even after six," Ballantrae said. "Good match."

Scarne was content. After blowing the first hole, he righted the ship. He strategically conceded a few short putts to Ballantrae, not wanting him to get in a rhythm making them. A short putt at a crucial time late in the match might be daunting. Despite the underlying tension, Scarne was enjoying himself. Alana Loeb was a wonderful golfer and often embarrassed both men with her precise shot-making, particularly around the green. Suddenly Ballantrae's golf bag started playing Ravel's *Bolero.* He reached in and pulled out his cell phone.

"Jesus! It never ends."

He walked off behind a towering ficus tree.

"I thought they didn't allow cell phones on the course."

"There are rules for Victor and rules for everyone else," Alana said.

She put her hands behind her head and leaned back, tilting her face toward Scarne. The day had warmed and he could see a glisten of perspiration on her arms and legs. In the close quarters of the cart, he caught an intoxicating whiff of soap, sweat and sex. She stretched her long legs out over the front of the cart. A greenish black bird with a sinewy neck broke the surface of the pond with a large fish speared in its beak.

"*Phalacrocorax auritus*," she said. "Double Crested Cormorant."

"You don't say."

She laughed and pointed.

"That huge bird over there is a Great Blue Heron. *Ardea herodias*."

"I knew that."

"Sorry. I'm showing off."

She proceeded to describe, in scientific detail, the beautiful plants and animals that surrounded them: brightly colored lilies, hibiscus, milkweed, sycamores, pines, palmettos, palms, anoles, geckos, herons, alligators, egrets, ibis and spoonbills.

"And that's only what we can see," she said.

Scarne asked her where she had picked up all her knowledge.

"I've always loved nature," she said. "Very close to it as a child. Almost a *Green Mansions* upbringing. And when I came to Florida I studied botany and biology at the University of Miami. Did you know that there are 4,000 species of flowering plants in Florida? Even after I switched to business and law, I kept up, with electives. Nature is so raw. Some of the most beautiful trees and plants are the most malignant. See that pinkish-red flowering shrub over there? *Ricinus communis*, which sounds political but isn't. It's a castor bean plant. Chew on its seeds and you would die a quick but very painful death."

"I'll never look at a bean salad the same way."

She laughed and squeezed his knee playfully. He felt an electric jolt at her touch. He hoped it didn't show.

"Well, it all is certainly beautiful," Scarne said. "What are these flowers, Rose-of-Sharon?" He pointed to some large pink-purple flowers just to the right of their cart.

"Very good. Many people confuse them with morning glories, which are vines and not all that common around here. Rose-of-Sharon is a bush." She paused. "We used to call them pecker plants in school."

"Excuse me."

"Look at the unopened buds behind some of the flowers."

Scarne got out and walked over. The pink-to-purple buds did indeed look like small and recently circumcised male organs. He got back into the cart.

"Well, that explains the botany courses. But let's talk about something more edifying than peckers."

Just then Ballantrae walked up to them.

"Too late," Alana said, and burst out laughing. So did Scarne.

The seventh was a short par 4, just 298 yards long, with trees along the entire right side of the fairway and bunkers flanking a landing area 230 yards out. The green was small and narrow and sloped towards a large pond on its left. Ballantrae elected to go with a driver.

"I drove this sucker once," he said as he waggled his club.

Not this time. He pushed his ball into a thick clump of the trees well right of the green. Scarne considered his options. He wanted to leave himself a full shot in so he pulled his 4-iron and hit a beautiful straight shot (where did that come from?) right between the fairway bunkers 120 yards from the pin. From there, a perfect wedge left him a relatively simple uphill 12-footer. He could do no worse than a four, which should win the hole easily.

Ballantrae's ball had flown into a heavily wooded area. Scarne and Alana drove over to help him look for his ball.

"It's like Guadalcanal in here," Scarne commented as he hacked his way in with a club. Ballantrae would surely have to take a penalty drop, even if he was lucky enough to find his ball.

But when they found Ballantrae he was ready to swing, with a clear shot to the green from an open space in the thicket that had obviously been cleared by a maintenance crew. The ground was sandy but it was the only spot within 30 yards where a golfer would even have a backswing. And the ball was sitting up on a little mound. Ballantrae's shot was anticlimactic. He hit a sharp low pitch between the bunkers that stopped in the fringe just short of the green, but only eight feet from the hole. He could certainly putt from there. As they walked to the green, Ballantrae stated the obvious.

"Got a great break. Must have hit a tree and kicked straight left."

"Did I say Guadalcanal," Scarne said to Alana. "I meant Lourdes."

Alana was away and two putted for a par. Scarne's straightforward 12-footer now looked about twice that length. He left it a miserable and unforgivable 18 inches short.

"Never up, never in," Ballantrae said. "There's a little chicken left on that bone." He didn't concede the putt, almost a tap in. Scarne made it.

"Nice par," Ballantrae said. Then he made a point of marking his own ball and showing it to Scarne. It had a scuff mark consistent with a ricochet off a tree. "I'm gonna replace it to putt, if it's OK with you."

Scarne nodded and the ball went back into Ballantrae's bag. He wondered how many times that same ball had played the part.

Ballantrae hit a strong putt. Scarne knew it was good from the start.

"Great three," Scarne said, without inflection.

But he was seething. He had the hole won easily but for Ballantrae's miraculous recovery. The hell with it. Down one with 11 holes to play was nothing. Scarne promptly lost the next hole, a tough par 4 on which Ballantrae's bogie held up when Scarne found a fairway bunker and took a double bogie 6. And he missed a sweaty-palmed six-foot downhill sliding putt to lose the Par 3 ninth!

In the blink of an eye Scarne was now three down and the wheels were coming off.

The two men in the maintenance truck watched the threesome pull away. They were only able to get close to Ballantrae's group on holes where there was water in play. Fortunately, in Florida, that wasn't a problem. The state is basically one big aquifer draining into the Gulf of

Mexico or Atlantic Ocean. Developers advertise the beauty of the lakes on their golf course communities but the truth is water naturally collects in the holes they gouge. The builders provide a little landscaping, maybe add some fish and plants, but basically let nature take over. The men were dressed in coveralls and occasionally got out of the truck to inexpertly throw a net in the water. They were ostensibly clearing the ponds of tilapia, a fast-breeding invasive fish. Although a staple in many restaurants, tilapias were a nuisance to golf courses, where their nests –they were prodigious and protective egg layers – eroded the banks of ponds, occasionally collapsing greens and fairways. The men in the truck weren't after tilapia. In fact, when they accidentally caught a few, they surreptitiously threw them back. They were after bigger, and less smelly, game.

Scarne managed to win one hole out of the next four, halving the others. Ballantrae had gone into a shell, playing conservatively. It was a good strategy. Scarne knew he was being forced to be aggressive; he couldn't afford to lose any more holes. He coldly evaluated the front nine and comforted himself with the rationale that he had not played that badly. The match could turn on a dime with a bit of luck for himself and a missed putt or two by Ballantrae. That he would leave to the gods. But Scarne would be ready to pounce. He had been lulled by the beauty of the day and allure of his companion. Now he was counting on his rival's complacency. Blusterers and cheats believe their own press. Ballantrae was probably feeling pretty good about the way he was playing. But Scarne knew his opponent's score had been inflated by conceded putts and chicanery.

Still, two down with five to play! The thought that he might have to write out a $20,000 check to the big oaf – and Scarne could imagine Ballantrae telling Alana to take it – brought acid to his throat.

†

PUBLIC HUMILIATION

THE 14TH AT Pelican Trace was a par 5, and a mirror image of the opening hole. Alana's drive landed only a few yards short of a fairway bunker about 220 yards out. She would have to lay up. Ballantrae was next. He hit an almost perfect drive. But almost is the most feared word in golf. His ball landed hard in the middle of the fairway and caught the down slope, running through the dogleg and obviously into the lake beyond. It was a bad break.

"Pity," Scarne said, without any.

Scarne pulled his driver. He had used it sparingly on the front. But he wasn't going to hold back anything now. He placed his ball on the right side of the tee and hit his drive down the left, at the lake in the distance. His natural fade pushed his Pinnacle away from danger into the middle of the fairway.

"Where the hell did that come from," Ballantrae said.

"Even a blind squirrel finds an acorn once in a while," Scarne replied cheerfully.

Driving to their balls, Alana said, "You've figured Victor out by now. He'll do anything to win. But I hope you don't think I'm a party to all this."

Scarne looked at her.

"We both know this isn't about 20 grand. He's playing to impress you."

"What are you playing for, Jake?"

For the briefest of moments, she looked vulnerable. He smiled.

"Go hit. The son of a bitch has his ball on the back of a turtle by now."

She recovered her composure almost immediately, pulled a club from her bag and hit an excellent lay up. They drove in silence over to Ballantrae. His ball was sitting tall on a severe slope leading into the water. There was no way it could have stopped short of the pond. Scarne reflected that playing with Alana had one disadvantage. It meant that Ballantrae usually got to his ball first, and unobserved. It was undoubtedly part of his plan.

Ballantrae hit an excellent shot off a sloping lie to the back of the green, 30 from the pin. Scarne had only 165 yards to the flag. His six-iron landed 10 feet below the hole. Both he and Ballantrae were on in two. Alana hit a lovely wedge to within eight feet. Ballantrae lagged his first putt to two feet, a virtual gimmee. Scarne watched his own eagle putt slide past the hole by a few inches.

"Pick it up, Ballantrae said, looking at Scarne for a reciprocal courtesy.

"Alana's away," Scarne said. He'd make Ballantrae putt, hoping that all those short ones conceded earlier would come back to haunt him.

Alana two-putted and then Ballantrae stood over his birdie putt.

"For Christ sake," he muttered, "I'd concede this to Helen Keller."

But the hole probably looked like a thimble to a now-nervous Ballantrae. Muscles tensing, he missed badly. Scarne was now only one down.

"Too bad, Helen," he said as Ballantrae angrily swatted his ball away.

As he was teeing up on No. 15, Scarne knew he had shaken Ballantrae's confidence. He couldn't afford to let up. Using driver again, Scarne hit another long fade just into the short rough on the right. He only had about 120 yards to the green. Ballantrae angrily sliced his drive well into the woods. He found his ball (or at least said he did, Scarne thought cynically) but lacking a chain saw was able only to pitch it back sideways to the fairway. He made a creditable bogey 5 from there; Scarne an easy par. They were even.

Scarne had a bad jolt on the next hole, a relatively straightforward Par 4. Both men found the fairway; Scarne with driver, and Ballantrae with a 3-wood. My, how things have changed, Scarne thought. Ballantrae was away. He fanned a 7-wood into the right bunker. Scarne pulled out his 5-iron and lasered a shot 20 feet past the hole. Alana, who had uncharacteristically hit her ball in the rough, had come up short of the green with her second, but hit a nice chip to a foot. It was an obvious concession, so she picked up.

"In case you guys haven't noticed, I'm having a hell of a round," she said.

Her good humor had returned. What a woman, Scarne thought. Ballantrae paid her no mind. Once again his short game came through. Scarne's heart almost stopped as his blast out of the trap almost flew into the cup on the fly before stopping two feet from the flag. Now Scarne needed to make his putt. It was severely downhill. If he missed the cup, chances were he'd roll well past and be lucky to get a par coming back. From birdie to bogie was the bane of every golfer's existence. He took a deep breath. His putt looked center cut. But at the last second it slid a bit left and started heading to China. Miraculously it just caught the lip and pirouetted 360 degrees before dropping in the front edge. Ballantrae swore under his breath.

"Sometimes you have to use the whole hole," Scarne said.

Inwardly, his heart was racing. That was as close as they come.

Ballantrae still had his chance to tie the birdie. This time he took his time over the two-footer and rattled it in. They were still even.

The next hole was a devilish Par 3. It was only 148 yards long, but it was fronted by a large pond that extended almost all the way back to the tee box. Its tiny green sloped back to the pond and was surrounded by several deep bunkers. Golf instructors are fond of telling their students to ignore the water. To imagine it's not even there and play their regular shots. That usually has the effect of turning a pond into the earthly equivalent of a black hole. Scarne knew that Ballantrae, with his great short game, had a distinct advantage.

The hole's dangers were soon evident, as Alana's good-looking shot – straight at the pin – was caught by a gust of wind and came up short. It rolled off the front of the severely slanted green back into the water. She teed up another ball and promptly hit that one into the water as well.

"The hell with it," she said. "You two finish the hole."

Scarne normally hit his 7-iron about 150 yards. After seeing what happened to Alana, he decided to take an extra club. Hit his 6-iron dead flush, and straight. It was a beautiful looking shot. He was momentarily elated. Then to his horror the wind died. He was going to be long. He watched miserably as his ball flew over the pin and sailed into the sand trap at the back of the green.

Golfers are never supposed to wish ill luck on an opponent. But the thought of losing to the boorish, cheating bastard overcame Scarne's innate sense of sportsmanship. He prayed fervently that Ballantrae would dunk his ball. For his part, Ballantrae began to show his nerves again. He backed off twice before settling in over the ball. Scarne was sure he would flub the shot. So he watched in disbelief and despair as Ballantrae's shot arched toward the green, landed just past the cup and spun back about six feet below the hole. It was a gritty play and for all his disappointment Scarne felt obliged to say "great shot." Ballantrae's returning crocodile grin went right through his heart.

They rode to the green together past a truck and two men who were throwing nets into the water. Ballantrae was chattering away. He knew he had the match in hand. With a straight uphill putt with no break to it, he had an easy par and a possible birdie. Scarne would be lucky to get down in two. Ballantrae could then play the last hole for a half and win the match.

When Scarne got to his ball, he was further discouraged to see that it was lying on a downslope in the sand. He now faced one of the toughest shots in golf. The ball would come out "hot." He stood a good chance of running it by the flag right into the damn pond. Scarne dug his feet into the soft sand and opened the blade of his club so it was almost facing straight up. His only chance was to flop the ball just over the lip of the trap and hope it didn't run out too far. A slight miscalculation and the ball could pop straight up and stay in the trap. Or he could blade it into the water on the fly.

His shot landed just outside the trap and started rolling toward the pin. For a moment Scarne thought it would actually go in! But the slope was too severe and the ball glided past the hole and kept rolling. And rolling. It finally stopped just short of the fringe, a good 15 feet past the cup. Scarne ordinarily would have consoled himself by realizing that even a pro couldn't have done much better from his horrible lie. But the bitter ash taste of defeat prevented that.

"That was a wonderful shot from there," Alana said sincerely. "You didn't have much to work with."

"Yeah, nice try, Jake," Ballantrae said, with mock generosity. Then, cruelly, "But I think you're still away."

Scarne walked glumly over to his Pinnacle.

"Gonna have to sink that, bucko," Ballantrae said. Scarne took a deep breath and went through his routine. He brought his putter blade back as Ballantrae started whistling "Waltzing Matilda." Scarne backed off and looked daggers at Ballantrae. "Do you mind?"

"Sorry."

Scarne went through his routine again and blocked Ballantrae out of his mind. With nothing to lose he hit a bold, firm putt that went in! It was a world-class par from where he had been, but he knew it probably wasn't enough. Ballantrae could win with a birdie.

Scarne's face was rigid as he awaited the crushing blow. It never came. Obviously remembering Scarne's speedy second putt and worried that he might go long and be faced with a tricky downhiller, Ballantrae babied his putt. It stopped an inch short of the hill.

"Nice lag," Scarne said. "That one's good. We're still even."

Ballantrae swatted his ball into the pond. As they walked off Scarne hummed "The Marine Corps Hymn."

Alana Loeb looked at him and just shook her head.

The crosshairs settled on Scarne's forehead and then slipped down to his smiling mouth. The man in the truck adjusted the focus, took a deep breath and squeezed a trigger. There was a series of rapid clicks. Then he swung the digital Nikon with the telephoto lens to the others on the green.

"That is one hot lady," he murmured. "I don't know how they can concentrate on golf."

"Man, he is pissed," the other man said, focusing his binoculars on Ballantrae. "I wonder how much they're playing for. He looks like he wants to kill the other guy. I wonder who it is."

"That's what we're here to find out," the man with the camera said. "Come on. There's a pond near the 18th green. We can get more shots there."

"I'll get the nets. If I never see another fucking tilapia again it will be too soon. Remind me never to order one in a restaurant."

The mood was poisonous on the 18th tee. It had all come down to the final hole, winner take all. Unless they halved, of course. But Scarne was determined not to settle for a tie. This was a once in a lifetime match; the closest he'd ever get to the pressure of the real tour. He didn't even think about Randolph or Josh Shields. All he wanted to do was beat the son of a bitch. For himself? For the woman? It didn't much matter at this point, he realized. This is the only place on the planet I want to be right now.

The last hole was a short but tricky Par 4, measuring a modest 340 yards on the card. But it doglegged to the right around a lake and there were out-of-bounds stakes along the left side of the narrow fairway. A diabolical layout. Alana's tee shot almost ended in disaster. The wind had picked up and was blowing strongly from the left. It nearly pushed her ball into the water. Scarne couldn't afford to get wet at this point, so he aimed well left, counting on the breeze to compensate. And, of course, the wind died and the ball held its line.

"The dreaded straight ball," he muttered as the well-struck shot went out of bounds left with sickening, unwanted accuracy. He'd have to hit another!

Scarne couldn't even look at Alana Loeb. He'd just lost the match, unless Ballantrae also hit it out of bounds or put it in the lake. But he sensibly put his driver back in his bag and hit a nonchalant 4-iron down the middle of the fairway. It was short but he didn't care if it took him two more shots to the green. Scarne would be lucky to make a six or seven.

"Position A," Ballantrae gloated, his humor partially restored.

Scarne glumly teed up another ball. Even if he hit a perfect drive, with the stroke-and-distance penalty for going out of bounds, he'd be laying three in the fairway and be lucky to get a bogie. It was over. He'd lost.

Unless.

Scarne estimated that it was about 220 yards from the tee box to the green – if a golfer hit directly over the lake and was suicidially inclined.

"A faint heart never won the chorus girl."

"What was that?" Ballantrae said.

"Nothing," Scarne said, putting his driver away and pulling out a 2-iron.

Even tour pros didn't carry the notoriously hard-to-control 2-iron anymore. (Thus the old joke: hold a 2-iron over your head in a lightning storm; even God can't hit it.) The look on Ballantrae's face was one of relief; Scarne was giving up. Only when he teed his new ball on the right side of the box and took his stance was it obvious that he planned to get to the hole by sea, not land. He looked at Alana and winked. Ballantrae's jaw actually dropped.

Scarne went into a zone. *Take the club back slowly, and hold the finish. Imagine the shot and execute.* He knew immediately it was a great shot. He heard it, felt it and now watched it. *If it has enough legs, if the wind stays calm, if I haven't misjudged the distance, if I don't hit a fucking pelican, it would be all over the flag.* The ball landed on the green and ran 15 feet past the cup. It was the best golf shot of his life. He was on in three and could save par!

He felt the silence. Without looking back, but knowing Ballantrae could hear him, he said, "Damn. Too much club. Should have used a 3-iron."

Caligula would have said "nice shot." Not Ballantrae, who was stunned.

In the cart Alana said, "That was the greatest pressure shot I ever saw."

"It will mean nothing unless I sink that putt."

"You will!"

They all drove up to Ballantrae's ball. For the first time, Scarne noticed a sheen of sweat on the other man's face. His 4-iron left him almost 170 yards from the green and some of it was over water.

"Still planning to lay up Victor?" Alana said. It was almost a taunt.

Ballantrae looked at her. His eyes glittered. He angrily pulled a 5-wood from his bag. He hit it flush and the ball tracked right at the pin. It landed softly and rolled to about eight feet from the hole. It was a gutsy play.

"Great shot."

Scarne meant it, even as he hated saying it.

Alana also reached the green in two. When they got there she walked to the pin and pulled it. Her ball was five feet past Ballantrae's, on the same line.

Word of the high-stakes match had spread and there was a considerable crowd standing around the green, including Lee Rodriguez and his friends. As Scarne walked by, Rodriguez asked, "What did you hit off the tee?"

"A 2-iron. But it was my third shot. I was out of bounds on my drive."

"That makes it even better," the old pro said.

Alana was away. She asked Ballantrae to mark his ball, which was in her line, off to the side.

"For Christ's sake. You're not even in the goddamn match. Just pick up!"

Ballantrae's bad manners elicited disapproving murmurs from the crowd.

"I'll putt out, if you don't mind."

"Sure, sure. Just hurry up."

He placed his marker behind his ball and then used his putter head as a measure to move the mark out of her line. She lined up her putt and boldly sank it. There is a smattering of applause from the crowd. She quickly picked up her ball and walked past Scarne.

"You're up." She lowered her voice. "Just be quiet when he putts."

He looked at her. What did she mean?

Scarne's putt was downhill, with a left to right break towards the water. As he knelt to read the putt, perspiration trickled down his spine and his heart pounded. He walked over to the hole and looked at the rim. The grass seemed to be growing towards where his ball was. That meant the "grain" was running against the ball and any putt would be marginally slower, even downhill. At least he hoped so, because he wasn't planning to leave the putt short. He needed to hit the putt strongly enough to hold the line. If he missed it wouldn't matter if the ball rolled to China. A par four was his only chance.

"Jesus Christ! Are you going to putt or not?"

"Soon as you move out of sight line," Scarne said.

Ballantrae grumbled and walked to the side.

Scarne took a deep breath and took a practice stroke. Grounding his club behind the ball, he willed himself to relax and putted through the ball firmly. It took off like a cue ball on a pool table! This ball is going in the hole or in the lake, he thought wildly. But the grain slowed it a fraction and at the last second the ball curled in the middle of the cup with a satisfying clunk.

By now the crowd had taken sides and roared approval of the miracle par.

"Great putt, Jake," Alana blurted, drawing a scathing look from Ballantrae.

But Scarne was realistic. Ballantrae could still win with a birdie and was assured no less than a tie. And his putt was straight uphill. Needing only a two- putt to tie, there would be no pressure. He could be bold and confidently go for the winning birdie. In that situation, most people make their putts.

Alana is holding the pin and standing next to Victor, whispering to him. He looked distracted. Finally he walks over to his marker. As he bends to replace his ball, she drops the pin, which clatters. Disconcerted, he stared at her.

"Sorry."

Ballantrae put his ball down and angrily snatched up his marker. Then he looked at Scarne with what only could be described as a sneer. *This birdie is for you*, it implied. He was just about to putt when Scarne suddenly realized the ball was not in the proper spot – Ballantrae had moved it by the length of a club head to accommodate Alana's putt. If he hadn't been distracted by what she had whispered to him and then the dropped flag, he might have realized his mistake. So, that's what she'd meant when she told Scarne to remain quiet! Seeing the opportunity presented by the positions of the balls on the green, she had set Ballantrae up. Amazingly quick thinking by a devious mind.

Sportsmanship decreed that even your opponents remind you to replace your marker in the right spot. Having been cheated for almost the entire round, Scarne never entertained the idea. He was now fervently hoping that Ballantrae made his birdie. He idly wondered how Alana Loeb would play the scene.

Ballantrae stroked through the ball.

"Victor! Wait!" It was Alana.

Too late. The ball tracked right into the hole. Ballantrae whirled around.

"Bloody hell! You almost cost me the goddamn match! It's damn lucky I made it." He looked at Scarne. "Too bad, pal. I make them when I have to."

"I was just trying to warn you."

"Warn me? About what?"

"Victor...your mark."

There was excited chatter among the bystanders. Doubt started to cross Ballantrae's face. He walked toward her.

"What the hell you talking about?"

"You forgot to replace your mark after you moved it out of my line. You putted from the wrong spot."

"I replaced the mark." He looked at Scarne for help. "You saw me."

"You know...I think she's right. I was so annoyed at myself I wasn't paying attention...or I would have told you. Sorry."

"Bullshit!"

He turned to the crowd, now entranced at the spectacle.

"Who saw me replace the mark?"

"You forgot, Victor."

It was Rodriguez.

"Why didn't anyone say anything?" Ballantrae's voice had a wheedling tone. "Lee?"

"With $20,000 on the line?"

"I hate to say it," Scarne said, not hating it at all. "But you lose the hole, Victor. And, unfortunately, the match. Pity, really. You played so...well."

"I'll place the ball back." Ballantrae was so desperate Scarne almost felt sorry for him. It was such a public humiliation. "You know I could two-putt from there and get a tie. Let's just call the match even."

"Doesn't work that way," Scarne said officiously. "Rub of the green. You caught some miraculous breaks out on the course. Guess it all evens out."

He extended his hand. Ballantrae stormed away.

Rodriguez walked over to Jake.

"Miraculous breaks? You mean he cheated the entire match."

"Only when he wasn't in his cart."

Rodriguez laughed.

"Alana's timing was priceless," he said. "She made it sound like she wanted to stop him in time."

Alana approached them. The great golfer patted Scarne on the arm.

"That 20 grand may be the least of your winnings, my friend." He lowered his voice. "But be careful. She just proved how cruel she can be."

He kissed Alana and walked away.

"What did Lee say?"

"He saw through your little charade. I'm sure Victor did, too. Why did you do it? He's your boss."

"No one's my boss. And I wanted you to win."

BOSTON AT THE BEACH

AFTER DROPPING THEIR clubs off at the starter's shack to be cleaned, Scarne and Alana agreed to meet in the grill room in 20 minutes.

"I want to freshen up," she said.

Since that probably meant he had closer to 45 minutes, Scarne took the opportunity to take a quick shower. He put on a pair of fresh grey slacks and a light V-necked burgundy sweater. He slipped into his loafers without socks as he checked his cell phone for messages. There was no display. He turned it back on. Funny, he didn't remember turning it off. He went to the grill and ordered a celebratory drink. He began to muse about his winnings. It would certainly buy a kick-ass vacation somewhere, although thinking about a vacation outside a gorgeous country club in Florida seemed a bit much. Hit Atlantic City on the way home and try to run it up? It was found money. That would probably be very stupid, but Scarne, like most gamblers, did not dismiss the idea out of hand. Invest it wisely? Please. Buy some art? The apartment in New York could use some sprucing up.

Ballantrae walked in wearing a business suit.

"Can I buy you a drink, Victor?"

"No...Thank you. Something has come up. I have to go to New York. My plane is waiting for me in West Palm. I wonder if you will do me a favor. I don't want to leave Alana in the lurch. Can you take her home?"

"Of course. It will be my pleasure."

Ballantrae took out his checkbook and, leaning on the bar, wrote out a check, which he handed to Scarne.

"I play by the rules. Same in business. We have nothing to hide."

Scarne folded the check and put it in his pocket, as if it were an everyday occurrence.

"Then you won't mind me nosing around your company?"

"Talk to Alana. She'll set it up. You two seem to have hit it off."

Just then she walked into the grill. She has showered and changed into a simple, strapless blue cotton sundress. Scarne couldn't help but stare. She languidly sat on a bar stool, crossing her legs.

"Ah, the rules chairwoman herself," Ballantrae said. "Alana, Jake has offered to take you home. Maybe he will even buy you dinner. He certainly can afford it."

With that, he offered a brusque handshake to Scarne and left.

"How about dinner in Paris?" Scarne said, pulling out the check and waving it in the air.

"I know a nice place that's a bit closer," she said, laughing. "But I want a drink first." She looked at his glass. "I never would have figured you for the Planter's Punch type, Jake."

"Want my cherry?"

She reached across and pulled it out of his drink by the stem and popped it in her mouth, smiling mischievously. He ordered two more and they took their time drinking them.

"I guess I should thank you for this $20,000."

"You were a fool to bet that much. Male pride. I'll never understand it. But I couldn't let you be cheated."

"Why does he do it? Everybody around here apparently knows. Soon he won't be able to get a game."

"Why do any of you do anything?" She put her hand on his arm and he felt the electric jolt again. "Come on. I'm hungry."

Only Scarne's clubs were waiting for them at the valet station.

"Where are yours?"

"I leave a set here. I'm not a member, but I never know when I'm going to be asked to play with Victor. They're nice about it. They let me keep some clothes as well. Like this little old thing."

"You look lovely."

Scarne's car pulled up. An attendant put his golf bag in the trunk and Scarne threw his duffel in the rear seat. Alana looked at the Rouche Mustang.

"I didn't realize NASCAR had a rental division."

"A friend is letting me use it," Scarne said noncommittally.

"Must be a good friend," she said as the valet held her door. "But isn't it difficult to tail a suspect in this."

"Not when they're in the car with me."

"In that case," she said, laughing, "let's keep the top down? It's lovely out."

With that, she kicked off her sandals and stretched out her long legs. She had exquisite ankles and long toes, which she flexed. Scarne found that oddly erotic. As he drove away the wind caught her hair.

"Are you in a hurry, Jake? If we take the Dixie Highway down the coast I know a great spot in Delray Beach. I just don't feel like rushing back."

Looking at her, Scarne didn't feel like rushing back, either.

†

It took a half an hour to get to Delray. Alana was silent much of the way and seemed content to enjoy the wind blowing through her hair. She set a striking figure with her blond and tan good looks and aviator-type sunglasses. Other drivers stared at her. She also got a going over when they walked into the restaurant, a place called Boston at the Beach. Considering that this was Florida in season and the place was full of spectacular looking women, Scarne got a new appreciation of how attractive his companion was. They were shown to a table on the second deck facing the ocean. When a waitress wearing a pink tank top and black shorts tried to give them menus, Alana looked at Scarne.

"Are you choosy about your seafood? I come here a lot. I'll order for the both of us if you like."

"That's fine," he said, taking a wine list from the waitress. "Just make sure it goes with champagne."

"What's the freshest fish in the house?" Alana asked the waitress.

"All our fish..." She stopped when she saw the look on Alana's face. "The cobia just came in," she finished.

"A dozen oysters, the Apalachicolas, to split." She looked at Scarne. "It is winter, the Gulf Coast oysters are safe now." She turned her attention back to the waitress. "And two conch chowders. Then have the chef broil two cobia filets with lemon, butter and a little white wine. Sides of coleslaw and Spanish rice. Plenty of tartar sauce and some lemon and lime wedges. Thank you."

Scarne was surprised to find a bottle of Brut Heritage on the wine list. He ordered one and asked the waitress to keep another in reserve.

"You must be planning to get me drunk, Jake," Alana said.

"Hell, you're the one who ordered oysters and conch chowder."

"The aphrodisiac powers of oysters and conchs are overrated," she said. "As are champagne's. At least with me. And you proved today that you probably don't need extra stimulation. You like to live dangerously."

She gave him a bold, challenging look that told him that she did, too.

"You must relate to that, working for Ballantrae. He's an interesting guy. How did you wind up with him?"

"Ah, the interrogation begins. I was wondering when you would start."

"I'm just interested."

"As a spider is interested in a fly." She put her hand along her cheek and studied him with an amused smile. Scarne wondered just who the spider was. "I worked for a Miami law firm and was the lead counsel in an employment suit against a Ballantrae subsidiary. Victor is always firing people. I won a large settlement. He doesn't like losing, as you know. He asked me to head up his legal department."

"Seems like you've carved out a niche. How did you jump from house lawyer to chief operating officer?"

The waitress appeared with their champagne in an ice bucket on a stand. She set out glasses and poured some in Scarne's. He tasted it and nodded and she filled both glasses and left. Alana took a sip and looked at Scarne.

"Where were we? Oh yes, you asked me if I fucked Victor to get ahead."

An elderly man and a bejeweled younger woman, who had Palm Beach trophy wife written all over her, were dining at the next table. The woman, who was closest to Alana, held a shrimp on a fork poised to go in her mouth. She looked over at Alana and almost put the crustacean in her ear.

"That wasn't quite the question," Scarne said equably.

"The hell it wasn't. But before I answer I want to ask you a question. Is this interrogation for business or pleasure? Are you on the job, or on the make?"

Scarne had to laugh at her directness. He realized he wasn't sure.

"I don't have a clue."

"Funny phrasing for a private investigator. But I'll take it to mean that you want to know for personal reasons. So I'll tell you. Victor is now my boss, period." The emphasis on the *now* was unmistakable. "I admired him a great deal. He's a handsome man. I was flattered. It was obvious he could get any woman he wanted. I also like to think that I offered more to the company than merely hauling the chairman's ashes. Victor wouldn't risk his company or his dreams on a piece of ass."

That got another look from the shrimp lady. Their food came. Alana raised her glass.

"Eat hearty, Jake. Then it's my turn to ask the probing questions."

They ate in virtual silence. When they finished, Scarne asked Alana if she wanted coffee and dessert.

"It's getting chilly. And I've had enough champagne. I'd rather go to the bar for a drink."

Scarne signaled for the check. Then he reached across the table and squeezed her hand, which was pleasantly warm and soft.

"I'm sorry if I was out of line. I'm sure now this isn't business."

She turned the full force of her eyes on him.

"I'm going to powder my nose. Meet me inside." She got up, and as she passed the lady next to her smiled and said sweetly, "You're going to miss the good part."

The woman laughed and said, "Damn."

The man with her cupped his hand to his ear.

"What did she say, Doris?"

"Nothing, darling. Do you want my greens?"

Scarne paid the bill and went to the bar. Alana was already seated at the far end sipping a reddish drink from a highball glass. He sat next to her.

"It's an Americano," she said, holding up her glass. "So popular among Americans in Italy in the 1890's they named it after them. But definitely an acquired taste. Campari and sweet vermouth, the bitter with the sweet. Fitting for us I thought. Want a taste?"

He shook his head and ordered a brandy.

"Where did you acquire the taste? Italy?"

"I read about them in a novel. They sounded so romantic. I ... lived ... in Buenos Aires for a time and a woman I ... worked for ... used to make them. Liked them ever since."

A strange look came over her face as she remembered.

"What were you doing in Buenos Aires?"

"Oh no," she said with a smile. "Now it's my turn."

Scarne clinked glasses with Alana.

"Shoot," he said.

She asked him about his childhood. She seemed fascinated by his grandfather.

"He must have been an amazing man. I always thought the Italians were maligned unfairly in World War II. Their navy did quite well. I think some German generals made a laughing stock out of the Italian army to deflect criticism from their own shortcomings. I met some German and Italian officers in Argentina. They were old, of course, but their memories were sharp. They bore no animus towards each other. They had been lower ranks during the war and saw things better than the generals."

Scarne was impressed by her grasp of history.

"You are part German, aren't you?"

"Yes, my family was Bavarian. But my great-grandmother was Jewish. So they left for Argentina when Hitler still felt compelled to treat Jewish World War I veterans decently. They were well ensconced in South America when many Germans fled there after 1945."

"Some of them were war criminals. What did your family think of that?"

"My grandfather made a nice living helping them get, how should I say, readjusted to civilian life all over South America. He knew many politicians and was very friendly with the police in many countries."

"He sounds very forgiving."

"Business is business, Jake. Besides, many of the people he helped – for a profit – were low level. Some were probably Nazis, but they had families, wives, children. He wasn't doing anything the Vatican or the Pentagon wasn't. Nazi scientists helped America land on the moon, no?"

"But your grandfather was part Jewish."

"Yes, he lost relatives in the camps. Hilton is opening up hotels in Hanoi, so what? Besides, he also had contacts with Israeli intelligence. Some people even think he helped them find Eichmann, who was an embarrassment to everyone. I think he aided the little fish, and got his revenge on the big ones."

"And, of course, the Israelis are very good payers."

"The best."

"That's quite a story, Alana. One I hadn't heard before."

"Americans are so wound up in their own history and lives they don't realize that the rest of the world is fascinating. I bet my grandfather and yours could have traded some wonderful tales. They would have liked each other."

"Probably. Is yours still alive."

"No." She left it at that. "But you are good, Jake. I'm back talking about myself. Let's get back to you. Where did you go to school? How did you become a dashing private eye?"

He told her, leaving little out, except his military service. She was easy to talk to. She had the ability to focus all her concentration on the person who was talking, as if he was the only one in the world. Even when she turned away to sip her drink, he felt that she was absorbing everything. At times she was coquettish. Then sympathetic. When he spoke of an interesting case, she appeared fascinated, and her questions were always on point. He finally realized that they had been talking at the bar for almost an hour.

"Have you ever been in love, Jake?"

He was startled. She was looking into his eyes with a bemused expression.

"Yes. What about you."

"God, no. And I hope never to be. It implies a loss of control. I don't lose control."

She said it so matter of factly he was stunned. Scarne knew many people said they'd never fall in love – usually after a terrible breakup. They didn't really mean it. But Alana said it like it never crossed her mind.

"Maybe you haven't met the right man."

Scarne knew he sounded ridiculous. Alana laughed.

"Or the right woman, or Great Dane. Why limit me to men, Jake? Next thing you'll be waving a white picket fence and snot-nosed little kids at me."

"You're a man killer and you know it, lady. You can play them like a fiddle, like you're playing me right now. Aren't you?"

She leaned forward, an elbow on the bar, and brought her face close to his. He could smell her perfume and the sweet essence of vermouth on her breath.

"Absolutely. Actually, I like children." She smiled. "Just as long as they're someone else's."

That was too much for Scarne. They had been reduced to talking in clichés, trying to impress each other. Instinctively he knew that this was a woman who used her beauty and intelligence to build a carapace around her feelings. He stared at her until her smile evaporated.

"You know, Alana, we have something in common. Both damaged goods. Orphans, raised by grandparents. Loved, surely, but, of course, it's not the same. There was a duty to their love. Grandparents have already spent much of their emotional capital on their own children. We get what's left."

He had her attention. The restaurant sounds faded into the distance.

"It doesn't matter how old you are when parents die," he said quietly. "You lose the only people who are always on your side, who think the world of you and can forgive anything. Love without strings. We may be able to give that kind of unconditional love, but we'll never have it again. We spend the rest of our lives trying to find something remotely like it. You're kidding yourself if you think you're any different from the rest of us."

If looks could kill, Scarne thought.

She stood up.

"I know a wonderful place in Hollywood Beach where we can stop on the way home. You've never seen anything like it. Are you game?"

EVEN THE WAITERS STOPPED

THERE WAS A good breeze coming off the Atlantic as Scarne drove. Alana hugged her legs to her chest but insisted he leave the top down. She did allow him to fetch a sweater from his bag, which she draped over her shoulders. Suddenly she sat up, eyes bright with excitement, her good mood restored.

"There it is. That long white building."

Cars were lined up by the valet stand, but boys ran back along the line and handed out claim tickets. Scarne and Alana walked toward the entrance to the restaurant, which a large neon sign identified as "Taverna Opa." Dozens of people were waiting to enter and Scarne heard Middle Eastern music wafting through the screens. He began to have his doubts. Alana walked to the head of the line. A man holding a clipboard moved the rope amid much grumbling.

"If you need anything, Alana, let me know," the man said as he held the door for them.

Inside, Scarne was startled to see people belly dancing on tables while people ate below them. Some of the dancers were obviously professionals but most were patrons, an eclectic mix of families with children and a jet-set crowd. One grandma was shimmying precariously near the end of a table, while a couple of anxious children, probably her grandkids, hovered nearby, ready to catch her. On another table, two wildly gyrating toddlers kept threatening to bump each other off their perch, although grandpa dogged their every move. The water of the inter-coastal shimmered out the back windows

"What is this, the road show of *My Big Fat Greek Wedding?*"

"Let's go to the bar. It's a bit quieter. I never take a table, even when I come here to eat. The food is superb, by the way, especially the lamb and fried smelts. But I don't like people's feet in my food. Do you like fried smelts?"

"Not particularly. But I bet it would be a great pickup line here."

They sat in the bar and watched the dancers, sipping ouzo. Scarne marveled at the efficiency of the staff as they served delicious-smelling platters amid the swaying arms and kicking feet. One waiter opened a bottle of wine, poured four glasses, left the wine in a bucket, all the while pirouetting as various servers and dancers swirled around him. A minute later the same waiter was dragging a recalcitrant woman onto a table, where she promptly began dancing with wild abandon to the music, which was provided by a DJ.

Some of the scantily clad belly dancers, all of whom were lovely and had hips that wouldn't stop, drew dozens of eyes. But the "civilian" dancers seemed lost in their own world, as if they were the center of the room's attention, rather than that of perhaps their family and a few friends, if that. It wasn't Scarne's cup of tea, but everyone seemed to be having a great time, especially the family groups, which included some well-dressed swells undoubtedly out slumming. Suddenly there was loud shouting and waiters ran down between the tables throwing napkins in the air, which floated down over dancers and diners alike. Most wound up on the floor. He looked at Alana.

"They used to smash plates on the floor, but I guess the insurers put an end to that. It was pretty wild. You can imagine the noise. Another reason I prefer the bar. Napkins are quieter, but it does seem silly now."

"When do they bring in John the Baptist's head on a platter?"

"I think you have to special order. And he might not be in season."

"More ouzo and my head will be on a platter. Yours is like a rock, Alana."

"Good genes. But I may have to dance some of it off. Care to join me?"

"I've had enough excitement for one day."

Alana reached down and took off her sandals, handing them to him. She walked out to the dining room and grabbed two young teen-age girls who were sitting at a table. Laughing, she yanked them up on a table near the center of the room. One of the real dancers joined the trio and paired off with one of the girls. People nearby started clapping in time with the music. The girls got down and the belly dancer brought two little children, obviously brother and sister, up to the table. She and Alana soon had them dancing like dervishes. The little girl was a natural. Even at her tender age, she had all the moves, twirling her belly and hips and looking provocatively at men in the audience. Her family roared approval. Alana helped her down and gave her a kiss on the cheek. She had the table to herself until one of the waiters, at the urging of his fellows, joined her. He was apparently the Travolta of the wait staff and began a sensuous dance with Alana. They swayed in sync, dipping past each other as if on cue. Alana's skirt twirled up, revealing her luscious legs. Her face took on an abandoned look as her hair swirled around her eyes, which took on an Asian cast in the light. As she tossed her head, her earrings twirled. Everyone in the restaurant was looking at her. Even the waiters stopped serving.

Scarne reached her just as the music ended. She looked down at him, breathless, and then fell into his arms. Her body was warm and her skin glowed. There was applause as they walked back to the bar. He handed her the sandals. She picked up some napkins.

"Let's sit on the dock," she said, walking out barefoot.

When they got there, she handed him the napkins and sat at the edge, swishing her feet in the water. He sat next to her, leaning back against a piling. She kicked water at him, laughing. Then she twirled around and extended her legs to him.

"Would you mind?"

As he dried her feet her eyes glistened in the reflection from the lights on the dock. When he finished he put on her sandals.

"Where did you learn to dance like that?"

"Someday I will tell you. Now I am tired. Take me home."

It was almost 10 P.M. when they got to her house on the bay across the Indian River from Miami Beach. Her neighborhood was heavily treed but he occasionally caught a glimpse of the bright lights of the condos and hotels on the stretch where his apartment was. A low stone wall backed by thick hedges surrounded the property. A well-lit courtyard beyond the gate fronted a large two-story house. There were three cars in the circular driveway and he could hear the faint strains of Caribbean music. He walked Alana to the door. She pushed a button on an intercom. A metallic voice answered in Spanish.

"It's Alana," she answered, and the door buzzed open.

She turned to face him, smiling.

"A good day. I hope you don't mind if I don't ask you in. I have people staying over for a party tomorrow. I'm going to take a hot bath and go to bed."

Hopefully hiding his disappointment, he replied, "That's quite all right. We're both pretty tired, I'd imagine."

She gently slipped a hand behind his neck and pulled him in for a long kiss. He started to reach behind her, but she quickly broke free, laughing.

"I had a wonderful time, Jake." She started to go in, then turned abruptly. "It's a pool party. Why don't you come? Lots of interesting people. Some from work. You can look for clues." She paused. "Victor won't be here."

"Sounds like fun. What time?"

"Anytime after noon," she said. "Don't forget your bathing suit."

After she went in, Scarne leaned back on the warm body of his car, staring at the house. The night was very still and he could hear small creatures rustling in the heavy tropical foliage. There was a slight sweet smell in the air, a combination of both flowering and dead vegetation. Would she have invited him in had she not had company? Did she even have company? Should he have asked her to see his place on the way? He went through all the second guessing men do when they think they may have blown the chance to sleep with a special woman. For whatever else Alana Loeb was, she was special.

Alana Loeb stood by a window in her second-floor office looking down at Scarne. The hook was set deep; she wondered how long it would take. Ordinarily, she would consider such a matter dispassionately. But, unexpectedly, she felt the first flush of arousal. She realized, somewhat to her consternation, that she wanted him. He slowly got into his car and drove off.

She had recognized the painful truth in what he'd said at the bar. She had been angry but suspected that she was the first to hear it from him. Why her? She opened the window and let the warm, fragrant night air wash over her.

With it came long-suppressed memories and a foreboding that was completely alien to her.

CANAPÉS AND CALL GIRLS

SCARNE SLEPT LATE and woke feeling groggy. The champagne and ouzo might have relieved the tension of the insane golf match, but he was now paying the price. He drank two glasses of orange juice and changed into running gear.

Once at the beach, he jogged north near the waterline. The hardpan near the buildings would have been easier, but he wanted a good workout. It wasn't long before he was sweating, even though there was a nice breeze and it was in the 60's. He passed a few strollers, plenty of sea birds and, as he got nearer the public beaches, some newspaper-wrapped bums. His calves burned from fighting the sucking sand. Occasionally, he misjudged a wave and was rewarded with a refreshing splash up to his shorts. After a couple of miles, breathing hard, he cut over to Collins Avenue. He spotted a Cuban bakery and bought a fruit empanada. Then he walked back to the apartment, made coffee and ate on the portion of his terrace that overlooked the Indian River. He thought he spotted Alana's house in the distance, but wasn't sure.

†

Scarne arrived at the house just before 1 PM. Cars were parked up and down the street, some on lawns. A large white truck was in the driveway. On its side were the words, "Parties by Rico," and a line of men in white coats were unloading trays of food. The driveway was full of Jaguars, BMW's and Mercedes, and one Bentley. A valet gave him a ticket. Scarne took his bag and walked into the courtyard past a board holding dozens of car keys on hooks.

The two-story house was much bigger than it looked from the street, where it was hidden behind hedges and trees. He was happy to see that it was an older house and not a McMansion. The stucco walls were spotted with ivy. A sign near the front door directed him to a path that led around the side. He could hear music, laughter and an occasional splash. He passed a small pool house and then was in the thick of the party.

There were perhaps 50 people in the backyard, most of them wearing speedos or miniscule bikinis. Some of the more beautiful women were topless. A few guests who were more fully dressed stood around awkwardly. Waiters walked around the pool and nearby gardens passing out drinks from silver trays. Looked like champagne, apple martinis and, of course, mojitos. There was a Tiki bar near the back of the house, complete with thatched roof. The music came from a small Calypso band set up near the bar. A buffet table was just outside the kitchen. In its center was a large ice sculpture of a dolphin surrounded by lobsters, shrimp, clams, oysters and other delicacies.

A small stretch of lawn separated the huge pool from a bulkhead and boat dock on the bay. Scarne walked over to the dock and looked down at the greenish brown water. His shadow spooked a school of small baitfish that rippled the surface. There was a series of pipes with shower heads at various levels adjacent to the dock with a sign in English and Spanish that said: "Please shower before entering the pool!" As he read it, he heard a splash and looked up to see a man swimming from a small cabin cruiser at anchor about 75 feet out. Another man was poised on the gunwale and soon followed the first diver into the water. Further out in the bay a larger yacht streamed by. Several men on deck passed binoculars back and forth. They were looking at the topless women at the party. The boat's horn tooted cheerfully and a couple of the men waved. Scarne smiled and waved back.

The two men from the smaller boat reached the dock after a few short powerful strokes and climbed up onto land. They walked past Scarne shaking their hands and heads, catching him with some spray. They seemed not to notice, and took turns standing under the top shower head, which poured out a strong stream when they pulled a chain. They seemed to barely glance at Scarne, although he had the feeling they got a good look at him. Both men seemed very fit. Their bathing trunks were fashionably tight. That was where the similarities ended. The taller, thinner of the two was very blond and his hair was cut short. He looked vaguely familiar. His companion was more muscled and had thick black hair that glistened as he stroked it. He was dark complexioned and had a trim mustache. Both moved gracefully. Dancers? Scarne didn't think so. There was something menacing about them.

The men went to the pool and dove in, then climbed out the other side and made for the bar, picking up towels from unoccupied chairs. What were they doing at Alana's party? The thought occurred to him that they had crashed. It would be so simple to park your boat and the swim into a party. Anybody in a bathing suit would blend in. He headed after them.

"Hot shit, ain't it?"

Scarne turned to see that a man has fallen in beside him. He barely came up to Scarne's shoulders and was wearing pink trousers, a flowered shirt and white sneakers. A substantial martini, thick with olives, was in his hand.

"Alana's parties get all kinds. Euro trash, Rio trash. They come out of the woodwork. But see that older guy holding court with the babes in the corner. Thomas Harris. *Silence of the Lambs*. Lives a few blocks away. And over there near the food is Iggy Pop, the singer. I think one of the Bee Gees is roaming around, too."

The man held out his hand.

"Tony Goetz."

Scarne introduced himself, saying, "Remind me to skip whatever comes with the fava beans. Where do we fit in?"

"Hell, you'll have to speak for yourself. I'm local Miami trash."

They reached the Tiki hut and Goetz crooked a finger at the bartender.

"Pablo, another one, por favor. S'il vouz plait. One more olive."

The bartender, whose nametag didn't say "Pablo," rolled his eyes and looked at Scarne, who shook his head. Three topless women strolled by.

"Six abreast," Goetz commented.

The bartender puts his martini on the bar. The glass was half full of olives.

"Like olives?" Scarne said.

"Hate the fuckin' things. The glass holds about 10 olives. Then I know to stop, or switch to beer. Doesn't work with lemon peels. I'd be dead."

"Jake!"

He looked over to the pool to see Alana Loeb springing out of the pool. She grabbed a small towel from a chair and began vigorously drying her hair as she walked slowly over to the two men. She was wearing a bikini, both parts. But it was very wet and left little to the imagination. Her nipples were boldly outlined in the fabric. The effect was more erotic than the bare breasts of the other women. The bottom part of the suit was severely V-shaped and accentuated her long legs.

"Goddamn," Goetz said under his breath in open admiration.

As she reached them she draped the towel around her shoulders.

"I'm so glad you came. I see you have already fallen into bad company."

She gave Scarne a brief kiss on the cheek, then leaned over to buss Goetz.

"I know I'm irresistible, honey, but you already kissed me when I came in," the little man said. "Not that I'm complaining, mind you."

"I just heard that you led all the salesmen this quarter. That deserved another kiss. Now, can I borrow Jake for a minute? I want to show him around and get his things put away. I'm sure he wants to take a swim."

She took Scarne's arm and led him across the patio past a spiral stairway with decorative wrought-iron railings leading up from a loggia to the second floor. In the kitchen, waitresses were busily unwrapping platters or pulling pans from the stove. She stopped to pluck a canapé off a platter that was sitting on the island in the kitchen. After plopping it in her mouth, she uttered a purr of delight, grabbed another and raised it to Scarne's lips.

"Let's get out of here before they send out empty platters," she laughed.

There was a small room just off the kitchen with a pullout couch, a chest of drawers and a computer desk surrounded by bookshelves. A curtained door led out to the patio. Another opened to a small bathroom.

"Drop your bag and I'll show you the hacienda. You can change in here rather than the pool house. And don't forget to grab one of my towels out of the chest. They're nicer than the ones we put out on the deck." She walked over to the chest and opened it to show him his choices, then reached in and pulled out a small half-robe, which she put on but did not cinch.

"I leave these all over the house. Sometimes I forget myself and walk around in my bathing suit. Or less. Not very lady-like. Of course, nobody would notice with this crowd. Are you shocked by some of the guests? Things are pretty casual in Miami Beach. It's like Rio. Cuban girls, especially, like to flaunt it. Suicidal, when you think how jealous Cuban men are."

"These are all friends?"

"Not hardly. People from the office, to be sure. But mostly clients and a few neighbors I invite so they can't complain about the party. Old college trick. Wouldn't be surprised if there were one or two call girls out there. Men like their arm candy."

She sat on the couch and used her towel to dry her feet.

"I should leave some flip flops or sandals around too. I'm liable to break my neck slipping on the stairs with wet feet. This will have to do. Come on, let me act like the nouveau riche I am and show you around."

It was a beautiful house, with an open floor plan that led to several spectacular rooms. The dining room featured an octagonal recessed ceiling with hand-painted panels and deep burgundy walls. A large glass-topped table with scrolled wood bases was surrounded by Tuscan-style chairs with green velvet backs and woven chenille fronts. A gold-framed painting of Venice sat on one wall opposite a triple wide china closet. Across from the living area was a family room with a mahogany pool table and antique bar. Through that room was a home theater, with lounge chairs at floor level and plush sofas on an upper tier. Another door led into a library with Caribbean rosewood flooring and recessed tin panels in the ceiling. A large fireplace framed with a hunter-green lambrequin dominated the room. Each room made a statement and stopped just short of ostentation. Much like the woman, Scarne thought.

"You have exquisite taste. I liked the Richard Prince in the library."

"I adore him. And thank you for the compliment. I did most of the decorating myself."

They emerged into the front foyer where a huge iron chandelier hovered above a mosaic floor. They took the marble staircase to the second floor.

"There are four bedrooms, but I'll just show you the best. Mine."

She led him to a large master bedroom at the rear of the house. The room was done in all yellows and celadon. A bright floral print for the draperies matched the accent pillows on the king-sized bed and its Louis XVI-style headboard. A door opened out to a small terrace where the decorative staircase spiraled down to the pool area. Scarne spotted the two men who had come off the boat earlier. They were looking up at them.

"Alana, who are those two men standing down at the bar? The blond and the swarthy one."

She looked down. Her good cheer evaporated.

"What's the matter?"

"Nothing. I know them. They work for us. But they usually don't come to my parties. I didn't see them come in."

"They swam from that boat. Thought they might be crashers."

"They tend to be loose cannons."

"I think I might know the blond fellow from somewhere."

She looked at Scarne with a funny cast to her eyes.

"I'll have to introduce you," she said, starting down the stairs. "I'll meet you at the bar after you've changed."

✝

A HELLUVA PARTY

SCARNE PEELED OFF from Alana at the bottom of the stairs and went to change. Once outside again, he threw his towel over a vacant chair near the deep end of the pool. He waited while a bare-breasted woman doing a backstroke glided past, then dove in and swam the length of the pool underwater. Then he did a normal lap on the way back and climbed out, refreshed. As he toweled off he headed toward the bar, where Alana was in animated conversation with the two men from the boat.

"Those guys are bad news." It was Goetz, who had fallen in step with Scarne, martini firmly in hand. "Ballantrae's Mutt and Jeff."

"What do they do?" Scarne asked. He shortened his stride. Goetz walked like a penguin; only his legs below his knees appeared to move

"Damned if I know. They're listed as brokers, same as me. But I hardly ever see them in the office. Thick as thieves, those two. Pair of faggadoons. Don't give me a look. Everybody knows and nobody cares in this town. But they give me the creeps. I'd like to know how they make their dough. In fact, I'm still trying to figure out how Ballantrae makes all its money."

"What do you mean?"

"Can't be from the brokerage business. Retail, investment banking, institutional and research are all burning money. But the well never seems to run dry. And it should, with the rates we pay out on our C.D.'s. They're way over market. I ask them how they do it and I get a lot of malarkey about overseas investments, hedges and proprietary computer trading. Like we can corner the market on that stuff. But what the hell, I'll leave it up to the lawyers. I'm just an asset gatherer. They call us 'financial consultants,' but all we do is get people to deposit their money. Most of it goes into those C.D.'s. If they buy stocks from us, it's accidental."

It came out "*ashidental.*" There wasn't much olive room left in his glass. Scarne wanted to draw him out further but they had reached the bar. Alana said something sharply in German to the blond man, then flashed a smile.

"Jake, I'd like you to meet Jesús Garza and Christian Keitel. I told them you thought they were crashers."

"You gringos always worry about Cubans jumping off a boat," Garza said.

They all laughed and shook hands. Garza's accent was barely noticeable.

"Be nice, Jesús," Alana said. "Jake was just looking out for me. Besides, I think he won half the company from Victor in a golf match."

"You are a marked man, Mr. Scarne," Keitel said "Victor doesn't like to lose, at anything."

He looked at Alana as he said it. Then he looked at Goetz.

"Tony, you beat us out again for the quarter. How do you do it?"

"The question is, 'How do you guys even get close to my production?' I bust my balls, while you guys jet around the world and work on your tans."

Garza slapped the little broker on the shoulder.

"We'd love to tell you, Tony, but then we'd have to kill you."

He turned to Scarne.

"Tony is getting nervous. We're nipping at his heels. He's afraid we'll get a bigger bonus or win one of the incentive trips."

"What the hell do you need a trip for," Goetz snapped. "You've been everywhere. Except maybe the office."

"Enough shop talk," Alana interjected. "I'm famished. Will you get me a Chardonnay, Jake? I'll fix us plates and we'll eat by the fountain."

She walked away, greeting people as she went. There was a low growl from a powerful marine engine. Scarne looked out at the water. A sleek cigarette boat with a large black tarp stretched amidships pulled up just offshore. He ordered two Chardonnays. Goetz looked at his two rivals.

"Well, if I have to stand next to a couple of boobs, I can do better than you guys. I think I'll go to the pool and do some research on silicone. One thing's for sure, Alana can throw a helluva fuckin' party."

After he walked off, Garza said, "Tony is a malestar – a pain – but he can produce. Lands a lot of Jewish money. There is still plenty of it in Miami."

"Who do you guys go after?"

"Oh, we have a big European and South American clientele. Some Middle Eastern. We travel more than Tony. Our pickings aren't as easy as his."

"I guess you do pretty well, to judge by your rowboat out there."

"Oh that. Sorry to disappoint you, but we don't own it. We belong to a boat club. Allows us to use a variety of boats for an annual fee that covers a certain number of hours. Anything from skiffs to yachts. When we bring them back, we're done with them. Don't have the time or the patience to own a boat. We have better things to do than scrape barnacles."

"Well, it's a nice boat. What is it, a 50-foot Hatteras?"

"You've got a good eye, Jake. It's a 50-footer, but not a Hatteras. It's a Sealine. Hatteras would have cost more hours, and the Sealine is a nice craft."

"That's not a bad way to do it," Scarne admitted. "They say the two best days of your life are when you buy a boat and when you sell it. What's the name of the club?"

"Yacht Net," Keitel said. "Although some of their boats, like that one out there, don't qualify as yachts. They have branches and berths in marinas on both coasts. You interested? The local office is in Key Biscayne."

"Maybe sometime in the future. Well, I'd better find Alana."

"Nice to meet you, Jake," Keitel said. "Good luck with your investigation."

Scarne nodded and walked away. He could feel their eyes on his back. Despite the friendly boating banter, he knew something wasn't right about them. He'd lay good money that they barely knew the difference between a stock and a bond. And then there was the mention of the investigation. That was a slip. There would be no reason that a couple of ordinary brokers would know why he was in Miami. Certainly Ballantrae and Alana wouldn't spread it around to just anybody. That meant that Garza and Keitel were in the inner circle privy to very sensitive material.

Alana was sitting at the table with several people. Scarne was relieved to see that the women all had their tops on. The food Alana had selected for him was delicious. For the next 20 minutes he ate and chatted. The men talked real estate and football; the women, fashion and diets. All were loud and animated and had uniformly atrocious table manners. The combination of braggadocio, spittle and suntan lotion eventually got to Scarne. He turned to Alana, who was disinterestedly listening to a woman extolling her bikini wax.

"Excuse me, but I think I'll go jump in the bay."

The woman who was talking to Alana said, very seriously, "You're not supposed to go in the water right after eating. You could drown."

"One can only hope," Scarne replied.

The woman looked confused. Alana suppressed a laugh. As he walked to the pool, she caught up to him.

"It's a pretty shallow crowd. Believe it or not, I have to do some more mingling. Do you mind if I ignore you for a while?"

"You don't have to babysit me. I'll be fine."

The party picked up. Some people were dancing. A woman screamed as she was pushed into the pool. Two men jumped in and all three began tussling amid much laughter. One of the men twirled a bikini top above his head. The woman kept jumping up for it, her ample breasts jouncing in the man's face. Many of the older people seemed to have left. He couldn't see Thomas Harris. Probably departed with plenty of ideas for table fare for Hannibal Lechter.

Scarne found a chaise in the sun and dropped his towel. He dove into the pool, came out on the bar side and ordered another glass of wine. Then he went to stretch out on his chair. It didn't take him long to spot all the hookers. Their bodies were firmer, they laughed too loudly at their companions' jokes and smoked incessantly. Scarne noted cynically that girlfriends were less effusive and wives tended to ignore their husbands. They had landed their fish. He wondered what, if anything, Alana saw in these people. Business, probably. Or maybe they appealed to her wild, table-dancing, side.

Garza, Keitel and Goetz were standing by the pool, engaged in a lively conversation. The stocky broker was wagging a finger at Garza. Scarne was amused to note that though the animated Goetz was swaying, the hand holding the martini glass – which even from a distance looked green with accumulated olives – was on a relatively even keel. He thought about going over, especially when he saw Alana join the group, but decided that he wanted to get Goetz all to himself for a while. Besides, the food, sun and wine began to do their work. He put his head back and started to doze off.

He was in that twilight zone that just preceded sleep when he heard the shot. He was instantly alert. There was no mistaking it. From the sound of it, a high-power rifle. Then he heard real screams, followed by the sound of crashing platters and broken glass. All the time the band played on, but finally one instrument stopped, then another until the music died out discordantly. People scrambled out of the pool and cautiously moved backwards, some pointing uncertainly into the water.

Scarne immediately looked for Alana. She, too, was staring into the pool. Goetz had disappeared and Garza and Keitel were prone on the pool deck, low to the ground, like cats. They were looking out at the bay. Scarne turned to see a glint of reflected light under the tarp of the cigarette boat he'd noticed earlier. He came out of his chair and reached Alana in three strides, propelling her violently into the pool. Just before they hit the water he felt more than heard the zinging passage of a bullet, followed by the sound of the shot and a loud splintering crash. Then they were plunging together to the bottom and came face to face with Tony Goetz.

He was lying on his back, arms outstretched, eyes wide open. He looked surprised. Scarne was momentarily disoriented by what appeared several other "eyes" bobbing near the man's head. They were green and had red centers. Scarne thought he was hallucinating. Then he realized they were olives. Goetz had taken his martini glass with him, still clasped in his hand. Alana pushed toward the surface. He grabbed her and signaled her to stay behind him. She put her arms around his neck and he surfaced at the side of the pool. Peering cautiously toward the bay, he saw the cigarette boat roaring away at full throttle. Garza and Keitel were sprinting to the bulkhead. They dove in, swam to their own boat and were soon in hot pursuit.

"I'll have to take your broker-training course, Alana."

She didn't answer. Her arms were shaking. He loosened her grip and climbed out of the pool, then pulled her up.

"Go inside," Scarne said.

"What about Tony?"

"I'll take care of it. Call the police." It would be redundant, he knew. Cell phones were popping out all over. "Go on," he said, shaking her. "Now!"

After she left he dove in the pool. There was still surprisingly little blood in the water. Scarne put his arms under Goetz and kicked to the surface, thinking, *well, I've got him alone now.* The cocktail glass came out of the hand and twirled toward the bottom. By the time he got to the side of the pool, a few guests had pulled themselves together. Several men and a woman – one of the ones he knew to be a call girl – jumped in to help. Hookers had some sand, he thought. The intrepid little band, with the help of the bartender, managed to haul Goetz onto the deck. The girl began mouth-to-mouth as the bartender compressed Goetz's chest.

"C'mon buddy, you can make it," the man said. Blood immediately seeped between his fingers. No water came out of his mouth with the compressions.

"No, he can't," Scarne said. "Don't bother."

He put a finger on the carotid. Nothing. He ripped open Goetz's shirt. There was a small hole below the breastbone. He rolled the body partially over. There was no exit wound. Not a military or steel-jacketed round, which would have gone straight through. More likely a hunting slug that mushroomed. From the size of the entry wound and sound of the shot, probably a high-velocity .243 or 6 mm. Small but devastating. The shock of 80 grains of lead and soft polymer tip traveling at 3,300 feet per second blossoming to a sudden stop internally would be enough to kill. The pressure wave alone could break the spine and stop the heart. Goetz was dead before he hit the pool. No chance to breathe in water. The seeping blood came from the pulverized heart.

"He's been shot. The police will want to talk to everyone. No one should leave. The cops wouldn't like that. They won't be interested in recreational drugs or your occupation." He winked at the call girl; she winked back. "Only what you saw or heard. But some of you may want to put more clothes on."

"Somebody hand me a towel," he said.

When one was offered he placed it over the dead man's face. Not strictly procedure, but the hell with that. He had liked the little guy. Some others apparently did as well. He heard a women sobbing and commiserating male sounds. Probably co-workers.

He heard a man say, "Jesus, they got Flipper. I was right next to it."

The dolphin ice sculpture on the buffet table had been decapitated. Some people were still pulling shards out of their hair. One hysterical woman was screaming "I don't match" repeatedly. In her panic she had put on someone else's bikini top.

Scarne heard the first siren. He looked down at the dripping body.

"You were right, Tony. She throws a helluva party."

"What's the use, Jesús? We'll never catch the fucking thing. It must have 10 miles an hour on us."

Not to mention that the speedboat was already moving away at high clip by the time he and Garza even climbed aboard their Sealine, Keitel reflected.

"Knots, Christian," Garza said. "We're on the water. The term is knots, which means nautical miles per hour. He has us by eight knots, maybe."

"Oh, for Christ's sake!"

Keitel was keenly aware they were on the water as both boats raced up the crowded river, scattering pleasure craft before them. The only knot was in his stomach and he felt that familiar twinge in his tailbone. I'd rather be shot, he thought, than endure another crazy boat ride with Jesús.

"We might get lucky, if one of the bridges is down," Garza said, ignoring the horn blasts and angry shouts of boats they nearly swamped. "Plus he only just realized we were chasing him amid all these goddamn boats."

And, in fact, a highway drawbridge loomed ahead, and it was closing. The speedboat would have to slow, Keitel realized, and so, thank God, would they. He reached under a tarp, opened a storage locker and pulled out an M-14 rifle. Bracing himself as best he could against a railing (well, they do call it a gunwale, he mused) he tried to get the speedboat in the crosshairs of the 10-power telescopic sight. But with both boats bouncing and swerving it was virtually impossible. But when they slowed, he'd have them. He would put 20 rounds into the speedboat and its occupants in 10 seconds.

Keitel lowered the rifle. Funny, the other boat seemed to have widened the gap. It was speeding up, heading right into the descending roadway. He watched in fascination and frustration as their low-slung target shot under the roadway, which was almost completely down, and into the waterway beyond. Damn it! His frustration soon turned into horror as Garza poured on the power. The lunatic was going to try to make it through as well!

"We're not going to make it," Keitel shouted. The drawbridge roadway, perhaps 100 feet away, was almost fully down.

"Piece of cake," Garza said.

Keitel saw people on the bridge waving and heard a woman scream somewhere above him. Garza jumped down from behind the wheel and, quite calmly, said, "Duck!" Keitel dove for the deck. The boat's cockpit smashed into the bridge roadway and was sheared off. Wood splinters, glass and metal shards rained down on the two men as the mangled cabin cruiser emerged on the other side. With its engines still on full power it zigged sharply to the left toward a rock bulkhead. The two men looked at each other and jumped overboard. A moment later the boat smashed into the bulkhead spectacularly and seemed to accordion. Garza and Keitel had just pulled themselves onto shore nearby when its fuel tank exploded. They watched it sink amid bubbles and steamy hissing.

"Pity," Garza said. "By the way, did you see who it was?"

"No. But I have a pretty good idea."

"Seattle?"

"He may be smarter than you thought."

A smoldering plank floated by.

"Piece of cake," Keitel said, plucking it from the water and handing it to his partner.

Garza shrugged.

"Come on. Let's find a cab."

A TOUGH TOWN

THE FIRST SIREN had been joined by several others. Their wavering pitch indicated that the cruisers were weaving through local streets as they neared the house. Scarne briefly considered melding with the crowd inside the house to avoid a prolonged grilling by the cops. But he'd liked Goetz. It didn't seem right to leave him lying there all by himself.

Tony Goetz? Who would want to shoot him with a high-powered rifle from a speedboat? It didn't figure. There were easier ways to kill stockbrokers. Gut instinct told Scarne that Goetz was just what he appeared to be – a loud, funny and cynical salesman. A good guy to get drunk with. But not a player. True, he wasn't very discreet. But a company party was no place to permanently silence a malcontent. If someone wanted to kill a broker, tossing him out a high-rise window might be the perfect crime. Scarne couldn't dismiss outright the possibility that a jealous lover, disgruntled client or man from Mars shot Goetz, but thought it more plausible he was not the intended target. Besides, there was that second bullet that, in effect, "iced" the dolphin sculpture.

Garza, Keitel and Alana were standing next to Goetz when he was killed. Scarne looked at the water in the bay. It was fairly calm, and had been all afternoon, but there were small swells, mostly generated by boats. Such swells were unpredictable, but could throw off even an expert marksman's aim by a few inches, up or down – or side to side.

The sirens grew louder and then stopped. Scarne could see flashing lights through the bushes at the side of the house. He shook out a cigarette from a pack left in haste on a nearby table. He lit it with a candle and was about halfway through the smoke when two uniforms walked over to him. Miami Beach cops. They looked down at the body. Scarne dropped the cigarette in a half-full glass and rose. The older of the two cops looked at him.

"Who are you? Why aren't you inside with the others?"

"Name is Jake Scarne. I was on the job once, so I tried to protect your crime scene. No one touched the body after some CPR."

"What did you see?"

Scarne told them. They took notes and asked a few questions. Their job was to nail down the time frame and secure the area.

"All right. Have a seat. The detectives will want to talk to you."

As they walked away, one of the waiters tentatively approached them. He was holding Scarne's shirt. The poor guy was nervous as hell. He was probably undocumented and wanted nothing to do with anyone in uniform. The younger cop spoke to him in Spanish. The waiter relaxed when he heard the comforting language. The cop pointed to Scarne and the waiter walked over.

"Miss Alana asked me to give you this, sir."

It was chilly and Scarne was glad to get the shirt. He thanked the waiter, who hurried away. Scarne wondered why he had not vamoosed right after the shooting. "Miss Alana" probably laid down the law.

Within a half hour the pool area was crawling with police. A five-person CSI unit taped off the area and scoured the area for evidence. Two of them, a man and a woman, knelt over the body and began examining it, as another man took photos. Just like on TV. The other two looked into the pool and started arguing, in a friendly way. Finally, they faced off and Scarne heard one of them say, "One strike three, shoot." Two arms shot out with hands displaying fingers. After three plays, one man said, "Shit, I never win." He walked back to the front of the house. In a few minutes he was back wearing a bathing suit and a mask and climbed into the pool, giving the finger to his smiling buddy.

The two cops who were first on the scene returned. With them were Detectives Frank Paulo and William Curley.

"This one probably wasn't an accident," Scarne said.

"What the fuck are you doing here?" Curley said.

Scarne debated how much to tell them. He knew he'd have to feed them something, or he might wind up answering questions "downtown," wherever the hell that was in Miami Beach.

"Before he died Josh Shields was working on an article about Victor Ballantrae and his company."

"The financial mucky-muck?"

"Yeah. Ballantrae and the Shields family are pretty close. I thought he might give me some useful background." As with most good lies, it had the element of truth and might even hold up. "Met with him and his chief of staff yesterday. This is her house. She invited me to this party. I thought it would be an easy way to meet a lot of employees. Get a feel for the company. Just covering all the bases."

"Except a guy gets murdered right in front of you."

"I've heard Miami is a tough town."

Scarne could tell that they didn't quite believe him, but there wasn't much they could do about it.

"OK," Paulo said, opening his notebook. "Lead us through it."

Scarne did. He told them how he met Goetz. The two shots. The panic. The cigarette boat. How Garza and Keitel pursued the shooter. How he dove in the pool and found Goetz's wound. How he secured the crime scene. He even ventured a guess at the caliber of the bullet.

Then Paulo said, "Quite a shot, don't you think? From a boat."

"It was pretty calm. But good shooting nonetheless, I'll give you that."

Curley said, "Did the two heroes come back?"

"Not that I saw."

"And the second shot came after the vic was already under water?"

"Yeah."

"So maybe he wasn't the target."

"Maybe we were all targets. Some nut with a rifle."

Both detectives stared at Scarne so long he finally had to smile.

"Well, maybe not."

"Go through it again," Curley said.

Scarne did.

"So, the dead guy, Goetz, was standing right between the Loeb woman and the two guys who chased the shooter. That right?"

"Among."

"Among what?"

"She was standing among the three of them, not between."

"You know, Scarne, it's not hard to understand why you got the boot from the cops in New York. But this isn't New York. You're here at our sufferance."

Scarne figured he said “sufferance” to regain the rhetorical high ground, but let it go.

“Let’s get back on point here,” Paulo said.

“My point is that if Goetz or the fuckin’ frozen dolphin weren’t the target, then one of the other three standing with him were. You got any idea why?”

“No,” Scarne said. “But it wouldn’t surprise me if Garza and Keitel had enemies. They didn’t react like your typical brokers. More like Navy Seals. They’ve been shot at before.”

The CSI man from the pool walked over holding a clear plastic bag full of what looked like green marbles.

“What have you got?” Paulo asked.

“Olives.”

“Olives?”

“Yeah, 10 olives and a martini glass. All on the bottom at the end of the pool where the vic went in. Nothing else.”

“Manzanilla,” Scarne interjected.

“Manza-what?” the two detectives blurted almost simultaneously.

“Manzanilla. Spanish olives, with pimentos.”

“Manzadead,” the tech said, looking at Scarne. They both laughed.

“Goetz had them all in his glass before he went in,” Scarne explained. The detectives looked annoyed. “I prefer a twist, but he used the olives to keep count. He’d stop when he couldn’t fit any more in the glass. One per drink.”

Curley looked at the dripping CSI tech, who was still chuckling at his witticism.

“Ten fucking martinis? Are you sure the bullet killed him?”

“Yeah. They can go easy on the formaldehyde at the funeral home.”

“I think he was Jewish,” Scarne said.

“So?’

“Means he probably won’t be embalmed after the autopsy.”

"Oh, yeah. I forgot they did that. Religious thing, right. Course, he might not be Orthodox."

"Enough with the embalming crap," Paulo said impatiently. "What about the second bullet?"

"We're looking," the tech said. "But don't get your hopes up. Could have gone anywhere after it hit the ice sculpture. Might be in the side of the house or in a tree."

"I'd check right around the buffet table," Scarne said. "The first one didn't go through the victim, so it mushroomed. The ice might have stopped the other bullet. Look in the shrimp pile."

"Not bad," the tech said, walking away.

"You guys through with me?"

"Yeah, for now," Paulo said. "I made some calls after our meet. You still got friends in New York. But I got a feeling you're not telling us everything you know. I won't hesitate to hit you with a hindering charge if I find out you're holding back on us. This is a homicide."

"Hey, I gave you a solid lead on the olives, didn't I?"

Paulo and Curley finally cut him loose and went to interview the guests who had stuck around. Scarne was fairly certain they would now look at Josh's death in a new light and seek a connection to Goetz's murder. He wasn't sure what that would accomplish, and it might prove embarrassing to Ballantrae, but there was nothing to be done about it. He reflected that if Shields Inc. was a publicly traded company, it would probably be a good time to short its stock. Any planned merger would surely soon be as dead as Josh – and Tony Goetz.

He changed his clothes and went to mingle with the guests and staff. Many of the Ballantrae employees knew Goetz and liked him. Garza and Keitel were also well known in the company. No one spoke ill of them but a few echoed Goetz's inability to explain how they made all their money given their erratic work habits. The "clients" and other hangers-on were uniformly circumspect about their dealings with the company. Scarne heard a lot of meaningless Wall Street palaver about trusts and hedge funds. Only one man, obviously in his cups from depleting Alana's brandy supply, let slip that the only reason he dealt with the company were the incredible rates on its certificates of deposit.

"Man, get one of their CD's. The return is almost three percentage points higher than at regular banks. Do the math."

Scarne asked him how that was possible.

"Hell, I don't know. Something to do with their offshore bank and investing overseas by using computers to find the highest worldwide returns balanced against political and economic risk. Who cares?"

Scarne went back out to the pool. Goetz's body had been removed. The CSI tech was talking to the detectives and eating a shrimp.

"You were right," he said when Scarne walked over to them. "Well, almost. The bullet was in a pile of clams. Really flattened. Almost a dum-dum. The one inside the vic must have done a lot of damage."

"You sure it came from the same gun?" Curley asked.

"We'll have to run some tests on both bullets, but the sculpture was on basically the same line. My guess is same gun, same shooter. I don't see any grassy knolls out there in the bay."

After the tech walked away, Casey said, "Everyone's a comedian. It's those damn TV shows."

Alana Loeb walked up to the three men.

"Detectives, all the guests have gone. I wonder if I can send my staff home. They are very upset."

"Of course, Ms. Loeb," Paulo said. "We have all their names. I'm sure this must have been trying for you as well. But we do have a few more questions for you."

"Thank you," she said. "I'll see Mr. Scarne out and then meet you in the house. Is that all right?"

After the detectives went into the house, Scarne said, "I think I should stick around, Alana."

"I appreciate all you've done, Jake, but that's not necessary. Christian phoned. He and Garza will be here shortly. They chased the other boat up the Indian River, but apparently had some sort of accident and it got away. I'm sure the police will want to get a statement from them when they get here, and then we have some business to talk over. So you might as well go home."

"What's going on Alana? We both know Goetz wasn't the target."

"Let it go, Jake." She touched his cheek. "You saved my life. Now I will return the favor. What happened tonight is none of your concern. I don't want you involved. Forget about me. Forget about the company. Just go back to New York."

"But I am involved. You remember Josh Shields, don't you?"

"You will get nowhere with that. And nowhere with me. Goodbye, Jake."

He was left staring at her back. He went to the valet station. No one was there, but his key was on the rack. As he walked to his car, he noticed Garza and Keitel getting out of a cab. They appeared to be dripping wet.

‡

FIERCE LOVE

SCARNE WAS BACK at La Gorce 10 minutes later. Instead of entering the garage, he pulled into the semicircular driveway, his mind racing.

"Do you want me to park the car for you, sir?"

He barely heard the valet standing next to his window.

"Sir?"

Scarne shot onto Collins Avenue, to a cacophony of angry horns. Weaving in and out of traffic, he roared toward the drawbridge over the Indian River. He jammed on his brakes as the bridge road gates came down amid clanging bells. The span began rising as a cabin cruiser idled toward it. Son of a bitch. After what seemed an eternity, the small boat passed and the roadway came down. Traffic began to move slowly over the bridge. He got stuck behind two cars, side by side, driven by old men strictly observing the 25-mile-per-hour limit on the winding road. Hitting his horn wasn't an option. They wouldn't hear him, even with their hearing aids. The last time those old coots were in a hurry the Berlin Wall hadn't been built. The driver on the left had his right signal on and the guy on the right had his left on. Maybe they planned to crash into each.

Disgusted, Scarne didn't wait to find out. He made a right and headed toward the bay. After a few minutes of aimless wandering in poorly lit neighborhoods, he got lucky and hit the street that paralleled the waterway. He soon spotted Alana Loeb's house. There were four cars in her driveway: three squad cars and a nondescript sedan. He doused his lights, rolled to a stop behind a neighbor's car a few houses away and scrunched down. After an hour, only the sedan was left. He waited. Fifteen minutes later, Curley and Paulo left in it. Finally, a cab pulled up and he spotted Alana walking out with Garza and Keitel. He could hear the anger in their muffled voices. She turned on her heel and they drove off.

Scarne strode to the front door. He rang the buzzer. Nothing. He pounded. Nothing. The front of the house was dark. He tried the door. It was locked. He thought he heard music. He followed the path around the side. Small creatures scuttled away in the grass into the bushes and flower beds. A large insect brushed his hair. When he turned the corner of the house he saw that the pool area was unlit. He could barely make out the yellow crime scene tape. A small green light on a pole flickered on and off, casting an intermittently eerie glow on the dock and the shimmering water beyond. He thought of Gatsby. As he passed the spiral staircase, he heard a rustle.

"I knew you would come back."

Her voice was hoarse. He didn't trust his own. She was standing halfway up the staircase, leaning back against the rail, backlit by the light emanating below her from the kitchen. She was wearing a white kimono-like translucent robe. He could see her legs through the fabric. She was barefoot. One arm was relaxed at her side; the other lay on the railing. The music came from her bedroom. What the hell was he doing?

He started up the stairs. She backed up, spiraling silently away from him. As they pirouetted, she undid her robe and dropped it off her shoulders. Whatever reservations he had dropped with the robe. She was naked. Her nipples were fully erect. He had never seen anything like them. They were like pencil erasers, he thought irrationally. The flickering lights from scented candles in the room behind her gave it an eerie, exotic glow.

She stopped at the top landing. He took her in his arms. He felt her hard points dig into his chest. He reached behind her and cupped her buttocks, pulling her tight. She put her head into his neck and then looked up at him, her head tilted suggestively to one side. She wasn't smiling. He felt dizzy. His throat tightened. Her lips were moving. She was whispering.

"Some love is fire. Some love is rust. But the finest, fiercest love is lust."

He kissed her violently as he swung her up into his arms. She wrapped her arms around his neck. Her nails dug into him as her tongue snaked into his mouth. He carried her into her room and placed her on the bed. She swung her legs to engulf him and drew him deep inside her before he even managed to get all his clothes off. They both climaxed almost immediately, like randy teenagers. Her orgasm was so intense he actually felt it internally despite his own excitement. She arched her back and emitted a protracted moan.

When, after lessening cries, she quieted, he tried to withdraw. "No," she said fiercely, clenching her legs tightly around him and then raising them almost to her shoulders so that he settled in even deeper.

She spoke to him quietly, in several languages, and kissed him gently, clenching her internal muscles until he was ready again and could start moving. They lasted a very long time before completion. Only then did he stumble away from her to finish undressing. Then they lay in each other's arms and caught up on the foreplay missed in their frenzy. They explored each other's bodies, they toyed with each other, they played, until they couldn't stand it anymore and joined again. She rolled on top of him. He remained passive. She was relentless with her movements. At the end, she cried, "See what you do to me. Feel that. Feel that!"

It was almost 4 A.M. when Alana Loeb left the bed, gently covering Scarne and pulling on a wrap. She walked down to her office, which also served as an upstairs library. She closed and locked the sliding double doors. As she walked to her desk she ran her fingers along a shelf that contained her most prized books. An insatiable and eclectic reader, Alana was also collector.

She paused in front of a first edition of *Gone with the Wind*. It had cost a small fortune but she had loved the story since childhood. Now, suddenly weary, she pressed her forehead against the novel, remembering the comfort it gave her with every re-reading. Her pampered back-country Argentinean life – at least before its brutal denouement – bore a passing resemblance to the romantic portrait Margaret Mitchell painted of the Old South. She identified with Scarlett O'Hara's fall from a life of luxury and self-indulgence, and, more importantly, with her rise from the ashes of defeat and humiliation. Her eyes fell on another first edition, paradoxically her second-favorite: *The End of the Affair*. If Scarlett is the woman I am, Alana bitterly reflected on occasion, Graham Greene's noble Sarah Miles is a woman I might have been.

Sighing, Alana moved to her desk and turned on the large green shaded banker's lamp that had been her grandfather's. Next to it was an antique gold picture frame containing a photo of the tough old gentleman holding the reins of a spirited black Argentine Criollo mare on which sat a ridiculously dressed but beaming girl of nine. The background was slightly out of focus, undoubtedly the result of the unease of the photographer – her mother – at seeing her child on such a steed. That was the only time I wore that gaucho outfit, Alana thought, and only because he insisted for the photo.

Smiling, she opened the top drawer of the desk, lifting out a leather-bound Smythson of Bond Street diary from its false bottom. She had kept diaries since childhood. The earliest ones were filled with the innocent thoughts, little secrets and golden hopes common to young girls the world over. Her narrative skills improved dramatically after the kidnapping. The writing was now stronger and more direct than it had been, and incredibly candid as it related to sexual and business affairs. Of course she excelled, as in everything, with computers, on which she composed reports and speeches. (Every activity of the Ballantrae organization was also scrupulously detailed on flash drives deposited in safe deposit boxes in the United States and abroad.) But her diaries were written in longhand using only white gold Tebaldi fountain pens. Her penmanship was exquisite; the good sisters had taught her well.

Anyone reading the diaries from the beginning would assume that another woman had picked up the tale in later years. Alana, herself, occasionally reread the pre-teen passages, not out of mawkish sentimentality, but rather as a reminder of what she had lost. She found it particularly useful when she and Victor took one of their incredible risks. As she wrote now, it occurred to her that some of those risks might be coming back to roost. She had no explanation for the shooting at the pool, but knew that Jake was right: poor, drunk Tony Goetz was not the target. It was either her, Garza or Keitel – or all three of them. She might have found out had it not been for Jake's courage.

She paused in her writing. Garza and Keitel had reacted predictably and properly, like the mercenaries they were, by going after the assassin. She couldn't fault their instincts. But Jake was quicker – and his only thought was to protect her. She undoubtedly would have been killed had he not reached her in time. She was, of course, grateful, and had proved it repeatedly in the bedroom. But she felt something else. They had shared more than sex in the previous few hours. She knew enough about that to recognize something entirely different. They had made love. He seemed to want to devour her, but unlike her previous partners reveled in her pleasure.

For her part, she couldn't do enough for him. The realization frightened her. Who was Jake Scarne? She had just met him and told him she didn't believe in love and never lost control. I have got to get a grip, she thought. The shooting has unnerved me. But why? I have been through much worse.

She bent to her diary. Whatever happened at the pool was a new and more immediate threat than the Shields investigation. Her thoughts went back to Scarne. She felt safer with him around. She smiled at the absurdity of the situation. Her new lover – and protector – was also hunting her. Her smile faded. But he was now in as much danger as she from the unknown assassin. Perhaps more, since Victor would also want to get rid of him. Business aside, he was undoubtedly jealous. She would have to find a way to protect Jake.

Goddamn him! She had tried to warn him off. But had she, really? When he came back tonight she was thrilled. She wanted him as much as he wanted her. She wanted him now. She couldn't lose him.

Goddamn him! Goddamn him! Goddamn him!

‡

THE CROSS OF LORRAINE

ALANA LOEB GREW up privileged, loved without reservation by her widowed mother and paternal grandfather on a sprawling vineyard outside the city of Mendoza 600 miles west of Buenos Aires. The province, also named Mendoza, generates almost three-quarters of Argentina's annual wine production.

Long-limbed and coltish, Alana was an enchanting combination of spirited country girl and, thanks to the nuns at Saint Adair Scots School for Girls, an incipient and beautiful lady of the manor. When not in school or charming tourists at the winery, she could usually be found in jeans tearing around the countryside on Mirari, her wild mare, or on skis at Las Lenas Mountain with cousins and friends. Utterly fearless, her spectacular tumbles in both pursuits terrorized her mother and delighted her grandfather, who saw in the not-so-fragile blonde beauty the possible realization of the dreams he'd once held for his dead son, his only child. (But Joseph Loeb was secretly grateful that Alana was also showing a growing affinity for golf.)

A German Jew who escaped the Nazis as a teen-ager in the nick of time after Munich, Loeb knew the world was no place for cowards. His boy, Eduard, looked his cancer straight in the eye before succumbing just short of his 36th birthday and his granddaughter was made of the same stuff, unlike her mother. Of course, as a widower himself, Josef sympathized with his daughter-in-law. But he had opposed Eduard's marriage to Catalin Lavalle. Her beauty was undeniable – she had been a finalist for the title of queen of the Fiesta Nacional de la Vendimia, the National Grape Harvest Festival – but her Basque antecedents were murky and her family poor.

"Eva Perón was a Basque," Eduard, thoroughly smitten, had reminded him.

"So was Ché Guevera," Josef retorted.

But, as he knew it would, love won out and Josef would not trade Alana for anything in the world. He fought a constant battle with his daughter-in-law over the child's upbringing. The girl would someday inherit a small empire – the vineyard was but one family holding – built with guile and toughness in a region that rewarded both traits. She had to be prepared. Although still too young to fully understand, Alana knew her grandfather was a feared and respected man in the halls of power in Mendoza, Argentina's fourth-largest city. She had been bounced on many a knee of men addressed as "Senador" or "Comandante." And there were other men who visited the hacienda, usually at night, around whom the servants tread carefully. In the end, all of Josef's planning went for naught. There was one battle that to the end of his days Josef Loeb wished his daughter-in-law had won.

It was annual tradition at Saint Adair that students who excelled were rewarded with a trip to Santiago to visit a sister school in a poor

section of town, as well as the museums and churches of the vibrant Chilean capital. And perhaps, the girls knew, to do a little shopping at the city's famous malls. Most of the students came from the upper grades but occasionally a younger student of exceptional achievement and maturity was selected. At just 13, Alana was the youngest ever chosen – and her mother was adamantly opposed.

"You are too young," Catalin said. "It is a six-hour bus ride, through the mountains. And Santiago is no place for a child."

"But Mama," Alana pleaded. "I ski in some of those mountains. And we will be staying at the Convent of Saint James. The nuns and teachers will be with us the whole time!"

Josef, of course, sided with the girl.

"Catalin! You do not give your own daughter credit for common sense. The good sisters will watch over her like a hawk."

Of that he was sure. Alana's excellent marks were probably enough to have her selected for the trip, he knew, but his generous contributions to the school didn't hurt. Eventually, they both wore Alana's mother down.

"Did you remember to bring fresh underwear?"

Alana cringed as she handed her suitcase to the driver the Mercedes sedan. The man exchanged a glance with Josef Loeb and both suppressed smiles.

"Yes, Mama."

"Two changes?"

"Mama!"

"Cait," Josef said, "let the poor child go. She will miss the bus."

Alana tried to get in the car, but her mother grabbed her.

"Be careful, my baby."

"I will, Mama. Don't worry. All my friends will be there."

"Don't fret," Josef said. "She will be all right. She is a Loeb. It will do her good to see how other children live. And I wager she will buy you something nice in Santiago. And maybe something for her grandpa."

"Oh, I will," Alana said, kissing her mother and then Josef. She got in the car and rolled down the window. "I love you both so much."

†

The bus chartered by St. Adair wound its way along a twisting, forest road. It was a lovely day and the dozen young girls inside opened the windows to savor the fresh air and wave happily at villagers in the small towns they passed. But as they rose higher into the mountains, the air grew cooler and they shut them. Alana was glad of that. There was too much dust and she was wearing her best clothes. Besides, there was now nobody to wave to anyway. They were alone on the road except for a small white van behind them.

"Girls! Please keep it down!"

Sister Rosemary and the other chaperones were having little success quieting the kids, who were chatting, laughing and singing, all the while constantly seat-hopping. "Remember, when we get to Santiago, act like Christian ladies. The children you will visit do not have all that you have."

Alana's best friend, Bella, whispered loudly, "Including bossy nuns."

Alana stifled a laugh as Sister Rosemary stared at them. The nun turned and walked up the aisle, trying not to laugh herself. She lost her balance as the bus lurched to a halt. Students reached out to keep her from falling.

Alana looked out the front window. A truck was straddling the road ahead. At its rear a canvas tarp was thrown open and men with rifles began jumping down. She heard a screech of brakes and turned. The white van had pulled up to the bus bumper. Four men got out. They were also carrying guns. Other armed men were coming out of the forest and converging on the bus. One of them walked up to the door and started pounding on it with the butt of a rifle.

"Open up!"

The driver hesitated and several of the gunmen began firing into the air. Girls screamed and clutched each other as the teachers tried to calm them. Fear was on every face. Finally, the driver opened the door. Two men reached in and dragged out the screaming man. Then they threw him to the ground and riddled him with bullets. His body bounced in the dust long after he was dead.

"God help us!" It was Sister Rosemary.

A grubby bandit wearing a cowboy hat stepped into the bus and looked down the aisle at the terrified passengers. Smiling, he crooked a finger at them and said, "Senoritas, por favor."

The men, laughing, lined up the women and girls against the bus. A few used the barrels of their rifles to lift the skirts of the older girls. A nun who tried to stop them was slapped to the ground. A bandit raised his rifle butt.

"Enough! Stand back!"

The order was barked by a man dressed in military fatigues. The other gunmen fell sullenly silent at the approach of their leader, who stepped casually over the corpse of the driver. He looked down the line of women and girls. A few of them looked hopefully at him. He smiled.

"Take the women into the woods."

Grinning wickedly, his men pulled the women out of line and started to drag them away. Some girls fruitlessly clutched at their arms.

"What about these," one of the bandits asked, pointing to the girls. "They all have bee bites on their chests. We'll make women out of them."

"All right," the leader said. "Take two more. But no children."

The other bandit moved down the line of girls. In a brutal sexual triage, he lifted skirts and jammed his hand down their underwear. He finally reached Alana, last in line. She stood calmly as his filthy hand felt for pubic hair.

"Ah. Peach fuzz. A little young, maybe, but I think you will do, girlie." His hand lingered and his face broke into a leer. What few teeth he had were stained by juice from cocoa leaves.

"Your breath smells like my dog's anus," Alana said, and spit in his face.

The startled bandit withdrew his hand and brought it back to strike her. His arm was grabbed by the leader.

"Pick two others. Go have your fun."

The bandit tried to protest but was pushed away roughly. Grumbling, he grabbed two other screaming girls and dragged them away. The leader turned to look at Alana. He lifted her face with a grimy hand.

"Such beauty," he said. "No tears." He turned to another gunman. "Put the rest of them in the truck. But not this one." He took Alana gently by the arm and walked her back to the white van, where a much older bandit stood.

"My grandfather will find and kill you."

"That is why we do not kidnap for ransom, little one. Too dangerous. I want nothing to do with families." He nodded to the old bandit. "Mateo, put her in the van. Give her something to drink. She is too valuable for the houses in Santiago. She will fetch a fortune in Buenos Aires. I know a place that likes them young and...unspoiled. Don't let any of those animals near her."

He walked away. Alana looked back at her friends being herded to the truck. Screams, and an occasional gunshot, echoed through the nearby trees.

"Don't look back," the old bandit said, not unkindly. "It won't do anygood. Just count your blessings."

Alana turned to him, her face impassive.

Vera Pappas, the Greek-born madam of the most exclusive bordello in Buenos Aires, languished in her spacious bed, carelessly playing with the girl's fine blond tresses and looking at their reflection in the ceiling mirror. The room was adorned with surprisingly tasteful Impressionist art. The faint, but pungesnt, aroma of high-grade Columbian gold

wafted from a recently snuffed cigarette in an ashtray next to the bed.

"You are special, Alana. That is why I have not let them turn you out yet."

"If I'm so special, why can't I have a joint?"

Pappas laughed.

"You are too young, and it is not good for you."

"But I'm old enough to fuck. Is that good for me?"

In the brothel Alana had been singled out for her innocence and ethereal beauty. Her only sexual partners handpicked by Pappas, who was also training boys. Alana knew that while she would eventually be marketed as nubile "virgin" – her hymen surgically repaired to facilitate the illusion – she would also be expected to perform as a sexual athlete.

"It doesn't seem to have done you any harm, darling. I've never had a girl who enjoyed sex as much as you do. I'm pretty sure you will never have to learn how to fake an orgasm." Pappas gently ran a hand over Alana's pubic mound and leaned over and kissed her left breast. "Am I wrong?"

Alana laughed and brushed the hand away. Vera was right, of course. The training had been an enjoyable experience. The boys were handsome and endowed, and tried to outdo each other in pleasuring her. Pappas, a mature beauty in her own right, seemed genuinely fond of all of them, and often joined their romps.

"You are soon to be 15, and will have to earn your living," Pappas sighed, laying back against the pillows. "But it will not be too bad for you, my little princess. You will entertain only the richest. Maybe a young potentate will take a liking to you and bring you home. You will be set for life."

"I'd rather an old impotentate, if it's all the same." Alana yawned and stretched her naked body languidly.

Pappas laughed delightedly. "Oh, Alana. You have been paying attention." She got up and threw on a bright red robe. "Stay here, I have a treat for you."

A moment later she returned with a handsome young boy of Alana's age.

"Carlo!" Alana squealed with delight. "You are back."

The two embraced. The older woman started to leave.

"Where are you going, Vera?" Alana asked. "Don't you want to join us?"

"Not tonight, dears. Enjoy yourselves. I will see you are not disturbed."

Alana and Carlo had been brought to the bordello within weeks of each other. After realizing that rescue was not forthcoming they found some solace in each other's arms. Although their training included other young men and women, as well as private sessions with the madam, they were allowed exclusive time with each other. Highly sexed as she was, Alana enjoyed all her encounters with the other trainees, but none more than those with Carlo.

After an hour of teen talk, they had sex. Despite rising passion, they heard loud noises, including screams, coming from elsewhere in the huge compound.

"No wonder the old bitch didn't want to stay," Carlo said, slowing his movements. "There must be a big party going on. Rowdy bunch. Probably some sado shit."

"Who cares?" Alana said. "Don't move. I want to show you something I can do. We can come together."

A few moments later, as they reached their peak, the door crashed open. Before either could react, a man in black fatigues rushed to the bed and pulled Carlo off by his hair and calmly slit his throat, then dropped him to the floor. Alana screamed and reached for her lover, who was gurgling horribly. The killer grabbed her and threw her on the bed.

"Go easy with her!"

Another man entered the room. A tall, commanding figure holding a smoking machine pistol.

"Put her in my jeep."

Carlo's killer wrapped Alana in a sheet and picked her up effortlessly. She clawed at his face. The other man patted her gently on her cheek.

"Easy child. You are going home. Cover her eyes."

"Yes, Capitán."

She felt herself being carried down the stairs. The man's hand on her face smelled of cordite, the odor reminiscent of her days hunting rabbits or deer with her grandfather.

"Alana, for the love of God, please help me."

Alana ripped away the hand. Vera Pappas and several other men and women, in various states of undress, were kneeling on the floor at the bottom of the stairs, guarded by men with automatic weapons. Vera's hands were lifted in supplication.

"Please talk to them. Tell them what we mean to each other!"

Alana was rushed out the door and placed in the back of a camouflaged Humvee between two burly men. She started to shiver. One of the men shrugged out of his tunic and wrapped it around her. Looking out, she could see that the compound's courtyard was packed with several similar vehicles and was swarming with armed men. Moments later the "Capitán" climbed in and sat across from her. Taking off his own jacket, he wrapped her legs and feet with it. Then he reached into a compartment and brought out a thermos. He poured something into a cup.

"Brandy."

Alana nodded and took a deep swallow, gagging slightly. The men laughed. One of them pounded her gently on the back and said, "Good girl."

"Your grandfather would be proud," the captain said.

"You know Grandpapa?"

"He sent us. It took us a while to find you. But he never gave up hope."

They were interrupted by gunfire and screams from inside the bordello. Then silence. A gunman came to the window. The leader looked at him.

"Meurto," the man said.

Alana looked at the captain.

"Did you have to?"

"Your grandfather is not the forgiving kind, I'm afraid. Now rest. He waits for you."

"And Mama?"

The three men exchanged glances. The captain gently took Alana's hands.

"I'm afraid your mother...passed away."

Alana Loeb had not cried in years. But now a lone tear rolled down her cheek. One of the gunmen patted her on the knee. The leader rapped on the window behind him with his ring finger and the Humvee started to move. His hand dropped to his lap and Alana's gaze drifted to the ring. In its large oval center is a cross with two horizontal bars... the Cross of the Lorraine.

After her rescue, Alana was happy to be home. But things were different. It was more than the loss of her mother. Her presence was a suppurating wound in the community. She was coddled by her grandfather and other relatives, but they – and their retainers – watched her closely, lest she resort to "evil ways." No longer the innocent child, she found herself scrutinizing every word, every gesture for a hidden meaning. She suspected that the boys who came calling knew everything, and wanted it all. Her grandfather treated all of them with barely concealed hostility.

It didn't matter to Alana; mere boys no longer interested her. She took up with a series of powerful men, most married. She soon became an embarrassment to her grandfather and was shipped off to a private religious school in Europe, which she hated, but where she honed her facility for languages, math and science. Eventually, she declared her independence and moved to the United States. In Miami, with its rich mix of cultures and decadent lifestyle, she thrived. She studied the law, slept with all the right men and turned her back on her family, except for her grandfather, who provided her with a liberal allowance and showered her with gifts. Her last sense of connection to her earlier life died when he did. She had no desire to run a winery or participate in any of the other family businesses, most of which had suffered from the neglect of her dispirited grandfather. His "empire" was crumbling and she knew her feckless cousins would finish the job. She sold her interests to them, as well as her beloved hacienda.

Alana Loeb, now free of any emotional restraints, would make her way in America, where her innate intelligence, newfound sexual prowess and disdain for men almost guaranteed success.

In both her personal and business life Alana now assumed everyone's intentions were malignant or at best selfish. It was easy to deal with the world that way and certainly a good way to make a lot of money. If she had a soft spot it was for children, especially the youngest. But ever the realist, she knew she was just compensating for her own truncated childhood. Her relationships in the adult world were all business or sex, and often a mix of both. She enjoyed relationships with many men, some just to further her career, and some more casual. She was not against having fun. But as pleasant and charming as some of her lovers were she never considered that they might love or value her. She understood that their primary instinct was to bed her first and get to know her later. She often gladly allowed the first, never the second.

So it was with Victor Ballantrae. Some of what Alana told Scarne about her recruitment by Victor was true. He had indeed been impressed by her skills and did want her to set up a legal department. But he wanted to fuck her first. He made that quite clear early in the negotiations about her compensation. His approach was so direct and vulgar she told him bluntly he was risking a lawsuit. Never missing a beat, he said he'd make her rich. At the time he had her pinned on the couch in his office. It was after hours; they were alone.

She thought about crippling him. Vera Pappas had taught her a few tricks. *("Remember, precious, it is you who will be using them. Make sure they always treat you well. And, if they don't....")*

Alana knew she could leave any man – even one as powerful as Victor Ballantrae – writhing in pain. Briefly, she contemplated using the notorious "nut knot" on him. But she had done her homework. Ballantrae was the kind of man who could make her rich. So, Victor was pleasantly surprised when Alana's resistance lessened and she became an enthusiastic participant to an activity that moments earlier had bordered on rape (not that he had anything against rape). More than enthusiastic. After they finished, a dazed and sated Ballantrae wondered if *he* had been raped. It was the most incredible carnal experience of his life. And Alana Loeb became his highest paid employee. He never knew how close he had come to being made a eunuch.

As their physical relationship progressed, Alana and Victor realized how much alike they were, and developed a real affection for each other, albeit one always tempered by self-interest. Victor amused her. He had told her about his background. She smiled at his braggadocio, but approved. To her mind, no family worth its salt lacked ancestors who ended up on the gallows. She suspected that in Victor's case the law missed a few.

And for all his faults, Victor was a real man, in and out of bed. For his part, Victor was astounded to realize that Alana ruined other women for him. Previously he had devoured them like burritos. After Alana, he still tried, but was invariably disappointed. She was the best sex partner he'd ever had; there wasn't a second place. She was a different woman in bed every time, a trait that never failed to amaze him. As for the other women in his life; Alana tolerated them, unless she had occasion to meet them. Then it wasn't pretty.

Victor was at one point so taken with Alana that he even broached – in the broadest possible terms and with the caution of a minnow approaching a bass – the possibility of marriage. He might as well have asked her to pass the ketchup. He never brought it up again.

Their partnership, such as it was, had proven incredibly lucrative. Alana Loeb had brought structure and order to the Ballantrae organization, solved the legal and other problems (often with Garza and Keitel's help) caused by Victor's recklessness and penchant for larceny, and managed the flow of political contributions and bribes. With her financial acumen and common sense, she also vetted Ballantrae's endless stream of new schemes.

And occasionally came up with one of her own.

THE MAN IN COACH

SCARNE WAS CONTEMPLATING his nakedness (and was mildly relieved to see that his sexual organs were intact) when Alana padded into the room carrying a tray, on which sat glasses of orange juice, mugs of coffee, pastries and silver bowls with cream and sugar.

"Just leftovers," she said. "I'll make us a proper breakfast later." Placing the tray on the table nearest Scarne she looked lasciviously at his crotch. "Sit up, Jake, I don't want you spilling hot coffee in your lap. I have plans for it."

He pulled up the covers and did as he was told. She sat on the bed next to him. The juice was delicious. It was Florida, after all. And the coffee was strong. She picked up a croissant and moved it toward his mouth. He took a bite then grabbed her hand. He turned it over and kissed the underside of her wrist. Then he bit the soft fleshy mound under her thumb. She cried out, pulled back her hand and handed him the rest of the pastry.

"So, you know about the 'Mound of Love,'" she said.

They ate in silence for a few minutes. When they were finished, she picked up the tray. On her way out the door she looked back.

"Why don't you start the shower? I'll be right in. We can wash each other. Then we can make love all morning. I owe you a bite."

†

Her lovemaking skills were remarkable. Scarne knew that she was a woman of the world, and he had long ceased to be surprised by feminine passion. But Alana took pleasure-taking to a new level. And pleasure-giving, for she was unquestionable generous. She usually allowed him to be dominant – and often near her climax put up a show of joyous resistance – until they were both spent. Then she often took over, first gently, then more urgently as her needs were reawakened. She was multi-orgasmic and very vocal. Afterwards, in post-coital languor, her soothing voice and feathery touches enveloped them in a cocoon of contentment.

Alana never fully let her guard down in these quiet moments, but she alluded to an earlier, tougher life. When he pressed her about her upbringing, she simply said, "My childhood was cut short, Jake, so there is nothing to tell." She clutched him tightly, as if his presence could erase horrible memories.

When he walked into the bathroom, he caught her reflection when he opened the medicine cabinet mirror. She was lying on her side in a *Naked Maja* pose staring after him. Her eyes said everything. But by the time he got back to the bed, she had recovered. She pulled her legs up to her chin and smiled mischievously at him.

"Looking for Viagra, Jake?"

"I'm thinking more in terms of CPR."

But he jumped her and they fell back laughing, and were soon asleep. It was late afternoon when he awoke, again alone. He threw on his pants and walked to the top of the stairs leading down to the pool area. She was sitting at a table, talking on a phone. The crime scene tape was gone and workers were cleaning the area. She waved him down. She was dressed in a shorts and a T-shirt and looked freshly scrubbed. The workers kept glancing at her. He leaned down and nuzzled her neck, inhaling her scent.

"Yes, I understand. I'll be along as soon as I can. It would be easier if I had one of the jets, but I'll make do. I'll see you there. No, I don't think there will be any problem leaving. If there is, I'll call you. Yes. Yes. Fine. Goodbye."

She hung up and looked at him.

"I have to go to Antigua." She took his hand and smiled. ""Darling, come with me. We can stay at the nicest place. I'll only be working a few hours. You know how it is in the islands. Nobody puts in a full day. Oh, please!"

The transformation from efficient businesswoman to sultry lover and temptress was unsettling, but also irresistible.

"Alana, I'm working. Things have happened. The police may want to talk to us."

"By staying with me, you will be working, no? We're not suspects in what happened to Tony." She put her hand to his face. "Please. I need you now."

Scarne weighed his options. He convinced himself that sticking close to Alana was the right move. But he also knew that he just wanted to be with her.

"I'll have to go back to my place and get some things."

"Thank you, darling! All the corporate jets are in use, so we'll have to fly commercial. I'll have the office make arrangements for the flight."

Scarne told her he'd be back in an hour to pick her up.

†

Once back at La Gorce, he packed and called Evelyn.

"How long will you be gone?"

"Day or two, tops."

"I don't like it, Jake."

"What don't you like?"

"First the fellow at the church, now the murder at the pool. Don't you think this is all just a little bit strange?"

Scarne had almost forgotten the incident at St. Christopher's. Something began to coalesce in his thoughts.

"Oh, by the way, Sheldon Shields stopped by. What a nice man."

Scarne lost the thought.

"What did he want?"

"Just said he was in the neighborhood and wanted to drop off a package. Said it was a gift. It's in on your desk. Would you like me to open it?"

"No, I'm in a hurry. I'll do it when I get back. Right now I want you to take something down."

Scarne spent the next 10 minutes dictating an abbreviated version of what he had learned up to that point about Josh's death and the Ballantrae organization. Evelyn made no comment until he finished, and then simply said, "Jellyfish, Jake?"

"Yes, I know. It all sounds so bizarre. But something is not right. I no longer think Sheldon Shields is wasting his money."

"Have you told him any of this?"

"God, no. I haven't come across anything that even remotely looks like a clue. I don't know what, if anything, all this has to do with Josh Shields. I'm just going to keep pulling the string to see what's on the other end."

"Be careful it's not a noose."

"You might want to let Dudley take a gander at your notes. Just in case."

Alana and Scarne were booked to fly American Airlines first-class to Antigua, through San Juan. The traffic was heavy and neither of them spotted the two cars that followed them to the airport. One, a maroon Cadillac, stopped a few lengths behind their cab when it pulled up to the departure building at Miami International. The man in the passenger seat got out with a small carry-on bag and followed the couple into the terminal. He was only steps behind them in line when they picked up their tickets. He spent a lot of time looking at Alana, but neither noticed him. It was to be expected that men stared at her. A moment later he booked the same flight.

The three occupants in the second tailing car had concentrated on the cab carrying Scarne and Alana; they didn't notice the Cadillac. One of them, dressed in a dark blue suit, as were the others, also followed Scarne and Alana at a distance to the counter. Once the line dissipated, he showed his credentials and jotted down the information he needed. When he got back to the car, his companions were also flashing wallets to airport security cops who wanted them to move the car. He climbed into the front seat and pulled out a cell phone to call New York as the car pulled away.

The flight to Antigua took just under six hours. Alana and Scarne, exhausted by their lovemaking, and sedated by food and wine, slept most of the way.

The man following them had a seat far back in coach. He didn't sleep. He was thinking. Unarmed, and with no connections in Antigua, he would have to improvise. He assumed he could get his weapon of choice from a street urchin or someone hanging around the docks. For now, he felt naked without it. Escape from the island might be a problem. But given the well-known incompetence of Caribbean cops, he thought he had a fighting chance. Those idiots in Aruba still hadn't found out who killed that American girl. That was a shame. From all accounts, she was apparently a nice kid.

He then thought of his own loss and his face hardened.

ROUGHING IT

"I'M SORRY, MS. Loeb, but it can't be helped."

The desk clerk at the Blue Water Hotel looked miserable.

"That's simply not acceptable. Let me speak to Maurice."

Scarne walked over.

"What's going on?"

"The suite I asked for isn't available. It's my favorite. I always stay there."

The clerk returned with "Maurice," whose name tag said Hotel Manager.

"A broken pipe," he said, wringing his hands. He had undoubtedly dealt with Alana before. "Water damage. Quite uninhabitable. We are so sorry. But we have a very nice cottage right near the beach. Much larger. At no extra charge. And, of course, you will be our guest at dinner tonight."

"Sounds wonderful, darling" Scarne said, kissing her cheek. "Let's rough it." He didn't care where he slept, as long as it was with this woman.

She smiled.

"All right. Why don't you get us settled? I have something to do at the bank. I'll be back in an hour." She looked at the manager. "Would you arrange a taxi for me?"

"No need, Ms. Loeb. I'll have one of the boys run you into town and wait for you."

The Blue Water was an older resort. The cottage was simple but charming, with a small living room, kitchenette and a well-stocked wet bar. Off to one side was a large bedroom with an inviting king-sized bed, above which a large-paddled fan swirled slowly.

Their bags had been placed on a wicker chest at the foot of the bed. Both rooms had sliders that opened to a common lanai overlooking the Caribbean. A path that connected all the cottages ran down to the beach. Scarne took his toiletry kit into the bathroom. The step-in tub had a dual shower curtain held up by a tensile rod. Someone had left the clothes line extended from its small chrome grommet by the shower head to its receptacle on the opposite wall. It brought back memories of drying socks from the many nights Scarne had spent in motels across the United States. He thought about hanging something naughty for Alana to see but instead released the line and it fell to the bottom of the tub before slithering up sharply into its nest.

Scarne changed into a pair of blue cotton trousers and a light yellow Greg Norman golf shirt. He slipped his loafers back on and poured three fingers of Appleton premium rum over some ice, adding a squeeze of lime and a sugar cube. Twirling the homemade rum punch with his finger, he opened the sliding door and screen to the porch and sat down on a cushioned wicker swivel chair, kicked off his loafers and put his feet up.

He was on his third drink when Alana returned. She took the glass from his hand and led him by the hand to the big bed. Her eyes were hungry. The next several hours were a blur of lovemaking. They hardly spoke. The only sounds were sexual, augmented by the slow swishing of the fan paddles above them. She did things to him, and with him, that he could not have imagined – and, like most men, he imagined plenty. Near the end, she caught a look of surprise on his face, finished what she was doing, rolled away and started to cry softly.

"Alana, darling, what's the matter?"

"Go to hell!"

He lay there confused, afraid to even touch a woman whose body moments before had eagerly accepted every exploration by his fingers and mouth. Finally, he let his hand slip to the base of her spine to the small tattoo, which he massaged gently until she fell asleep.

Scarne was awakened by the sensation of someone gently caressing his face and running fingers through his hair. Her face loomed above him, her blonde hair gently stirring with the breeze from the fan.

"I'm sorry, Jake."

"There's no need."

"You are a beautiful man."

"We missed dinner last night."

"Did you mind?"

He slid his hand to her breast and began playing with a nipple. She laughed as they both watched it harden. He pinched it hard, like she liked. Then she swatted his hand away.

"No! I have to brush my teeth. And I want a shower. I can't imagine what the maid will say about these sheets. You'll just have to wait until after breakfast. I'm starving."

She sprung out of bed as he reached for her, almost falling out of bed.

Just then the phone rang. She picked up the receiver and threw it to him.

"Answer it. It will get your mind off other things."

"Not for long," Scarne replied, but picked up the phone and said hello. He listened for a moment, looking increasingly perplexed.

"And he asked for me by name? Who did he say he was? Yes, you did the right thing. OK. I'll be right over. Thank you."

He sighed, looking at a naked Alana grinning mischievously.

"What is it?"

"The front desk. They said there is a man from Government House who wants to see me. Says it's urgent. He's waiting for me in the coffee shop. Something to do with my passport. Asked me to bring more identification. Can't imagine what it's about. Damned nuisance."

"You must be on a watch list. The custom people are a little slow. They let you in the country and then they question you. Have I been making love to a terrorist?" She covered her breasts and pubic area in mock fear.

Scarne laughed. "You are the one who has terrorized me. I'll be back in a few minutes. Do you want me to bring back some breakfast?"

"Oh yes, something decadent and gooey," she laughed. "We can disguise the sheets."

Scarne pulled on a pair of shorts and a golf shirt and slipped on his sandals. He grabbed his cell phone and went out through the sliders to the lanai and began walking down the path toward the main buildings. He barely noticed a small car idling in the road just below the path. He went down the stairs leading to the main walkway that led directly to the main hotel lobby. He was halfway there when he ran into the hotel manager.

"Good morning, Mr. Scarne. I hope you found the cottage to your satisfaction."

“Yes, Maurice, it’s fine. Can you tell me how to get to the coffee shop?

“It’s just to the left of the lobby where you checked in. But it won’t be open for another 15 minutes. I can have something sent to your room.”

“That’s funny. The desk clerk said a man was asking for me and is now in the coffee shop. Maybe he was confused. Where else would he be waiting?”

The manager frowned.

“I have been on the desk until just now, Mr. Scarne. There was no one asking for you, and we didn’t call you. Are you sure?’

“Listen, it had to be ....”

Scarne stopped. He remembered the car idling near the cottage. Christ! He turned and ran, leaving the manager with his mouth agape. When he reached the lanai, the sliders were open. He heard a muffled scream and the sound of glass breaking. He dove through the bedroom and burst through the door into the bathroom. A man had Alana by the throat and was bending her body backwards over the sink. She was naked, but the man seemed oblivious to that. The floor was wet and slippery from Alana’s shower, and the assailant was sliding on the floor. His hands did not have a firm purchase on her neck.

The man seemed stunned by Scarne’s arrival. But instead of simply letting go of Alana he flung her towards him. Scarne automatically tried to keep her from falling. That gave the man enough time to reach into his waistband. Had he come out with a gun, there was little Scarne could have done about it. It would have been game, set and match. But the hand came out with a knife, which flicked open, straight from its scabbard, like a serpent’s tongue. Except that this tongue was five inches of polished tungsten steel and glittered.

Scarne pivoted and pushed Alana towards the door as the man slashed at his eyes. The turn saved his sight as the blade just nicked his eyebrow. The man immediately whipped his arm in the other direction. A pro. Scarne leaned backwards. The blade missed his throat by a fraction of an inch. The attacker squared himself, preparing for another assault. A small predator's grin bared his teeth. He was in his element, his surprise at Scarne's arrival now an inconsequential memory. Scarne took a quick inventory of his opponent. Much shorter and at least 50 pounds heavier. If it was fat, it was hard fat. The man's agility was obvious, as he rolled on the outside of his feet and swayed toward Scarne, the knife making lazy eights in front of him.

Scarne knew that the knife movement and swaying were intentional. A target's instinct is to back away from an assailant while keeping his eyes riveted on the threatening blade, like a mongoose on a cobra's head. But this cobra had two hands. The blow would come from the empty hand, and would be meant to disorient and stun. Then the deadly thrust. But Scarne was no stranger to hand-to-hand combat and had been taught by the best – Marine non-coms who had killed in many countries. He could almost hear the grizzled gunnery sergeant named Lunsford reciting the Marine Corps mantra: "Always close with an enemy. Straight up the middle, high diddle-diddle." Less effective against a machine gun certainly, but not a bad tactic against a man trying to kill you with a bayonet or a knife. "Never let him thrust it into you," Sgt. 'Lungsfull' as the young Marines dubbed him, had yelled. "Slashes hurt, thrusts kill. Eat the pain and spit it back at the motherfucker."

Scarne suppressed the instinct to back away and looked straight into the man's eyes. Then he charged. He was on the man before he could pull the blade back to where he could stab Scarne straight on. But it did some damage, cutting an ugly rent into Scarne's side. Pain seared his flank. There are no rules in a knife fight, except winning. Scarne jabbed his outstretched fingers his into the man's eyes. He shrieked and lurched backward, hands going to his face.

Scarne grabbed the knife hand but the man, still protecting his face, twisted away. He put his other arm around the man's neck, burying his face in his thick brown hair. Scarne smelled expensive cologne, mingled with sweat. If he let go of the knife hand, he could use his right forearm as a pivot and strangle the man or maybe even break his neck. It would be close. The man could easily get lucky and slash Scarne badly before succumbing.

He never had to make a decision. The man pushed backwards and both men fell into the tub, with Scarne on the bottom taking the worst of it. His back and neck hit the tub wall hard and his breath whistled out between his teeth. He came close to losing consciousness. Only the white hot pain from the slice in his side and the cold spraying shower water kept his mind focused. As he went over, he caught a quick glimpse of Alana backed up against the sink but then had to concentrate on avoiding the knife the man was wildly swinging back over his shoulder in an attempt to slash his face. One thrust barely missed Scarne's right eye and nicked his ear.

The man switched tactics and the blade moved downward out of Scarne's vision and he braced himself for a cut into his groin. He twisted desperately and was rewarded with another bolt of pain, in his upper thigh. He became enraged. He let the man's knife arm go and removed his grip on the man's neck. The man, straining away from Scarne, lurched out of the tub. Scarne drew his knees to his chest and braced his back against the wall. He put his feet on the man's buttocks and pushed his legs out savagely, sending him violently across the bathroom into the vanity and mirror on the opposite wall.

The man's head smashed the mirror, which spiderwebbed, and the knife clattered to the floor. The man was momentarily stunned, both by the impact and the reversal in fortune. But then he whirled around and came at Scarne snarling with both hands, his face a mask of blood and hate. Scarne barely had time to get to his feet before the man had his hands around his throat. He started pushing Scarne into the corner nearest the shower head. Scarne's sandals had come off and his feet began slipping on what he knew was his own blood, now mixing freely with the gore streaming from his assailant's shattered face. He could see bits of glass embedded in the man's cheeks and eyebrows. He put the heel of his left hand under the man's chin and pried the head backwards while at the same time desperately reaching his right hand up to grab a purchase on the shower head. Instead, that hand closed on the circular escutcheon that surrounded the clothesline grommet.

Scarne felt the little button that started the line and grabbed it. He pulled it out just enough to wrap it around the meat of his hand. He swung that hand under the man's left arm and used it to break its grip on his throat. Then he twisted violently to his right and stood up straight. Now his height became an advantage. He also had the added benefit of being in the tub, which gave him a few crucial inches. The man's feet came off the floor and Scarne turned him around easily. The man's arms shot out in a natural reaction to losing his balance. It cost him his life.

In another move that came instinctively from his military experience, Scarne wrapped the line around the man's throat. He placed his other hand on the line and held the man off the floor. The man frantically tried to pry his fingers between the line and his neck. The line was thin but strong, like heavy-duty fishing line, and it bit deeply into the neck. Blood seeped down the throat. Scarne could see the man's eyes bulging in the unshattered portion of the mirror across the floor. He looked into Scarne's face in the mirror as his tongue started slithering out of his mouth. If he was seeking pity, he found none. Scarne was all business now. The strain in his own neck and shoulders pulled his cheeks back in a savage grimace. The man's arms flopped and his legs collapsed, and almost pulling Scarne out of the tub. Scarne's forearms looked like steel cables and felt like they were on fire, but he didn't let up. He had once throttled a sentry who feigned unconsciousness and later shot one of his men in the back. He would never repeat that mistake. He closed his eyes and tried to block out the horrible gurgling sounds.

Soon all he heard was the shower. He looked into the mirror again. This guy wasn't faking it. A warm stream ran down Scarne's leg and he smelled the dead man's urine. The line had disappeared entirely into his assailant's neck. His face was a horrible blue. Above the sound of the shower water and the roaring in his ears, Scarne heard his name, as if from a distance. Alana was still standing naked at the entrance. She hadn't fled. She stared at him with a strange fascination.

"Jake. Enough. For God's sake. Enough."

"Get out of here," he said harshly through gritted teeth.

She lifted one of the complimentary robes hanging on the door and walked out. He heard her on the phone. He tried to let go of the cord, but it had bitten into his hands and he could barely unclench his fingers. He knelt in the tub to lower the dead man to the floor. Water from the shower cascaded over his body. He let it. He felt defiled. It took several minutes to open his hands. Then the pain hit. His side, his leg, both hands. He stood up, turned off the shower with his elbows and stepped out of the tub over the body. He leaned against the sink, breath rasping. The room stank; in death the man had lost control of more than his bladder. Scarne had trouble using his numbed hands and arms but managed to turn on the water in the sink and let it run over his cut and bruised palms. He knew he wouldn't be swinging a golf club any time soon.

Despite the pain, he pulled his wet and bloody shirt over his head. He used it to wipe off his face and then threw it into the tub. His vision swirled and his legs buckled. He pivoted, sank to his knees and vomited violently into the toilet.

†

BAD FOR THE TOURIST TRADE

WHEN SCARNE FINALLY emerged from the bathroom, he found Alana sitting on the edge of the bed with a drink in her hand. She extended the shaking glass to him and he drained it. She stood and put her head into his chest, holding him tight. They stood like that, silently, until they heard the pounding at the door.

"Ms. Loeb! Ms. Loeb! Are you all right?"

It was Maurice. Scarne gently untangled from her.

"Are you OK?" She nodded and he kissed her. "Go sit out on the lanai."

When he opened the door, the hotel manager recoiled. He was with a young man and behind them were two curious cleaning ladies.

"Mr. Scarne. What happened? When you dashed off I didn't know what to think. Then Ms. Loeb called and asked for a doctor."

"There was an intruder."

"My God. Is he gone?"

"In a manner of speaking."

Scarne listed against the door frame. He was woozy.

"Hey, easy, pal," the other man said. "Let's take a look at you."

"This is Dr. Bonamo," Maurice said. "He's a guest. I asked him to help."

Scarne led them into the cottage.

"Would you like me to call the police?" Maurice said.

From his tone, Scarne could tell that the manager would rather not involve the authorities in a simple break-in. It would be bad for the tourist trade.

"Do what you think is best," Scarne said, pointing into the abattoir of a bathroom where a nearly decapitated body hung from the wall.

"Holy shit," the doctor said. Then he turned to Maurice, whose face was a mask of horror. "Call the goddamn police, you idiot." Then he sat Scarne on a chair and began tending to his wounds.

"Nothing appears to be broken," he said after a few moments, "but you're going to need some sutures. I'll wash out the wounds. They don't look too bad. Got any Listerine or alcohol?"

"In the bathroom," Scarne said dryly.

"The hell with that," the doctor said. "How about some vodka"? Then he smiled. "For internal and external use. What the fuck happened in there?"

For some reason the fact that the doctor was a fellow American pleased Scarne. He gave a short version of the event. It took his mind off the stinging of the vodka as the doctor, using some clean pillow cases, patted down Scarne's slashes. He was particularly gentle with Scarne's hands.

"Take a slug of this," he said, putting the vodka bottle to Scarne's lips. "It's a sin to use it only as an antiseptic."

Scarne took a deep swig. The doctor also took a belt.

"Drinking on the job. I hope your malpractice premiums are up to date."

Bonamo laughed and told Scarne to hold a vodka-soaked napkin to the wound on his ear.

A woman shrieked. One of the cleaning ladies had chanced a peek into the bathroom. Maurice was now dragging her away.

"Would you mind looking at the lady on the lanai?" Scarne said. "She has had quite a shock. The man tried to strangle her."

"Your wife?"

"No."

"Way to go."

He spent a few minutes with Alana and came back.

"She's shaken a bit and there's a little bruising to the neck, but she'll be fine. Tough lady."

The local constabulary finally arrived. A tall black officer in a crisp tan uniform, complete with matching cap and baton, started barking orders.

"Don't nobody touch nothing." He walked over to Scarne and pointed at the bathroom. "You do that in there?"

"This man has to get to a hospital," Bonamo said. "He was attacked."

"Who are you, man?"

"I'm a doctor, and I want you to call an ambulance."

The policeman started to object, but Bonamo interrupted him.

"Now!"

The cop turned to an underling and told him to get on the radio.

Bonamo winked at Scarne and said, "My wife and I are in 211. There are a bunch of us sawbones from Pittsburgh down for a week." He picked up the vodka bottle and took another healthy swig. "If you need anything, give us a call. We can send in the Marines if these people start fucking with you." He tapped Scarne gently on a part of his arm that didn't hurt and left.

Another man walked into the cottage and started talking to the police officer. He, too, was obviously an American. He was sturdily built and was wearing a lightweight tropical suit. Scarne could see the bulge under his left shoulder. He heard the word, "Ballantrae" and the cop walked over to Scarne. His whole demeanor had changed.

"The ambulance will be here directly. Apparently the lady was attacked and you saved her life. The man had a knife and you were unarmed. That was very brave. We can wait until later to take your statement."

†

Scarne spent two hours in the local hospital. In addition to the more than 60 stitches in torso and calf, his badly bruised hands were X-rayed and bound with gauze. His upper back and neck, which had taken the brunt of his fall into the tub, ached. He knew that by the next day the pain would be much worse. He was given a tetanus shot and a prescription for Cipro.

"No sense in messin' around," the emergency room doctor said. "If you won the fight, Mon, I'd hate to see the other fella." He also provided some suspiciously large orange-colored pills.

Scarne looked at him.

"Who was your last patient, Secretariat?"

The doctor laughed. "Don't take more than one at a time. No booze."

"Doc, I won't be running at Epsom Downs, but I'm gonna have a drink."

"Well, not too much booze. And don't drive."

When he and Alana finally left the hospital, the kid-glove treatment continued. They were allowed to drive to police headquarters in St. John in a Ballantrae corporate car without escort. Once there, they gave their statements in each other's presence, which broke every rule of interrogation procedure. The man in the suit never left their side. Alana introduced him as the head of security for Ballantrae Antigua. His name was John Merryman, and if ever a name didn't fit, this was it. He didn't smile and spoke mostly in monosyllables. Scarne wondered when Alana had called him. The local cops obviously knew him. It was almost his meeting. And since he obviously answered to Alana, she was subsequently treated very gingerly by the Chief Inspector who debriefed them over a pot of very good tea. To keep up appearances, the Inspector, a distinguished looking and highly starched man named Wilmoth Baldwin, initially was more formal with Scarne.

"And you found it necessary to kill the gentleman by garroting him in the bathroom?" British accent, perfect diction. "Why was that, sir? Could you not have merely immobilized him?"

When Scarne started to reply, Merryman interrupted.

"Don't answer that."

Scarne said, "Excuse me Inspector," and slowly turned to Merryman. "I don't take orders from you. Let the man ask his question."

The room got quiet. The only sound was from an overhead fan and the tinkle of Alana's spoon as she stirred her tea. The Inspector cleared his throat.

"Well, yes, then. Suppose you tell me why you had to kill your, ah, assailant."

"It seemed like the right thing to do, given the circumstances."

He looked at Merryman, who nodded imperceptibly. Scarne turned his attention back to the officer. He had noted the use of the term "assailant." The man was going through the motions. After a few more desultory questions, the interview was over.

"I will have your statements typed up and send someone round to your hotel for you to sign them," Inspector Baldwin said. "This appears to be a simple case of a burglary going bad. The man panicked when Ms. Loeb walked in on him. He got more than he bargained for, and probably what he deserved. I think we may even be able to do without an inquest, although I certainly can't speak for the Chief Magistrate's Office."

"I'm sure we can rely on your judgment in this matter, Inspector," Alana said. "We will be happy to fulfill our legal obligations, whatever they may be."

No questions about who the dead man was. Or why he would break in to a cottage early in the morning, when every guest at a sold-out resort was likely in bed. The man had been well dressed. Then there was the matter of Jake being called to the hotel just before the attack. It was only chance that brought him back in time. Which meant Alana was a deliberate target.

The Inspector wished them "the very best of luck." As they walked out, Scarne remarked, "Next time I kill someone, I'll be sure to do it in Antigua."

Merryman didn't smile, but Scarne thought he came close.

They had to wait almost four hours before a Ballantrae corporate jet arrived from Venezuela. The next commercial flight out wasn't scheduled until the next day and despite the home-team treatment they had gotten from the authorities, Alana and Merryman were anxious to get Scarne off the island. He wasn't about to argue. He didn't know the nationality of the man in the shower and until that was resolved he would feel safer back in the States.

The Ballantrae hanger at the airport was almost as large as the main terminal, and much better appointed. It had a bar, conference room and lounge. Attendants provided them with a decent lunch and some much-needed drinks. The only time

Merryman left Alana's side was to speak to two tough looking men who were obviously security. Scarne had little time alone with her.

There were no local police in sight. Their only visitor was a man who brought their suitcases from the hotel. Scarne went into the men's room and changed into fresh clothes. It was a painful experience, but he felt a lot better for doing it. He thought about asking for his cell phone, which was probably now buried in one of his bags. Then he remembered it had not survived his fall into the tub during the fight. The face was smashed and the whole device now sounded like a baby's rattle when he shook it. He considered using a hangar phone or borrowing someone's cell but decided against it. He'd wait until he got to Miami. Besides, he was dead tired. The adrenaline had long since worn off and the horse pill he had been given at the hospital made him groggy. The double bourbon he inhaled didn't help.

There was a small room off the main lounge for pilots and other staff. It had a couch and Alana went in to lie down. An attendant covered her with a blanket. Scarne made do with a deep leather seat in the lounge. No one gave him a blanket. He put his feet up on a table and was almost instantly asleep. He was awakened by a whining roar in his ear and a sharp pain in his shoulder. Momentarily disoriented, he sat up and lashed out in self defense.

"Hey, easy pal. I'm on your side." Merryman was shaking his shoulder to wake him. The roar was from a mid-size Citation as the craft taxied towards them. The sleek corporate jet didn't pull into the hanger but swung into position just outside, engines idling. "Come on pal, time to go."

"Let's get a couple of things straight, Merryman. I'm not your pal. Touch my shoulder again I'm going to feed you into one of those turbofans."

Merryman took the crankiness well. He was a pro.

"Sorry. I forgot about your arm. Please get on the plane."

"What about the police statements?"

"I wouldn't concern myself about any statements."

‡

RUSH HOUR

THE MOOD OF the rush hour crowd pouring down the stairs at the 34th Street station could best be described as sullen. It was an abominable Spring, with only brief flashes of warmth to break up days of cold drizzle. The jet stream, which had dipped farther south than normal in the winter, bringing absurdly frigid temperatures to the Northeast, was apparently still on vacation.

The elderly man was jostled on his way down the stairs. The steps were slick with muddy rain and he held the railing. There were no apologies as sodden people brushed past him. Manhattan subway riders, not the most civil of urban animals anyway, were being sorely tested, and not only by nature. A recent fire at a crucial Midtown switching complex had severely curtailed service at two major lines that served a million people. One out of every five trains were dispatched and routed manually. In effect, much of the system was being run the way it had been in the 1920's. In some locations, conductors could not leave one station until a dispatcher at the next called and said the line was clear. Needless to say, savvy straphangers avoided the first and last cars.

The fire was caused by a homeless man using newspapers to heat a can of soup right under the antiquated switching box. Even had he cared, the vagrant would probably have assumed the rusted mass of metal and wires above his fire was an abandoned relic from another era. He barely survived the explosion and subsequent meltdown. When the head of the Transit Authority predicted it would take five years to fix the prehistoric wiring in the damaged switching station (which now resembled molasses) the tabloids went berserk. The Mayor's security detail wouldn't let him take the subway to work anymore.

With service so unreliable, many platforms were crowded. The old man, who in normal times would have made his way to the front of the platform so he could exit nearest the stairs most convenient to his destination, was now content to stand near the stairs he had just descended. A young girl with a backpack shouldered past him. She was a cute thing, he noted, who would be even cuter if she ever learned some manners. He almost said something but then caught himself. Kids, he thought. I shouldn't be too judgmental. She's in her own little world. He moved just far away from the stairs to avoid the flow of people, edging closer to the yellow line behind which passengers were supposed to stand for safety.

Many people ignored the line as they craned their necks to look down the tunnel for an approaching train. One of them was the young girl who had bumped him. She kept looking into the void and then down at her wristwatch, a look of annoyance on her face. She was late for something. School? Work? A young man? The elderly man hoped it was the latter. What the girl lacked in comportment she more than made up for in looks. Not for the first time he felt that pang of envy that youth invariably stirs in the mind, and loins, of the old. Oh well, I had my innings. Some young fellow is probably stepping up to the plate with this gal. Lucky bastard. His thoughts were interrupted by a comforting rumbling. A train was heading toward the station. He leaned forward and peeked down the tunnel but couldn't see any headlights. As he straightened up he felt someone brush up against his back.

"Sorry," a man said.

Well, at least someone had manners. He caught a whiff of expensive cologne, which stood out amid the general mustiness. Now he could see as well as hear the train. Its lights shimmered and wobbled in the tunnel as it approached the station.

"It's about fucking time," the young girl just down the platform said.

The old man gave her a disapproving look and smiled sadly. The girl saw the look. The old fart didn't like my language? Who was he to judge? She thought about flipping him a surreptitious bird but then caught herself. He looked a little like her gramps. No harm, no foul, she thought. As the train roared into the station, the man instinctively stepped back a bit, and bumped into the fellow behind him. It was now his turn to apologize.

"Excuse me."

He turned to the right and looked back over his shoulder, catching a glimpse of a wintry smile and a red ski cap. The man leaned past as if looking down the tunnel.

"You're excused," he whispered, and shoved his victim off the platform.

It all happened too quickly for distinct impressions to register with witnesses, which worked in the killer's favor, as he knew it would. The old man tumbled to the tracks silently, too stunned to cry out. He landed on his feet but almost immediately his knees buckled and he pitched forward, arms outstretched to break his fall. He was splayed across both rails. He might have cried out when his face hit the ground, but in any event it would have been drowned out by screams from others on the platform and the screeching from the train's brakes as the motorman made a valiant, if futile, effort to stop the hurtling metal monster. The train finally stopped three quarters of the way down the platform. By then, it didn't matter to the man on the tracks. The motorman leaned out of his cab and vomited, splattering boots and trousers.

After the train came to a halt, Christian Keitel casually dropped a manila envelope between the train and the platform. In the ensuing pandemonium no one noticed. He had considered planting it in the man's pocket before pushing him but didn't want to chance the enclosed disk being crushed by the subway car's wheels. The police would move the train to recover the body and would undoubtedly collect everything from the track area. Since the envelope had the man's name on it, it would be added to his effects.

Keitel pulled off his red cap, pirouetted and started up the stairs, yelling, "Oh my God, a man jumped! Call 911!" When he got to the top, he removed his ski cap and pulled another one out of his pocket – this time it was blue. As he put it on, two cops rushed by him, heading down to the platform. He doubted anyone would chase him, and if they did, they would be looking for a red ski cap. He debated reversing his dual-zippered jacket but decided against it. Somebody might notice him doing that. On the street he hailed a cab. There was plenty of time for a swim in the hotel's indoor heated pool and perhaps a massage. Then a leisurely dinner at his favorite French bistro on 61st Street.

On a subway platform crowded with hundreds of distracted, miserable people, there was only one real eyewitness to the murder. The girl whose curse had earned her the old man's rueful smile had glanced back to see if the old gent was still looking at her. His head was turned in her direction. He was apparently saying something to the man behind him. She saw him pitch forward with a startled look on his face, right into the path of the oncoming train. Later, she would remember certain things. How the old man's arms shot out to brace himself. How he landed awkwardly, almost on his knees and then pitched full forward on his face, an umbrella flung to the side. Then, it was all a jumble of screams, screeching metal, a horrified look on the motorman's face – eyes wide open, mouth making a perfect O! – as the train roared past her.

But she was sure she saw a hand on the back of the old guy, pushing. The man the old guy was talking to. The left arm of the stranger straightening against the old man's back. The black glove. She even started to call for someone to grab the man with the red ski hat, but was drowned out by more screams. And the man lingered. He looked like he was peering down along the side of the car in front of him, not even interested in the man he had pushed to the tracks. But when he started shouting and running away, she excitedly began telling people what she saw. Two young black kids actually believed her and ran up the stairs looking for a red ski cap. But they came back empty handed. They went to get a Transit cop for her. Finding one was no problem. The platform was now swarming with them, in an out of uniform. A couple looked like panhandlers, real skells, but, of course, that was the idea. Two uniforms jumped down to the tracks between one of the cars, and came back looking ill. She thought she heard one of them say, "Just a leg."

Another cop walked up.

"Did anyone see what happened?"

Someone said, "I think he jumped." Others chimed in, turning what they heard second and third hand into gospel.

The girl was beginning to doubt what she saw, but after things settled down she approached a young cop (he was very cute).

"Are you sure, Miss?" he asked politely. (She was cute herself.) When she said she was "pretty sure" he told her to wait around until a detective could take her statement. "Meanwhile, could you describe the man?"

She did, and the young cop spoke into his radio. Cops topside found only one white male wearing a red ski hat, and he was pushing a stroller with a squalling infant whose face matched the cap. A very fat woman, apparently his wife, was berating him. Something about his mother. He didn't appear to be making a getaway, although they wouldn't have blamed him.

When the detectives arrived on the platform, the young cop pointed the girl out. They introduced themselves, and the younger of the two, a tough-looking Hispanic, pulled out a notepad.

"What's your name, miss?"

His voice was mellifluous, not at all in keeping with his appearance.

"Nancy Lopez, like the golfer. I don't golf, though. I mean, I took lessons at Dyker Park with my boyfriend. I just can't seem to find the fucking time. Sorry. He's not my boyfriend anymore."

The cop smiled. The kid was nervous. Better get her back on track before she forgot.

"That's fine. Just tell me what you saw."

She did. It started to come out in a rush, but the detective soothed her to a manageable rate. It was embarrassing to tell them why she was looking directly at the old man, but it needed to be said, especially when one of the detectives pointed out that everybody else was saying the man jumped. Actually, she started feeling pretty good about herself. She was going to miss her first class at Pace, at least, but she was doing her civic duty. She hoped the cute young patrolman noticed. He was still hanging around, a good sign. Then she felt bad. She hadn't even been thinking about the poor old guy who was killed. I wonder what his name was. He looked like my gramps. And how horrible was the death! I bet they won't be able to identify him. That's silly, he was well dressed. He must have had a wallet. I'm glad I didn't say or do anything to him. What a shit I can be! She thought she might start blubbering, but didn't.

The detectives noted the glistening eyes, but were firm with the girl, trying to make sure she wasn't just looking for attention. Her description of the "assailant" was pretty good, considering. White, not as tall as the old man but not short. Blonde hair sticking out under the red cap. High cheekbones. Thin mouth. Blue, mean, eyes. (The detective noted the color and discounted the characterization; you push somebody in front of a train, you are, per se, a mean S.O.B.). Dark blue jacket, pretty nice, but nothing special, dark sweat pants, couldn't see his shoes. She could only guess at his build, what with the jacket and all. But he didn't look particularly heavy. Oh yes, black gloves.

"Definitely not a homeless guy, but no Beau Brummel, either," she said.

The cops looked at each other and smiled. This girl was a bit rough around the edges, but sharp as a tack. They eased up just before she was going to tell them to go fuck themselves if they didn't believe her. They liked her. When they asked her to go down to the precinct and make a more formal statement "and maybe look at some pictures" she took a deep breath and frowned.

"I'm going to miss all my classes," she said, although she had just made up her mind to go home. She felt ill. The shock of what she had seen was finally seeping past the adrenaline. She took a deep breath.

"Listen, honey, you don't look too chipper," the older of the two detective said gently. He reminded the girl of Lenny Briscoe. The show wasn't the same without Jerry Orbach. "Officer Long can give you a ride to the precinct, and then maybe drop you off at home. He'll even give you a note for school."

He hooked his thumb at the cute patrolman, who seemed eager to help.

"No problem," the girl said.

‡

BODY COUNT

A PREOCCUPIED ALANA LOEB spent much of the flight on the phone in the front cabin arguing with someone. Scarne occasionally caught her looking over at him. He had a couple of stiff bourbons with Merryman, who began to relax the further they got from Antigua. Both men thought the Dolphins needed a new quarterback. After a while they nodded off and slept most of the way to the States. Scarne was awakened by the slight bump of their touchdown at Miami International. The small jet taxied to the General Aviation area and pulled into the Ballantrae hangar. Merryman asked him if he wanted to go to a hospital. Though he felt like he had gone a few rounds with Mike Tyson in his prime, Scarne declined.

"Are you sure? You look like a pile of shit."

"Thanks. Just get me a ride to my car, will you?"

Alana came over.

"Jake, I have to go to the office. There is a lot to straighten out."

I'll bet, Scarne thought, with two dead men in three days. He looked pointedly at Merryman, who took the cue and left the plane.

"Alana, we have to talk. When can I see you?"

"Go back to your apartment and rest up. I'll come to you tomorrow."

She kissed him. He started to protest. She put a finger to his lips.

"I can't talk here. Just wait, please. I need you. But I have to go."

When Scarne deplaned, Merryman was standing by a limo where a driver was holding a door open. Scarne told the driver to take him to the parking garage at the main terminal. He retrieved his car and was at Josh's apartment 20 minutes later, and fast asleep five minutes after that.

He dreamt he was in a large room, a boardroom of some sort, with plush carpeting and period furniture. It was dark. He walked toward the end of the room, where there was a light. As he got closer, he saw the bed, with a woman on it. She was clothed, though her feet were bare. At first he thought it was Alana, but the hair was darker. It took him forever to reach the bed. Emma Shields looked up at him, smiling. There were red striations on her neck. Had he done that? He started to say something, but was interrupted by someone pounding at a large red door behind the bed. He hadn't noticed the door before. He woke. The dream receded but the pounding continued.

"Mr. Scarne! Mr. Scarne!"

He threw on his crumpled pants. He was almost at the front door of the apartment when he heard a key in the latch. He looked out the peephole and saw Mario, the concierge. Scarne opened the door.

"Mr. Scarne, I am so sorry. I thought there might be something wrong. The night man said you came in and looked, well, injured. No one saw you come down this morning. And your secretary just called. Said it was urgent. She said you were not answering your cell phone. When you didn't answer the door right away, I grew concerned. I have a pass key. Please forgive the intrusion."

He looked Scarne up and down and his eyes widened. Scarne was bare-chested, and his bandages were prominent. His hands and face were bruised.

"Madre Dios! What happened to you?"

"I took a full swing at a golf ball in a tile bathroom."

Mario looked confused.

"Never mind. Let me grab a shirt. You didn't do anything wrong."

When he came back, he said, "Is there a phone I could use? My cell phone is smashed."

"Please use mine." The concierge reached into his pocket and produced a cell phone. "Just drop it off in the lobby whenever you can." He turned to leave, then slapped his hand against his forehead. "Idiota! I almost forgot. There were two police detectives here looking for you. Said they had tried your mobile phone and your office. Said you gave this address to them. I'm to call if you returned. I have the number downstairs. What do you want me to do?"

For a moment Scarne drew a blank. Then he remembered the homicide cops at Alana's house. They must think he was on the lam. He rubbed his eyes. Still half asleep, he was having trouble focusing.

"You should sit down, Mr. Scarne. Have you eaten? Can I get you something from across the street? That little hotel has a wonderful café. Good Cuban coffee. I don't think you feel much like cooking, no?"

Scarne was famished. He instinctively reached in his pocket and brought out a wad of cash. He pressed it into Mario's protesting hands.

"Coffee, egg sandwich. Make it two, any kind of meat. Keep the change. Don't argue. You've been very kind. Use your key. I'm going to jump in the shower. Call the detectives and tell them you saw me. Do it right away. That way you are covered. I have their cards. I'll call myself in a few minutes."

After a painful shower, Scarne dressed gingerly. His stitches seemed to be holding. He went to the refrigerator and poured a glass of orange juice. He was refilling the glass when Mario came back. The smell of the food made Scarne dizzy. The concierge began opening the bag and Scarne took it from him.

"Mario, you're a lifesaver. I'm fine. You've been away from the front desk too long. I'll take it from here. I'll get the phone back to you soon as I can."

He ushered the still-commiserating man out the door and ate the sandwiches standing at the kitchen counter. The Cuban coffee came in a container but was accompanied by the thimble cups from which it was traditionally savored. Scarne ditched the cups and drank half the potent brew. It was incredibly sweet. He immediately began to feel much better. He picked up Mario's cell phone and dialed his office. Evelyn answered immediately.

"Jake, where have you been? I've been trying to reach you for two days. I was about to call Dudley."

Evelyn was never flustered, but he could sense the tension in her voice.

"My cell phone is broken. What's the problem?"

"Well, you didn't call me about the funeral, so I took it upon myself to send flowers. I thought you'd probably come up for it, but when I didn't hear from you, I became worried. Especially after a Miami Beach detective named Paulo called looking for you."

"Funeral? What funeral? Who died?"

He hoped it wasn't a friend.

"Jake, it was in the papers and all over the telly. Didn't you see it?"

"For God sakes, Evelyn!"

"Sheldon Shields fell under a subway train yesterday. The service is tomorrow. Jake, are you there?"

"Fell under a train?"

He knew he sounded ridiculous. He gulped the rest of the coffee. He could feel his heart racing. It might have been the coffee.

"They're saying it was a possible suicide. I feel terrible. I really liked him. Such a gentleman. Can you make the service?"

She gave him the details and he told her to make travel arrangements. Then he dictated an expurgated version of the events in Antigua. When he was finished, he was greeted with silence. That was unlike Evelyn, who, during his occasional catastrophes, could usually be counted on for at least some droll English sarcasm.

"Evelyn?"

"I'm beyond speechless, Jake. Would you like me to list the bodies in alphabetical or chronological order?"

That was more like it.

"Just get me on a plane this afternoon."

"Shouldn't you see a physician?"

"I'm all right. This coffee will probably kill me before anything else."

"And what about the detective?"

"I'll take care of it. I know who it is. I think it's related to the shooting at the pool. The local cops are probably wondering what I'm doing."

"They are not the only ones."

"I'll need a new cell phone. Mine is toast. I'm using a friend's."

"Just remember to bring your old phone with you when you come to the office. I'll run it down to the dealer and have him switch out the SIM card so you'll have all your contacts. And, Jake..."

"Yes?"

"I'd be careful of my friends."

Scarne wished he had thought to ask Mario to get cigarettes. Sheldon Shields! That made four deaths, all somehow involving Ballantrae. But two of the deaths, while obviously connected, seemed unrelated to those of Josh and Sheldon Shields. Scarne no longer had a client, but he knew he was in the case, or whatever it was, until the end. After all, he himself added to the body count and would possibly have to answer for it some day. Moreover, he had to find out if he'd done anything that precipitated Sheldon's murder. For he was certain it was murder, no matter what the media said.

And he was also certain that Victor Ballantrae was capable of murder. What he was lacking was any sort of proof. He could hardly tell the police that he was suspicious because Victor Ballantrae cheated at golf. But he certainly could report to Randolph and Emma Shields. He owed it to Sheldon to warn them about the kind of person they were dealing with. Randolph would now surely unleash his investigative cannons.

But where did Alana fit in to all of this? He called her office.

"I'm sorry, but Ms. Loeb is unavailable."

"Please find her. Tell her it's Jake Scarne. I think she'll take the call."

"I'm sorry, Mr. Scarne, but Ms. Loeb is traveling. She and Mr. Ballantrae flew out this morning. I'm not sure when they will be back."

Scarne had a sinking feeling.

"Do you know where they went?"

"I'm sorry. I can't divulge that information. I can try to reach her and let her know you called."

He had a thought.

"Can you connect me to Jesús Garza or Christian Keitel?"

"Certainly, but I think they are out of town, too."

"That's fine. I need to speak to their assistant. They gave me an investment idea and I'd like to see if they sent out some follow-up material."

"Of course, please hold."

Even before she came back on, Scarne knew what she would say. And he knew the timing was right.

"Mr. Garza and Mr. Keitel's office. How may I help you?"

"Hello. This is Jake Scarne. I know that Jesús and Christian are in New York, but they asked me to call if I had a question about a trust agreement they are preparing, and I do. How can I contact them?"

"Actually, only Mr. Keitel was in New York, but he already left. Not that he's here now. I believe he is flying to meet Mr. Garza somewhere. Do you want me to try and reach them?"

"No, that OK. It isn't that crucial. I presume they are with Mr. Ballantrae on his trip. They mentioned something about it."

"They did? I don't think they knew they were going. It was quite sudden."

"I bet that happens a lot. Victor sure does get around, doesn't he? So, Christian had to cut short his Manhattan trip. What a pity. How long was he there?" He hoped he wasn't laying it on too thickly.

"Oh, he was coming back anyway. He was only scheduled to be there Monday and Tuesday."

Plenty of time to push a helpless old man in front of a subway train.

"Well, thanks for your help. Tell Chris and Jesús I said howdy. By the way, did they leave word when they'll be back in town?"

"No, I'm afraid not. Next thing on their schedule in Miami is the annual client party next Sunday."

"Oh, yes. They told me I should stop by. I doubt if I can make it, but just in case, where is it again?"

"The Forge in Miami Beach. Starts at 8 P.M. Have you been to the Forge? It's wonderful and Mr. Ballantrae pulls out all the stops."

"Oh, Victor will be there?"

"He never misses it. People come from all over. You should try and go."

"Well, you never know. I just might."

Scarne wasn't looking forward to his next call, but knew it was unavoidable. Detective Frank Paulo got right to the point.

"Where the hell you been, Scarne?"

"I went to the islands for a couple of days. My cell was on the fritz. I just got your message. What's up? You didn't tell me not to leave town."

"This isn't a movie. We don't say things like that anymore. But everybody kind of disappeared all at once, and after a homicide we don't like that."

"Who else?"

"Well, the mistress of the house for one. And the two heroes on the boat, for two and three. You made four. Care to explain?"

Scarne saw no harm in answering honestly. Somewhat.

"I went to Antigua with Ms. Loeb."

"Business trip?"

"Not entirely. But what you should know is that someone tried to kill her down there." He gave Paulo a brief rundown. "Before you ask, yes, I think it's tied to Goetz. But I don't know how. Garza and Keitel weren't with us. Keitel may have been in

New York." No harm in having Paulo check that out. That's all I know." Not true, but enough for the cop to digest.

"Jesus. I thought we were investigating a simple homicide, not a massacre. You think they all skipped?"

"No, they travel a lot. They'll be back. I think Goetz and the Antigua thing came out of left field for them. Something is unraveling. You make any progress on the shooting?"

"Found another olive."

"Come on. I've given you what I've got." Or most of it. "Maybe we can help each other out. I'm not a suspect, am I?"

"A few more bodies in this thing, and I'll put you down as a serial killer."

Scarne was glad he hadn't mentioned Sheldon Shields.

"Antigua going down as self-defense? You know who the guy was?"

"Yes to the first, and no."

"Well, I don't like you for Goetz," Paulo said, "and the other thing is off my reservation, though I'm gonna find out who he was. This is a colossal shit storm. You and I know Goetz wasn't the target. Sounds like it was Loeb. I can tell you that you got the bullet right. Didn't find the rifle. Probably at the bottom of the river. Tracked down the speedboat to a hotel dock, where it had been tied up illegally. Stolen earlier from a marina controlled by some wiseguys. Don't know if that means anything. Garza and Keitel aren't your typical Wall Street types. Nothing much on them. Their history is a black hole, but I've got them pegged for ex-military, maybe mercenary. We're checking with the Feds now. Other than that, bupkus. What are you going to do now?"

Scarne didn't want to tell Paulo about the funeral. He had given him just enough to keep the pressure on Ballantrae and maybe off himself.

"I'm going home to get some rest. This is out of my hands now."

"Sure," the cop said, not believing a word. "And you'll keep in touch, too."

"Of course. And you know how to find me."

"I'll just follow the bodies."

†

CANDID CAMERA

AFTER ARRANGING WITH Mario to ship his golf clubs and most of his clothes separately, Scarne managed to catch a late afternoon flight out of Lauderdale. His battered visage and bandaged hands earned him extra scans and pat-downs from T.S.A. personnel at the airport and nervous glances from his fellow passengers. By the time the plane landed at LaGuardia, he could feel wetness inside his shirt and knew some sutures had given way.

Evelyn had already left, but he had his cab wait while he dropped his damaged cell phone off at his office; she could remove the SIM in the morning. His next stop was the emergency room at St. Vincent's Hospital near his apartment in the Village, where he was re-patched, jabbed with more antibiotics, given some painkillers and told not to drink alcohol. Then he went to Knickerbocker's for a couple of martinis and a steak. Before he left he ordered a third martini.

"This one's for you, Sheldon," he said, draining the drink.

Then he walked, unsteadily, to his apartment and slept. It wasn't until the next morning that he realized that someone had been in his apartment. He stood for a long time at his chess set, reading the note explaining the brilliance of a move he hadn't made, before he angrily swept the pieces off the board.

†

Scarne almost never drove in Manhattan; keeping an automobile there was an extravagance. The airports were easily accessible by limousine, taxi or train. As for road trips outside the city, renting was infinitely less expensive than the cost of ownership. But he loved cars and felt naked without one of his own at his beck and call. Fortunately, the garage rates in Greenwich Village were among the most reasonable in the city.

The underground lot Scarne used was adjacent to his building at 2 Fifth Avenue. He paid a $100 premium over the regular $400 monthly flat "courtesy" rate the garage offered to his building's residents. That got him a sheltered spot on the ground floor next to the cashier's booth, where it was unlikely to be dinged. He also made sure to meet all the attendants and learn their names. His $10 tips on the infrequent days he used the car, plus various gifts (bagels, cookies, cakes, wine), insured that he was treated like family.

The object of all this affection was a perfectly restored and lovingly maintained 1974 MGB Roadster, painted in classic British Racing Green. The two-seater convertible zipped in and out of traffic and was easy to park. And when liberated from congested city roadways, it was an invigorating ride.

When Scarne walked into the garage's 8th Street entrance, the attendant on duty immediately took a set of keys from a drawer. He flipped them to Scarne and began pulling the tarp off the gleaming MGB. It would be folded neatly and stored in a special bin in the cashier shack.

"How's the family, Emmanuel?"

Scarne never called the attendant "Manny," as some customers did. He knew how proud the man was of his Haitian lineage.

"They fine, Jake. We were very blessed."

Among Haitians, losing *only* two second cousins in an earthquake was considered providential.

Scarne smiled and handed him $10.

"You need another letter or anything, let me know."

Scarne had pulled some strings to help get some of the parking attendant's family out of Haiti.

"I 'preciate it. I'd like to get my sister out now. It's lookin' good."

Emmanuel Moliere watched Scarne pull out into traffic. He could hear the muted, but throaty, rumble of the MGB's engine long after it was out of sight. Jake sure loves that car. Good man. Always polite and interested. Even when recouperatin' from something bad. Moliere had seen his share of wounds, from bullets to machetes. Looks like Jake just went through another grinder. Dish it out, too, I bet. He got that look in his eyes.

St. John the Divine, in Fairfield, Connecticut, serves one of the richest congregations in the nation. The service for Sheldon Shields was set for 11 A.M. Cremation would follow. Parking near the church was nonexistent, so Scarne flashed his P.I. license to a town cop directing traffic and said he was on the family's security payroll. He was directed to a handicapped spot in the lot right next to the church. Given his bruises, he didn't think the consideration was completely undeserved.

As he expected, the church was filled. He was standing in the back when Emma Shields came in with the family. When she spotted him, a look of disbelief, then consternation, crossed her face. It wasn't the reaction he expected, but maybe he'd surprised her. The service itself was simple and moving. Emma and her father gave elegant eulogies that brought out the humanity of Sheldon. Scarne was surprised at the emotion shown by Randolph as he remembered his brother and their early years together. Emma held up well, until she noted that Sheldon, his wife and son – "the entire family" – were all gone within a few months of each other.

"Uncle Sheldon is now with Aunt Adele and their beloved Josh," she said, her voice faltering briefly.

That kind of loss, Scarne knew, could not be completely mitigated by anything he accomplished. But it would be something.

A choir sang "Battle Hymn of the Republic," undoubtedly in honor of Sheldon's fascination with the Civil War. Finally, a piper played "Amazing Grace" and then everyone filed out. Randolph Shields and the rest of the family congregated at the foot of the stairs outside the church talking to well wishers as the limousines pulled up. Scarne started to walk over to offer his condolences when Nigel Blue intercepted him.

"Mr. Shields would like to see you at the house. Follow the cars going back for the repast."

It was less an invitation than an order.

The Shields family compound was located in Southport, a tony Connecticut community on Long Island Sound that is part of Fairfield, which itself is 20 miles east of Greenwich. After entering the estate grounds, Scarne drove up a long tree-canopied road toward a huge gabled mansion that could only have been Randolph's. The access road itself was flanked by acres of fields, on some of which white-coated valets were parking cars. After dropping off his roadster with a valet who miraculously knew how to drive stick, he walked through a foyer to a large dining room, where a groaning board heaped with food was beginning to attract the attention of the growing crowd. A bar set up in the corner was doing a brisk business. Scarne had just started nursing his wounds with a stiff bourbon when Nigel Blue spotted him.

"Mr. Shields wants you in the library."

They walked toward the back of the house and stopped in the hallway outside a small den. Blue handed Scarne a DVD disk.

"You're to watch this." He pointed to a small entertainment center in the den. "Then go through there." With a hook of his thumb he indicated the double doors opposite the den behind them.

Blue left. What the hell! But Scarne did as instructed. The TV was already on and he inserted the disk. Video images appeared on the screen. They weren't of the best quality but were clear enough so that the hairs on the back of his neck rose, and he got a sick feeling in his stomach. The first 10 minutes of the disk showed a couple making love. It was shot from above, at a slight angle. The action had been spliced, as there were quick cuts to various positions and activities. There was a strange, constant flickering throughout, as if a camera shutter was rapidly opening and closing.

Scarne felt sweat running down his back. Only moonlight and ambient light streaming over the bed made the activity visible. But the light and the shadows – and especially the damnable flickering – had the effect of making the couplings highly charged and erotic. It was, Scarne thought wildly, like watching an old black-and-white stag film or a peep-show at a carnival. Could the pair of lovers be identified? There were blessedly no sounds. But Scarne's hopes were soon shattered by the last few minutes of the video, shot in the morning as dawn began bathing the room.

Tangled in the sheets in post-coital exhaustion were he and Alana. And the flickering continued. What kind of camera produced that effect? Then Scarne remembered the fan over the bed. That's where the bastards had placed their camera. The flickering was nothing more than the fan's blades lazily cooling the lovers. But who would do something like this? Scarne's mind raced. The room had been a last-minute change. Or had it? And what was the connection with the man who tried to kill Alana in the shower? Scarne felt his rage building. He had been played the fool. Then he forced himself to calm down. His humiliation was not over. He ejected the disk and put it in his jacket pocket. He then walked out to face the music.

CELL CLONE

THERE WAS A fire blazing in a stand-up hearth in the library. Randolph Shields was standing with his back to a large desk, looking out a bay window towards the fields beyond. A rich man's view. Scarne could see horses doing horsey things. The word gamboling popped unbidden into his head. Shields turned when he heard Scarne enter. He was holding a manila envelope.

"Emma, I wonder if you would let us have a few moments alone?"

She was sitting in a high backed chair.

"I'd rather stay."

"I don't want you to hear this, Emma."

"Dad, I'm as much a part of this as you are. I saw the disk, after all."

Jesus, Scarne thought.

"Suit yourself. You're a big girl."

Shields walked over to his desk. He did not sit down and he didn't offer Scarne a seat. Emma crossed her legs and put her hands in her lap. Scarne made a concerted effort to not look at those legs. It was, he reflected, hardly the time. Instead, he looked at her face and read disappointment and pity in her eyes. He would have preferred anger. Randolph provided the anger, tossing the envelope on the desk toward Scarne.

"Open it."

It was addressed to Sheldon Shields. In it were glossy photos and a single sheet of note paper. The photos were stills taken from the disk, carefully chosen to minimize interference from the fan. The note was neatly typed:

"Dear Mr. Shields:

Do not trust Jake Scarne. You have placed a great deal of faith in him. As you can readily see, that faith was misplaced.

A Friend"

"I don't suppose you know who sent this to your brother."

"I don't think it matters. It was found on the tracks near Sheldon's body. My brother sent you off on a wild goose chase. You saw a big payday, complete with a vacation in the sun. You're the kind who takes advantage of other people. Sheldon trusted you. When he saw the disk and the photos it robbed him of his last hope. He was very fragile emotionally. He never got over the death of Josh and his wife. This betrayal must have devastated him. He killed himself. I hope you had a great time with your little strumpet."

Strumpet? What was this, a Dickens novel? But Scarne held his tongue. Emma had remained silent during the tirade, but now she spoke.

"Dad, we're not sure it was a suicide. It could have been an accident. And one detective said they were looking into the possibility Uncle Sheldon was pushed. What Mr. Scarne did was despicable but until we're sure what happened we should leave the hyperbole out of this."

It was a rational statement, by a woman not afraid of her famous father. But the only word that stuck with Scarne was "despicable." He would have preferred 50 lashes. Randolph

Shields shook his head dismissively. Before he could spout more Victorian dialogue, Scarne cut him off.

"Mr. Shields, your daughter is right. I am despicable." They both stared at him. "But that doesn't change the fact that I think your brother was murdered, as was his son before him. There are too many dead bodies turning up in this case to think otherwise. Four, at last count, including your brother. Yes, it's possible he thought I had been stringing him along and he killed himself. But it's just as likely that the people who sent him the photos wanted you to think that. I won't be able to sleep until I find out how he died."

"It doesn't look like you get much sleep anyway," Shields said.

A cheap shot. As badly as he felt, Scarne didn't need any moral lectures from "Randy" Shields, whose own sexual exploits were legion. But he let it go.

"Who else died?" It was Emma.

Scarne told them everything. He saw the incredulity on their faces. When he finished, Shields spoke.

"Victor Ballantrae is a tough, shrewd businessman, with more money than God. You expect me to believe that he is a killer. The only one he might reasonably want to kill is you, and I'm not sure I'd blame him. You diddled his chief of staff, who is probably his mistress, and did your best to damage his reputation. And for all that, he's not holding it against me. He was one of the first of my friends to offer his condolences after Sheldon's death. He reiterated his support for my company. He knew my brother was mentally unbalanced. You must think I am! You actually think that by spinning this fantastic yarn you can get me to continue funding your so-called investigation?"

"How do you explain the murder at the pool and the man I killed in Antigua?"

"Probably a jealous boyfriend," Randolph said. "Now, get the hell..."

"Dad, just a second," Emma interjected. "Do you have any proof of anything, Mr. Scarne?"

"Not yet."

"There is no 'yet,' Scarne," Randolph shouted. "You're fired. I don't want you anywhere near my family. You've done enough harm to us. And I intend to take this matter up with the proper authorities. I'm going to get your license, if you even have one. And I'm going to recoup every cent of the money my brother paid you. I'm sure he never expected you to buy the most expensive piece of ass in Miami with it. Now get out! Your appearance at Sheldon's funeral was an abomination."

Scarne could have pointed out that Randolph wasn't his client, so he couldn't fire him. What was the point? He couldn't look at Emma. So he turned and walked out.

Scarne got back to Manhattan at 4 P.M. He waved Evelyn into his office.

"Things may get rough around here for a while. Randolph Shields may try to shut us down. And I may have given him enough ammunition to do it. Get Don Tierney on the phone for me."

Evelyn had a strange look on her face.

"Jake, there's a problem with your cell phone."

"I know that. I told you to get me a new one. Use the land line, for God's sake. What's the matter with you?" It was the first time he'd ever raised his voice to her in anger. He immediately apologized. "Sorry. It's been a rough couple of days."

"You don't understand, Jake." She held out her hand and opened it. In her palm was a tiny wafer. "The phone tech found this in your old phone when he switched your S.I.M. card. He said it was very sophisticated. State of the art, he called it. He also said you probably know what it is."

Scarne did. He picked the miniature transceiver bug out of her palm. His cell phone had been cloned. Someone had been listening in to all of his calls. But for how long? He'd only bought the phone recently and the last time the tech had switched S.I.M. cards nothing was amiss. Since then it was never out of his sight or not on his person. Then he remembered the locker attendant at Pelican Trace who told Scarne that the club didn't allow cell phones on the course. He'd left it in his locker. Except there was no club rule. They'd been one step ahead of him. Bugging his phone, burgling his apartment.

"What are you thinking, Jake?"

He looked at Evelyn. He hadn't used the phone much, except to make appointments in Miami, and most of those preceded the golf match. But he did call Evelyn and dictate a memo on his progress. And in that call he mentioned that he had not yet reported to Sheldon Shields. Had someone decided to cut off the investigation at the head? Killing Scarne would have raised too many questions. Sheldon, and probably even Randolph, wouldn't have let that go. But killing Sheldon and disgracing Scarne solved everything. It was a brilliant gambit. And it looked like a winning one.

"Jake?"

"Evelyn, I need some time to think. Don't call Don just yet. Where is my new phone?"

"Right there." She pointed to a small brown package. "On top of the gift that Sheldon Shields dropped off." She gave him a concerned look and walked out, closing the door quietly.

I haven't exactly covered myself in glory on this one, Scarne thought as he idly pulled the package over. I never took the case seriously from the beginning. Basically went through the motions. Perhaps that was a bit harsh, but he didn't feel like cutting himself any breaks when it was possible he'd gotten his client killed and destroyed his own livelihood.

He opened the cell phone and checked its contact list. Everything seemed to be working. He began to unwrap the package.

What about Alana? Did she know about the video? That seemed unlikely. After all, it was he who insisted they take the cottage when she was arguing with the hotel manager. And he was convinced that their lovemaking was genuine. Of course, he had saved her life in Miami, and she expressed her gratitude physically. But the things she said in bed, the reactions to his touch, the murmurs, the tears, the pure happiness, seemed to be as surprising to her as they were to him. And, now, after saving her again from the man in the shower, he was sure she loved him.

Inside the package was a book, swathed in hunter-green tissue paper. There was a note in a small Crane envelope:

"Dear Jake,

Thought you might like a copy of Pullen's "Twentieth Maine." It's a first edition. I had two. I kept the one I gave to Josh. I wanted you to have mine.

Best,

Sheldon"

Scarne stared dully at the book and felt sick to his stomach. What must that bereft old man thought of him? But he still couldn't believe that Sheldon Shields killed himself, even if he viewed the video. Still, deep in his gut, he knew that whatever happened on that subway platform was his fault.

He had to prove it was murder. He owed that to Sheldon. But what if Alana Loeb had a hand in that murder? And Josh's?

The woman he now also loved.

DONUTS TO THE RESCUE

THE PHONE STARTLED Scarne. The clock radio said 9:24. He sat up quickly in bed. That was a mistake. The searing pain behind his eyes, parched throat and stomach biliousness of the hangover almost made him forget his cuts and bruises. Sweating and with heart racing from alcohol dehydration and nicotine, he took the phone to the window and opened the blinds. Another mistake.

"Mother of God," he said, momentarily stunned by the glare.

"No, it's only Evelyn. Tough night, have we?"

"I didn't get the license plate of the truck that hit me."

"I think you'd better get in here. We've got visitors."

"Get rid of them."

"They all have badges."

"I told you Randolph Shields would play rough."

"I don't think he's behind this. Two of them are F.B.I. and the third is a Seattle police detective."

"Seattle? Jesus, I wasn't that drunk last night."

"Perhaps you should put your wit on hold for a while. It's Seattle Homicide. I told them all you were running late."

"I can be there by 10:15. Order up lots of coffee and donuts."

"The donuts are beneath you, Jake."

"They're not for them. I need a sugar fix. And some orange juice."

"You poor baby. How about an intravenous line?"

Seattle Homicide? What the hell was going on now? Scarne reeled into the kitchen. The bile in his stomach rose at the sight and smell of the open and almost empty bottle of bourbon on the counter. He quickly grabbed a blessed Coke in the fridge. He used the Coke to wash down a handful of vitamins as he headed to his bathroom. Throwing off his shorts and undershirt, he turned on the shower and let it run on his head and body even before it warmed up, trying as best he could to keep his dressings dry. The shock to his system started to clear up the cobwebs. In 15 minutes, after downing four Advil, he was out the door. He estimated he could stay a half hour ahead of the hangover's inevitable return. On the cab ride to his office Scarne thought over his behavior the night before. It had been years since he let himself go like that.

"We're here, mister."

Scarne came out of his trance. He was feeling shaky. The hangover had closed the gap. Black coffee and an artery-clogging donut were now necessities. When he entered his waiting room, he was surprised to see it empty. He checked his watch. It was just 10:10. Evelyn walked out of the small conference room.

"I put them in there. Sit at the head of the table. I left the blinds up. The light will be in their eyes." She looked at him appraisingly. "And if they don't lock you up, take the rest of the day off."

"I intend to. Thanks, you're a pip."

He started toward the conference room, and Evelyn said, "Wait a minute."

She went to her desk, opened the top drawer and grabbed a pack of cigarettes and a lighter. She slipped them in the right side pocket of his jacket.

"Just in case," she said.

He opened the door to the conference room. Bookshelves lined one wall. Centered on the other wall was a large wooden-framed Mercator map of the world, dated 1939. It had been his grandfather's. In the corner of the room nearest the door was a small table, on which sat a Dunkin' Donuts coffee box and a tray containing what looked to be two and a half donuts. Since Evelyn never bought less than a dozen, it was apparent that these lawmen had not been insulted by the gesture. One was just closing up a cell phone and brushing some white powder off his jacket. Another was reading the backs of books on one of the shelves. He turned to Scarne.

"You must have all the Spenser novels. My wife loves the fact he's so loyal to his girlfriend, what's her name, Susan something?"

He walked over to Scarne and extended his hand.

"Special Agent Jack Casey, Federal Bureau of Investigation. The guy cleaning sugar off his pants is my partner, Tom Valledolmo. And that's Noah Sealth, Seattle Homicide."

A large black man in brown pants and a tweed sports coat nodded to Scarne but made no effort to rise or shake hands.

"Silverman," Scarne said. "Her name is Susan Silverman." He walked to the head of the table and shook the other Federal agent's hand. "She has Spenser wrapped around her finger."

"That's funny, coming from you," Sealth said, chewing a cream donut.

"What the hell does that mean," Scarne said. "And what's going on? Where's the CIA and the Secret Service?"

"With you, only a matter of time," Sealth said.

The two Federal officers put their cards on the pad at the head of the table. Sealth rather dismissively threw his in the general direction. Scarne didn't even look at them. These guys were right out of central casting. Besides, Evelyn would have vetted them. He reached for his wallet. Casey waived him off.

"Your secretary gave us your card. She's very good, by the way."

Scarne walked over to the coffee service. The only donuts left were plain dunkers. Damn! He drained a small bottle of orange juice and poured a coffee. Then he sat at the head of the table and looked at the black cop from Seattle.

"You flew all the way in from the coast to eat the good donuts?"

"I was starving. I caught the red eye and been in meetings since. All the F.B.I. had was granola and shit. You could tell these guys are deprived. They hit those sinkers like they were going to the chair."

Evelyn walked in holding a napkin with a jelly donut covered in sugar and half a caramel cream donut with sprinkles. She put them in front of him.

"You don't need the other half of the cream donut," she said. "It is delicious, though."

He could have kissed her. She smiled at the other men and walked out.

"She's very, very good," Casey amended.

All were now seated. Sealth was eying the jelly donut, so Scarne took a quick bite, and then to be careful, took a nibble out of the cream one as well.

"Well, I guess you want to know why we're here, Mr. Scarne," Casey said.

Scarne nodded, and took a long sip of his coffee. It was hot and strong.

"Does the name Carlo Brutti ring a bell with you?"

The question came from Seattle. Scarne drew a blank on the name, although he didn't like the sound of it. When a cop asks about a guy who sounds like a regular on the *Sopranos*, he's probably not talking opera.

"No. Should it?"

"Well, we thought it might," said Valledolmo, "since you strangled him in a bathtub in Antigua."

THE BLADE

SCARNE THOUGHT HE took the news well, considering. Carlo Brutti was obviously someone he shouldn't have killed. He hoped the sugar and caffeine would kick in soon. He had to start thinking clearly.

Valledolmo put a briefcase on the table, opened it and slid a photo to Scarne. It showed a photo of burly man in an expensive suit walking down the stairs of what appeared to be a courthouse. He was smiling at a gaggle of reporters surrounding him. It was the man from the shower.

"Does this refresh your memory?"

"He didn't look this happy the last time I saw him," Scarne said, testily. "And I forgot to ask his name while he was slashing at me with his pig sticker." He was tired of being everyone's punching bag, even if he deserved it. "Now, before we go any further or I run out of donuts, whichever comes first, tell me what this is all about. If you know the man's name, you know it was self defense and I was cleared by the local authorities."

Sealth sat up loudly and pointed a finger at Scarne.

"Listen, dickwad, we'll do the asking. In case you don't realize it by now, you're in deep shit. I don't give a rat's ass what a bunch of Caribbean craptown constables think happened. Local authorities, indeed. Those guys wouldn't know a homicide from a hemorrhoid, and they're bought and paid for anyway. Brutti was Seattle beef and I don't need any New York hotshot P.I. who can't keep his dick in his pants dripping all over my investigation. These two Feebies may be impressed by the fact you're a pal of the police commissioner, but he ain't my commissioner, so I don't give a flying fuck."

Should have let him have that jelly donut, Scarne thought. A familiar hot flash began in his chest and spread toward his face. His blood roared in his ears. Could he slug an out-of-town cop? As he started to rise Casey jumped up.

"Whoa, hold it, Mr. Scarne. Please sit down. We're only here to gather information." He smiled pleasantly. "We're not trying to be confrontational."

Sealth's scowl accented high cheekbones that hinted at a mix of races. American Indian?

"I want to apologize for Detective Sealth," Casey continued. "He's had a couple of long days. Probably jet lagged. Anyway, Mr. Scarne ..."

That was as far as Scarne let him get.

"Cut the crap, Casey. Aside from some minor jurisdictional problems – a guy from Seattle killed by a New Yorker in the Caribbean – you can't do good cop, bad cop with three cops. What's he here for?" Scarne pointed at Valledolmo. "To hold you guys apart when you come to blows?"

Casey sighed.

"Hell, we'll start over. I didn't think it would work. You were on the job once and we know all about your reputation, good and bad. But I figured we'd take a shot. But listen, Jake ... can I call you Jake?"

"Sure." He smiled at Sealth. "It's a step up from dickwad."

Casey shook his head, and went on. "This is serious business. You may not have done anything wrong, but the Brutti family controls the Mafia in Seattle. Carlo was heir apparent and chief enforcer."

"Skip the horse-head-in-the-bed crap," Scarne said. "I've had a rough week. It sounds like I saved you a lot of trouble. What's the problem?"

"The problem is Victor Ballantrae. You may have saved *him* a lot of trouble and we'd like to know why?"

The name had its desired effect. Scarne looked at the three men and considered his options. He had to balance the possibility of learning things that could save him weeks of legwork, and perhaps his life, against revealing the confidences of his client. Of course, the client relationship had been severed by a downtown local. Scarne was now his own client. An unpleasant thought, given his recent incompetence. But at least the checks would clear.

"Look, fellas, I'd bet we're on the same side of whatever this thing is. You didn't come here to arrest me. I'll play straight with you and not lawyer up if you give me some idea of what this is all about."

Casey looked at the other two men. Valledolmo shrugged and Sealth said, "Why not? He probably knows more than we do."

Casey got more coffee.

"After the financial meltdown in 2008," he said, "the Bureau set up a special unit here in New York to look into financial crimes."

"Too bad it didn't do it *before* the shit hit the fan," Sealth said.

"Spilt milk. Anyway, Tom and I decided to take another look at some anonymous tips and rumors that the S.E.C. and other regulators had previously ignored. Victor Ballantrae popped up on the radar."

"What kind of rumors?"

Casey waved his hand dismissively.

"I don't want to go into details, but the usual crap: money laundering, insurance fraud, Ponzis, etc."

"I hear the West Coast mobs use his offshore bank to hide cash," Scarne said, "including millions of dollars stolen from the government of the Ukraine in the 1990's."

The three men stared at him.

"See, I told you he knows shit," Sealth said.

"Where did you...?" Valledolmo blurted. "Oh, forget it. You're not gonna tell us."

"In any event," Casey said, resignedly, "we don't have nearly enough hard evidence for wiretaps or bugs. And Ballantrae is a hard man to pin down. He travels around a lot on his own planes. But his base is in Miami so we asked our field office there to keep an eye on him. They put a semi-permanent tail on him and his close associates, some of whom have some pretty interesting jackets. When you showed up to play golf with him you became a person of interest, as they say. Figured it was a business deal of some sort."

"Don't take this the wrong way," Valledolmo said happily, "but the agents figured you for a hood."

"Some of my best friends are hoods."

"No surprise there," Valledolmo said. "Anyway, Ballantrae does a lot of business on the course. Tough to be overheard. But we got some nice long- range video of the three of you. The S.O.B. cheated his ass off, you know. Hope you weren't playing for a lot of money. Great shot on 18, though. Took real balls. What did you hit?"

"A 2-iron."

"A 2-iron! What, you planning an insanity defense for the Brutti thing?"

"If you guys are through," Casey said, exasperated, "can I go on? When Ballantrae hopped on to a corporate jet after your match we put a loose tail on you. Picked you up the next day when you headed to Loeb's house."

"Voila, your first dead body," Sealth said.

"There's obviously a party going on," Casey went on. "All sorts of shady characters. Too good a chance to pass up. Our Miami guys braced the caterer. After they asked him about his staff's green cards, he was happy to give a waiter's uniform to an agent, who waltzed in with an itty bitty camera. By day's end he has photos of everybody. Very thorough. Some topless gals he photographed more than once."

"I don't remember anyone taking photos at the party."

"You didn't pick up our tail in Miami, Boca Raton and Antigua either. That's what happens when your mind is on other things, my friend."

Scarne wasn't prepared to argue that.

"Our 'waiter' took his shots from inside the house. Just slipped up to the second floor, picked a room with a view of the pool area and fired away."

"I don't suppose you have any shots of the murder? Your man must have thought he died and went to heaven to be on the scene."

"We wish. He was taking a leak when that happened. And before you ask, the only boat in the background in any photos is the cabin cruiser Garza and Keitel used to chase the speedboat. Oh, yeah. We know all about them. They were identified early on in our database. Lovely couple."

He turned to Valledolmo.

"Tom, fill him in."

"Jesús Garza worked for Cuban intelligence. He specialized in infiltrating the expat community in Miami before he decided there was no future in that line of work, at least financially. He switched sides and gave up his network. Half the murders in Miami for a decade were political reprisals disguised as gang warfare or muggings. Some he did personally, to validate his bona fides and take care of any old mates who suspected him."

"Murder is murder. Why didn't someone stop him and his friends?"

It was Casey who answered. He looked unhappy.

"I know. It sucks. But the feeling at the time was that they were doing God's work. What can I say? Miami isn't the United States. Anyway, Garza made a name for himself and went free-lance. Somehow, he was recruited by Ballantrae. He brought Keitel on board later."

Scarne looked at Valledolmo.

"What's his story?"

"Christian Keitel is former German military. Was in the KSK Special Power Commando, an elite unit trained for secret combat operations. It was active against Eastern European countries during the Cold War. Highly decorated. Apparently fearless. Came to this country about 10 years ago. Lots of Germans gravitate to Florida. It's heaven to them. We figure he met Garza in one of the gay hot spots in South Beach."

"So, Garza and his boyfriend are Ballantrae's muscle?"

"More than that. They apparently have some operational responsibilities."

"How did you finger me? You get my name from the Miami cops?"

"Hell, no," Casey said. "From your wallet. Remember the waiter who brought out your shirt? That was our guy." He was justified in bragging; the man had been good, playing the scared illegal to the hilt. "He didn't wait around to collect anyone else's name. Didn't want to let the locals know we were interested in Ballantrae. You know how city cops can screw things up." He glanced at the Seattle detective. "No offense, Noah."

"None taken," Sealth said mildly. "But they might like photos of the crime scene."

"We checked the photos. Nothing in them that had anything to do with the murder. Mostly head shots taken before Goetz bought it. Homicide and CSI talked to everyone and took their own pix. We wouldn't have added anything."

"Right," Sealth said, with a tinge of disgust.

Scarne asked, "How did your man leave without being interviewed?"

"He changed clothes in the catering truck and flashed his credentials to the uniforms doing perimeter security," Valledolmo said. "They thought he belonged. He just walked away."

"I didn't know you from Adam," Casey continued, "but my boss recognized the name. She had trouble believing it, until your photo came through. But, lo and behold, it's the famous, or should I say, infamous, Jake Scarne, P.I. extraordinaire."

"Lo and behold?"

"He talks that way," Valledolmo said. "I take it out of our reports."

"If I might continue," Casey said. "Nothing piques our interest like an assassination in broad daylight while we're passing out canapés, so we were able to free up some more assets to follow you and the delectable Ms. Loeb to Antigua. That was my boss's idea. Not one of your bigger fans, I might add. She said that you could fuck up a wet dream. But she also said that you always seemed to be where the action was and probably wouldn't do anything too illegal. So, we went with it. At first, we thought we drew a blank in Antigua. Our guy reported that you seemed to just having a good time with the lady."

Casey saw the reaction and held up a hand.

"Hey, I'm not being judgmental. You're over 21, even if the lady is bad news. Nobody is blaming you. I was pretty sure the whole thing was a waste of time from our angle. Our guy was actually getting antsy to go home."

"They have it cushy in Miami," Valledolmo added, sourly.

"But then you killed the guy in the tub," Casey continued, "and it turned out to be Carlo 'The Blade' Brutti."

"The Blade," Scarne thought. That explains the shower fight.

"Body No. 2," Sealth said. "You were averaging being at the scene of a homicide about once every 36 hours. Course, it helps when you kill somebody yourself. Speeds things up. You can see why we might want to talk to you."

They were having a fine time, Scarne realized. Wait until they hear about Sheldon Shields and his son. He tried to buy a little time to think. He got up for more coffee. Jesus! Princess Diana in the tunnel had fewer people following her. And he hadn't had a clue.

"Needless to say," Casey went on. "Brutti's killing opened up a whole can of other worms. Our Organized Crime guys got interested. They contacted our Seattle office who, as it turned out, had been asked for help in locating Brutti by local homicide cops. Enter Detective Sealth here. By the way, Noah tells me that Brutti was about 20 and zip in knife fights for his career until he ran into you. You are either very lucky or very good. I bet we'll find some interesting stuff in your military records. Anyway, Noah knew Brutti and his pals pretty well. I'll let him pick this up from here. Quite a story."

EPTATRETUS STOUTI

"WHAT THE HELL was it?"

Scarne had been both fascinated and horrified by the story the homicide detective told him. He took out the pack of cigarettes and walked over to the bookshelf in the corner nearest him. There was a small ashtray on the top shelf. He put it on the table and then offered the pack around.

Valledolmo said, "Isn't that illegal in this city?"

"A local law. Another jurisdictional problem for you boys."

"Screw that," Sealth said, looking at the pack like it was a life preserver. "Gimme one of those. Every time I think of that slimy thing, I need a smoke."

After lighting up, Scarne threw him the pack and the lighter and slid the ashtray between them. Sealth greedily pulled a cigarette, lit it and took a deep drag. The two Feds looked at each other but didn't say anything. Scarne assumed they started each day with a run around Manhattan.

"It was a hagfish," Sealth said. "*Eptatretus stouti*, the scientists call it," Sealth said, smoke hissing between his teeth. "I'd never heard of it in Latin or in English. But after it popped out of Maria Brutti I became the department expert on the fuckers. They're like eels, but without the personality. You heard of lampreys, those things that killed all the trout and salmon in the Great Lakes? Attach themselves to the outside of a fish and suck out blood and other fluids. Leave terrible circular scars on what they don't kill. Kissin' cousins of the hagfish, but much more lovable. Everybody I talked to about hagfish looked like they wanted to throw up. Did you know they have five hearts, no eyes and no stomach? They work from the inside, slithering into dead fish and sea mammals on the ocean floor and then eat their way out. They can pump out a quart of slime in less than a minute."

Sealth took a long drag.

"They're a big delicacy in North Korea, which is all you have to know about North Korea. Fisherman run into them every now and then when they pull up their nets. And there have been rare cases of them being found in human corpses pulled from deep water after a ship or sub goes down. But we had the first recorded case of a hagfish found in a dead Mafia princess. I think it'll probably stand for a long time."

"Why was it still alive?" Scarne dreaded asking the next question. "And how did it get in her?"

"Probably by accident. Maria Brutti was killed only a couple of hours before the viewing at the morgue. Ice pick through her pump. Then she was covered by hundreds of iced fresh fish leaking seawater. I spoke to a guy at the Seattle aquarium. He said hagfish can live quite some time inside a dead body before running out of nutrients and oxygen. Said human blood is a lot like seawater. This one did quite a bit of damage to her internal organs. Probably thrashed around looking for a way out. It didn't come out the way it went in."

"My God," Scarne said. His jelly donut didn't look quite so appetizing. "Her brother must have gone crazy seeing that."

"We all went a little nuts. It took my partner and three lab techs to control Brutti. Dispatch got so many calls they sent a S.W.A.T. team for Crissakes! Somebody had seen *Alien* once too often. Although I got to admit the thought did cross my mind. Brutti went completely off the reservation. Nobody, and I mean nobody, fucked with Carlo Brutti, inside or outside the family. He was not just muscle. He was sharp enough to realize that his family was facing a lot of competition from the Hispanics, Russians and even the Viets. Because of him, the Eye-tals made some shrewd deals. Some of the other crime kings value them for their financial expertise. There is a lot of revenue sharing."

"That fits with what we heard," Valledolmo said. "A confidential informant told us Victor Ballantrae became the banker for the Ukrainians based on a recommendation from the Bruttis. Carlo may even have handled the transfer of hot funds out of the country."

Sealth automatically reached for his coffee cup, which had been empty for some time. Scarne went to get the pot but the cop waived him off.

"Forget it. I don't need anymore caffeine. I've had about 20 cups since midnight. I'd probably have a cardiac." He grabbed another cigarette instead. "Brutti loved his sister, who by all accounts was a nice lady. He wasn't married; she was always trying to fix him up. They were very close. When that damn fish came out of the girl, he went right after the Ukrainians."

"I thought they were in business together. Why would he assume they killed his sister?"

"The body was found in a building owned by Andriy Boyko, the Uke warlord," Casey said. "The relationship between Brutti and the Ukrainians had been going sour. Our C.I. told us that for some reason the Ukes couldn't access their funds in Ballantrae's bank. He kept stalling them. They apparently suspected that Carlo double-crossed them. Boyko went to old man Brutti about it and that pissed Carlo off. He prided himself in always keeping his word. In fact, in his circles he did have a reputation as a straight shooter, or straight-stabber, if you will. He lost his temper at a meet and told Boyko to go fuck himself. Boyko took umbrage."

"Still, you don't go after family."

"You've seen *The Godfather* too many times," Sealth said. "We're talking Ukrainians here. But, you're right. I can't see Boyko stepping over that line. Not to mention keeping a body in a fish cooler in his warehouse. He's actually become a real businessman."

Valledolmo slid another photo over to Scarne.

"When he has to, Andriy can dress up. Favors three-piece suits. Looks like he could fit in at a bank board meeting, don't he?"

Another shot taken outside a courthouse.

"Don't you read the papers," Sealth said. "He'd fit in perfectly at a bank board meeting. They're fucking thieves."

"Brutti wasn't thinking straight after the morgue fiasco," Valledolmo said. "He went right after Boyko. Sliced and diced one of his lieutenants in the warehouse where Brutti's sister was found. That's when he probably found out that Boyko didn't kill her."

"How?"

Valledolmo sighed.

"Would you believe the Boyko lieutenant Brutti killed was our informant! Took us years to get him that high in the organization. He'd told us Boyko had nothing to do with Maria Brutti's murder and he undoubtedly also told Carlo."

"I don't want to burst your Federal bubble," Sealth said, "but your man's days were probably numbered anyway. When I spoke to Boyko I got the distinct impression he wasn't too devastated by the guy's death. I think he wondered what he was doing in the warehouse to begin with."

"There a huge difference between having your days numbered and having the M.E. numbering your body parts," Casey noted. "The poor bastard was probably snooping through Boyko's office when Carlo found him."

Valledolmo slid another photo over to Scarne. It was a crime scene shot of what was probably a body on a table. It was hard to tell. It could have been a salmon spread at a buffet.

"Not much you wouldn't say when you're being turned into laboratory slides. Our informant would have also told him that Garza was in town."

"Garza killed the sister," Scarne said, without hesitation

"Yeah, that's what we think," Casey said. "Both sides knew him. In addition to his other duties, he was the go-between and bagman for Ballantrae and knew his way around both operations. He'd even been to the warehouse before. Our C.I. said he showed up unexpectedly and acted like he wanted to mediate the dispute between the two mobs but we think he was really sent out to start a war between them, maybe to buy time for Ballantrae. We figure that when Brutti found out Boyko didn't kill his sister, he put two and two together. He headed East to settle scores."

"Then it was Brutti who was the sniper at the pool," Scarne said. "He was after Garza."

"He was probably after anyone he could get," Casey said. "After missing his chance in Miami, he must have tailed you and Loeb to Antigua. He wasn't thinking straight. Making it up as he went along. Didn't even have time to arrange for a gun in Antigua. Lucky for you and Loeb."

"Listen, Jake, I think you'll agree we've been forthcoming with you," Valledolmo said, pulling out a notebook. "We did check you out. Your friend the Commissioner said we could level with you, and we have. Now we need your help. Our informant is dead, Brutti is dead. The West Coast families have clammed up. Ballantrae's offshore assets are well hidden behind a phalanx of lawyers and some bought-and-paid-for American Senators and Congressmen. What can you tell us?"

☨

For the next hour, Scarne told them about the initial contact by Sheldon Shields and the blond-haired man in the church in New York. (The three cops looked at each other, and Casey mouthed "Keitel.") He told them about the Miami M.E.'s suspicions about the death of Josh Shields and his talk with the editor of Josh's paper in Miami. He told them about Josh's relationship with the intern at *Offshore Confidential* and their shared suspicions.

"I went to one of Sink's conferences," Valledolmo said.

He again went over the pool shooting and the trip to Antigua, and the fight with Brutti. He told them about the cloning of his cell phone. His burgled apartment. When he told them about the death of Sheldon Shields in the subway, they just stared at him.

"Keitel was in New York when Sheldon died," Scarne said.

"Son of a bitch," Sealth said. "Father and son. Whatever happened to just shooting people?"

"Goetz was shot," Valledolmo pointed out.

"And Brutti was strangled," Casey rejoined, shrugging apologetically to Scarne. "But they could be the proverbial 'innocent bystanders.' I bet that's a designation Carlo never expected to earn. Where does your gir—I mean, the Loeb woman, fit in all of this?"

Scarne hesitated. But there was no getting around it. Alana was no fool. Or an "innocent bystander." He took a deep breath.

"She has to be aware of his activities. At the very least she knows he stretches the laws in every country he operates. She might even do the stretching. But a killer? It just doesn't fit with what I know of her."

"When are you seeing her again," Sealth said.

"Look, I'm off the case. I don't have a client anymore. You guys take it from here. I have to earn a living."

The other three men exchanged glances.

"Haven't you fucked up enough?" Valledolmo said.

‡

As they walked out of the room, Sealth stopped and turned to Scarne.

"Sorry I gave you such a push early on," he said quietly.

"Dickwad?"

"The jury's still out on that, but I'll give you the benefit of the doubt. Maria Brutti's murder jerked my chain. You can't feel too good about screwing up either."

When Scarne said nothing, the detective went on.

"Be careful with the Loeb woman. She's a player. But even if she isn't, there are a lot of dead bodies piling up in this case, or whatever the fuck it is."

"When do you go back to the left coast?"

"Tomorrow. I got as much from these guys and you as I need. Nothing I can do here and my chief ain't gonna send me traipsing around Florida or the Caribbean. My partner is pissed enough at me that I got to make this trip on seniority. I should have told him to go. I haven't had a decent night's sleep or a decent meal since I got here."

"Are you free for dinner tonight? I can get us a good table at Sparks."

Sealth recognized the invitation for what it was. Quid pro quo time.

"That's the steak joint where Gotti set up the hit on Big Paulie Castellano."

"Don't worry. I have a rib-eye in mind, not a rub out."

"It ain't that. I've got a hankering for a good French meal."

Scarne grinned.

"Jean Georges? Eight o'clock?"

"Jean Georges will be just dandy."

As they got to the door, Sealth stopped.

"I was looking at your map. I know it ain't politically correct, but I think the Belgian Congo had a sexier ring to it, don't you?"

Scarne closed the door in his office. He stared at the photo of his grandfather, taken when he was about the same age as Scarne was now. He thought of all the man had accomplished after being defeated and imprisoned in a strange country. What would he say to his grandson about this fiasco? He was sure his grandfather would tell him to set it all right, no matter what it took. There was light tapping on his door and Evelyn stuck her head in. She was carrying her pad.

"Jake, I'm sure you will figure a way out of this."

He gave her a brief rundown of what had happened, leaving little out.

"Perhaps I spoke too hastily," she said when he finished.

"Call Dudley and see if he's free for lunch tomorrow. Then book me a late afternoon or evening flight to Miami. Get me a room in South Beach, preferably the Delano."

"I take it this time you won't need your golf clubs."

‡

'THE FINAL ONE KILLS'

JEAN GEORGES WAS in the lobby level of Donald Trump's International Hotel and Tower at 1 Central Park West. With floor-to-ceiling windows facing the park, its airy, modern décor was all angles and light. But what set the restaurant apart was the food, simple dishes elegantly prepared by Jean-George Vongerichten himself. Scarne and Sealth ordered the prix fixed dinner, which featured venison with spring fruits and vegetables. Sealth asked if he could see the wine list. He looked up at the hovering sommelier and said, "Let's have the 2002 Hawks View Pinot Noir."

"You came 3,000 miles to arguably the best French restaurant in New York," Scarne said, "and you want a California wine?"

"It's from Oregon, Willamette Valley. You'll love it."

"Your friend knows his wines, sir," the sommelier remarked. "It is perfect for the venison. We only have a couple of bottles. I'll put them aside."

"I spent a year in France on an Interpol exchange program with the Sûreté Nationale," Sealth said. "I got into wines over there and try to keep up back home. Turns out Oregon has pretty ideal climate for the Pinot Noir grape, which is very cantankerous."

"How did you like working with French flics?"

"I liked it fine. Tough guys and smart, most of them. Not like Inspector Clouseau. More like that detective in *Day of the Jackal*, the first one. Anyway, it's a different legal system, but the French police are first-rate. Their Government can be stupid, but they don't have the monopoly on that, do they? People are nice enough if you make the effort. I tend to give the frogs a bit of a slide just because I think I might have a bit of French trapper blood in me. Course, the women are wonderful. Almost married one."

Scarne raised his eyebrows.

"I met her at a party the Interpol guys gave us. We went out for almost the whole time I was in Paris."

He paused while the waiter returned with their wine. Sealth tasted it, and nodded. They both drank after the man left.

"So what happened," Scarne said. "Great wine, by the way."

"Seattle ain't Paris."

Sealth stared into his wine, lost in thought.

"Any chance you'd trade Seattle for Paris?"

"Not then. I was an up-and-comer, poised to make the great leap to Homicide, a real coup for somebody like me. Hard to throw that away. Timing is everything, ain't it? Anyway, that ship has sailed. It's been five years. We exchange Christmas cards."

"May mean you're not the only one carrying a torch."

"Who says I'm carrying a torch?"

"It's written all over your face, Noah. Don't be defensive. You didn't mention her boobs, or how great the sex was. She still means something to you. I'm the last guy to be giving advice, but why don't you go for it? How many hagfish homicides do you want in your life? I don't see a wedding ring."

Their food came they made small talk. It turned out that Scarne was right about Sealth's bloodlines. When the big cop found out that Scarne had Cheyenne in him, he loosened up again.

"Jesus, between the two of us we could start a casino," he said. "I've got some Duwamish or Suquamish in the woodpile. The original Noah Sealth was Chief Seattle, who signed the treaty that gave all the tribal lands to the white man before the Civil War, not that he had much choice. I don't know if I come by the name Sealth legitimately or it was adopted by one of my slave ancestors who went west and married a squaw. Like I said, the Injun' blood had been diluted by French trappers somewhere along the way, hopefully voluntarily."

They skipped dessert in favor of Armagnac and coffee.

"I want to tell you something I didn't tell the feds, Noah."

"Here it comes. I hope I don't have to arrest you. I'm getting to like you."

"You keep forgetting your jurisdictional problem. Besides, if stupidity was a crime, you'd already have cuffed me."

Scarne told him about the sex video. Sealth's shoulders shook with suppressed laughter.

"I'm sorry, but you just made my day. And you're giving me advice about women! Somebody has got you by the short hairs. What now?"

"I'm going to find out why they don't want to whack me outright, just get me off the case. The video not only discredits me, it also provides a rationale for Sheldon's suicide."

"You don't think it's possible that the video, pardon the expression, sent him over the edge?"

"Why would he be carrying it around? I don't believe he ever saw the damn thing. Keitel must have planted it at the scene after he killed him."

"You think the broa – I mean Loeb – knew about the video?"

"If she did, I'd like to think she would have told me after I saved her life. I'm certain the room change was news to her. If she were in on it, why the charade? But I guess I can't be completely sure. She's an unusual woman."

"Do you love her?"

Scarne sat back and twirled his brandy glass.

"Yeah."

"Then you really are between a rock and a hard-on. At the very least she's complicit in covering up financial crimes and maybe turning a blind eye to murder. At the worst, she's ordering the murdering. She may love you, which may be the only reason you are still alive. And that could change. She could decide you are not worth the risk. Women can be more practical than us in that regard. To them, if it can't be, it ain't. Or somebody could decide that for her, or the both of you. That whole organization seems unstable to me. Getting careless or arrogant, or both. Either is dangerous. In combination they are fatal. Maybe to you."

Sealth sipped his Armagnac.

"You want my advice? Forget her. Forget what happened. Take whatever the Shields family throws at you. Better to lose your license than wind up with a hagfish up your ass. You still have friends in high places. You'll bounce back. Let the Feds handle Ballantrae. It's a miracle you're not dead already. You want to hear my odds on another miracle? And I don't care if you are part Cheyenne and part Sicilian. The Basque have a saying: 'Every hour wounds, but the final one kills.' The secret is putting off that final hour, my friend."

The waiter appeared. Somewhat to Scarne's surprise, Sealth made an honest effort to split the check.

"Buy me dinner next time I'm in Seattle," Scarne said, grabbing the bill.

"It was a one-time offer, dickwad," Sealth said.

†

Outside on the sidewalk, Scarne turned to Sealth.

"I told you about the video because I may need your help."

"What a surprise."

"I want to turn Alana. If I can get her to testify against Ballantrae and the others in the Brutti killing, can you claim jurisdiction in Seattle? I want her clear of the Feds to start. Once you have her, she may even be able to bargain for witness protection with them. They want Ballantrae. You get Garza. I'm sure Keitel will take a fall, too. Then everybody is happy."

"And why do I need you? I'll get them eventually."

"Eventually is a long time. And no offense to Seattle's finest, but you don't have the resources the Feds have. We both know they're going to cut you out just as soon as they can. Brutti's sister is a sideshow to them. I have an edge right now with Alana. I want to get her clear, but whatever happens I'm going to beat the Feds to the punch. You can go along for the ride. We have a deal?"

Sealth looked disgusted.

"Yeah. Why not? Can't deny a condemned man's last wish."

MACK'S RULES

SCARNE SPENT THE next morning tying up a loose end. A few calls located one of the detectives who was at the scene of Sheldon's death. He grudgingly told Scarne that there was a witness who claimed Sheldon Shields was pushed.

"Didn't you pursue it?"

The silence told Scarne he could have phrased it better.

"Hell, no. We always let murderers go. Especially when they push old men in front of the downtown local. We rushed it because we were out of donuts. You fucking P.I.'s are all the same."

"Sorry."

"Of course we 'pursued' it. But the girl's description didn't pan out. Nobody else saw anything and the family told us the guy was probably despondent. We put a little extra on it because of who he was, but there was nothing. What's your interest in this again? You got something for us?"

"Sheldon Shields was my client. I'm not sure it was an accident."

"Wait a minute. You're the guy on the family's shit list, right? What's the matter? The old guy's check didn't clear?"

"I don't suppose you could give me the girl's name?"

"Blow me."

Reluctantly, Scarne called Dick Condon at home. After reciting a long list of Scarne's shortcomings, the Commissioner said he would do what he could.

"Her name is Nancy Lopez," Condon said without preamble when he called back. "You can skip the golf jokes. Take down this number." He gave it. "I had to speak to the detective personally to pry it out of him. He figured it was you who was asking. Don't think I've ever come that close to being told to go fuck myself by a second-grade. Guy has balls. I like that. Thinks you're an asshole. Another plus in his favor. Anything else you need? Luckily, I don't have much to do as Commissioner."

"Thanks, Dick. I owe you."

"Yes, you do. Although you may not be able to repay me anytime soon. Randolph Shields wants your head on a platter. He went to our mutual friend on the City Council. I'd lay low. Maybe leave town for a while."

"I'm heading to Miami."

"That's still in this hemisphere. Try harder."

"Who are you again?"

Nancy Lopez's voice on the phone was polite, but suspicious.

"My name is Scarne. I'm investigating the death of Sheldon Shields, the man you saw fall in front of a subway train."

"I told the other cops everything. They didn't believe me."

"I don't think it's a question of the police not believing you. Nobody else saw what you did. But now some facts have popped up. I believe you, and that's all that counts."

The girl, briefly and succinctly, described how a man pushed Sheldon onto the tracks. She was staring right at him when it happened. There was no mistake. What did the man look like? Again, she gave a solid description of what little she saw of the assailant. It meant nothing to the cops but she could have been describing the man who followed Scarne into the church. Scarne smiled grimly. Keitel.

"You've been very helpful. The Police Department could use you."

"That's what my boyfriend says. He's a cop. Met him the day of the subway thing, in fact. I'm gonna switch to John Jay. I hope you get the prick – uh, sorry – the perp who pushed the old man."

"Don't worry about it, Miss Lopez."

†

"Now, why do I find myself agreeing with everything a tomahawk-throwing cop says, and nothing you say?" Dudley Mack took a bite of his roast beef sandwich. "What the fuck is the matter with you?"

"I don't think he throws tomahawks," Scarne said.

They were standing at the bar in Fraunces Tavern, a New York landmark that was a favorite of George Washington and earned its patriotic stripes honestly when a British frigate put a cannonball through its roof. The restaurant was also a favorite of Mack's, especially on weekends when there were no loud Wall Street brokers at the bar. When Scarne had arrived the few tourists walking by were casting nervous glances at Bobo Sambuca leaning against Mack's Lincoln Town out front. No wonder, Scarne mused as he waved hello; Bobo looked like he could catch a cannonball.

"Whatever," Mack said. "Sealth sounds like a smart cop. If he thinks you're going to get killed, that's probably the way it's going down."

In addition to his sandwich, slathered in horseradish sauce, Dudley was sipping Jameson's. After a decent night's sleep, Scarne was feeling, if not quite human, at least like a primate. But he wasn't quite up to drinking Irish whiskey for lunch. He sipped his Diet Coke and picked at a chicken pot pie.

"I know the Loeb broad got inside your head, Jake, but come on. Life isn't *Casablanca*."

"Pick another movie. Bogart gave up Ingrid Bergman."

"With much less reason. My point is, you keep ignoring Mack's three laws. They bear repeating. Never play poker with a man called Doc. Never eat at a place called Mom's. And never, ever, sleep with a woman with troubles worse than your own."

"What happened to pissing into the wind?"

"Sometimes that can't be helped," Mack said and took another dainty bite. It always amazed Scarne that his friend had excellent table manners. He even dabbed a bit of horseradish at a corner of his mouth.

"You stole the line about women from Nelson Algren."

"So what? I didn't spend all my time in college getting laid. And I bet old Nelson stole it from someone else. But you're the one proving us right."

He put down his sandwich, took a sip of whiskey and placed a hand on Scarne's shoulder.

"Let me recap. There is a porn video of you that will probably be on You Tube. You strangled a mobster who was trying to avenge a sister who was eaten by an eel. Your girlfriend and her boss may be homicidal maniacs with two professional assassins on the payroll. Said assassins may have pushed your elderly client in front of the downtown local. The FBI is all over your shit. You're probably going to lose your license. I left out a couple of killings, but I have a ferry to catch."

"Well, when you put it that way."

"Don't be a smartass. What do you hope to accomplish? And please, don't give me any bullshit about honor, or a damsel in distress. We both know that ain't the case. You just have to see this through with her to the end."

"How about revenge?"

"You son of a bitch. You know I'm a sucker for that kind of thing."

"You don't mind if I restore a little of my honor along the way, do you?"

"Just don't let it cloud your judgment, kemosabe. Come on, finish up. I want to make a call before we take you to the airport. I know you won't be smart enough to take Bobo with you, but there are some people in Miami who can help you. Can't let you get in any more knife fights unarmed, can I?"

†

On the flight to Miami, Scarne considered his options. He knew that it might be months, even years, before the Government made a case against Ballantrae that could stick. And they might never succeed. Administrations changed. All Casey and Valledolmo had were unsubstantiated rumors and dead bodies. And dead bodies can't testify. The Feds had been right. He did Ballantrae a favor by killing Brutti. Well-paid lawyers and lobbyists could probably explain away everything else. It wasn't likely the Mafia or the Ukrainians would turn state's evidence. He thought about that. What would the mobsters do now? And what should he do about Alana?

It occurred to him that it didn't matter what anyone else did at this point. With both Josh and Sheldon Shields dead, and himself disgraced and ostracized by the family, Scarne knew he had to bring Ballantrae down, and quickly, before Randolph Shields made good on his threat to ruin him. But how? The only way, and it was a long shot, would be to find out what Josh had discovered about Ballantrae, if anything.

Since most writers were paranoid, he was willing to bet that Josh had backed up his files. Perhaps the killers missed something. The backup could be anywhere, but the likeliest place was the Miami apartment. Scarne's initial search of the flat, before the case turned so murderous, had been desultory. Now he was determined to tear the place apart. Fortunately, Randolph Shields had not asked for the keys back. Maybe he didn't know where Scarne had stayed. He figured he had a couple of days before the lawyers started going through Sheldon's affairs and contacted La Gorce's management.

Scarne's plane landed in Miami at 7 P.M. and he asked his cab driver to find the nearest Home Depot. Telling the cabbie to wait, he went in and bought a small tool kit. He then had the cab drop him at the Intercontinental Hotel on Biscayne Boulevard. He walked through the lobby into the open restaurant area beyond. A waiter came and he ordered coffee and a club sandwich. There were avocado slices under the turkey. He was almost finished when a small, very thin man wearing white slacks and a colorful short-sleeve shirt walked over. It was exactly 9 P.M.

"Mr. Scarne?"

Scarne nodded and the man sat and placed a small toiletry bag on the table.

"Welcome to Miami."

He didn't offer his name or his hand. Scarne gestured toward the pot of coffee and the man poured himself a cup.

"You don't look like a Sambuca," Scarne said.

"I married one."

Since the Sambuca women were only slightly smaller versions of the males of the family, Scarne suppressed a mental image of the marriage bed. Probably a sawed-off shotgun wedding or a career move.

"Nice bag," Scarne said. It was a Louis Vuitton. He lifted it. "Feels like you overdid the toothpaste."

The man flashed a small grin, for half a second. He leaned slightly forward.

"The automatic is a .380 Bersa, with a Brugger & Hock silencer. They call it their 'Thunder' model." He shrugged. "Don't know who they're trying to impress. It's basically a Walther by another name, made in Argentina. Figures, the place is lousy with Krauts. But it's a very good piece. Better than a Walther, in my opinion. It's got a blowback action like the Walther but it won't knick your hand on recoil. That's a problem with the Walther." He held up his right hand in a shooting pose and used the index figure of his left hand to rub a spot near the back of his right index finger. "See these little scars? Those are Walther bites. Can make you gun shy. Think too much about it and you'll miss what you're aiming at. Bersa engineered the bite out. Amazing for a gun so light. Easy carry, only weighs 23 ounces without the silencer."

He saw the look on Scarne's face.

"Don't worry. It's a solid piece of metal. You know what they say. 'A .380 in your pocket is better than a .45 in the truck.' They kept the weight down with the magazine. It only holds seven rounds, plus the one in the chamber. But it has straight-in chambering, which means it takes the best hollow points. You need more than eight hollows you're in big fucking trouble, friend."

"Don't some of these lighter guns have a tendency to jam with hollows?"

The man nodded approvingly.

"Yeah, some new Bersas jam in the first couple of dozen rounds, until the recoil spring gets broken in. Then, never again. Weird. Don't worry about this one." He deadpanned. "Spring's broken in."

"Ammo?"

"I gave you two boxes of Cor-Bon 90 grains, hollow, and two extra magazines, in case you run up against Tom Cruise. You ever notice how he kills five guys shooting at him with Uzis and he's only got a pistol."

"Probably has a Bersa."

"Yeah, whatever. Ammo velocity without the silencer is 965 feet per second, 12 feet from the muzzle. At 25 yards, it will group just under three inches. Closer than that, even Stevie Wonder can't miss."

"You know your guns."

"This is Miami."

The man got up to leave.

"By the way, there is toothpaste in there, brush, disposable razors, other stuff. Thought you might need them."

"Thanks."

"Gun's clean. No serial numbers. Keep it or fish it. Good luck."

Scarne finished eating and walked out to the cab line in front of the hotel.

The Delano, among the most beautiful hotels in Miami Beach, was a favorite of Scarne's. It was noted for severe but luxurious rooms, all done in white, as well as the flowing white floor-to-ceiling drapes and soaring columns in its famous indoor/outdoor lobby and common areas. Even the staff wore white. Scarne thought that only the brightly colored Dali furniture prevented snow blindness. He went up to his room and unpacked. A half hour later he was sound asleep. It was going to be a busy Sunday.

‡

DIRTY BUSINESS

SCARNE WAS UP early the next morning. After a cobweb-clearing swim in the ocean and a quick room-service breakfast, he opened his "toiletry bag." The blue/black gun was in a Houston paddle holster, designed to fit on a hip or in a waistband. The Bersa slid out easily. He worked the action and ejected the magazine. The thin man was right. It was a quality piece and amazingly light. He opened the box of shells and loaded the magazine. He left the chamber empty. The silencer screwed on easily. He went through the routine three more times with his eyes closed. Removing the silencer, he put the gun, holster and ammunition in a small overnight bag, then called the front desk for a cab.

Fifteen minutes later, after crossing the Rickenbacker Causeway, the cab pulled up in front of a small, one-story building that was part of the Crandon Park Marina on Key Biscayne. The building housed a bait shop, small seafood restaurant and various sightseeing and fishing charter offices. The air smelled of diesel fuel and French fries. Scarne told the cabbie to wait and went through a door that said "Yacht Net, Inc. (Boat Ownership That Makes Sense)."

A weather-beaten woman was sitting behind a counter looking at a computer screen. A small yellow Post-It note pinned to her blouse said "Marge." She looked up at him and smiled. At least Scarne thought she smiled. There were so many creases in her tanned leathery face he couldn't be sure. There was a rustling sound behind Scarne. He turned to see a large, sinewy dog with an absurdly small head struggle to stand in a plush canine bed. The fragile-looking animal made its way over to him and sniffed his leg. He reached down and let it smell his hand before gently petting it.

"Is this a ..."

"Yup, a greyhound," the woman said. "Belongs to the owner. Once they're finished racing the tracks put them up for adoption. Make wonderful pets. Happy to sit around all day. Not surprising after running a million miles chasing fake rabbits they never caught. Course, Lancelot here couldn't catch an armadillo now. Eats too much and has arthritis to boot. But he's a sweetheart and makes the effort to check out anyone who comes in the door."

Lancelot gave Scarne a rheumy but not unfriendly look and then ambled unsteadily back to his bed, where he lay down in stages.

"Now, what can I do for you, handsome?"

The wall behind the woman was almost entirely covered with nautical maps, all liberally punctured with variously colored pins. Scarne noted the distance between the marina, which was marked with a large "YOU ARE HERE!" and a red star, and the section of Miami Beach where Josh Shields died. It would have been an easy trip.

He wanted to ask Marge if she was Quint's mother, but instead said, "If I were to give you a date within the last year or so, could you tell me who took out one of your boats on that day?"

"What, no foreplay? Just wham, bam, thank you m'amm. Hold the KY jelly?" The old woman cackled and punched Scarne on the arm. "Just funnin' with you. Now what do you need?"

Scarne couldn't help but laugh.

"Sorry, my name is Jake Scarne and I'm a private investigator." He pulled out his wallet and showed her his license, holding it close for her to see. "I'm trying to find out if two men involved in a case I'm working used one of your boats on a particular date."

"Sonny, you don't have to shove that in my face. Old Marge's eyesight is probably better than yours. I can still spot a herring slick a mile away. What did these guys do that a New York private eye needs to know about their sailing habits? Drugs? Murder? Illegals? Or something really bad, like credit default swaps?"

Scarne was about to lie when she said, "Don't matter. It's privileged information. We have an exclusive clientele. They pay a lot of money to be able to use one of our boats whenever they want. It wouldn't be good for business if we go around telling tales on them, now would it? And did you know that it's against the law in Florida for a boat rental operation or boat club to reveal that kind of information to a third party without a subpoena? You got one of those?"

"No, I don't."

Scarne was debating how much cash it would take to get the woman to subvert the ridiculous law when she cackled.

"Well, that don't matter either, cause I made that shit up about the Florida law. I'm making minimum wage here. You think I give a rat's ass about boater privilege? Goddamn government knows when we take a crap. Nothin's a secret anymore. What's their names?"

Scarne could have kissed her (well, maybe, he thought).

"Jesús Garza and Christian Keitel."

"Why didn't you say so at the beginning? They're famous around here. Sank one of our boats, for Crissakes. Gave us some cock and bull story about losing control. Way I heard it, they ran full tilt into a bridge. Probably all coked up. Thank God for the insurance."

Scarne recalled Alana telling him that Garza and Keitel had an "accident" chasing the sniper at the pool.

"They give me the creeps, those two," Marge said. "I don't even want to know why you're asking about them. Come across so smooth. But they can't fool me. Pair of barracuda. Hold on a sec, honeybuns." Her hands flew across the computer's keyboard and she worked the mouse like a teen-ager. "Here it is. Take a look-see." She motioned Scarne behind the counter. "See, this is their account. It shows how many hours they've purchased, how many hours they've used, how many are left, blah, blah, blah. I hit this thingamajig and we get to the page showing past usage. Dates. Type of craft. Hours used on those dates. All sorts of stuff. What date you interested in?"

Scarne told her and she scrolled backwards. Garza and Keitel took out boats about twice a month. He asked about the (WR) notation next to the dates.

"Means weekend rate. It's higher than during the week. Your boys only went out on weekends. Here we are. Hey look at that. I spoke too soon."

The date she pointed to with a bony finger did not have a (WR) next to it. Scarne knew it was a Wednesday. It was the only weekday Garza and Keitel had ever taken out a boat. Even the time fit – 2 P.M. to 8 P.M.

She looked up at him and saw the smile.

"Well, Sherlock, you look like the cat that swallowed a canary. Something tells me you found a clue. Am I right?"

"It's been so long I'm not sure." But Scarne couldn't quite keep the excitement out of his voice.

"This even tells you what kind of boat they took," the woman said, getting into the moment. "See those initials – SL50 and HAT50 – that means..."

"...Sealine and Hatteras 50-footers."

"Well, ain't you the bright one. Regular *Jeopardy* candidate."

Garza and Keitel had discussed those very boats with Scarne at the party when Goetz was killed. From the list on the computer, it seemed that those were their craft of choice. So, they'd managed to sink a Sealine. Not easy to do on a calm inland waterway. But they hadn't taken such a large boat out on the date Scarne had given the woman. On that date, they had taken out a DSK24.

The woman had noticed as well.

"Wonder why they took a Dusky out that day? Another clue, Shamus?"

It might not hold up in court, Scarne thought, but on the day Josh Shields died, a day they never went boating, Garza and Keitel took a Dusky from a marina a half-hour away from where he was fishing. And where a witness said he noticed a Dusky or Grady White in the water a few feet away. Scarne couldn't help himself. He gave the woman a kiss.

"My, aren't we the bold one. Don't even know my name and you give me a kiss. Now you're gonna have to buy old Margie a dinner." She saw the look on his face and laughed. "Don't sweat it sweetie. You don't have to be there."

"Thanks, Marge," he said, handing her $100.

"Come back anytime, big spender," she said.

Lancelot didn't bother looking up as he left.

Scarne had the cab drop him off at a small public park adjacent to a fire station on Collins Avenue a few blocks short of La Gorce. He walked through the park to the beach and headed north to the apartment building on sand hard-packed by joggers. When he got to the back entrance at La Gorce, he waved his electronic "key" at the pad on the outside fence, and was rewarded with the familiar buzz. The same held true for the metal door that led into the garage. He didn't want to chance the lobby elevators and a run-in with Mario. So he took the "recreation deck" elevator to the seventh floor and exited by the pool. An employee was skimming the pool. The man waved to Scarne indifferently. He entered the building proper and took an elevator to Josh's floor. He walked to the apartment and tried the key. The lock hadn't been changed!

Scarne despised this kind of work, but he was good at it. The bathrooms would be the easiest place to start. They were mostly tile and there were few spots to hide anything. Scarne took off his blue sports jacket, khaki trousers, shoes and socks. This would be dirty business. He reached in his overnight bag and pulled on a pair of thin latex gloves and the tool kit, then headed to the small bathroom off the guest room. It contained a shower stall, toilet and cabinets above and below the sink.

He turned on the overhead light and then unscrewed the cover before the bulb became too hot. Nothing there. He put the light fixture back together and walked into the shower stall and unscrewed the shower head and tried to pry out the floor drain. It didn't budge, and looked like it never had. The soap dish was empty, and solidly entrenched. He then checked in and around the toilet bowl. He lifted the cover from the reservoir and dismantled most of the inner workings, paying particular attention to the ball cock. Nothing. He tried to lift the toilet. It didn't budge. He checked in, around and under the sink and cabinet. The drawers below the sink contained towels. He checked every one, and then took the drawers out. He looked behind and under them. The open space below the sink contained the usual things such places contained, including bottles of shampoos and liquid drain cleaner. The shampoos were see-through, so he let them be. But he carefully began pouring the drain cleaner into the sink. It was drain cleaner.

When he was finished, the drain was probably working better than it had in years. He moved on to the medicine cabinet, where, luckily, there were only a few bottles of pills and powders. He emptied every one. He squeezed the toothpaste. He didn't know what he was looking for but felt certain that he would recognize anything out of place. The mirror looked, well, like a mirror and didn't appear to have been tampered with. He checked the towel racks. They also looked undisturbed and firmly planted. He checked his watch. This one little bathroom had taken him almost 45 minutes! He shrugged.

Just outside the bathroom was a utility closet, with an over and under washer/dryer combination. That would be a bitch to search. He'd come back to that. He headed to the master bathroom on the other side of the apartment. Following the same routine, he cleared it in just under an hour, even though it was three times the size of the first one. A lot of wasted space, he thought. Had both bathrooms been about the same sizes, the designer could have fit another small bedroom or den in the apartment. He was certain he missed nothing, even unscrewing the water jets in the Jacuzzi tub. Another waste, he thought. The huge tub was impractical, considering that the room's walk-in shower could fit three people, and the building had a heated spa by the main pool.

He walked back to the guest bedroom. Josh Shields had only the best equipment, including Shimano reels and Loomis rods. Everything was meticulously maintained. There was no rust on any metal surfaces, including lures and hooks. Even a battered and ancient "Old Pal Pail" minnow bucket resting on a shelf was spotless. It now held only a variety of lead sinkers and cork bobbers. He guessed that the bucket was a cherished relic from childhood (Scarne had kept his own until it rusted through in college, where it had done yoeman's service as a beer bucket). He wondered if Sheldon had given it to his son, and probably couldn't bear to take it home. He checked the bucket, and every tackle box, rod, reel, lure and fishing vest.

He tore apart the bed and looked under the rug, in the drapes, rods and blinds. He looked behind pictures on the wall, in lamps and the smoke alarm. He unscrewed everything that could be unscrewed. Standing on a chair, he checked the ceiling fan. He would never trust a ceiling fan again, he thought bitterly. He opened all the air vents. On the way out, he checked the utility closet, pulling out the washer/dryer. He made a lot of noise, but it couldn't be helped. By the time Scarne headed back to the master bedroom another two hours had passed and he was sweating and filthy. His fingers ached and he had skinned his knuckles painfully despite the gloves.

Scarne was hungry. He stripped off his gloves and went to the kitchen and found some Genoa salami, provolone cheese and olives in the refrigerator. As he cut into the salami he half hoped a computer disk might fall out. It didn't. He wasn't looking forward to going through the cabinets and all the food and appliances in the kitchen but there was nothing for it. He put on a pot of coffee. He swirled a knife through the coffee can. Nothing. Fortified by his snack and two cups of black coffee he put the gloves back on and headed to the back bedroom and its large walk-in closet. When he emerged he was confident that he hadn't missed anything. The only thing of value, to him anyway, was an unopened pack of cigarettes, buried deep in a drawer. He found some matches in the kitchen and had a smoke with another cup of coffee.

Scarne had been in the apartment for more than six hours. He spent another hour in the living room, with all its electronics, bookshelves and bric-a-brac. He searched every book, vase, table and chair. He heard doors opening and closing in the hallway, and cooking smells began to waft into the apartment. He had a sickening feeling that he was on a wild goose chase.

He washed up as best he could, put on his clothes and headed down to the garage on the sixth floor. He had searched Josh's car briefly during his previous trip. There aren't many places to hide things in a car, unless you are a heroin dealer or Goldfinger, in which case you take off the side panels or the exhaust system, or perhaps rip up the leather and reupholster everything. And nobody who loves his sports car would do that to hide a disk or flash drive. Scarne spent an hour on the Mustang, checking the inside, engine compartment and trunk. Like the apartment, it was clean.

Scarne realized that the only thing he'd accomplished for a full day's work was not being seen. Perhaps the opposite would be more productive. If Ballantrae knew Scarne was mucking about he might do something rash. He looked at his watch. Ballantrae was hosting a company party at the Forge within the hour. Scarne decided to crash it and see what happened.

He knew that calling the lack of a plan a plan was a sign of desperation, but there was little to lose at this point. And Alana would probably be there. He looked at Josh's car. It probably now belonged to Randolph. Smiling at the thought, Scarne got in, turned on the ignition and drove out of the building.

An hour later he left the Delano showered, shaved and dressed for the lion's den at the Forge, the Bersa resting comfortably on his hip.

SHELL GAME

IT WAS STILL early. Miami's famous nightlife had yet to kick in and Scarne found a parking spot across the street from the Forge. He suspected that he might not want to wait for a valet to get his car. A hostess directed him to the Ballantrae function. As he walked through a small courtyard he saw waiters cleaning tables and closing two service bars. Probably a cocktail hour before the dinner. He could hear Ballantrae's voice through the door to a small salon just off the courtyard.

Scarne walked to the door. Ballantrae was standing at a table giving a speech. He had his free hand negligently touching Alana Loeb's shoulder, who was sitting at the table with three other couples. There were perhaps 60 other people at the other tables in the room listening to Ballantrae, who was saying something about "our best year ever." Scarne didn't like the look of Ballantrae's hand on Alana. It seemed intimate, or at least proprietary. He realized that in addition to everything else he felt, he was jealous.

Ballantrae kept talking even as his eyes followed Scarne, who casually walked over to another service bar and ordered a Jack Daniels. A few other men also turned their heads in his direction. They looked like men who stayed healthy because they noticed people like Scarne walking into a room. He felt the comforting weight of the Bersa on his hip. Among those who took an interest were Garza and Keitel, sitting alone at a small table opposite the bar. They looked at him impassively. After a moment, a small smile formed on Garza's lips and he raised his drink. Scarne returned the gesture. When he turned back to look at Ballantrae, who was now talking some claptrap about "the new paradigm of our financial services model," his eyes locked with Alana's. There was warning in her eyes, and something else that told Scarne he needn't be jealous.

Ballantrae finished his little speech with a flourish. There was a burst of laughter and overdone applause. As if on cue, waiters started descending on the tables. Alana got up and walked quickly over to Scarne. Ballantrae started shaking the hands of people who walked up to him.

"Jake, what are you doing? I didn't know you were back." She spoke calmly but there was tension in her body. "You should have called me. We have to talk. Why come here? This isn't the place." She lowered her voice. "I'm leaving the company. I have a few loose ends to tie up. Some things are out of control."

"Like the video in Antigua?"

"Video? What video? I don't understand."

She didn't know. He was sure of it. Out of the corner of his eye he spotted Garza and Keitel closing in. He leaned toward her and whispered, "We're about to have company. Someone taped us in bed in Antigua and has used the video against me. I half thought you were in on it."

Her eyes widened, either in surprise or anger at his accusation.

"It's nice to know you're not. Even if there is a lot I think you're guilty of. Now it seems someone is gunning for the both of us. Strange bedfellows, no?"

"Mr. Scarne, isn't it?"

It was Garza, smiling his pearly whites.

"Speaking of strange bedfellows," Scarne said.

Garza's smile disappeared, then came back with just a little less wattage.

"Did you hear that, Christian, he disapproves of our lifestyle."

Scarne had to laugh at the man's boldness.

"Your lifestyle is your own business and it's probably the only thing about you two that doesn't bother me. Tell me, have you killed anyone today, Jesús? What about you, Christian?"

A strangled sound came from Alana.

"The night's young," Keitel said quietly as he leaned past Scarne to take a glass of wine off the bar. He gave it to his partner and then got one for himself as Victor Ballantrae came up to them.

"Jake, how nice to see you," Ballantrae said, extending his hand, which Scarne took. "How are you feeling?"

He was in the company of three hard-looking men. Scarne's Bersa felt better by the moment. One of the men ordered straight vodka and leaned against the bar, staring curiously at Scarne. The other two didn't order anything but stood to the side and scanned the room's entrances. Scarne recognized the chiseled features of the vodka drinker from the F.B.I. photo: Andriy Boyko. He did look like a banker in his three-piece suit.

"I'm doing well, Victor. Thanks for asking."

Ballantrae adopted a pose of thoughtful concern.

"I think what you did in Antigua was wonderful. It must have been rough. But you saved Alana's life, and, for that, I will be eternally grateful. As we all are. You don't look too much the worse for wear. Amazing, after going up against a robber like that. Crime on the island is getting out of hand. I'm going to have a word with the Prime Minister about it."

Scarne smiled, but said nothing.

"But tell me, what brings you here? I'm glad you are, of course. I was going to ring you up. Where are you staying? We owe you something for what you did."

"The Delano. I'm clearing up some things related to the Shields murders."

"Murders? I know you think the death of young Shields was suspicious, but I was given to understand Sheldon Shields died in an accident. Or perhaps took his own life. A real tragedy. I sent a note to his brother. I liked the old gentleman. Does the family actually think they were both murdered?"

He said it in a way that made it clear he found the whole idea preposterous.

"In fact, no. They fired me. I'm currently unemployed, so I thought I'd kick over some rocks down here and see what crawls out."

"Why don't you just leave it all alone, Jake? The family apparently doesn't put much credence in your theories. Frankly, neither do I. You've had a tough time. You need a rest. Take some time off and then come talk to me. I could always use a man with your talents. Isn't that right, Alana?" He gave Scarne his best salesman smile. "I'm talking top dollar."

Alana stood there stone-faced.

"Thanks, Victor. That's very thoughtful. But I'm not comfortable working for anyone else. I think I'll be my own client for as long as I can afford myself." Scarne then decided to burn his bridges, and the roads leading up to them. "Besides, I know why Carlo Brutti shot up Alana's party and tracked her to Antigua. Poor Goetz. The only accidental death in this whole farce. And I know that you killed both Josh Shields and his father. What I don't know is why. But I will soon." He turned to the bartender, who was standing there, mouth agape, pouring wine into a glass overflowing onto the counter. "That's going to stain. Give the wine a rest and pour me another Jack Daniels, please. Try to keep it in the glass. Victor, do you want anything?"

If Boyko was surprised by anything Scarne said, he didn't show it. He merely smiled and stared at Ballantrae.

"Jake, I honestly don't know what you are talking about," Ballantrae said, glancing nervously in Boyko's direction. "I guess what happened over the last few days must have affected you more than you realize. You need help. But I have to warn you, despite my gratitude, I will defend my reputation vigorously, even to the point of a slander suit. Now, I think you had better leave."

"Victor, you lie even worse than you golf."

It was a weak parting shot, but Ballantrae reddened. Scarne brushed past Garza and Keitel and walked out the door. Very dramatic, he thought. Probably just got myself killed. As he left the room he glanced back. Ballantrae was talking rapidly to Boyko. No one followed him out to his car. If they wanted him, they would try the Delano first. When he hit Collins Avenue, he turned toward South Beach, just to be on the safe side. No one was on his tail, and he doubled back and drove to La Gorce. Once again, he entered unnoticed.

Back in the apartment, Scarne poured himself a drink and found the pack of cigarettes. He walked out to the deck, opened up a beach chair and sat down next to a small table before realizing he didn't have an ashtray. Then he spotted a large seashell on another table in the corner. It was a rather nondescript and discolored conch. It would do. He carried it to his chair. Before flicking an ash into it, he put the shell to his ear. He thought of Emma and Josh Shields as he listened for the hollow sound of the "ocean" – his own blood. Strange. There was only the faintest hum. Something fell into his ear, and he almost dropped the shell, thinking it was some sort of small animal or insect. He looked into the conch and something long and black spilled out, giving him another bad moment. But it just hung there and he immediately knew what it was.

"Son of a bitch."

With a rising sense of excitement, he gripped the end and pulled. Several more inches of black cord came out, but then whatever was at the end got stuck in the shell. It wouldn't budge.

Scarne walked to the kitchen. He wrapped the shell in a towel and put it in the sink. He found a meat hammer in a drawer and gave the bundle a sharp rap. He heard the shell crack. When he opened the towel, the object inside came loose easily. Scarne lifted it by the black mini-lanyard and smiled. It was two-inch long computer flash drive.

Scarne looked around the still-trashed apartment.

"Way to go, Josh."

PUBLISH OR PERISH

ALTHOUGH HE WAS almost certain no one knew where he was, Scarne didn't feel the least bit silly tilting a chair against the front door knob of the La Gorce apartment. He didn't bother about the sliders to the deck; he would take his chances if Spiderman was on the Ballantrae payroll. But he slept fitfully, and with the Bersa close at hand. The next morning he brewed coffee and took a cold shower. He'd have to stop drinking on the job. He couldn't afford any mistakes. He spent an hour doing what he could to clean up the apartment. Then he packed and called the *South Florida Times*.

†

"I heard about Sheldon Shields," Pourier said without preamble. "I presume there is a connection or you wouldn't be back here."

"This may tell us." The editor's eyes lit up when Scarne held up the flash drive. "Josh hid it in his apartment."

"Where?"

Scarne told him.

"Josh and his shells," Pourier said. "He was always bringing in a bag for me to give to my kids."

He quickly put the flash drive into the UBS slot of his computer. A list of 12 folders popped upon the screen: **DRAFTS, FRAUD (Insurance), FRAUD (Securities), GOVERNMENT REGULATORS, LEGITIMATE BUSINESSES, MISCELLANEOUS, MONEY LAUNDERING, OFFSHORE BANKING, POLITICAL INFLUENCE, PONZIS, RESEARCH** and **SOURCES.**He copied them to the computer's hard drive. Scarne didn't object. The more people with access, the better.

"Why do I think the LEGITIMATE BUSINESSES folder will be thin," Pourier commented, moving the cursor to DRAFT. He opened it, revealing three Word documents: *Ballantrae (First Draft), Ballantrae (Final Draft)* and *To Do.* He put the cursor over the *Final Draft* Word doc. "Only 28 kilobytes. Virtually empty."

"Ballantrae got to write Josh's *Final Draft,*" Scarne said.

The cursor moved to *First Draft.* It contained almost 800 KB.

Business Empire Founded on Fraud Expands in Criminality

By Josh Hidless

"This sounds promising," Pourier said dryly. "Although I'll never understand why reporters insist on writing their own headlines. We change them anyway."

They started reading:

"The Ballantrae Financial Group, a conglomerate of financial services, banking, insurance and trust companies, is nothing more than a front – a clearing house, in fact – for a variety of criminal organizations, sources within the company have revealed. The sources, who have asked for anonymity, said that Ballantrae, which has offices in New York, Miami, Dallas, Seattle, Chicago, South

America, the Caribbean and in many European countries, has, in effect, created a huge Ponzi scheme to hide its real operations and to launder what may potentially be billions of dollars in criminally sourced money from both foreign and domestic partners. The alleged mastermind of this financial plot is Victor Ballantrae, an Australian businessman who is the sole owner of the Ballantrae Group.

Although Ballantrae has been lionized in the financial press and is considered a rising star on Wall Street, he has also apparently caught the eye of several American and international police and regulatory agencies, these sources say. But his company's structure – it consists of more than 50 "affiliated" companies, all with their own boards of directors and lawyers – has so far thwarted any serious prosecutions, they contend.

According to public records, Ballantrae has lost only a few minor skirmishes with the Securities and Exchange Commission and the National Association of Securities Dealers, which have imposed relatively minor fines in a handful of small cases involving allegedly fraudulent securities transactions and aggressive recruitment of employees from rival brokers. In fact, a survey of more than 100 complaints brought against Ballantrae's securities brokers by clients during the past two years reveals that the company won approximately 75% of the cases. (Brokerage disputes rarely end up in court. Most are adjudicated by arbitrators who have worked in the brokerage industry. Clients who lose their cases must pay for the arbitration.)

"He's editorializing here," Pourier said. "But I guess that's all you have to know about Wall Street."

They continued reading.

Ballantrae's non-brokerage companies have also been the target of many civil suits, all of which have been settled or withdrawn.

"This is small change for Ballantrae," one source said of the settlements, which are confidential. "It's breakage, the cost of doing business."

This source, a former Ballantrae employee, said Ballantrae's aggressive expansion into financial services is part of its plan to launder money that is deposited in Ballantrae International Bank, based in Antigua. According to this source (and confirmed by others), the money that flows into that offshore bank is "invested" in the expansion of Ballantrae's financial services business in America. Approximately half of the money in the offshore bank comes from "legitimate" or "quasi-legitimate" sources, mainly very rich South Americans trying to avoid confiscatory estate taxation in their home countries or political appropriation of their wealth. These deposits are then commingled with other deposits from less savory "investors," reportedly including both the Russian and Italian "Mafias" on the West Coast of the United States.

"Holy shit," Pourier said.

"Originally much of the criminal money came from drug cartels, arms merchants and certain Middle Eastern 'charitable' organizations that were fronts for various terrorist groups," claimed one source. "But after 9/11 a lot of that money dried up." This source, who left Ballantrae after he became suspicious of the returns the company was promising its bank investors, said that Ballantrae is being forced to move into financial services in the United States, where it has created a growing broker/dealer business, complete with advisors who sell securities, investment bankers who structure deals, analysts who sell research (some of it quite good, he acknowledged), real estate developers, a marketing arm to attract new investors in the U.S. and a huge legal department that has, to this point, kept regulators and law enforcement officials tied in knots.

"It's a classic Ponzi," this source said. "The money coming into the offshore bank is sent onshore in the States, where it creates an aura of legitimacy. Real clients invest real money in real securities, and may even do well on their legitimate investments. Ballantrae earns commissions and investment banking fees, but nowhere near enough to cover the expenses of its rapid expansion. But it doesn't matter. That

legitimacy in America translates into even more deposits coming into the bank."

"Some of these quotes sound a bit too pat," Pourier said. "I wonder if Josh embellished them or put words into the mouth of his sources."

"Reporters embellish? I'm shocked."

"Yeah, I know. But I'm just saying we'll have to be careful. My lawyers will have a field day with this stuff."

"Maybe we should just ask Josh," Scarne said.

Pourier looked pained and then continued scrolling.

The scheme, he said, is furthered by the ability of the offshore bank in Antigua to pay very high rates on the company's certificates of deposit; often two or three basis, or percentage, points higher than similar instruments offered by mainstream U.S. banks. They can offer such rates because part of the bank money invested in the United States has been placed in some highly leveraged hedge funds returning 20% or more. But according to the source (and confirmed by the company's sales and marketing brochures) Ballantrae tells clients and prospective clients that it achieves its spectacular returns by using a "proprietary" computer-based trading platform that "has created a new paradigm of investment strategy."

"It's all bull," the source continued. "The program only works if the hedge funds continue to perform as advertised and legitimate investors can be lured into putting money into the offshore bank."

Since the interview with this source, there has been a huge shake-out in the mortgage industry and many prominent hedge funds have collapsed, causing problems for prominent Wall Street firms and shaking the very foundations of the world's economy. Ballantrae is not immune to the financial cataclysm. Indeed, it may be uniquely vulnerable. According to one source, Ballantrae takes a 'fee' for laundering mob money that amounts to maybe 10 percent, equal to hundreds of millions of dollars a year. Mobsters can put up with getting back only nine dollars out of every ten as long as it's untraceable and squeaky clean, especially when they're virtually recouping the 10% on C.D.'s. But they are presuming their principal is safe. If Ballantrae's offshore bank were to stop interest payments on its C.D.'s or, in the worse case, refuse to redeem them (offshore instruments are not guaranteed by the F.D.I.C., as are C.D.'s in U.S. banks), the reaction of some investors can only be imagined.

"They might not be too happy if they find out that Ballantrae is gambling with their money in hedge funds," the source said.

"That might be the understatement of the century," Poirior marveled. "If the mob decided to ask for its money back and it's not there, well, it's not going to seek arbitration."

Ballantrae Financial had its origins in a more modest, but still criminal, Ponzi scheme that started in Venezuela and then metastasized to Miami. Money from that original scheme, which was based on the notorious "La Vuelta" scam that defrauded thousands of Venezuelans and Miami residents (mostly Venezuelan expatriates) was then used to fund an even grander fraud involving the sale of $200 million in zero-coupon Venezuelan bonds that the Venezuelan government has disavowed.

The rest of the story was devoted to a detailed explanation of "La Vuelta" and the bond scheme. There was also an incomplete section briefly profiling the various Ballantrae subsidiaries and some of the organization's major players, including Alana Loeb.

A last line in parenthesis read: **(MORE TO COME)**.

"Afraid not, kid," Pourier said quietly.

"Open the 'To Do' doc."

- *Although the story is well sourced, nobody is willing to go on the record. One source said she had heard stories about employees who threatened to spill the beans about the company who then disappeared, or died unexpectedly. She also said that there is something fishy about mortality rates in Ballantrae's insurance unit. I think she might have read "The Firm" once too often.*

- *Tie up loose ends. Have called the company several times for comment. Provided the basics of the allegations. No response, except a threat to sue. Next step may involve a trip to Antigua.*
- *Still awaiting copy of suit brought against Ballantrae brokers by clients burned in lottery scam. Clients withdrew suit (paid off?).*

They started going through the other folders, which each had subfolders and were full of news clippings about the Ballantrae companies and personnel; the Caribbean, Switzerland and other money havens; fragmented interviews; explanations of financial terms; records of phone calls and emails; profiles of politicians and regulators; securities regulations, and examples of financial frauds from the Middle Ages to Madoff.

"This could take hours," Pourier said, quitting half way through the list. He tilted his chair back and putting his hands behind his neck. "I wonder when he had time to sleep, let alone go fishing. That was his passion, you know. That and the godamn seashells. This has Pulitzer written all over it. It's a story any reporter would die for."

Scarne sat on the edge of the desk facing him.

"He apparently did, John. The threat this would reach print would force Ballantrae to stop him, and not with a lawsuit. He couldn't afford to have his mob investors find out he was gambling their money. In effect, he was running a Ponzi on gangsters. I don't know what Ballantrae told the mob but I guarantee it wasn't that they were now in the sub-prime mortgage market and could lose 100% of their money. Criminals are very conservative with their ill-gotten gains. If they found out Ballantrae was gambling their hard-stolen money – after paying him 10% to wash it – they would go nuts."

He suddenly looked thoughtful.

"What? What it is?"

"I've been trying to figure out why so many bodies are piling up. I wouldn't be surprised if there has been a run on Ballantrae's bank."

"What are you talking about?"

He told Pourier about the shooting at Alana's house and Brutti's death in Antigua. He left out the video. Pourier picked up a pad from his desk and balanced it on his knee. As Scarne spoke he wrote continuously, pausing only to shake his head.

"Who knows you have all this information?"

"Nobody but you. But I may have overplayed my hand. Last night I shot off my mouth in front of some of his investors, or partners, or whatever the hell they are, including the head of the Ukrainian mob in Seattle. I was bluffing and guessing. Not that it matters. I'm sure they are looking for me."

"Then it's both our interests to get this in print. Once it's out there, they'll have more to worry about than you or me."

"You shouldn't underestimate these bastards, John. Take whatever precautions you can. When is your next edition?"

"Friday."

"I think this may be a case of publish or perish."

"That refers to academics, and I don't think that's funny."

"I guess not. But I don't see how a story could hurt now. Sheldon Shields is dead. I'm probably next on the list. Whatever happens between now and Friday, one way or another I want Ballantrae finished. But do you have enough to go on? You still have to check things out, don't you?"

"Of course. We'll start a full court press. If we can get hold of Josh's sources, and they confirm what he wrote, there's enough. We'll have to talk to the company, of course. And I want the civil suits, but that should be public record. That will give us enough to turn over some rocks."

Pourior smiled and pointed his pen at Scarne.

"Hell. Even without the sources, we probably have enough to run a 'where there's smoke there's fire story.'"

"Goddamn it!"

"Now what!"

"The sources. If we have their names, then so does Ballantrae."

"Oh, Christ."

Pourier slammed his chair forward and reached for his mouse.

"Maybe he used a code or something," he said, hopefully as he opened the **SOURCES** folder.

It was a list of six names, with phone numbers. The two men looked at each other. Scarne spoke first.

"He wouldn't have known what he was dealing with. In his world, companies that feel threatened call their lawyers, not hit men. Ballantrae didn't realize who Josh was. He considered him just a gnat."

"It's been three months since they got his computer?"

Scarne nodded. Pourier sighed and hit a button on his phone.

"Meg, come in here, please."

Meghan Pace walked in and nodded at Scarne. After a few minutes of background, Pourier printed out the list of sources.

"Grab anyone who is breathing in the newsroom and try to contact these people. Explain what happened. Try not to frighten them, but tell them they should take precautions. Tell them their best bet is to talk to us."

"They've been blown for three months?"

"I'm afraid so."

Meghan Pace shook her head and walked out.

For the next two hours Pourier and Scarne went through everything else that was on Josh's flash drive. On a separate laptop, Pourier hammered out the outline of a story and various notes to staffers. They were finally interrupted by a somber-looking Meghan Pace. She walked over to them holding the list.

"None of these people are in danger," she said. "Anymore."

Both men stared at her.

"Spoke to several widows, in fact. No fun."

"How'd they die?" Pourier said, looking decidedly less cheerful than usual.

"It wasn't on the Bridge at San Luis Rey." She scanned her list. "Car crashes, a drowning, an electrocution, a cardiac and, I kid you not, a bungee-jumping accident. That one actually was a bridge. Must have been a sight."

Scarne automatically patted his pocket. It was empty.

"Damn it!" he said, in frustration.

Pourier recognized the gesture, opened up a drawer in his desk and threw down a pack of cigarettes and a disposable lighter.

"For emergencies, and this sure qualifies. The smoking lamp is lit."

All three used a communal coffee cup as an ashtray.

"I wouldn't venture a guess on the odds of six people on any list dying in separate incidents within three months," Scarne said. "Astronomical. And this isn't any list. It's a list of whistleblowers. Maybe they got lucky with the coronary, but bungee jumping?"

"I guess we'll hold our lead story on the fucking yacht show," Pace said.

After she left, Scarne said, "Contact the F.B.I. office in New York. Ask for agents named John Casey and Thomas Valledolmo." Pourier was jotting notes furiously. "Tell them what you have. I'd bet they will work a quid pro quo with you. It's not like you have to protect any sources. They're all dead."

"What about you?"

"I don't need the First Amendment privilege. And I don't plan on dying. Mention my name. The Feds might open up. Do you need anything else?"

Pourier looked at him incredulously.

"You must be joking. Dead reporter, dead sources, Feds, assassins, the mob and Wall Street! I don't know whether to run this in the news section or the comic pages."

Scarne pulled the flash drive from Pourier's computer.

"Can I borrow an office and a computer and an internet connection?"

THE TRADE

WHEN HE FINISHED with the computer Scarne called his office.

"Jake! Thank God. I've been frantic. I didn't know how to reach you."

Evelyn didn't sound frantic. She might have been reciting the phone book. But he took her word for it.

"Why didn't you try my cell?"

"Alana Loeb called. She wanted to know if I'd heard from you. She told me that your cell was compromised. Not to use it. I didn't know if she was talking about your old phone or the new one. And I certainly couldn't ask her!"

Scarne had to laugh at that.

"What's so bloody funny?"

"Nothing. Listen, Ev, I just left *The South Florida Times*. They're getting ready to blow the lid off Ballantrae. I emailed you what they have. Get it over to those F.B.I. guys and to Sealth in Seattle."

"He called a little while ago. Said he has to talk to you. It's urgent."

"I will. Also Huber at *The New York Times*. But tell him he can't print anything until Friday. That's when it will hit the fan down here. I owe that to Josh and Pourier. Huber probably wouldn't run anything without checking, but at least he'll have a head start. Hell, no reason Dudley and Dick Condon can't have a gander. And Reginald Sink at *Offshore Confidential*."

It might not be enough to prevent his getting killed, but at least his obituaries would be a hell of a read.

"Jake, Ms. Loeb sounded anxious. Maybe even desperate. She wants you to stay away from your hotel."

‡

The street was empty. The only car in Alana's driveway was her blue BMW. Scarne heard a lilting Caribbean melody coming from the back of the house. He walked around back. She was swimming laps, gliding through the water effortlessly. She finally stopped and buried her head in her arms on the far side of the pool.

"Alana."

She turned slowly as he walked toward her. She swam to the shallow end and walked up the submerged staircase, seemingly oblivious to her glistening nudity. When she reached him, she stood silent for a moment. Then she slapped him hard across the face. Something seemed to go out of her and she reached up gently and touched the red welt on his cheek. She put both arms around him and put her head on his chest.

"I thought you were dead. Victor will try to kill you, if only to save face."

She clung to him fiercely. He felt her body through his now wet clothes. He put his arms around her. His right hand gently massaged the cleft between her buttocks at the base of her spine, where the tattoo was. He knew she liked that. She shivered and pressed into his groin. He felt his control going. He reached up and pulled her arms down.

"Alana, we have to talk."

His voice was hoarse. He picked up a towel from a nearby chaise and held it open. She walked into it and he wrapped it around her.

"You look so serious, Jake. We love each other and you are going to destroy that, aren't you? But I am selfish. I've never loved anyone before. I want it to last a little longer. So, before we talk, make love to me. You won't want to do it after. You may hate me then. You can do anything you like. Treat me like the lowest whore in creation. Or a queen. Whatever you want. It won't matter, because I know you love me. I see it in your eyes. Carry me upstairs."

They made love slowly and silently, totally absorbed in each other. Unlike their previous couplings, she remained passive, and seemed to enjoy his dominance, taking pleasure in being loved. The only sounds came at the end, when they couldn't help themselves. After a while, lying on her side facing him, she began to speak. She told him about her childhood, the massacre and kidnapping, the rescue from the bordello. He listened in morbid fascination.

"When one of the men my grandfather hired burst through the door, I was with a boy. We were fucking. He was a nice boy. The man pulled him off me by his ponytail and slit his throat. I guess he thought I was being raped. I can still see that poor kid spurting from the neck and his penis at the same time. Not many women can say that. Perhaps it was a reflex. They say some men ejaculate when they are hanged. I've never told anyone that story. I have more like that, if you want to hear them."

"Alana. Don't."

"The leader of the soldiers who rescued me was a former Legionnaire. We became lovers before he went off to fight in some stupid war."

Without thinking Scarne reached behind her and touched the Cross of Lorraine tattoo. He'd always wondered about it.

"I didn't love him. He was paid to find me. I've never loved anyone. Until now." She smiled. "You may have been paid, but not to save my life, twice. You reminded me of him. I saw it the day I met you. After the shooting at the pool, I rewarded you with sex. But with Brutti you risked your life for me and were almost killed. Since then I have rewarded you with love. Can you not feel the difference when you are inside me? I know I can. So strange. Tell me again you love me. No, show me again. One last time."

"Victor and I recognized each other for what we were, right off."

Alana's final cries of passion had dissolved into bitter tears, but she quickly regained her composure and was now calmly explaining Ballantrae's many schemes and her part in them. Scarne's blood ran cold when she described how she recruited Garza, and what the Cuban assassin and Keitel had been doing over the years. She saw the look on his face and for a moment he thought she would break down again. Instead, she laughed harshly and got up and put on a silk wrap. Then she sat at the end of the bed, tucking her legs beneath her.

"Get me a cigarette, please, Jake. They're in the nightstand."

Scarne lit her cigarette and she took a long drag, letting the smoke out in a luxurious hiss, then nonchalantly flicked an ash off her sleeve.

"I won't give you any nonsense about my childhood traumas," she said. "We are all responsible for our actions. I did what I had to do to survive. I fought my way to the top. But I was willing to risk it all to protect you. That must count for something."

"What happened to Josh Shields?"

She looked disappointed but then resumed her dispassionate narrative.

"The questions he asked us were too pointed. We felt we had to do something. There was simply too much at stake to let a no-name reporter derail all our plans. Of course, in retrospect, we know why he was so dogged, so well informed. You must appreciate our shock when we found out who he really was. It's funny, when you think about it. The people who took me when I was young didn't realize how powerful my family was. It cost some of them their lives. And we made the same mistake with Josh Shields."

"How was he killed?"

Scarne's voice sounded like it came from someone else. She told him, in clear concise terms. She might have been discussing the settlement of a nuisance lawsuit.

"Of course, the method was all their own," she said. "They are quite mad."

Scarne made a mental note to let the medical examiner know he had been close to the truth. He wondered how the Miami Beach Chamber of Commerce would take it.

"Eventually, despite our blunder, we felt we were in the clear. Then you showed up. I told Victor you were dangerous. But he wanted to play games. He was angry with me because I had ended our affair. He told me to seduce you. That was the easy part. Oh yes, it was all part of the plan. I decided to have some fun. You were attractive, and every smile I got from you was a dagger to Victor's heart. I don't like many men. Silly poseurs, most of them. But I found myself liking you. By the time you came for me after Goetz was killed, I wanted you. If you hadn't come, I don't know what I would have done. Taking you to Antigua was lunacy. But if you weren't there, I would have been killed. You were so savage in protecting me. Now, I had to protect you."

Alana looked at Scarne to see his reaction. There was none.

"I told Victor that if anything happened to you, I would expose him, even if I went to jail. Or worse. I think he wanted to kill me then. But I told him I'd taken the normal precautions. Copies. Safe deposit boxes. Letters held by lawyers. Bluff mostly. I bet the authorities have a lot on us now. Our political influence is waning with the changes in Washington. We're not as protected as we were. We buy off most investigations with campaign contributions. The rest die on the vine of our lawyers' delaying tactics and smokescreens. Every new crop of politicians needs watering. But it takes time. Victor couldn't take the chance. Things are very dicey right now."

Alana motioned for another cigarette. Scarne also needed one.

"Josh Shields was right about some things," she continued. "We did invest some of the money from our less-than-savory 'investors' in hedge funds. How else could we offer the phenomenal returns on our C.D.'s we needed to attract more deposits? I warned Victor about that, but he pictured himself as a buccaneer. He didn't realize that those Wall Street stars profiled in the *Journal* and the *Times* and on the cover of *Fortune* were bigger con men than he was. Ironic, when you think about it. He made much of his fortune by selling bad paper, backed by nothing. And then he risked the mob's money on hedge funds that invested in sub-prime mortgages. Talk about worthless paper!"

Alana let out a long stream of smoke, then smiled.

"But his story wasn't entirely accurate. We never took money from the Mid-East 'charities.' Oh, yes, I read his story.

Had it seen the light of day, we might have insisted on a correction about that part of it. I guess you don't think that's funny. But there were plenty of legitimate crooks we could service. Baby killers, we're not."

"A fine distinction, Alana. What about Josh's sources?"

"Disloyal employees," she shrugged. "We made them rich, and that's how they repaid us?'

"And Maria Brutti?"

Scarne saw incomprehension on her face.

"Garza killed Brutti's sister and planted the body in Boyko's warehouse."

She looked genuinely stricken.

"No! After all we had survived last year our Ukrainian and Italian friends recently had a burst of patriotism. The Government wanted them to help monitor ports on the West Coast for terrorists, like Lucky Luciano did in New York during the Second World War. It was Nazis back then, of course. Our clients were pressured to do the right thing by Government agents sniffing into their deposits offshore. The sniffing would stop once they started helping out with port security. But the damage had been done. They didn't like the Government knowing where their money was, so they started to make arrangements to relocate it. That would have created a liquidity crisis because after the hedge fund debacle Victor had decided to go somewhat legitimate by building a mainstream Wall Street presence. That takes money, and he had again dipped into their funds. As you might imagine, they weren't the kind of people who take I.O.U's. Fortunately, their withdrawals were gradual; they needed time to find safe havens for their money."

She paused to light another cigarette. She rearranged her feet under herself and absentmindedly began rubbing one of them.

"We needed time to refill their accounts. Victor sent Garza to Seattle to sow trouble. Jesús was supposed to set the Italians and the Ukrainians at each other's throats. By the time things calmed down we would have been able to sell things, restore the funds in their accounts. I assumed he would blow something up. You have to believe me, I knew nothing about the killing. He and Keitel are becoming more macabre as they go along. But how did Brutti find out it was him? Garza is usually very careful."

Scarne told her about the autopsy and Brutti's subsequent rampage.

"So, Garza unwittingly precipitated a vendetta against us. We wondered about that. Until he figured out what was going on, Victor didn't need me upsetting the apple cart. So he promised to leave you alone. I negotiated for your life on the flight back from Antigua. But I had to give him a bone."

Scarne had a sick feeling in his stomach.

"Sheldon Shields."

"Yes. I traded his life for yours." Alana looked at him coldly. "Isn't this the point where you tell me that we killed your client and you have to do something about it? Like in the movies. But you can't, can you? Sheldon Shields died for our sins, my darling. Pity. I liked Sheldon. He was a gentleman. More than I can say about his brother. The horny old toad made a pass at me on the yacht."

Scarne started to say something, but she cut him off.

"I warned you off, several times. You knew what you were getting into. Don't hide behind your clients, or your honor." She laughed. "You have the look you had when you killed Brutti, Jake. Do you want to kill me? You won't. Because you still love me."

'I CAN LEND YOU SOME HANDCUFFS'

THEY WERE SITTING in her library, drinks and cigarettes in hand. Scarne needed both, badly. Alana was once again remarkably composed.

"It's over, Alana. Josh Shields made a copy of all his notes. I found them. He didn't have everything, but he had more than enough."

"We went through his apartment."

Scarne told her about the flash drive.

"Priceless. What did you do with it?"

"The newspapers have enough to bring Ballantrae down. And the Feds have it, too. They were closing in anyway. The F.B.I. was at your pool party, taking pictures, and followed us to Antigua. For a time, we were giving Brad and Angelina a run for their money."

"Do you think they'd give me some for my album? For my grandchildren."

"Then there's the Seattle police. They're going to want Garza. The New York cops will want Keitel. And they'll all want you. They'll look closely at all those suspicious deaths of Josh's sources."

Alana looked at him calmly.

"What do you want me to do?"

"You have to cut a deal. Your best bet is in Seattle. There's a homicide cop there with a one-track mind. He wants to settle accounts for Maria Brutti. He may be able to get you immunity while we work out something with the Feds, if you can convince him you didn't know about what happened out there. You can probably put a lot of bigwigs in jail. Some Federal prosecutor can make his bones on your testimony. Might even offer witness protection. It will be a rough few years, but you'll be free, and alive. But you have to act fast."

"And where will you be?"

"Back in New York, trying to forget I ever met you."

She smiled. No one ever forgot her.

"Somehow, I can't see myself running a hair salon in Iowa."

She tilted her head, looking up at him with doe eyes. She never looked more beautiful.

"It might not be quite that bad. You don't have a choice."

"And if I say no? Do you 'take me in'? I can lend you some handcuffs."

"This isn't the movies, Alana. I can't arrest you. But after Friday, everyone connected to Victor Ballantrae will be radioactive. It may be weeks before you're arrested. But by then, you will have few options. Victor, Garza and Keitel will cut their deals. You'll be on your own."

"You may think you know them, Jake, but you don't. They will cut no deals. And I won't betray them."

"Honor among thieves, Alana? They took a video to use against you. You don't owe them anything."

"Office politics. It was the right move for them. After all, I was acting irrationally. I guess I still am. Love makes you do funny things, right Jake? It's why I avoided it so long. After all, they didn't try to hurt you, physically. They kept their part of the bargain, after a fashion. Of course, after your performance at the Forge all bets are off. Garza and Keitel want you dead, in the worst way. And they are experts in worst ways, as you know."

"I'm pretty good at taking care of myself. Besides, after Friday, they will have other things on their minds."

"Just the same, don't go back to your hotel. Stay here. They would never do anything in my house. Maybe you can talk me into that Iowa hair salon."

He knew he couldn't. She was going to run.

"Whatever it is you're planning, Alana, don't do it. Turn yourself in. I'll do everything I can."

She put her drink on a table and leaned forward, searching his face.

"Darling, come away with me. We can have a wonderful life. I have plenty of money. I'll do just about anything you want. But I'm not going into any fucking witness protection program. This isn't an episode of *The Sopranos*. If I disappear, it will be to a beach somewhere, where it is warm, with a change of hair color, a new name and half a dozen passports. We'll leave many well-paid lawyers behind to muddy the waters. In five years, everybody will forget about us. Who knows, maybe we'll slip back into the country as illegal immigrants. Nobody ever finds them."

"You are whistling past the graveyard. What about the Shields family?"

"You overestimate the power of the press, darling. Media properties go on the block all the time, at bargain prices nowadays. Who knows who will own that company in a few years? Maybe us."

"And the various mafias you've bilked? Not to mention the people they've lost. Do you think they will forgive and forget?"

She waved her hand dismissively.

"They will be made whole financially. That's all that matters to those people. We shouldn't have panicked. A wire transfer here, a wire transfer there, and it's done. It is being accomplished as we speak. Some other depositors, who are, let's say, less prone to violence will find their accounts bare, but that's what they get for evading banking laws. We will blame the recent disconnect in the credit markets. There is nothing that anyone can do about it. In this country if you steal a little money, especially if you are poor, they throw the book at you. And if you steal in the billions, well, then even your moribund regulators may be moved to action. But if you steal somewhere in between, like us, then you stand a fair chance of getting away with it. As for Garza and Keitel, they killed for years before we even knew them, and it didn't seem to bother anyone. They leave few tracks. The only one to catch on was Brutti, a killer himself. I'm not particularly worried. You yourself said that it will be weeks before the police will rouse themselves to action."

There was nothing more for Scarne to say. He realized that some of what she said was an act, perhaps to make it easier for him to despise her. He stood up. She didn't meet his gaze. When she spoke it was as if he weren't there.

"Just go. Stay away from your hotel until tomorrow. Then, it won't matter."

Scarne drove back to La Gorce and parked the car. He went back down to the lobby. Mario came out of the concierge cubicle.

"Mr. Scarne. I thought you were back when I saw the car gone. But I was getting concerned, so I called Mr. Shields. They told me he died! I couldn't believe it. I spoke to a Miss Emma

Shields and she said not to worry about the car until I heard from her. She said if I saw you that you should call her."

So Emma was watching his back. He would make sure she got Josh's files.

"Has anyone been looking for me?"

"No. Are you expecting someone?'

It was unlikely Garza and Keitel would check the apartment after his breach with the Shields family, but he gave Mario a description of the two killers anyway.

"If you see either of them, let me know. And there is something else I want you to do. I had to search the apartment pretty thoroughly." He smiled at the understatement. "Arrange a cleaning service, the industrial kind, to straighten things up. You might also want your handyman to check it out. Here's $500. Keep $100 for yourself and if you need more bill my office."

Scarne gave Mario his business card.

"You have been one of our more interesting guests, Mr. Scarne. I'll miss you."

When Scarne got to the apartment, he took a shower and then remembered to call Noah Sealth. He told the detective to expect the files.

"Alana doesn't want a deal. I think she's going to run. Ballantrae and the boys, too. Not much any of us can do about it in the short term."

"They're not going to get far, Jake, and they have no long term."

"What are you talking about?"

"That's why I've been trying to reach you. Ballantrae overreached out here. The Brutti thing struck a nerve with our mob bosses. They don't mind occasionally whacking each other but draw the line at outsiders bumping off locals, especially when trying to set them against each other. Ballantrae accomplished the impossible. He got these skels to work together. Their first joint project is him. One of my informants told us Boyko promised old man Brutti he'd settle accounts for all of them, personally. He's heading to Miami."

"He's already here, Noah. I saw him last night."

Scarne explained what happened at the Forge. As he did he watched an Air France 747 turning in over the ocean on its descent in Miami International.

"Jesus. I wish I could have seen that. What did Boyko do?"

"Nothing. Just took it all in."

"That's not a good sign. The calmer Andriy is, the worse things are sure to get. I don't know what he's planning to do, or when, but based on past experience, it's going to be like Nagasaki. Ballantrae's two homos aren't the only ones with imagination."

"Alana told me that they are going to pay off the Bruttis and Boyko."

"Won't matter. That may just speed up things. This is personal. Ballantrae fucked with the wrong people. She did, too. Don't go anywhere near her."

They were silent for a moment. Finally, Sealth said, "Hey, don't beat yourself up. What happened last night doesn't matter. It's a done deal. Go home. Let the Miami cops pick up the pieces."

"You want to countenance murder, Noah? Isn't it your duty to warn them?"

"Don't fucking lecture me." He sounded angry. "These scumbags have crapped all over my town. If I could get them myself I would, but I have to go by the book, and they'll be long gone, one way or the other. You're not exactly a hero in all this, my friend." Sealth relented. "Listen, I made a call. All I got was Ballantrae lawyers and PR pukes. They clammed up, even though I told them they had nothing to gain since they, and a couple thousand other Ballantrae employees, were about to join the ranks of the unemployed. Loyal or afraid, take your pick. I called the Miami cops, too. Said they would look into it. Don't hold your breath. Go ahead, give it a shot. Maybe you can convince the woman, get her out of it, cause that's what you want. You don't give a shit about the others. But Boyko probably wouldn't mind a piece of your ass, now that he knows you. If I was you, I'd go back to New York. She made her bed, and you're well out of it."

TURKEY SHOOT

Scarne tried to reach Alana at home. Answering machine. Left a message warning her. Same with her cell phone. He got his jacket, checked his gun and pocketed extra rounds and headed to the garage.

Her front door was locked. He rang the bell and pounded on the door. He went around back and tried the sliders to the kitchen. The house was dark. He picked up a wrought iron chair from the patio and hurled it through the glass. An alarm sounded. The house was deserted. He checked her bedroom. It bore signs of a quick exit. As he drove away, he heard sirens approaching. He called her office. Everyone was "away on business."

Miami was a big city. He'd never find her. Then he remembered her warning. He drove to the Delano, and spotted Keitel lounging against a red Lamborghini parked out front. Garza was behind the wheel. Every now and then Keitel walked into the hotel. Often he came back with a cell phone glued to his ear, smiling at the beautiful people pulling up in their exotic cars. Scarne wondered how long they would wait before joining their bosses. He assumed they would all be leaving together, wherever they were going. He had to assume that; it was his only chance of finding Alana. He briefly thought about walking over to them and telling them about Sealth's tip. But once they had the information they'd probably just shoot him many times, this stretch of town being one of the few places on earth where you could be unobtrusive making a getaway in a Lamborghini. And if he killed them, he'd never find her.

At 6 p.m. sharp Keitel came out of the hotel for the last time and climbed in the car, which pulled away from the curb. Scarne followed them down Collins Avenue. They left Miami Beach via the Venetian Causeway, which travels through six small islands in Biscayne Bay on its way to Miami proper. Scarne had to be careful not to get too close. Halfway across, he was startled by a sign that read "Dildo Island," until he realized that some wit had whited out the second "I" in "Dilido."

Once off the causeway, Garza went south on US1. Scarne wondered if they were headed to the Ballantrae office, but they soon cut over to I-395 and then to I-95 South and sped up. Scarne had to weave in and out of traffic going 80 to keep them in sight but wasn't worried about being spotted. On this stretch of I-95 maniacal driving was the norm. At one point, some lunatic passed both Garza and Scarne at probably 110 miles an hour. Soon, however, all the southbound traffic had to slow as I-95 merged into US1. Because of the traffic and lights, he almost missed their turn toward Coral Gables. There were few cars in this neighborhood, one of the richest in America. Scarne turned off his headlights, hoping he wouldn't plow into one of the massive ficus trees that defined the area.

Garza entered the grounds of the Biltmore Hotel and drove up through the famous arched driveway and stopped at the entrance. Keitel got out, said something to the valet, and walked inside. Garza pulled off to the side. Scarne drove past the driveway and into a small lot that said, "Guest Self Parking." He had a clear view of the driveway exit. He got out and put the top down on the car. There was nothing he could do about the vehicle's color, but with convertibles a dime a dozen in this part of Florida, he hoped the change in appearance would help. After 10 minutes he decided to chance a closer look. Well screened by trees and shrubs, he walked to the bottom of the driveway and was debating what to do next when Garza came out of the hotel, followed by Alana and Ballantrae. Just behind them were Boyko and his two thugs. Ballantrae was smiling, but Alana looked tense. A large limousine pulled up to the group and Ballantrae held the door for Alana, as the other men crowded around. She got in, and so did the men. Scarne ran to his car and watched as the limo, followed by Garza and Keitel, left the driveway and headed away. Soon the little convoy, with Scarne bringing up the rear, was back on US1, once again heading south.

They passed the huge University of Miami campus. The drive rapidly became boring, with long stretches of car washes, auto shops, restaurants, check cashing stores, strip malls, motels and gas stations. Scarne checked his fuel gauge. Just over three-quarters full; plenty, unless they were headed for Cuba. The traffic wasn't bad. They had missed rush hour. They passed Kendall and Homestead, with its huge Air Force Reserve base. Their destination was obvious: The Florida Keys. It made sense to Scarne. There were small airstrips in the Keys. And calm inlets for a float plane. They could fly out with less notice. And there were plenty of places for a boat to meet them.

Whatever their plans, Scarne was almost certain that not everyone would make – or finish – the journey. He thought about calling the police. State troopers might stop the cars on a tip of drugs or gun running, but that would only delay the inevitable. He had no proof. He had to wait for the end game.

†

They rolled past Florida City and headed into the Keys. They passed Key Largo. Bogie wouldn't have gotten in this jam, Scarne thought. The caravan kept on, past the towns of Tavernier and Islamorada, then on to the academic-sounding Lignumvitae Key. Traffic had thinned, as weekenders and vacationers peeled off to various resorts and marinas. He smelled the salt water, the Gulf of Mexico on one side, the Atlantic on the other. He lit a cigarette to help stay awake. The distraction almost caused him to overtake the cars ahead, which were stopped at an accident scene. He could see the flashing emergency lights. He jammed on his brakes and heard a screech behind him. He waved an apology. Scarne knew he would have to be more alert. It's considered bad form to crack up your car while tailing someone.

An ambulance and several Florida Highway Patrol cars passed him going in the opposite direction. Soon, he was on the move again, passing dozens of small islands: Fiesta Key, Conch Key, Duck Key and Key Vaca. The town of Marathon was next, a dusty strip of shopping plazas, gas stations and tourist traps. Before he knew it, Scarne was on the Seven-Mile Bridge, with only three cars separating him from his quarry.

A few minutes later he saw their brake lights. They turned off into Big Pine Key. Now they were the only three cars on a road, which got narrower and more isolated. Scarne wondered if he should chance turning off his lights, but a vision of his car shooting off the winding road into swamp deterred him.

In the front seat of the lead car, Andriy Boyko spoke into his cell phone. A closed glass partition separated him from Ballantrae and Alana in the back.

"Is he still behind you?"

In the second car, Christian Keitel looked in his rear mirror.

"Yes, maybe a quarter mile back."

"Amazing." There was respect in the Ukrainian's voice. "But now it is time for the hare to turn on the fox. There is a sharp bend just before the cutoff. You will have to slow. If you go straight there is a road, but it has been blocked by a barrier of logs. Just past the turn is the road to the dock, on the left. There is no sign, but you can't miss it. Pull in and you can go back and catch him when he slows for the bend. Take him out there. Then meet us at the dock. I have something else for you."

"What about his car?"

"Pull it into the cutoff. Won't be found for days. We'll be long gone."

Garza and Keitel saw the log barrier and slowed for the sharp bend. Almost immediately they saw the entrance to the small road on the left. As they pulled in and stopped, they could see the taillights of Boyko's car diminishing in the distance. They got out and popped the trunk of their car. With practiced precision, they pulled out two 12-gauge pump shotguns and fed large shells into the magazines. Garza loaded with hollow point deer slugs; Keitel, heavy lead buckshot. They were taking no chances. Running back to the road, they could see the headlights of Scarne's car, coming fast. He would have lost sight of their taillights and probably was speeding up. With any luck, he'd plow right through the bend into the logs. Then they could finish him off at their leisure.

They positioned themselves on either side of the road just past the turn. Keitel, with the buckshot, was closer to the bend on the right side of the road. He could fire the first blast without endangering his partner with the pattern spread. It would be a turkey shoot.

Now they could hear Scarne's car. Its headlights began to illuminate nearby trees and brush. Garza thought he saw small pairs of eyes reflecting the beam. He wondered what animals were about. Not that he cared. His slugs could stop a car, let alone a raccoon. Scarne's car was almost at the bend. Would he see the turn and the log pile in time?

The two killers heard a low whine from Scarne's car as he downshifted coming into the turn. He had seen the obstacle. But it wouldn't matter. Keitel edged nearer the turn, raising his shotgun and bracing it solidly against his shoulder. He hadn't used a 12-gauge in quite some time. It would have quite a kick. One never got used to it. It might leave a bruise, he thought resignedly.

There was a rustle in the undergrowth directly in front of him, and a small animal broke cover and ran directly onto the road into Scarne's path.

Both gunmen heard the screech of brakes.

The Key Deer is a miniature breed indigenous to South Florida. An endangered species, the last wild herd of perhaps 300 individual animals lives only on Big Pine Key and surrounding islands. Mature adults rarely top two feet at the shoulders and weigh only 50 pounds.

The frightened deer spooked by Keitel darted down the road right at Scarne, who swerved and jammed on the brakes. The car slalomed through the turn, missing the animal but finding the log pile, smashing into it broadside. Some of the smaller logs at the top of the pile were dislodged by the impact and rolled into the convertible.

The car's headlights were now pointing down the main road, into the ditch at its side. Caught in the beams was a startled Garza, who began moving towards the car, raising a shotgun to his shoulder. In the dusty haze on the other side of the road, there was also movement. Keitel! Scarne had stopped 50 feet short of their killing zone.

With one motion, Scarne unbuckled his seat belt and flung open the driver's side door. But he didn't go left. Instead he jumped onto the passenger's seat and vaulted over the log pile.

The diversion worked. Garza, expecting Scarne to come out the driver's side, pumped out three quick booming shots. Two of the heavy slugs clanged into the door with such force it almost closed. Keitel had a better angle as Scarne went over the woodpile. He got off two shots, but at a greater distance than he had wanted. The windshield exploded and some of the big double-o pellets caught Scarne in the lower legs as he dove over the pile.

But his landing behind the pile did the real damage. He felt, and heard, the sickening pop as he dislocated his left shoulder. He couldn't suppress a moan. Keitel also kept firing and Scarne heard glass shattering and metal-twanging. This time Scarne moaned loudly, for effect, hoping they would assume his wounds were serious, maybe fatal. But all that the fusillade accomplished was to knock out three of the car's tires and its headlights, plunging the area into blessed darkness.

Scarne drew his gun. He knew the odds weren't good if he went up against the two killers. The Bersa held seven rounds. He had put his extra magazines in the center console for easy access, but it would be suicide to go back to the vehicle. Keitel and Garza had pump shotguns. He had a pistol. The effective killing distance of the respective weapons was about the same, but as Scarne knew from the throbbing of his legs, his assailants didn't need to be all that accurate. If it wasn't for the woodpile, Scarne would be dead with a hundred holes in him. Safety for Scarne meant heading up the trail he was on, away from the killers. They would be crazy to follow him. And they weren't crazy. They were pros. They would carefully check around the car and woodpile to see if they had gotten him. They would listen for a while. But then they would go back to the car they presumably parked a short distance up the main road.

Scarne didn't hesitate. He switched his gun into his almost-useless left hand. He reached down with his right, picked up a small piece of wood and threw it to his left. He was moving in the opposite direction before it even landed. When it did he heard shots. He plunged into the swampy woodland, and was relieved to find he could move almost silently. He was only a few yards from the road. He holstered the Bersa and put his good arm out to ward off collision with trees. It didn't prevent branches from slashing his face, and he stumbled on roots. In some places the water was up to his knees.

He heard a shotgun boom. It was close, but no leaves rattled and no bark flew. They were shooting at other sounds. There were animals about. But Garza and Keitel would give that up soon, as pointless. It was so dark that Scarne decided to take a chance. He cut to the road and looked back. He couldn't see the two men. Or even his car. Which meant they couldn't see him. He broke into a run, eyes down at the barely-visible road. He almost missed the small cutoff where Keitel and Garza had left their car. It was parked about 20 feet in. He tried the door. It was locked. He looked down the road. He thought he saw light, and maybe a glint of water, perhaps 200 feet ahead.

Scarne remembered the silencer. That might be his only advantage. With agony in every movement, he slipped his left hand into his pocket and pulled it out and put it between his teeth. Then he put the gun in his left hand, which would barely close, and using his right clumsily screwed on the silencer. He was debating whether to head for the boat sounds, or wait and try to finish Keitel and Garza. Then the car chirped and its headlights flashed. He swung around and in the dim light saw Garza pushing the remote on a set of keys.

The two men, perhaps 10 feet apart, saw each other for only a second. Garza raised his shotgun but Scarne's pistol coughed first. He heard a grunt. The shotgun boomed and Scarne was hurled back against the cars, his side burning with pain. He fired at the flash of the big gun, twice, and rolled off the side of the road. He wondered why he wasn't dead, then realized Garza must have been using slugs. The heavy bullet had taken a chunk out of his side. A pellet spread would have splattered him all over the landscape. Where was Keitel? He crawled over to Garza, who was lying on his back staring up with one eye open. The other eye was a bloody crater.

Scarne lay prone next to the body and heard the footsteps of a man running and the metallic clack of a shotgun being pumped. Keitel presumably hadn't heard Scarne's silenced shots and was looking for a target at eye level. He would also be loath to fire without knowing where Garza was.

Scarne, head down so that his eyes wouldn't give him away, listened to Keitel's steps slow. He must see something lying in the road. Now! Scarne raised his gun and shot Keitel twice in mid-body. The man screamed and sank to his knees, jamming the shotgun into the dirt, where it went off and spayed bits of dirt and rock into Scarne's face, momentarily blinding him. Now Keitel saw Garza's bloody face and red hate boiled in his eyes. He raised his gun, his mouth open in the beginnings of a howl as he pumped another shell into the chamber. Scarne got to his knees and quickly put a bullet into the howl.

Keitel pitched forward on the body of his partner.

Scarne slowly got to his feet and looked down at the two dead killers.

"Checkmate," he said.

'WHAT DID YOU DO?'

SCARNE WAS HAVING trouble breathing. But he knew he was lucky to be breathing at all. If it wasn't for the deer, he would have driven into their ambush. It was a miracle they hadn't killed him anyway. His wounds weren't mortal, but he couldn't take much more damage. He was leaking blood and losing strength. But he hurt in so many places, it wasn't that bad. The body couldn't concentrate on one particular pain.

With only one round left in the Bersa, he needed more firepower. With a useless left arm, the pump shotguns would do him no good. He rolled Keitel off Garza and patted him down. Nothing. He tried the Cuban. Only the shotgun. The car! He went to the open trunk, and had just started rummaging around when he heard a large marine engine rumble to life. Scarne decided. He turned and sprinted down the road. One bullet would have to do. Or, rather, the fact that his opponents wouldn't know there was only one.

He stumbled twice. Each time the breath whistled out between his teeth and it was a struggle to rise. They must have heard the shotguns. No matter. They would assume it was Garza and Keitel. He was counting on the element of surprise. If his exertion didn't make him bleed out first.

He almost ran full tilt into a small shack that loomed out of the dark. Light drifted around the edges of the structure, which appeared to be nothing more than a fishing cabin. He heard voices and harsh guttural laughter from the water side of the shack, which was on a spit of land. He could hear boat sounds: the low coughing of an idling engine; wooden piles knocking; water sloshing; the almost lyrical twang of straining hawsers. He slid along one wall. More voices. Russian? And Ballantrae's. He was arguing with someone but sounded slightly defensive.

Scarne went through the minor agony of removing the silencer. It had served its purpose but would slow the bullet; now accuracy and killing power were all that mattered. He edged his head around the corner of the shack. What he saw helped make up his mind, while at the same time greatly reducing his chances of survival. A large modern sport fishing yacht was tied up at a small dock under a bright light. There were five men arranged in a rough semicircle around Alana and Ballantrae. One of them was Boyko. Two others were just climbing onto the boat, straining with the weight of a large black metal cooler. They placed it against the gunwale near the rear of the boat. One of the men lifted its lid and looked in, grimacing. The boat was rocking and some water sloshed out of the cooler. The man looked at Alana and Ballantrae and smiled. But he closed the lid after a sharp rebuke from Boyko.

Scarne weighed his options. None were particularly promising. Two of Boyko's men carried short-barreled automatic rifles. The others had pistols in their belts. He could rush the boat, kill the nearest man, take his weapon and try to shoot it out with the others. It was suicide. He might get one or two, but certainly would be cut down by the others and get Alana killed in the process.

Then, the decision was taken out of his hands. Boyko said something to the man standing by the tub, who put on a pair of heavy work gloves, visibly shuddered, and reached into the tub. It took him several minutes to get hold of whatever was in the tub, which appeared to slip from his grasp as he cursed loudly. Boyko laughed and said something that brought cackles from his men. Finally the other man wrestled a pinkish-grey eel-like creature above the lip of the tub, where it wriggled obscenely and started exuding slime, which dripped all over the deck.

"Jesus Christ!"

It was Ballantrae. Alana's hands went to her throat.

The man holding the creature struggled to maintain his balance in the slime at his feet. Scarne knew what it was. Noah Sealth had described a hagfish in great detail. Scarne also knew what was coming. Alana's eyes were wide with terror. Insanely, he recalled how he went to Florida thinking he was on a wild goose chase. Well, now there was nothing for it.

Scarne stepped out and pointed the Bersa at the man with the hagfish.

"Put it back in the tub."

Everyone froze and all heads turned his way.

Startled, the man with the hagfish slipped on the dripping slime. It was a classic pratfall and his back hit the cooler, which overturned and sent its contents across the deck. Scarne saw three other hagfish slither toward the stern. The man who fell lost his purchase on his captive and it came to rest on his chest. He screamed and twisted away as the prehistoric fish plopped to the deck and slid toward its companions, where they all wriggled madly gasping for oxygen in the ghastly pool of water and slime collecting in one corner. Everyone, including Scarne, watched the horrible tableau for a second before the other men brought up their weapons.

"Hold it!" Scarne shouted. "I'll kill the first man that moves."

They stopped, but Boyko, facing Scarne, smiled.

"You are a brave man," he said, in excellent English. "But only one. We are five. I don't doubt your ability with that pop-gun. You bested those two maniacs we left behind to kill you. I thank you for that. Saves me the trouble. You will notice we have four of these monstrous fish. Two of them were for Mr. Garza and Mr. Keitel."

There was a curious look on Ballantrae's face. He could add.

"Grotesque creatures," Boyko went on blithely. "But a fitting payback for Maria Brutti, don't you think? I have no love for the dagos but they will be very grateful for the gesture. What's that saying, 'What's good for the goose is good for the gander?' Maybe, now, things will get back to normal in Seattle."

"What the hell are you talking about, Andriy?" Ballantrae's voice had a wheedling edge of panic. "Kill him and let's get moving."

"Let the woman go," Scarne said. "You've won."

Boyko gave him an appraising look.

"She is not innocent."

"She had nothing to do with Maria Brutti. And what happened afterward was not intentional."

"Perhaps you would like to explain that distinction to the Brutti family. I would not. But it is of no consequence. I want to make a statement, for the Bruttis and myself. We are not to be trifled with. You East Coast people have no respect for us in Seattle. When word of this gets out – and I will make sure it does – it will be good for business. Call it a marketing ploy."

"You won't live to see that business. Here's the deal. Your lives for her. I will see that she is punished. But not this way. You have Ballantrae. I don't care what you do with him."

Ballantrae's mouth was working, but no sound came out. He started to move toward the boat's ladder but two men blocked his path.

Boyko shrugged.

"The woman asked me to spare your life, but Victor wouldn't hear of it. He knew you would follow her. If it's any consolation, she was a very unwilling bait. You want to rescue her. There is something between you. That is a pity. I, too, am a romantic. But she is too dangerous. She knows too much. If she can, she will do everything in her power to avoid punishment. She will further entrance you. Even if you mean what you say, she will hire the best lawyers. Perhaps plead insanity, or childhood abuse. I have found out some things about her. The Bruttis want vengeance, not an interminable series of appeals through your appalling legal system. My way is better."

"Don't be a fool. She has undoubtedly made provisions. Ballantrae, too. It's all on paper somewhere, or on disks."

"He's right. If anything happens to us, you will go down." Ballantrae had finally found his voice, although it was none too steady.

The thrashing on the deck was getting louder. Boyko looked amused.

"Victor, a moment ago you wanted to kill him. And now he's your new best friend?" He turned to Scarne. "Unfortunately for you, the Government now values my patriotism and is willing to overlook some misdeeds. But this is getting tiresome." He looked pointedly at Scarne's weapon. "That is a small gun. A Bersa, no? I have one myself. We heard many shots. You may have reloaded, but no matter. You can't shoot all of us."

"But I will shoot you, Andriy." Scarne smiled coldly. He centered the barrel on Boyko's face. He felt unafraid, detached.

The Ukrainian leaned back against the side of the boat and crossed his ankles, in a pose of resignation. And he smiled back.

"My friend, if you know who I am, you will also know that I did not rise to the position I have attained by being afraid to die. Nor will I live long by showing fear to my men." He nodded and his men began to fan out. "Now do what you have to do. It will change nothing for the woman after you are dead."

Scarne knew it was over. The bluff had failed. He turned toward Alana. She had not said a word the entire time. Now she saw the look in his eyes and said, "Do it. Please."

The loud crack of the single shot refroze everyone. The wind had died. The smell of cordite was strong in the muggy nighttime air. Guns were raised as Scarne let his drop to his side. He would have been cut in half but for a sharp order from Boyko. One of the men said something quietly, almost reverently, that Scarne couldn't understand.

"Mother of God, what did you do?" Ballantrae cried.

Scarne walked toward Alana, who had crumpled to the deck. A gunman moved to block him but backed away at a gesture from his chief. Scarne bent down. Her eyes followed him. There was a small, almost delicate, hole in her blouse above her left breast. She was still alive, barely, a testament to her iron will. Her mouth moved slightly. Then it was still. Her pupils began to expand. The very last thing that Alana Loeb saw on earth was the first man she loved. Scarne felt someone take the gun from his hand. Boyko checked the magazine.

"So, that's how it was," he said.

Ballantrae looked at Alana's body. There was triumph in his face.

"So, you hated her too, Jake. She could do that to a man. Didn't figure it out to the very end, did you? I caught on a lot faster. You fucking sap."

Scarne was very tired. It was Boyko who broke the silence.

"You are a fool, Victor. The man had one bullet left. He spared the woman a painful death. It's your bad luck he didn't have another to use on you. Although I doubt he would have bothered."

He barked an order. One of his men moved behind Ballantrae and pinned his arms. Another grabbed Scarne. He hardly felt the pain in his shoulder.

"Andriy, we can work this out." Ballantrae's legs were buckling. "I have your money."

"Please, Victor, kindly shut up. For the very first – and, God willing, the last – time, I can say this is not about the money." He looked at the terrible writhing mess on the deck. A cruel grin cracked his face. "They appear to be fading, although with such creatures, who can tell." As if on cue, the hagfish began making sucking, smacking sounds. "In any event, they undoubtedly need nutrients." He looked at Ballantrae and sighed. "So many eels, so few orifices in a man. Well, we shall have to make do."

Boyko turned to Scarne. "You deserve better than what awaits this piece of trash." He spoke rapidly to the other men. Scarne's hands were quickly and efficiently bound behind his back and two of the gunmen roughly pulled him off the boat and prodded him down the dock with automatic rifles. He glanced back to see the others stripping the screaming Ballantrae and forcing him into a fishing chair. Scarne thought wildly that he had been right. Victor's hairy legs would look ridiculous in golf shorts.

"What are you doing? Oh, God no! Jake, do something! Please, please. Help me!"

Boyko's men marched Scarne down the shore around a small bend where encroaching foliage almost reached the water. Behind them an inhuman shriek pierced the night. One of his captors said something and both men laughed. Scarne tripped on a root of some sort and pitched onto his face. One of the men reached down, effortlessly pulled him to his feet by his collar and pushed him forward. The screams on the boat diminished with distance and finally, after a few chilling wails, stopped entirely. Normal tropical nighttime sounds slowly began to fill the void as animals and insects again went about their business. Death sounds were nothing new to them. Scarne looked at the small waves breaking on the shore.

"Kneel."

Scarne sank to his knees in a small depression filled with mud and water. Dozens of tiny fiddler crabs scurried a few feet away from him then stopped. In the moonlight their claws, waving in unison, seemed to be bidding him goodbye. But for his bound hands he would have waved back. So he just laughed. The two gunman exchanged glances.

A huge bug landed on his face and began lapping. Sweat? Probably blood. He could feel warm rivulets running down his flanks. He wondered which perforation they were seeping from. He looked at the foliage to his left, only a few feet away. He would never make it, and even if he did, he was in no condition to fight the thick roots that made up the bulk of the shoreline. And then there was the matter of his arms being tied. Idly, he wondered what kind of mangroves they were, white, black or red? Alana had taught him how to tell them apart by their leaves. Funny pillow talk. Florida has lost most of its mangrove forests, she told him. The trees are considered endangered species.

"Lot of that going around," he said aloud.

"Shut up."

One of the men stood directly behind him, so close Scarne could smell him, a not-too-unpleasant odor of diesel fuel, sweat and fish, with a whiff of sun block. Funny how one's senses sharpen at a time like this – and are obviously a bit more forgiving. The other man moved in front, his weapon held languidly in the crook of his arm. Scarne recognized it as a Vepr (in English, "wild boar") the Ukrainian-designed version of the ubiquitous Russian AK-47.

Any second now. Better get out of the line of fire, pal.

Scarne squinted at the trees. Hard to concentrate. He spotted small buds at the end of some leaves. Not even mangroves. Probably Green Buttonwoods, which also loved standing water and were often mistaken for mangroves. Or maybe that other tree, the one with the funny name. What was it?

"Gumbo Limbo," he said loudly, just to piss them off. Was the dance named for it? Interesting. She would know.

Hit by a wave of dizziness, Scarne began sagging to the side. That wouldn't do! He straightened up. The man in front of him noticed and gave him a nod of respect, then looked past him to his partner and smiled. There was a blinding flash.

†

"That's a croc," the charter captain shouted.

Al Russo was startled. He and his fishing partner were debating the respective pennant chances of the New York Yankees and the Tampa Bay Rays and he'd just boldly predicted a runaway for his beloved Yanks. They were going flat out just off Big Pine and he didn't understand how the captain could hear them over the wind and engine noise. Hell, I can barely hear myself.

"I didn't know you were a Ray's fan, Skipper," he shouted at the captain.

"What the hell are you talking about," the captain yelled, pointing toward shore. "That's a croc. Big bastard. Must be 12-foot if he's an inch."

Russo and the other man, Mike Carman, a fellow orthodontist from the Miami suburb of Kendall, followed the finger as the boat slowed and the bow turned toward what they could now see was a huge reptile.

There were a million alligators in Florida, or one for every 22 humans. (Hungry gators were beginning to narrow that ratio in their favor, not to mention decimating the poodle population in some upscale golf resorts.) But the American crocodile is rare; there are fewer than 500 left in the state. They reside primarily in the southernmost tip and the Keys where food is abundant and the habitat, consisting of swamps and inlets, ideal for ambush hunting.

"Grab your cameras."

The two dentists fished the Keys whenever they could and had seen as many alligators as teeth. They squinted toward the beach 200 yards away. In the early-morning light, it looked like just another alligator. But they weren't about to argue with the captain, a grizzled bear of a man with sun-hardened skin. The son of a bitch could spot a fish *under* the goddamn water. Neither had ever seen an American crocodile in the wild, let alone photographed one. The snook and tarpon could wait.

As they got nearer they recognized the long snout that differentiated a crocodile from the broad-nosed American alligator. The croc was moving slowly backward along the mix of beach and mud flats toward the ocean and appeared to be dragging a large bundle of clothes.

"Mike, flip me those binoculars," the charter captain said. "Quick!"

He looked toward shore and then cursed, gunning the engine. The fishermen fell to the deck.

"What the hell are you doing?"

Ignoring them, he poured on the power, aiming directly for the crocodile.

"That's a body he's dragging. Probably washed up. That croc is scavenging. Grab a paddle, gaff, whatever. We have to scare it away."

The two men looked at the crocodile, which as they got closer appeared to be a lot longer than 12-feet, and then at each other. But they did as they were told. This would be something to tell the grandkids. Hopefully.

The captain just wanted to spook the croc. His passengers appeared to be game. He sure didn't want to pull his .357 Magnum out of the sea locker. Probably would get 20 years for killing the damn thing.

All three men started shouting as the boat approached the shore. A wave caught the stern and it grounded onto the beach just short of the animal. Russo was pitched onto the sand, where he had a face-to-face with the annoyed reptile, which released its hold on the body and backed off a few feet, hissing.

"Watch it, Al!"

Russo needed no encouragement to "watch it." He sprang back, tripping over the body, which let out a low moan.

The rest was anticlimax. The crocodile, looking for a docile (as in already dead) breakfast, had no argument with three madmen. Even the breakfast was stirring. That was too much. The croc hissed again at the wildly gesticulating trio and then trundled majestically into the water, its powerful tail propelling it toward a nearby cut that would take it inland, where there was easier – and better mannered – prey.

The men bent to the now coughing bundle.

"Jesus, his hands are tied," Russo said.

"Clear his mouth but watch his head," Carman said. "Look at that gash. Somebody conked him pretty good."

"Probably a drug hit gone wrong," the Captain said. "Lucky bastard."

†

BREAKAGE

THE OCEAN WATER off Harvey Cedars on New Jersey's Long Beach Island is frigid in late April. The air is brisk and the beach deserted, especially at dawn.

Scarne ran a mile along the tide line before encountering anyone else, a lone fisherman bundled against the chill, standing knee-deep in the surf. From the size of the man's rod, Scarne knew he was after striped bass. The man, his breath condensing in the air, looked back at Scarne. His smile said, "Yeah, I know I'm crazy." Scarne, who had caught nice stripers off this very stretch of beach, sometimes in a freezing rain, gave him a friendly wave. He didn't think the man was crazy at all.

†

After his rescue by the dentists, Scarne spent a week in a Miami hospital, where he fielded a slew of questions from various incredulous Federal, state and local cops, including Paulo and Curley, who kept telling him to at least get a lawyer. He knew they were trying to help him but he refused. He didn't care. By the time Bobo walked in with one of the Florida Sambuca family retainers, he'd told the authorities just about everything that had happened since Sheldon Shields first approached him.

The Sambuca lawyer, a wizened old pro named Stanley Steckler, threw everyone but Bobo out of the room and read Scarne the riot act, calling him a "first-class idiot" and reminding him that "these fucking rednecks down here still use the electric chair for traffic violations" so in the future "just shut your fucking trap." Then he heard Scarne out and went "to see the D.A. and make a coupla' calls."

He came back the next day with a bag of knishes and a smile. Scarne still didn't have much of an appetite, which worked well for Bobo, who quickly commandeered the bag.

"There are no bodies and the boat dock was as clean as an Intel chip lab," Steckler said. "They found two cars, a Lamborghini registered to the Ballantrae Group, which is collapsing as we speak, and a shot-to-pieces, souped-up Mustang registered to Josh Shields. No blood stains on or near the cars, but it's been raining heavily in the Keys. There's just enough evidence to corroborate your story, but not enough to bring charges against you. Between your new friends down here and your old ones in New York, the various prosecutors don't seem inclined to pursue this. Considering the stuff I usually handle for the Sambucas on a regular basis, I could beat this rap with my eyes closed. I'm not sure the cops believe all of it, anyway. And I can't say I blame them. That leaves only the dead guy in Antigua, which everybody says was self defense."

Steckler looked at Scarne and shrugged.

"Of course, I'm not sure how his family back in Seattle looks at it. I know something about 'families'."

"Dudley knows some people out there," Bobo mumbled through a mouth full of knish. "He's making some calls."

Before leaving the hospital, Scarne heard from Sealth.

"The Bruttis are calling it a wash. Breakage. Carlo tried to kill you and you did what you had to do. Besides, you killed the guy who murdered Maria Brutti. And the call from your pal certainly helped. If he's got that much clout out here, tell him not to visit. I've got enough trouble."

"What about Boyko?"

"He's back, as if nothing ever happened. I can't be sure, but I think he also put in a word for you. After all, by killing Garza and Keitel, you solved a lot of problems for both families. Not to mention icing the broad."

Sealth paused.

"Didn't mean that, kid. I wasn't thinking."

Scarne ran another mile and then headed back to Dudley Mack's five-bedroom oceanfront home he'd been using for a week while trying to get back into shape. Dudley had left Scarne alone, except for alternately sending his sisters and Bobo Sambuca to check on him every couple of days and bring in some home cooking. The girls tried to tease him out of his mood. For the first time in their lives, it didn't work.

"I'm worried about him," Alice told her brother. "He's not acting like Jake. It's not the wounds. He's getting around. But it's like he's, I don't know, broken. What the hell happened in Florida?"

Mack was noncommittal.

"Jake has to work this out. He'll be OK. We just have to give him time."

Scarne started out sleeping a lot, and reading. Except for the occasional phone conversation with Evelyn, he spent his time on long walks on the beach that eventually became jogs, then runs. He tried not to think of Alana, but, of course, that wasn't possible. She had been a monster, no better in the beginning than Ballantrae, Garza and Keitel. And yet he loved her.

Scarne had no illusions. There was something about her that fascinated him when he should have been repelled. What did that say about him? A part of him had died on that boat. But which part? The man he always thought he was or the part that could love a woman like Alana? He knew exactly what she was, and yet if she walked in the door now he would rush into her arms. Who was the monster?

After two weeks, he called Dudley. They went for an early dinner at Kubel's, a seafarer's tavern near Barnegat Light. They took a table under the gaping, bleached white, skeletonized jaws of a whale shark.

"Just looking at it makes me hungry," Dudley said looking up as they sat. "Reminds me of a cheerleader who gave blow jobs at college frat parties."

It was the off season and the restaurant was quiet but for a few grizzled locals who glanced their way before going back to their shots and beers. From their table, Scarne and Mack could see several men in cloth caps and hip boots washing down two large fishing boats at the nearby docks. They had the look about them of men enjoying their work.

"Those boats were used in *The Perfect Storm*," Dudley said. "Swordfishing isn't what it used to be. Stocks have been virtually wiped out. Average fish caught now is about 250 pounds; used to be about a thousand. It's why I don't order swordfish anymore. I hear that most of the sword boats have been converted into shrimpers. They needed a couple to play the *Andrea Gale* and the other boat that had the woman captain." He pointed to the bar. "And this place was supposedly the inspiration for the tavern in the movie, although you'd think they could find a good seaport gin mill in Rhode Island. Anyway, those two boats made the trip to New England; the bar didn't."

Scarne looked at his friend affectionately. He knew Dudley was trying to cheer him up.

The house specialty was clam pot pie, which tasted a lot better than it sounded. They drank Rolling Rocks out of a frosted bucket. Scarne pulled a folded manila envelope from the pocket of his yellow rain slicker.

"I want to get this to Emma Shields, in person. Can you see to it? I don't want some secretary opening it."

Mack looked dubious.

"Why don't you call her? If you want to get something off your chest, are you sure you want anything on paper?"

"If the cops wanted to prosecute me, they have everything they need. I owe her an explanation but I'm not interested in seeing her. If you don't want to do it, say so."

Mack grabbed the envelope from Scarne's hand.

"Don't be a smartass. I'll hand deliver it to her myself. Given your recent track record, the broad's probably better off without you." He saw the look on Scarne's face. "Sorry." Then to lighten the moment, he said, "Why do I think there's also a check in the envelope? You're returning your fee, aren't you?"

Scarne almost smiled.

"That settles it. The way you throw around money, you buy the damn dinner."

Two days later Scarne went back to his apartment in Manhattan and his doctors reluctantly cleared him to go back to work.

'A FEARSOME PRICE'

EVELYN STUCK HER head into his office.

"Randolph and Emma Shields are here."

Scarne looked at her.

"Show them in."

"Are you OK, Jake?"

"Show them in, honey."

Evelyn held the door for them.

"Would you like some coffee?"

During his recuperation Evelyn had purchased a state-of-the-art machine that made everything from cappuccino to iced-tea. It looked like a Mars rover and she was proud she was the only one who knew how to work it.

"No, thank you," Randolph Shields said. "We won't be long."

Evelyn looked disappointed and closed the door as she left.

Scarne stood but didn't extend his hand. Neither did Randolph Shields.

"It's nice to see you, Emma. Please sit down."

Shields looked like he would rather remain standing but when his daughter sat so did he.

"My daughter told me about the letter. Why you didn't send it to me?"

'What can I do for you, Mr. Shields?"

Shields stared at Scarne. Finally, he said, "The people who murdered my brother and his son are dead. I know you had a part in that and my sources tell me you were injured in the process. I would like you to elaborate."

"Mr. Shields, I don't mean to be rude, but everything you need is in the letter, including the names of federal and state officers now dismantling what's left of the Ballantrae organization. It will keep your writers busy for months. I'm sure that with Victor Ballantrae dead, there won't be a conflict of interest."

Shields reddened.

"That's a cheap shot, Mr. Scarne. There ceased to be a conflict when my brother was murdered. A murder for which I must hold you partly responsible"

"Father! That's enough." Emma Shields hadn't raised her voice, but she now commanded the room. "Jake was almost killed trying to set things right. And I think he knows he was just out of line."

"Your daughter is right, Mr. Shields," Scarne said, and he meant it. "I apologize to you both for that. I'm tired. And I'm sick of the whole affair."

Randolph Shields sighed deeply.

"I loved my brother, Mr. Scarne, and Josh. When all is said and done, the people responsible for their deaths have paid a fearsome price. And I suspect you have, too."

He stood up, as did Scarne, and extended his hand. They shook.

"Come along, Emma."

"I'll be right there, Papa," she said, standing to escort her father out the door, which she closed and then walked over to Scarne. "I spoke to your friend, Mr. Mack, and a Detective

Sealth. I can't imagine what it's like to have to kill someone you love."

Emerald Shields put her hand behind Scarne's head and kissed him full on the lips, then walked out the door.

†

Evelyn came into his office holding a package.

"Messenger just dropped this off." She placed it on the desk in front of him. She looked as if she wanted to say something, then apparently thought better of it and went out, shutting the door quietly.

I seem to be getting a lot of packages lately, he thought. This one was about the size of a shoe box. Scarne picked it up and felt its heft. There was nothing other than his name and address and a bold "PERSONAL" on the brown wrapping. He used a knife to cut through the masking tape. Inside was a metal box. He opened it and stared at the blue-black Bersa Thunder. He finally lifted the gun out and saw the note, handwritten in a thick, but legible, scrawl:

"You have the balls of a Ukrainian. A firearm without serial numbers may be valuable to you. It is only a piece of metal. It has no memory. Nor should you. I would advise you to use it soon. But if you and I should meet again, let us try not to kill each other."

There was no signature, just the letter "B".

33732238R00270

Made in the USA
Lexington, KY
07 July 2014